"In *New Art*, Dorothy Dunn give glimpse into one of the most private and respected sisterhoods of modern times, the sisterhood of American Catholic nuns. If you think you know who was on the front lines of social, religious, and human rights reforms, you're in for a surprise. Gloria Steinem and company have nothing on our heroine, Sister Elizabeth Mary."

— KAREN RIZZO, author of *Famous Baby*
and *Mutual Philanthropy*

"*New Art* is a well- and carefully written novel, told by an insider, filled with knowledge and insights unknown outside the community of nuns who went through the huge upheaval and transformations of the 1960s. It deserves a wide audience."

— LOU MATHEWS, author of *Shaky Town*
and *L.A. Breakdown*

NEW ART

A novel

Dorothy Dunn

RAYMOND
·PRESS·

Published by Raymond Press
www.raymondpress.com

Library of Congress Cataloging in Publication Information

Library of Congress Control Number: 2021912217
The following is for reference only:
Names: Dunn, Dorothy, author.
Title: New Art: A Novel / by Dorothy Dunn.
Identifiers: ISBN 978-1-938849-70-1 (pbk.) | ISBN 978-1-938849-71-8 (ebook)
Subjects: Fiction / General | Fiction / Women | Fiction / Religious | Fiction / Feminist

Book layout and design by Amy Inouye, Future Studio.

Printed in the United States of America.

For Gertrude

I cannot recall the first time I saw a nun. They seem always to have been in my life, probably even in the delivery room before Mother saw me. In our old family album, there's a photo of me, five weeks old, bundled in my father's arms, with a nun on either side. Hefty old Mother Mary Brendan— or as Dad called her, "Aunt Maggie"—was his mother's sister. And Lucy, the skinny, white-veiled novice, is Dad's sister. The photo is marked simply "ELIZABETH MARY BYRNE, BAPTIZED, EASTER, 1928." The Lourdes grotto is behind them, so I know they've brought me to the gardens of the motherhouse of the Sisters of Mary in St. Louis.

After that, no nuns appear in family pictures until Christmas 1945: I'm there at that same Lourdes grotto, between Mother and Dad. I'm a postulant in the Sisters of Mary, having joined the order in August of that year. A year later, also by the grotto, I stand alone as a white-veiled novice. Finally, in the fall of 1947, in the black veil of a professed nun, I am nineteen-year-old Sister Elizabeth Mary, in front of St. Patrick's School in St. Louis, with my flock of seventy-two uniformed third- and fourth-graders.

Far more numerous than these few family pictures are the scenes lodged in memory. Here nuns fill the pages of my mind's album, often in the background, and occasionally, very much in the foreground. Within this album I can trace my choices, both large and small, that led first into and then, years later, out of the convent. For, after living as a sister among my family of sisters, I came to appreciate the wisdom of the Apostle Paul: "When I was a child, I spoke as a child and thought as a child, but when I became an adult, I put aside the ways of a child." Or, as the philosopher Kant put it more harshly: "Only with great difficulty can one loosen the bonds of tutelage." Choices all.

Chapter 1

1933

January 1933

Tommy and I live with Mother at Grandpa and Mimi's because Daddy's in the hospital and Mother's gone back to work. Each morning begins with early Mass with my grandmother, Mimi, always; Grandpa sometimes. Nuns fill the front bench. I see only the backs of their heads. I can't tell them apart. Except the old one Grandpa says is Irish. She nods at Mimi and Grandpa on her way out and always smiles at me. Saturdays after Mass we stop at the parish convent with a basket. "Surprises for the sisters," Mimi says. "A little treat for the good nuns," according to Grandpa. He writes a check to go with the basket of apple crunch that Mimi makes for them. They don't have the whiskey it's made out of, so sometimes there's also a small bottle tucked next to the crunch—good medicine, Grandpa says, even when the nuns don't look sick to me. I want them to open the basket while we're here, because there are other goodies inside. They might offer me some. But they just smile and tell God to bless me.

At home, I stay with Mimi in her garden. She lets me help her with her flowers, but then I get to play when she sits down with her sewing basket. She works crocheting those fancy things for the back of her good chairs, so Grandpa's oily hair won't ruin them, she tells me. Then comes her knitting—so fast, without looking! And I get to play with those teeny things she knits, those little boots and caps for babies up in St. Vincent's. That's where sisters take care of babies who don't have mothers and daddies.

After Mimi's done enough of her knitting for the day, she pulls a little French prayer book out of her knitting bag. She gets very quiet, just like the silent nuns on the trolley car with their small books. "Use the ribbons, like this." She shows me how to open the book without touching the pages, because my fingers might be sticky. Only sometimes she falls asleep, and her little prayer book falls off her apron onto the grass. (Can the sisters fall asleep like that?) When that happens, I get to be with Grandpa. He's taught me how to crank up his Victrola, so he can put on his favorite record and then lets me sing along about taking Kathleen home again. But when he puts on that one about Tralee, he tells me to come sit on his lap and we'll both just listen. At times I think he might cry when that one's over. Except men don't cry, especially not Grandpa.

Sometimes I get to "play-read" for Grandpa from his old Irish books. But only pages I already know by heart. When the print is too small or the words too long, I pretend. I'll learn to read the real way when I go to school next year. I've got to be able to read and memorize the catechism before I can make my First Communion.

When Mimi has chores downtown, I tag along. I'm the only one of her grandchildren who calls her by this name— her *secret* name. I heard her nun sister, Mother Mary Brendan, call her that when Mimi called her Maggie. They do that when no one else is around. Nuns don't use regular names, but then no one else calls my grandmother Mimi either. Not even Daddy. He calls her Mama. And Mother says Mama Byrne. Or, when she's mad, Mrs. Byrne. Mimi got this name from Maggie when she was my age back in Ireland. She looked like me too, she says. And our names are the same, almost. I'm Elizabeth Mary, she's Mary Elizabeth.

Nuns always come in pairs, like those candles on each side of the altar. They glide down streets and into trolleys and doctors' offices, two by two, never just chatting the way other ladies do. They hardly ever look at you, and on the trolley they sit looking into their laps, seemingly playing with their rosary beads. Mimi says they're praying. For nuns, prayer is not just in church. Their lives are a prayer, Mimi tells me. That's why they pull those little books out of their deep pockets when they stop gliding and sit down. "They are praying, Betty darling. Don't stare." But I see them anyway. They use the ribbon to open their little books the way Mimi showed me. Their ribbons aren't silky like Mimi's, though, and their pages aren't gold-edged.

Hardly anything they do is like other people. Nuns don't fumble in handbags for coins or talk to the conductor or listen to his stories. They are special, Mimi says, that's what "taking the veil" means. They get to ride free on the trolleys and trains. People are extra polite to them. Loud men lower their voices and don't use bad words. Even crabby old ladies smile when they give up their seats for them. Mimi and I always move so the sisters can sit down two by two. Sometimes she gives up her seat even when I know she's tired by the way she breathes. I like being with Mimi around the sisters. But I wouldn't like to be left alone with them. Some have mean eyes.

March 1933
"How do we know God wants her to be a nun?" Grandpa is raising his voice at Mimi. "She should leave the order—come home now!" I've never heard him like this.

"Not until I find out what's wrong with her," Mimi answers, just as cross.

Daddy tells me they're worried about his younger sister, my skinny Aunt Lucy—now Sister Immaculata. Mimi decides to go down to Kansas City to see her. She needs to find out if Lucy is taking her medicine. Even though Aunt Lucy is a nun, and lives in a convent, Mimi is still her mother. She needs to help her get well! She tells Grandpa she doesn't want any daughter of hers quitting and coming home. Having a nun in your family is a blessing, she reminds him.

I'm almost five and get to go with Mimi on the train to Kansas City. My big brother, Tom, isn't allowed to come, even though he's eight and in the third grade. For our trip, Mimi buys me my first overcoat—new, not a hand-me-down. It's navy blue with shiny brass buttons, but it's too big. "You'll grow into it," she tells me, sternly. "You're going to be tall, like all the Byrnes." Her black fur coat is big, too. I snuggle inside and she wraps me next to her when it gets cold waiting for the train. She says I look like she did in Ireland a long time ago. She wore the same kind of itchy white stockings and knit cap that almost covers up my eyes. She keeps pestering me: "Cover your ears, dear. Keep *all* your hair inside." She doesn't like my bangs or the way Mother bobs my hair. "You should let her hair grow long," I heard her tell Mother. "A natural curl will develop, like her father's."

Mother shakes her head. "That won't do any good," she says. She lets Mimi know that my straight hair comes from her side of the family, even if it is brown like Daddy's. Mother doesn't like the way the nuns tease with Mimi about how Irish I look. She just scolds me more about how I should drink lots of water and eat more vegetables. "That'll get rid of those dark circles under your eyes. They make you look hungry and sad. No wonder people think you're Irish."

But I *am* Irish. Mimi's told me. And I'm not sad. I'm on my first train ride. My first overnight stay—anywhere. Where will I sleep? Do nuns undress at night? Will I get to see them in their bare feet and pajamas? And what will I do all day while Mimi sees Aunt Lucy? Where do they eat? If nuns pray all the time, who will play with me? I stay close to Mimi's warm fur when we get to the convent. We go down breezy hallways, and my new shoes make noises that echo. So I tiptoe.

"You may wait in the chapel for Mother Brendan," the whispering nun tells us before gliding off. Mimi kneels. I stand so I can see over the high prie-dieu. It's not like our church at home. It's so clean and white and empty. It smells different, too. Do the sisters say their own Mass? They have no benches, no colored windows, no pulpit. None of those flickering candles that make pretty shadows on the walls and ceiling at our church. No magazines or envelopes for donations. Nothing to draw on. Just big and quiet and cold, like the middle of the night.

I hear the rustle of skirts and beads coming our way, and then I get all tangled up in crackling starch and scratchy wool that smells like mothballs. It's Mother Brendan, trying to kiss me. Mimi tells me not to squirm, and I blush under all the "darlings" and "dears" and "sweet little Elizabeths." "My name's Betty," I say, pulling back. Big Mother Brendan is nicer after that. But I still don't kiss her back.

"You can call me Auntie Brendan, if you like." She smiles at me and her eyes are sparkly blue like Daddy's and Mimi's. And she has the same funny false teeth as Grandpa. (Will she take them out for me, the way he does?) I'm beginning to like her. Her face is soft like Mimi's but without that powdery smell, and with none of Mimi's lavender. She smells like Grandpa's liniment and rubs her big knuckles the way he does.

"Where's the bathroom? I can go by myself." I'm off to explore while they stay in the dark parlors for their grown-up talk about Aunt Lucy. When I run down the long halls, I can hear my shoes echoing. I find the toilets—stall after stall, cconcrete floors, no mirrors, a funny laundry smell, and one little light bulb hanging down. The slick toilet paper hurts, and I have to reach to pull the chain, just like at Mimi's house. I peek under each stall. No nuns anywhere. I wait, but nobody comes. Do sisters have regular bottoms? How do they pee-pee with all those skirts?

Teatime is the same as at Mimi's, only the dishes aren't as pretty and the milk tastes funny. Nuns don't drink or eat in front of regular people. They just watch, so I watch back. They no longer seem all the same. Auntie Brendan says you can tell nuns apart by their walk. I try. Some swish more than others when they walk, and some make more noise with their beads. But no nun has noisy shoes. They can't make echoes the way I can.

"Now finish your tea, dear," says Auntie Brendan, and she sounds just like Mimi. She lets me play with her beads, wood beads with little holes in them and cracks like the ones in some of Mimi's dark furniture. I finger them all the way down her side to the heavy crucifix at the end.

"It's so smooth," I tell her, "Jesus is almost gone."

"Because I've rubbed it a lot, Betty dear. Over sixty-five years of hard praying," she tells me.

"Why don't you get a new one? Like hers?" I touch the beads of the tall sister, the one pouring tea. Old nuns have smooth crucifixes and wrinkled faces. Young ones have nice new rosaries but no wrinkles on their cheeks. The tall young sister smiles down at me while she pours tea and waits on Mimi and me. She's young and pretty, but her hands are red like my mother's and smell like that brown laundry soap out on Mimi's back porch. It can't be from washing diapers, though, because nuns never have babies. I wish I could play with her when she stops pouring tea. I'll bet she can run and jump even farther than Tommy, if her long skirts wouldn't get in the way. She looks like she laughs a lot. Did all her boyfriends become priests? I'm not supposed to ask what color her hair is. Or if it's curly, or straight like mine. A little bit of Auntie Brendan's gray hair sticks out, but I pretend not to notice. Nuns' hair is a secret, like their names.

Their talk goes on and on. They don't even notice how I'm playing with the tip of Auntie Brendan's veil. I hold it up to my eyes and then look all around the room. Mimi and her sister look squiggly and wavy, and so do the furniture and windows—like those old-fashioned pictures in Grandpa's den. When a big loud bell clangs, everyone moves out of the polished parlor. It's the voice of God, Auntie Brendan explains. He's saying, "Come into the chapel to pray." So they hand Mimi one of their little black books, and she takes me by the hand. The chapel isn't empty now. It's got more nuns than I've ever seen in one place. Spooky! I start to fidget, and Auntie Brendan nods at me. I can leave and go exploring on my own.

Outside in the yard, snow is falling, but gently, making a soft blanket around the statue of Jesus. Arches cover the walkway that goes all around the garden. I can hear the nuns chanting, but they can't see me, so I skip and dance to their chanting. I pretend that I'm playing with that tall young nun. She's quick and moves fast like my mother, only she's thinner than Mother—and prettier, even though she doesn't wear lipstick or powder and I can't see her hair. But she smiles more than Mother and her eyes are friendlier. I make believe she lets me try on that long pretty veil so I can play dress-up the way I do with Mimi's hats.

Chapter 2

1944

December 1944

I am in my usual spot in Sister Marie Gabrielle's ("Gaby," as we call her) senior English class, in my last year of high school at St. Mary's Academy. Like my Auntie Brendan—Reverend Mother Mary Brendan, the mother general and big boss of the whole order—Gaby does not let on to anyone that we met years ago in Kansas City. As far as I know, she might not even remember me. After all, I only *imagined* playing with her then.

When I met her again this past September, here in the company of her favorite authors, she seemed different from the other academy sisters, most of whom are feared by my classmates. Even today in her classroom, all decorated for the Christmas season, I am shocked by how she is anticipating the holidays: There are no Santas or snowmen around this classroom, or even lists of where to bring food for the poor. Everywhere else getting into the Christmas spirit seems mostly about getting and giving. Myself included. At home, and especially at my Saturday job, gift wrapping at Famous-Barr, I've been pushing for more hours, working after school these last two weeks, eagerly awaiting full-time work (and full pay!) once classes end—eager for more money for more gifts!

Instead, there on Gaby's bulletin board is Fra Angelico's *Annunciation*, with Latin words of the Angelus in beautiful calligraphy surrounding Mary and the angel. And on the cork borders above the blackboard, going all around the room, are sprinkled those little black square notes of plainchant that even I can recognize as *Veni, veni Emmanuel*....

Today she's been reading us a passage from Wordsworth's *The Prelude*, when suddenly she puts down the book and starts talking about the approaching feast of Christmas. She doesn't urge us to fill food baskets for the poor or gather gifts for the orphanage like the other nuns do. "This is the season of God coming into time. Of a young mother and her baby. Of empty inns, hillside caves. Of poverty and plainness. Of the young girl Mary, and old Joseph, and their very new baby. They are our link, every creature's link—" her voice becomes whispery, "—our link to the Creator of the universe. Why at Christmas we celebrate the sacredness of all earthly things, all that exists. Wordsworth calls this *natural piety*. We call it *religion*.

> *"My heart leaps up when I behold*
> *A rainbow in the sky:*
> *So was it when my life began;*
> *So is it now I am a man;*
> *So be it when I shall grow old,*
> *Or let me die!*
> *The Child is father of the Man;*
> *And I could wish my days to be*
> *Bound each to each by natural piety."*

She reels it off from memory! I'm impressed, dazzled, by the poem and by her. When a hush comes over the class, she becomes self-conscious and turns abruptly toward the board, printing in large script: RELIGION = RE *(again or return)* + LIGO *(to bind back, to tie, to fasten)*. "The word *religion* comes from the Latin *ligo*, 'to fasten' or 'to bind,' plus *re*, meaning 'back to a source,' " she explains. And then, back to us, and recites:

> *"Glory be to God for dappled things—*
> *For skies of couple-color as a brinded cow;*

For rose moles all in stipple upon trout that swim;
Fresh-firecoal chestnut-falls; finches' wings...
All things counter, original, spare, strange...
He fathers-forth whose beauty is past change
Praise him."

From memory, again! All of it! With all those odd words! Gaby's voice is so sure, the words spilling out as if practiced, especially when she turns to speak directly to us. It seems she's sharing some deeply cherished confidence: "We humans, like Hopkins, like Wordsworth, can *recognize* these connections! We alone among God's creatures can do this— recognize the great wonders of our world for what they are: Alive! Holy with life! Actual, existing, beings! All around us." The words linger before other words sing out of her. *"A world alive with the grandeur of God. To grasp this, and to proclaim it publicly. That is religion. That is prayer."*

So simple, yet so startling. For twelve years in my religion classes, I've learned how to identify, and then distinguish between matter and form of seven sacraments, between venial and mortal sin, plenary and partial indulgences, the Immaculate Conception and the Virgin Birth—endless facts about the creed, code, and cult of Roman Catholicism. But never until this moment have I glimpsed what *religion* is— and it has nothing whatsoever to do with Rome or the pope or the catechism.

"Incidentally," she begins, twisting both her hands back to point to herself, "this is why we, the nuns who teach you, are called *religious*. In official, legal Church language, 'religious' is a noun, not an adjective. Because, unlike those wondrous dappled things—the trout or chestnut or finch—that cannot make that connection, our very garb gives witnesses to our Creator, we've made a choice. Our public vows make explicit that we understand this connection between creature and creator. So, what Hopkins and Wordsworth do with their poetry, monks and nuns do with their lives: profess their *re-ligo* to their Creator." Suddenly she's flushed and self-conscious, and I am embarrassed for her. She's mumbling an apology for digressing, and quickly returns us to our term assignment.

It's no digression for me, though. She's shown me something very simple, yet something I cannot put into words. This odd but exciting feeling stays with me throughout the rest of English class. It's a sense of having found something I didn't even know I was looking for—which makes me want to talk with her in the worst way, as long ago I wanted to play and dance with her in those cloistered gardens in Kansas City. Though I'm not exactly sure of what I want to say. At any rate, it's impossible: School's about to recess for the Christmas holidays.

December 28, 1944
"Girls, girls, religion's supposed to help us love each other, not argue."

Dad is fed up with how I challenge Mother about what I call the "numbers thing." Mother crabs when I don't join her at morning Mass for the novena she started right after Christmas. She sees this practice of doing something special for nine successive days as her own "blitzkrieg of prayer," her personal contribution to the war effort. Ever since Pearl Harbor my freshman year, she has been dedicating nine days each month to this devotion. Then, after Tom joined the Navy, she put the pressure on my little sister Suzy and me to join in her novenas. It really frosts her when I say novenas are superstitious.

"What's so special about nine days in a row?" I ask. "Why not seven or twelve? Why can't you skip a day? Who's counting? God? If you miss one, what happens?"

She switches on the vacuum cleaner, stopping me cold.

Dad and Suzy and I are removing the metallic tinsel from the tree and smoothing it onto the cardboard holders to be used again next year. The decorations come off now; tree and crib stay up until the Epiphany on January 6.

"Lay off!" Dad mutters. "For Pete's sake, just help her out!" She's got a lot on her mind right now, he reminds us, referring to Mimi's presence in our home since her stroke a few weeks back. "Your mother loves you a lot, Betty." I believe him, of course, but it doesn't help much.

For Mother, religion is like the war—grim and serious, a deadly gamble where some win but most lose. I think she worries about my soul because I don't seem to stick at daily Mass during Advent or Lent. Dad says I question too many things that are important to her: Why a glass of water ten minutes after midnight has to keep me from Holy Communion when the same water ten minutes earlier is okay? Does she really think I'll go to hell for this? Or on Friday nights with my girlfriends at the drive-in, why must the hamburger sit there getting cold until a minute after midnight when it's Saturday and okay to eat meat? After all, it's already Saturday in New York, I tell her.

Mimi would understand, but just when I most want to talk to her, she's all shriveled up and can't talk. Unlike Mother, she'd know I'm not scoffing at religion when I call her novenas superstitious and get testy about the "numbers thing." She'd understand what Gaby means regarding religion and prayer being about *Praising God* more than it is about begging for favors. But Mimi can't even recognize me now. All the talk, even before she dies, makes me want to scream. The prayers at night about wanting a "happy death" for her stick in my throat. I'm expected to join in when they pray for a "speedy end to Mama's suffering" and for "God to take her to Himself." The words stifle me like the room she's in. Even the roses I bring don't help that awful odor. I want something else for her, too. But death? Maybe that's why I've been shirking my chores around the house, why I am seldom around "just to visit" when people drop by to pray at Mimi's bedside. Mother calls me selfish. She'd never believe that the nuns at school—most of them, anyway—think me generous and outgoing.

After the tiff with Mother about religion, I decide to go biking, saying I need to go to the library for our term assignment. That was slightly dishonest, of course. I do have a big assignment that's still far from finished, but most of all I need some fresh air. I need to be free of them all, to be out of that house! To think my own thoughts away from all that dismal talk of death. To imagine my choices for college: Catholic or public? Coed or all-girls? Boarding or day? Yet why so sneaky? I love biking in the cold, with the wind biting my face and tingling my legs—especially after gorging on all those holiday treats. But why sneak? And why decide to swing by St. Mary's? Do I really need that notebook from my locker? Or was I hoping all along that I'd bump into Gaby?

She was heading toward the staircase, when we surprised each other—she swathed in a coverall apron, and I in scruffy old Levis and a much too large peacoat of Tom's. By contrast, she's almost cute, reminding me a bit of Judy Garland in *The Wizard of Oz* in that crisp blue-and-white-check apron. She's holding a tray of dishes, covered by a clean white kitchen towel; I feel simply awkward and embarrassed.

"Your class seems more religious than religion class," I blurt out. Finally I've said it, and it was easy—a start on what's been buzzing around my mind since that class on Wordsworth before Christmas vacation.

"I know what you mean," she says softly. She lets me help with her loaded tray and invites me to join her down in the home ec lab. "That's where I prepare lunch for my patient— but now it's cleanup time."

I notice when we remove the towel that the dishes on her tray are all used, but barely. Is she feeding a bird? "Patient?"

I ask.

"In between other jobs, I am a tray-taker."

"I thought you were studying English literature?" I've heard St. Mary's gossip about Gaby: how teaching us senior English is not her whole "obedience"—as the nuns call their assignments; how she's also working on a master's degree at the university. But nursing?

"No, I'm *not* a nursing student!" she says with a laugh. "It's just every grad-school sister has some minimal duty at mealtime, usually an elderly nun in the infirmary as our charge. Mine's Sister Agatha. You probably don't know her. She's a dear, older than God, hasn't taught since I entered the order." With her veil pinned back, I see her "high color" is, in reality, very chapped skin, and what I thought were black eyes are really dark brown.

When we reach the home ec lab, she flips on the light and explains: "This is my hideaway during vacation." At the far end of the room, beyond a half dozen kitchen stations, is a miniature "practice" dinette where last year I learned more than I ever wanted to know about how to set the table for afternoon tea. Now the innards of her thesis are spread out on its small table: neat piles of paper, an ancient looking typewriter, a shoebox of index cards, and books stacked all around. Water runs into the dishpan while she drops the top part of her apron to attend to her huge billowing sleeves: deftly folding, then compacting, and finally pinning them atop, first right then left shoulders, ending up like some footballer ready for scrimmage. Those huge dark sleeves I've watched sweep across blackboards printing old English and Latin have completely disappeared up under the elastic of the puffed gingham coverall she's put back on.

But when Gaby starts shedding her tight-fitting inner sleeves that cover her lower arms, I feel I'm trespassing in forbidden territory. Never before have I seen a nun's bare arms—nobody has! And hers are not at all what I would have imagined—chubby and childlike, with dimples where I have only bony knuckle-like elbows. It's unfair: This cloistered woman has smooth olive skin, perfect for a tan, while I'm stuck with hairy white arms that blister and freckle at the mere thought of sunbathing. And her eyebrows—so perfectly shaped, not wayward like mine. Strange to be envious of a nun's beauty.

When we finish washing up the dishes, she asks if I want to share some brownies left over from "the feast"—convent language for Christmas. "They're slightly stale, but great if you dip them in cocoa or coffee. Which do you prefer?"

Can she possibly mean she'll *eat* with me? In all my twelve years of nuns' schooling, I've never seen one eat, even my aunts. I choose coffee—having only recently tried it out, but only with scads of milk, which I notice she doesn't have. She turns on the flame under the tall blue metal pot, chipped just like the one Mimi used to fix Grandpa's coffee. Before she settles herself on one of the counter stools across from me, she shoves a plateful of brownies between us.

"I understand, I think, about literature sometimes teaching us religion better than the religion class, or catechism," she says. I'm flattered: She remembers what I told her up in the main hall. "I often use that Hopkins myself for meditation." She puts down the brownie she's been dunking into her coffee mug and fishes deep inside the slit in the seam of her apron and then her habit.

Since the first grade I've watched nuns retrieve things from their pockets this way, but I never knew the "pocket" is a separate garment worn around the waist, underneath the habit. Like a cowboy's holster, Gaby tells me, pulling hers out for me to see. It has compartments, a slim one for a pencil, a somewhat larger one for a prayer book, with the rest a spacious pouch for her heavy book of poems. "Listen to this," she says as she leafs through hunting for precious gems. "You heard some of this in class, where he sings about dappled things and the beauty of cows, trout, chestnuts, and finches' wings. Now listen to him on a young woman's beauty:

> *"Winning ways, airs innocent, maiden manners,*
>   *sweet looks, loose locks, long locks, lovelocks,*
>   *gaygear, going gallant, girlgrace—*
> *Resign them, sign them...long before death...*
> *Give beauty back, beauty, beauty, beauty,*
>   *back to God,*
> *beauty's self and beauty's giver...*
> *See; not a hair is, not an eyelash,*
>   *not the least lash lost...."*

The strange words—plus the melody of her reading them—charm me even more than they did in class. But differently. Sitting so close to her and watching her face, I'm distracted by a detail: those straight, sweeping eyelashes. Dark, almost Asian in their downward slant, how perfectly they help me to grasp His line about every eyelash counting. The Maybelline people would want her to curl those straight blunt lashes. And miss entirely their special beauty.

"So, yes. A poem like Hopkins's can show us what *religion* is, better than the catechism," she continues. "*Praise* is at the heart of it, and *gratitude*, more than rules and rubrics. Maybe least of all rules and rubrics."

She must see that I agree because she rushes on, not restrained or embarrassed as she became in our class. Without effort she embroiders exquisite detail around her simple truth: Our world—because it is God's creation—is sacred. But only the human heart—among all God's creatures—can recognize this wonder, acknowledge it, and sing praise to our Creator for it. We can offer his creation back to Him! I sit transfixed by her words. So old, yet so new. She seems out of breath, lost for any further talk. Yet she continues: That's what *sacrifice* has meant from time immemorial—burning the first and best fruits of a harvest as homage and praise to the Giver of all crops, of all life, and all beauty. Abraham understood this and was prepared to sacrifice what was for him the most wondrous of God's creations, his son Isaac. He saw the connection—his son and his son's Maker. And that's at the heart of religion: making connections, connection with our Creator. Poets do it with their words; others with their lives.

I'm relieved when she puts aside her book and we return to dunking our brownies, neither thinking much nor chatting. I slip off my peacoat, warmed by her words and the hot coffee. When she stands and starts gathering up the empty dishes and moves over to the sink, I'm more comfortable. I'd be embarrassed to have Gaby see me with what I know must be very flushed cheeks and slightly jittery hands, most likely from all the coffee. After longing to talk, I cannot speak—like that day in her class.

A squawk from the intercom summons her back to her patient in the infirmary. Off comes her enveloping gingham, down come her large black sleeves. Her released veil falls gently over her shoulders. She's once again my English teacher. Yes, of course, I'll finish the cleanup, I say, and turn out the lights and slam the door behind me.

"Happy New Year!" she calls, floating out the door. "Happy 1945!"

"You too!"

Yet I'm much too excited to start the simple cleanup right now. I keep staring at the scattered remnants of our brownie treat. It's just as it was in that class of hers before Christmas, only more so: Her words fit perfectly in my heart, resting there as if they've been mine forever. I am excited, yet peaceful in a way I've never felt before, frightened by a challenge that seems way beyond me, yet deep down calm, even confident. My cheeks burn, I feel weak and breathless even more than I do after those laps at the Y.

However, I also feel strong, stronger than ever before. And clear about my future, about the choice I know I'm making. I can become a "religious" like Gaby, make a profession out of acknowledging my link with the Creator. My *choice*: giving beauty back to God, like her poet says, the beauty of my human life, my young life, my "girlgrace."

This is prayer I can understand. I see now why they call it her Profession Day, when a nun makes her vows. It's not so much what she's pledging to do as who she's promising to be: a "professional" who chooses by her vows—and even by her garb—to point back to our Creator, "Beauty's self and beauty's giver."

The shaky feelings are gone now, and I easily clean up. I turn out the lights, grab the peacoat but am stopped by the slow tolling of the chapel bell, telling me it's six o'clock.

It's part of a most familiar prayer, the *Angelus*: three single, evenly spaced tollings of the huge chapel bell, then three more, and then another three, followed by a final nine. Each prompting an *"ave"* uttered silently. The drawn-out bells ring every day, four times a day: twelve and six, a.m. and p.m. Of course, I'm never here at the motherhouse for this six p.m. dinner one, and certainly never at midnight or six a.m.—only the one at noon. Before the war, even though we had always heard this somber noontime tolling of the chapel bell, it was completely ignored by the kids, and even by some nuns, on our academy side of St. Mary's.

But things changed dramatically with Pearl Harbor on December 7 of my freshman year. The whole school voted to make this our special time to remember "our boys" and pray for their safe return. So ever since, throughout this long war, at noon every day you'd think we had become an ancient monastery. All the monks stop where they are, what they're doing, and lower their heads to pray silently. By this, my senior year, every girl, and probably every nun, has someone away at war—a father, brother, cousin, or boyfriend. Some

NEW ART

are dead. No teacher is needed to enforce the silence.

I've detoured over to the windows while my own silent prayer finishes and am standing now, gazing dreamily out at the stars in the cold winter sky. The same stars, I'm thinking, that are shining over servicemen everywhere, over wherever in the Pacific theater Tom is. Without warning, my eyes fill with tears, even as I smile at the absurdity of it. Tom has been my ever-teasing sparring big brother since I first opened my eyes on this world. The thought that I might actually start crying for him is beyond belief.

I stand sniffling by the window until I'm thoroughly chilled, then reach for the jacket, the Navy jacket he was so proud to wear even before he joined the Navy, and now was such a warm reminder of him somewhere out in the Pacific. Names I've heard on the radio and in newsreels tumble through my mind—Midway, Guadalcanal, the Solomons, Leyte, Guam, among the hundreds clustered on that map Dad secured on our dining room wall as soon as Tom shipped out. With each news story we'd locate the island and I'd picture those awful bombed-out ships in Pearl Harbor from three years earlier, imagining how trapped those sailors must have felt. Now I wonder: Does Tom—star quarterback and Eagle Scout—let himself be scared? I've never seen him scared, and have certainly never seen him cry. He probably did as a baby, but since I'm younger, I never saw him then.

Dad stays chipper, urging us to imagine he's just away at another football game and we're left at home, rooting for him. We have to keep up our spirits, he says, reminding us that moping around won't bring Tom home any quicker. Besides we should thank God that he's in the Navy instead of an infantryman in that horrible European theater. Mother, though, doesn't want to talk about the war at all, yet she writes Tom every day. She's always at it. Maybe she cries at night with Dad, but she never lets Suzy or me see her that way. With me, she harps about finishing my weekly cookie-making job for him: "Get that batch in the mail—early. And pray for him, Betty. He needs your prayers."

Now, all alone in this big, cold building, the awful thought that he might die out there, or be dead already, hits me and I sink down to the floor. Pulling my knees up tight, I try to envelop as much of myself as possible in my peacoat, not minding that my crying is getting noisy. I don't want him to die. I've taken for granted that he'll always be in my life, though I've fought with him lots—for as long as I can remember—and wail now remembering how often I've screamed at him to "drop dead."

Even though, truth to tell, I've been happy to have Tom out of the house these last years. Especially lately, when boys started to be in my life more, and I've begun at last to have a bosom. With him away, I've not had to worry about his teasing, like the way he used to call me "slats" even in front of his friends. I've been relieved that he's *not* around to deliver such cracks around the boys who have joined our crowd. Still, I don't want him to die.

I wrap my jacket tighter and bury my head on my knees, letting my sobs get louder and louder. I've not cried like this since I was a little kid. But I let it all out now without any fear of being heard or seen, drooling and sniffling unashamedly, until finally I am exhausted, all cried out. I get up slowly and dry my face on my big flannel shirt—also Tom's, meaning from his closet, which Dad tells me I should leave alone. Tears are indeed magical, because I feel so much better as I stand to gaze out again at the darkness. Tiny stars lead me out toward the Pacific, but instead of burned-out, mangled warships, I'm picturing proud ships of a powerful Navy, like the ones on those recruitment posters, with men in spanking-white uniforms all standing at attention with beautiful Fourth of July fireworks lighting the sky and "Anchors Aweigh" floating out over the ocean.

I know the song well, as I do those of the Army, Marine,

and Air Corps. On Friday nights when a bunch of us hang out at Bixby's, our favorite hamburger joint, we eventually end up going through the entire repertoire of service songs, along with "My Country 'Tis of Thee" and, always, always, "God Bless America." So it's easy now, all alone, to let loose and sing unselfconsciously, a hearty "Anchors," with Tom here in front of me standing straight like he does in that picture on our mantel, with the same kind of peacoat, smiling and handsome in his sailor hat. Tears again threaten. Now, though, they taste of pride in my great big brother.

The highs and lows of my unexpected emoting here in this darkened lab have allowed Gaby's words to settle even deeper inside me. They are now my own. They've made this cool decision inside me inevitable. I thank Tom and his Navy for helping me see things clearly. He didn't wait for the draft to get him. Even though it made Mother cry, he couldn't wait to join that "band of brothers" and serve his country. He enlisted as soon as they'd take him. So will I. I'll join Gaby's band of sisters, as soon as I graduate. Offer myself back to God—like the ancients sacrificing their crops to God as the poet Hopkins reminds me. There's no need to fret over choices ahead of me when I graduate—unless, of course the nuns reject me. But that seems about as likely as the Navy rejecting Tom.

Chapter 3

1945

February 6, 1945

"Find yourself a good, strong steamer trunk. Nuns do a lot of moving around." Sister Augusta is explaining how one goes about joining the order. Gaby's been transferred, unexpectedly, at semester break. So it's to this other, older nun, my twelfth-grade civics teacher, that I bring my big decision. "Better a used one. New trunks are terrible—since the war—no better than cardboard." Words as sturdy-sounding as the trunk she says I'll need, as sturdy as she herself seems to be. "Also, talk to your parents. You need their permission. You're aware of being underage, I trust?"

The trunk is easy: Mimi's old one—with its metal sides, wood slats, and huge knuckled corners—is certainly sturdy. It came with her from Ireland, holding her trousseau, and still, after all these years, connects her with things Irish. Just before her stroke, she gave me a bundle of Irish lace from it: "For your wedding, Betty dear," she said. "I may not be around then."

"Call me when you've had a chat with your parents, and I'll get you an appointment with Reverend Mother." That's Mother Pauline, Auntie Brendan's successor, the newly elected mother general. I don't know her. "If she thinks you're suitable, she'll give you an application."

I hold off telling anyone just yet. In a few weeks I'll be seventeen, which sounds so much more mature than sixteen and might make a difference to Reverend Mother. I had not counted on needing anyone's approval to carry out my plans.

※

March 7, 1945

My birthday, the perfect time to tell my parents! Right now, before dinner. Suzy's still outside playing, and I'm alone with Mother and Dad. In a moment, the news bulletin gluing them to the radio will be over. But Mother suddenly interrupts: "Listen!" She moves to the edge of her chair, letting her darning basket fall to the floor, and with urgency again demands, "Listen, it's something major." Excited voices are announcing that US forces have captured the only remaining bridge over the Rhine! "Jesus, Mary, and Joseph!" she screams. "They're inside Germany! On their way to Berlin!" She blesses herself, keeping her eyes shut tight, holding back the tears.

Mother is never teary like this. She's careful and tidy about everything she does, particularly with her darning basket (with her own nylons no longer available). She's scrupulously faithful to patterns or recipes when sewing or cooking, and really careful about money—"good with numbers," Dad says. (Was this why they married?) He credits her with getting us through those awful Depression years, and even now she has the final word on money in our house.

"At last!" says Dad, now out of his chair, staring down at the radio, from which important people are commenting on this dramatic news. "The beginning of the end," he announces. "And on your birthday, Betty m'girl!" He calls me that only when he's especially pleased with me. We stand right in front of the radio—as if we could grasp the news better that way. "What a gal—you turn seventeen, and the war ends!"

"Not yet!" Mother corrects, sternly. "This is just one battle, and over there, not where Tom is." She's returned the basket to her lap and is once again busy straightening it out so she can get to those socks. "It's not over for him. Or for all those others."

It's hard to see her eyes, now that she's wearing glasses

most of the time. They are sad eyes, and like mine, green—every bit as Irish as Dad's, but not sparkling Irish-blue the way his are. Nor is she proud of her Irishness the way he is. Perhaps because her family has not prospered as Dad's parents have, though they've been here a generation longer. Also, at her secretarial college, she couldn't have imbibed the sort of Irish blarney he did during his years with Notre Dame's fighting Irish. So maybe I can brighten up those sad eyes? I just blurt it out: "Listen to *my* good news. I'm joining the convent in August!" They stare at me. Not such a great idea, I instantly realize, and proceed to squelch my disappointment by chattering about the trunk I'll need. "Do you suppose I can use Mimi's?"

Dad recovers first, with a broad smile and warm embrace. "Grand news! Another blessing for the Byrnes! Betty, m'girl, I'm proud of you. We'll have to celebrate *double* tonight." Mother frets, as if she's annoyed that I've interrupted her darning. Dad continues, "Of course you can have Mama's trunk. Nothing she'd like better." His arm is around me, again, squeezing me uncomfortably. "She'd be proud of you."

"When did you decide all this?" Mother asks, clearly annoyed. "Have you told anyone else? Suzy? Your aunts?"

I want to scream: Don't you trust me to have figured out what I want! What's right for me before I tell anyone, including you? But I keep my mouth shut and move over to sit on the edge of the footstool in front of her as she returns to her darning. "Any other girls from St. Mary's going?" she asks. "Do we know them? Have they told their parents?" Her eyes remain fixed on the sock stretched tight over her darning egg. I reach up to take it from her and at last our eyes meet.

"I haven't told anyone but you, Mother. I can't answer your questions. I've not even applied yet."

"You are so young, Betty. How can you be so sure?" She looks directly at me now, and I can tell she's hurt and sad.

"I just am," I answer. "I'm very sure. Believe me."

Dad stands behind me with his large hands working my shoulders and neck the way I like, and says matter-of-factly, "Our own Joan of Arc." He must be remembering that same statue in the upstairs hallway of Grandpa and Mimi's house. Maybe he said his night prayers there when he was a little kid, as I did, staring at that serene, determined girl-warrior sitting so erect on her charging stallion, with the flag of Orleans rippling in the wind. I like Dad's comparison. "You should tell your aunts you'll be joining them." He seems proud of me.

"Not yet." Mother's eyes stay with her darning, though I don't think for a moment she's scowling because of the holes in the socks. "If you ask me—which of course you aren't— you are entirely too young, and too close to *them*, to all those nuns, to that school. You need to get away for a while, go to college." When she again looks up, the scowl is still there. "And don't write Tom, for heaven's sake. He's got enough on his mind. Nor Suzy. Things like this get around."

"Why is she so crabby?" I ask Dad the next night when we're walking around the block. He tells me Mother cried last night, thinks she's failed me because I'm turning my back on our family, not wanting to be, like her, a wife and mother.

"You've hurt her, Betty. She thinks you like the nuns better than us, that you don't have time for us anymore." He's partly right, but partly wrong, too. We walk for some time in uncomfortable silence. "You *are* rushing things a bit, don't you think?" He stops and grips my elbow as if I had a game leg or something. "Your mother and I would like you to have a chance to grow up more, to get the feel of being a grown-up woman, to know something of what you're giving up." More silent walking, before he stops again. He puts his arm around my shoulders and squeezes me close to him. "Papa left money in his will for all his grandchildren to visit Ireland. That's out of the question right now, of course. But after the war. Say you go to college next year. Then in the summer—it's sure to be over by then—you can travel. You'll only be eighteen—plenty of time left for the convent. What do you think?" I'm speechless at the change in him. He had been on my side! Mother's got to him. "Give it some thought, won't you, Betty, m'girl? It's not much for a dad to ask, is it?"

Not much! It's *my* life, I want to shout at him. Putting it off for a year! He tells me that deep down they're both happy for me, and then repeats the family line: Both he and Mother are grateful to God for this gift of a religious vocation to our family. But they don't seem happy, especially Mother. And now he's taking *her* side!

"Even good things can sometimes be hard for parents. Try to understand this, Betty. Be patient with your mother. She's got a lot on her mind right now—no word from Tom, her own mother's failing health, and now my mother's, your Mimi's, house to clear out." I've been thinking Mother was relieved by Mimi's death, though I don't say it.

He's quiet for a long time, but when we get back to the house, he decides we should go around the block again. Sounding confidential, he tells me she is going through "the change" and how that accounts for her moods. Also, he'd like to move our family into Mimi's big house on Lindell, but Mother thinks it's beyond our means. "That's been worrying her a lot, Betty, even before your news. We need to pull together, you and me. Get her to smile more. Give her less to scold us about."

So she scolds him, too. Is that why I feel so much closer to him? We walk briskly without speaking until he stops. "Why don't we give her some relief on that Lindell project? It could be your summer job—helping to clear out Mama's stuff. You'll get to drive her old DeSoto, and earn your trunk."

June 4, 1945

Graduation is behind me, and the clearing out of Mimi's house well under way. Dad with his brothers and non-nun sisters decide the major issues. Now I'm on my own, employed by the "estate of Mary Elizabeth Connor Byrne" to organize and inventory and finally distribute what remains of her earthly possessions. I sort and bundle in the mornings, then tool about in Mimi's old DeSoto in the afternoon. Piles of Mimi's religious stuff—prayer books, holy card, statues—and always some good, clean, fresh-from-the-bank American dollars go to the old-folks' home. It's run by the Little Sisters of the Poor, who beg for food and never eat until the old people are fed, Mimi once told me; then St. Vincent's Orphanage, and the Good Shepherd Home for Wayward Girls, and finally to the St. Anne's Monastery of cloistered nuns.

At each stop I hear stories about my grandmother, different stories, though always with the same ending: "She felt like one of us, part of our community." I feel no connection with any of these nuns as I do with "my" sisters at St. Mary's. They are all friendly enough yet somehow seem to me from another planet. Is it because their work is so tough and so noble, while my sisters are just teachers, obviously enjoying what they do? Sister Augusta told me each order has its own personality, so I suppose that's what I'm learning from these afternoon jaunts: learning what I am *not* choosing to do with my life.

I'm also learning how much I love to drive all alone, going as fast as I can down empty country roads. Which is why I left this trip to the cloistered nuns out in the country for last. I figure it's my reward, exploring roads I've never been on, wandering about until there's only enough gas to get back to the Lindell house. Dad thinks I don't know what I'm giving up by going to the convent, what I will be "freely forfeiting," as Gaby and her poet put it, what Reverend Mother referred to as "worldly pleasures." But surely speeding along like this, alone, with the windows down, the warm air brushing my face and messing up my hair, surely this must be one such pleasure. Some nuns drive, of course, but they don't race along like this, and never alone. I'm positive this is not part of convent life—any more than skiing or horseback riding, or ice skating, or floating on my back far out on the lake staring up at the sky while the waves gently lift me up and plop me down.

I may not know *all* the pleasures of a grown-up woman, but I've enjoyed enough of them to be able to "give beauty back to beauty's self and beauty's giver," as Gaby's poet says. I know more about all this than Dad thinks I do.

June 11, 1945
The doorbell startles me. Nobody but my family knows I'm working over here at Mimi's. At the door, in his white officer's uniform, is the "boy next door." He's not exactly family, but not a stranger either. It's Peter, the grandson of the widow Mrs. Atkinson, Mrs. A. to us, Mimi's longtime neighbor, whom she once described (as only an Irish native can) as very proper and *very* Protestant, *"yet even so,* a very good woman." She's also very arthritic, which is why we've all come to know her grandson and handyman helper, Peter. He's older than Tom and, before the war, worked on Saturdays for his grandmother and occasionally for Mimi as well.

Both women missed Peter terribly after he enlisted, so Mimi's cookie project for her grandsons came to include Peter as well. It was a weekly routine for her before her stroke, her contribution to the war effort, she said proudly. On Fridays after school I helped her address the small tins and bundle them into Grandpa's garden satchel before taking the bus to the post office. On one of his first leaves home, Peter "volunteered"—at Mimi's request, I later learned—to teach me how to drive her DeSoto, even though I was underage.

That way, the post office trip wouldn't take up so much of my free time. Mother didn't quite approve of this use of gas during wartime, or that I should be driving at fifteen, but she wasn't about to cross her mother-in-law, the formidable Mama Byrne to her.

So when I open the door, Peter is meeting his former student, now a seasoned driver. He's surprised to see me alone; his grandmother told him the whole family is working together to clear out Mimi's house. And I'm surprised by him! I know he went into officers' training, but I've never seen him in his dress uniform. Now he holds his brand-new ensign's cap over his heart, telling me he's sorry about Mimi's "passing." Then he says, "Wow, have you changed, Betty."

He hasn't seen me for well over a year. I'm glad I chose my favorite bareback sundress, a hand-me-down from my cousin Peg, even though it's sort of dressy for this work. But it's just so comfortable in this sticky weather, plus it makes me look older! I take him out to the kitchen, the least cluttered of all the downstairs rooms. He's tall, blond, and bony, how I imagine that all-American boy Jack Armstrong must look. Peter always seemed to me a bit bookish and boring, if terribly polite. Mimi thought him "a well-mannered young man"—no doubt because he was so prompt in thanking her after each cookie box. (The only one among "her boys," including Tom and my cousins in the service, to write me as well.)

Through these thank-you notes I've followed his V-12 program: at college, then his midshipman training, and finally his commission. My letters back to him have lengthened as I've become disenchanted with the local high school boys. Though far from stuck-up, Peter is, for me, way ahead of the juvenile products of the local Jesuit high school. He always seemed to enjoy my comments about his V-12 college studies, yet he's never asked me out when he's been home on leave. I've presumed he has other real girlfriends—older than I am.

But this afternoon, as we sit in Mimi's kitchen, I think how grown-up he makes me feel. I'm happy we've corresponded; I always sound older in my letters. He hasn't seemed to mind that I am serious about studies, even though Mother tells me, with boys, it's not good to be that way. When I apologize for not having anything other than lukewarm lemonade to offer, he asks if Bixby's is still in operation. Maybe we can go over there for something cold? He's seen Mimi's old DeSoto in the driveway. I close up the house and hand him the keys.

At Bixby's we discover the power of his uniform. By the time we get there, it's past three o'clock and the owner is pulling down the door shade with a sign saying "Closed until 5:00." But then he spots Peter's uniform and opens up for us, leaving the "Closed" sign in place. He's an old Navy man, he tells us, and recognizes Peter's rank. "If you don't mind the mop and bucket, sir, I'll get you anything you want. Even a beer."

Peter assures this gruff man, old enough to be his father, that we don't need beer, but would appreciate anything cold. And, please, skip the "sir." Peter insists on paying for our Cokes so I feel less guilty for getting the special treatment.

"Tell you what," the old man finally says. "Come in here until I finish." He gestures to his mop and bucket and leads us into his "overflow room," used for dancing in the evening. "The jukebox is on me—if you'd like to dance."

First a polka. Round and round we go in the hot, airless room. "No beer, no barrels, just good old St. Louis sweat," Peter jokes and takes off his jacket and loosens his tie.

"Not so fast for the next one," I plead. We sing with mock emotion: "Don't sit under the apple tree with anyone else but me, till I come marching home." Then "In the Mood," and we're off swinging. He flings me out, pulls me back— over and over—while we laugh like little kids. We are both dripping, but with the soft and soaring "The White Cliffs of

Dover," we skim round and round. I imagine my sundress to be a ball gown and myself Ginger Rogers. With little breath for talk, I blurt out that I don't want him to die, that I'd be scared were I in his place going overseas.

He stops abruptly and stares at me. I'm embarrassed: What have I said wrong? He takes my arm and escorts me to one of the booths, as if we're in one of those ritzy nightclubs you see in movies. "I'll dig up another Coke," he says and goes off toward the owner. When he returns and we're once again facing each other, he says he's relieved that I brought up the war—and being scared. "It's on everyone's mind but nobody says anything! Sometimes people can be just too polite." He's crunching his paper napkin into a ball, swallowing hard. "The Pacific's the hot spot now, right where I'm going. You're darned right I'm scared, Betty. Real scared."

"I think you're very brave," I mutter. Newsreel images play in my mind—of Japanese suicide bombers streaking out of the sky, plowing into our American ships; of ships with newly minted young officers like Peter; and of seamen first class like Tom. Suddenly I am ashamed that I've never told Tom I think he's brave. They could both be dead before this wretched war is over.

"I've often wanted to talk to you about religion and stuff," he says, eyes fixed on the paper ball he's made. "It seems real with your family."

I want to tell him about my new understanding of religion, but instead I brush off his remark with the crack, "Just because you're Protestant doesn't mean you're not Christian."

"Yeah, I'm Christian all right. But that doesn't keep me from feeling afraid of death. And then being ashamed that I'm afraid."

"Oh, Peetie." I'm shocked to hear me using his grandmother's name for him! "I'd be afraid too if I were facing what you're facing." Embarrassed, I reach for his arm. "Come on, let's dance."

Again I feel graceful and light, the way people tell me I look playing volleyball. The way I felt just a few minutes ago. Can Peter ever believe as I do, or want to believe, that every one of us is called to live our true lives in Heaven, that earthly death is only the entryway to a better life? And that some people—nuns for instance—are lucky enough to begin this heavenly life on earth? I wish he'd heard that choir at Mimi's funeral pleading with the angels of Heaven "to lead her into Paradise and receive her into the holy city of Jerusalem!" Right now, though, Bing Crosby is leading us: "I'll be seeing you in all the old, familiar places...in everything that's light and gay." Peter slows down, rocking us back and forth. I'm afraid of getting too sentimental, even weepy, so I quickly ask for another record.

"Fast or slow?"

"In between."

Too hot for jitterbugging, too sentimental for any more slow stuff, I think, and am glad for his choice of "Tonight We Love." When I start humming along, he tells me to hush up and holds me tighter. His slightly stubbled chin, which moved over my cheek and onto my bare shoulder, tickles me, and I'm sorry when we have to stop for a new record. As it spins around, he holds me even closer, his head nuzzling against my neck. "It's still the same old story, the fight for love and glory, the fundamental things apply, as time goes by." He stops our rocking to kiss my neck, gently. Instantly my face flushes. I'm glad he can't see me. I must look like a beet, and I'm afraid I might just start to cry. "Woman needs man and man must have his mate, no matter what the future brings, as time goes by." The tears that are about to spill over are for him, for Tom, for Mimi, for myself, for the little kisses he's sprinkling softly over my shoulders. "You must remember this, a kiss is just a kiss...."

But they aren't just kisses. They are so much more.

Suddenly I understand why that old foggy retreat master warned us against dancing cheek to cheek! It's so much more than dancing. It's sweaty necks to sweaty arms and wonderful warmth all over. This is nothing like dancing with those twerps at Jesuit High or the creepy USO guys. Soldiers' hot cheeks never made me feel like this. Peter's kisses and tickling chin make me feel different all over, inside and out. I could want so much more of this. My head is still wrapped around his as he resumes our rocking back and forth. When the record stops, he takes my face in his hands and kisses his way around my mouth, gently opening my lips.

"Peter, please." I take his hands down from my head, hold them tight and kiss them hungrily. I know for sure now that I'm not too young to appreciate what I will be giving up by going to the convent. By giving myself back to God. Peter maneuvers us back to the booth, and I look straight at him. He sees my tears rising and rushes with apologies. I reach across the table and put my hand over his mouth so I can tell him how very happy he has made me. No apology needed. "Just the opposite," I tell him. "I am sooo grateful." He's let me taste something I didn't know anything about—till just now. "But we've got to stop." If his kissing and hugging goes on, I'll be giving away something already spoken for. There are no tears in my voice when I go on to tell him about my plans of joining the convent.

June 15, 1945
History won't record this Friday as the day the war ended and "the lights went on again all over the world." But for my family that's exactly what it is. Because tonight, while we were at dinner, Tom called. He's back in the States. He is unharmed and will be home soon, at least to visit, before our move into the Lindell house. Maybe even before I leave for the novitiate.

"At last he has a real address," Mother announces. "It's okay to write him now."

But I've nothing to tell him. I have not heard from Reverend Mother Pauline since that day in April when Mother and Dad and I met with her. I took for granted then that she would accept me. But I've heard nothing. So there's nothing to tell Tom—or anyone. Wanting to be a nun doesn't mean the nuns want me, I guess. I go through the motions of being happy, kissing neighbors, relatives, and friends with the cheery news about Tom. But for me, the war is not over any more than it is for Peter. The battle for the Pacific rages on, with the struggle for Okinawa alone consuming thousands of lives. My battles are petty by comparison, yet they weigh me down.

Mostly Dad teases and Mother complains—about the same things they always have. Now, though, their gripes seem aimed at convincing me I don't have what it takes to be a nun. Does Reverend Mother feel the same way? Should I forget about wanting to do something special with my life? The memory of Peter's face scratching my bare shoulder distracts me. Could Dad be right about waiting a year?

After dinner, we kneel side by side in church for the regular Friday night Benediction, Mother next to the aisle with me at her side, Suzy and Dad on my other side. The priest reminds us to offer a prayer of thanks for the recent war news, and then turns to position the big gold monstrance high over his head, onto the tabernacle. While we all sing *"O Salutaris hostia,"* its familiar *"Bella premunt hostilia"* reminds me that "our foes press on from every side." Yes! Peter is still fighting off those Japanese dive-bombers, and I'm still battling with those kneeling right here, next to me. It's not yet over! And the hot tears roll.

"If you're going to give them up anyway, why do you need *more* clothes?" Suzy complains. Mother wonders why I still fiddle so much with "that paraphernalia" in the bathroom—meaning my collection of nail polishes, lipsticks, and hair curlers. "You'll be sharing space with a lot more than the three of us. Besides, for someone about to renounce the world, don't you think your appearance matters more than it should?"

Even Dad has a new twist on his old complaint about coming home late, missing family meals, staying too long on the phone. "If you can't obey us, how can you ever keep a vow of obedience?" At first I laughed off these cracks. But none of it seems funny anymore. I'm tired of keeping a stiff upper lip. Maybe I am unfit for convent life, because their attacks are definitely on target. I am vain, not very obedient, and a tad selfish. Of course, I could give Suzy my bike now and my tennis racket—she's constantly begging for them.

"It's easier for her to hand over the rest of her life than to give up her tennis racket," Mother tells Dad. But then she didn't hear Reverend Mother mention tennis courts at the novitiate. Reverend Mother's ideas help me most right now. "The convent doesn't require perfect people," she told me, "only willing people." I'm certainly willing. Still willing. But the nuns, are they willing to have me?

Benediction rolls on: *"Tantum ergo sacramentum."* I bend low, yet feel no humility, just humiliation. And shame—to have spoken about my plans, to have allowed myself be teased by my family like this before I know whether or not the nuns truly want me. I've offered to give up my life, only to find out I can't even give up my bike. My grand gesture is being ignored. Why don't the nuns want me?

The organ jolts me out of my melancholy with the rousing: "Holy God we praise Thy name...all on earth thy scepter claim." I pull myself up to stand beside my parents as the congregation, mostly old ladies, genuflect. Some of them smile in our direction; some, grasping Mother's hands, amble down the aisle. Everyone's happy about Tom. I can feel Mother's pride in Tom even as I hear her sniffle and glimpse her reaching back for the handkerchief in her purse. Tom is, after all, her firstborn. And he's coming home. She's singing too—which she doesn't usually—and, to my surprise, sounds great. And looks prettier than she has in years.

As usual Dad belts out the line: "Infinite Thy vast domain, everlasting is Thy reign." "The poor man's Caruso," Mother used to tease in the days before the war, when she was more often in a teasing mood. Most of all she teased him about his looks, how all the old ladies in her Altar and Rosary group insisted he was the handsomest "Irish lad" around. It's even more true lately, thanks to Hitler. As that nasty dictator's picture—with his tight little spit of a mustache—has become familiar to everyone, Dad's mustache has gradually spread out, along with his hair. He hasn't been plastering down his kinky curls so much lately, looking definitely less Hitler-like. A girlfriend of mine even says he's "cuter than Clark Gable," especially as his streaks of gray have increased. (Odd for your friends to have a crush on your father?) Both Mother and Dad are handsome and happy now. For them, the war is over.

Even Suzy is full of smiles, not fidgeting the way she usually does at church. She's shot up so fast this past year that she can elbow me in the ribs, as she does now, making me giggle against my will. Everyone is happy. But I'm not. And I'm ashamed that I'm not. I wish I'd never said anything to anyone about the convent. It's like a secret disease, eating away at me, this embarrassment. And I'm afraid it shows.

As my work at Mimi's house stretches on and on, I go to bed each night dejected. The rhythms of everyone around me are speeding up, while I feel stopped in my tracks. I have the peculiar sense of having changed places with my parents. Especially with Mother. She's always been weighed down with frowns and worry. Now, though, she's filled with schemes for their new house and about-to-return Tom. She's creating a new future for the family, while I'm stuck awkwardly somewhere in the past.

Of course, I'm glad they're happy. I only wish I could be happy with them—in their bustle and chatter and their "Happy Days Are Here Again" song. They even look younger, laugh more, spend money more freely. The war's been good for Dad's business, so he's full of plans to expand, to build new offices, maybe make Tom a partner in a few years, since it's looking like he'll settle here and probably marry Mary Kay, the girlfriend who's been waiting for him. It's all about the future—a future I'm tossing aside. Same with Mother. I'd like to be happy with her. Every letter from Tom, every mention of his name these days brings a look to her face that says at last her burden is lifted. Already she's stopped praying "for Tom's safe return" and prays instead "in thanksgiving" for his return. No longer does she scrimp and save "for the war effort," or nag us to save bits of string and tinfoil. All that has stopped. The rest of the country may still be fighting a war, but hers is over.

Was this how she was before we were born? Hair softer, lipstick remembered more often, even before breakfast? Friends who knew her then speak of her beauty as "classic"— something I've never understood, the word conjuring up statues of stern Greek gods. Mostly, though, her new look comes from being happy—so happy she hasn't even noticed that the nuns aren't responding to my application. And she's distracted with all the painters and plumbers around fixing up Mimi's old house. On my darkest days, I imagine she's glad I'm leaving home. This is unfair, of course. From the first she's included me in their plans for "our new house," even designating one of the bedrooms as mine. She's made it clear she doesn't want me to give away any of my belongings. "They're yours and I intend to keep them for you, convent or no."

When they were children, both my parents heard discussions about the nineteenth-century specter of nuns being turned out of convents in France without money or means of support. So Dad is careful about the war bonds in the bank account he had me open with the money I made from my first babysitting job. All my earnings since then have gone straight into war bonds. He promises they won't be touched, nor will my share of the inheritance from Grandpa and Mimi. He'll keep investing it for me. He's already put my Social Security card in the safe deposit box with all the important family documents. "You may be sent home, Betty. Novices often are, so remember: There will always be a place for you here. This is your home, understand?"

It doesn't feel like it, though. All around me, gears are shifting, people are making new plans—plans from which I've chosen to separate myself. At Bixby's, I hear my girlfriends planning good times ahead, not just because we are all now "college women," but because the war is winding down. Once again kids talk about "college away" and real careers, instead of "jobs for the duration." Best of all, the boys will be back. The worst shortage of all is almost over. I envy my friends their plans, their anticipation for the future, yet I feel isolated from them all.

If only I knew someone, anyone else, applying to the sisters. What are they like, the other applicants? Older? Out of college? Career girls? Farm girls? There's no one for me to talk to about all this, with both Gaby and Sister Augusta still at their summer missions.

The summer job Dad gave me makes me feel even worse. As I clear out heaps of family photos in Mimi's trunk—three generations of brides and grooms, new babies, first communicants, graduates—I ask myself: Why am I cutting myself off from this handsome family? Aunt Theresa's picture does it. She's the aunt I've always been told I resemble most. Here she is in 1924—not much older than I am now—holding her first baby. And there, in a snapshot from last Christmas, that baby is grown and holding her own first baby. It's easy to see what my kids would look like if I'd forget about the convent.

They'd have long narrow faces, high foreheads, and only occasionally a smile: that's what distinctive about all these Byrnes. And those intense, deep-set eyes that Dad and Aunt Theresa have. Those, I have.

Dad's words at a cousin's wedding last month sound so different to me now. Then I thought it was the champagne—too much for him, too new for me—that made us both so weepy. "It's not too late for you to change your mind, Betty m'girl. Before you turn your back on us, think about it: Wouldn't you like a wedding like this? So you could add your own little boys and girls to this clan?" He went on about Mother and Mimi, and how motherhood is also a holy vocation. "Nuns don't have the corner on goodness, you know."

The same thing old Dr. Maloney told me when I asked him to fill out the convent health form: "Two generations of Byrne babies I've delivered. I can vouch that you're from good stock, Betty. You can make it as a nun. You have what it takes. But the Church needs mothers, too. People like your own mother and your grandmother. Good women, unselfish women."

Even Mother begins to talk that way. After so many years of fussing about how selfish I am, she's started talking about how the neighbors say I am a good babysitter. How their kids like me, and the mothers find me so responsible: "Don't you think it might be God's will for you to be a wife and mother?"

But God and His will are pretty remote for me right now. I'm not sure what I'm praying for at this point. Every night I kneel by my bed and rattle off: "For the repose of Mimi's soul, for world peace, for Peter's safe return, for my own vocation." But my mind fills with images of babies. Sometimes I imagine—and actually *feel*—soft baby fuzz against my face, the tight clutch of little fingers, the whiff of baby powder. Is it those babies from the photos, or am I remembering my newest little cousins? Or Suzy, when she was an infant? Or myself? How can I remember being held and patted and sung to sleep? All over again I feel the warmth of Grandpa's lap, the bristle of his mustache, the stubble of his chin. (Or was that Dad's? Or Peter's?) What am I praying for? To have my own baby? Or to be babied?

⁘

July 15, 1945
"Dear Betty," begins Reverend Mother Pauline's impeccable script inserted above mimeographed mouthfuls. First I'm congratulated, then instructed about the order's responsibility in accepting members, especially minors. Finally, on two closely typed pages are the theology justifying, the timetables describing, and the canon law regulating the next five years of my life. First I will be a postulant, next a novice, and after that a junior sister with temporary vows for three years. Only then, if the community as a whole wants me, will I be allowed to make final vows.

Lists follow—the required "clothing, supplies, sundries," enough to fill Mimi's old trunk. At the moment, however, they make Mother fretful. "What on earth will you do with 200 name tapes? Or two dozen pair of lisle hose? Don't they know how impossible it is to get even one pair these days? And fifteen yards of sateen? And gingham? There's still a war on, for heaven's sake!" She's so vexed, but why? Can't she see I'm happy? Reverend Mother urges me to trust in the goodness of God, to pray to Mary, Our Mother of Good Counsel. Yet my own mother fusses, "I don't know how those nuns can expect all this. I thought they were supposed to be poor!"

Everything on the list has to last through my five years of training and beyond, I tell her. But she's still annoyed: bathrobes, wool and cotton; nightgowns, flannel and seersucker; petticoats, wool and sateen.

Dad chuckles at the mention of drawers and chemises. "Too bad your grandmother can't be here. She could explain a lot of this." But he is happy for me; I can tell by the way he immediately started working on the trunk. "We've got to finish this up, Betty m'girl. Let's go." He's brought his tools with him to the Lindell house. He prints my name on a card with our new address after I explain to him the convent custom of addressing a girl's trunk to her home during years of the novitiate and temporary vows. I pick out the yellowed isinglass cover held in place by a metal frame, eventually releasing several old address cards. When he pries off the last corner of the frame and the remaining bits of isinglass and cardboard fall like confetti, we stare together at the original name card. In a firmer version of what Dad and I can both recognize as Mimi's distinctive script, she had addressed her trunk to herself at Uncle Marty's:

MISS MARY ELIZABETH O'CONNOR
C/O MR. AND MRS. MARTIN O'CONNOR
ST. LOUIS, MISSOURI, U.S.A.

Years later this same trunk went back with her to Ireland when she and Grandpa and their children took off in 1910 for their grand pilgrimage to the shrines of Europe. Throughout my childhood, Mimi was still delving into this trunk, dispensing to her grandchildren—and later to her great-grandchildren—holy water from Lourdes, relics of the True Cross from Rome, rosaries from Lisieux, Miraculous Medals from Paris, scapulars from Assisi, and, always, linen from Ireland: handkerchiefs, doilies, table runners, hemstitched or lace trimmed or hand rolled. In a thousand small ways, Mimi's treasures from this trunk have propagated the pieties of Catholic Europe and Ireland within her Missouri family.

Dad studies the original address card. "This writing—it's just the way I was taught by those old Irish nuns." He gives a small laugh, but seems preoccupied, maybe even sad. Then casually, in a soft voice, he drops a bomb: Both Mimi and my own mother had, in their teens, wanted to be nuns, had actually entered novitiates intending to "take the veil."

"What?!" I'm stunned.

"Shhh," he whispers. "She doesn't like me to talk about it." He puts his arm around me and moves us both over to sit on top of the old trunk. "For Mama, it was that Irish curse of weak lungs, 'consumption' they called it." He brightens and grins sheepishly: "For which I've always been grateful. If the nuns hadn't sent her home, I'd never be here—nor you, Betty m'girl." But then his face clouds over. "Your mother, now, is different. I've never known why she quit. Maybe they sent her home? At any rate, she doesn't want to talk about it." With his thumb he makes a cross over his pursed lips— Mimi's gesture as well. It means shut up; big secret; don't repeat. "One thing more," he says. But I'm barely listening, still shocked at this huge family secret! How I would love to talk to Mimi about her long-ago decision like my own. "I don't want you changing your name, Betty. I told Reverend Mother, if they get you, it'll be as Sister Elizabeth. I don't want you ending up the way Lucy did—'Immaculata,' for God's sake! Or 'Redempta'! None of that for you, Betty m'girl. Understand?" His words are stern, but not his eyes.

Several nights later, Dad produces tickets for the Super Chief for the three of us—Mother and Dad and me. Travel for pleasure has been nearly impossible these last four war years. Yet somehow he's managed to get these. The plan is to vacation in California the first week of August. My last fling, he calls it. That mobilizes me to finish what Dad—but never Mother—jokingly calls my trousseau. I finish the trunk myself, covering the gray lining of the tray with flowered oilcloth and painting the old wood inside a bright green— something for my new life that connects me to Mimi and her Irish family. Day by day, I add items from the lists given me by the motherhouse: towels, blankets, sheets; an umbrella and galoshes; thimbles, thread, pinking shears, embroidery hooks, and pins of every kind, including tiny black "veil pins."

And I sew. With Mother, and alone: the black postulant

dress with its white pique collars and cuffs and elbow-length cape, then petticoats and aprons, and each with its own hand-sewn name tape. Mother fusses, but soon she's adding items not on any of the lists: a handy little handkerchief pocket hidden inside my cape; a small leather folding frame with family snapshots; and a tin of old-fashioned fruit candy wrapped in a wool kerchief for "cold nights." She sees to it that the waistbands and seams are generously sewn for letting out in stages. I'll gain weight in the novitiate, she says. She knows how I hate to sew. With a hot-water bottle tucked in among the blankets, she warns, "You won't get a hot toddy like your father makes for you when your period comes. That's for sure." Is she remembering her own novitiate? What we can't find in the local stores, we order from a nuns' outfitting catalog. She absolutely refuses, however, to let me mail-order the required arch preserver oxfords. Shoes must be tried on, she insists, and promptly calls around town to locate what I need.

Once settled in the old-ladies shoe store downtown, we're both stunned at the sight of the huge black objects the clerk brings us. Embarrassed at our embarrassment, he prattles on while waiting for Mother to stick her foot into them. "Fine leather here, madam, sturdy arches. Sensible for sure, and handsome to boot."

Mother doesn't seem to hear him, or his pun, so I quickly untie my saddle shoes and present him with my bobby-sock foot. This stops his chatter. In awkward silence, he laces onto my feet the pointed oxfords that remind me of nothing so much as shiny new submarines. When I stand to let his thumb discover my toe, I can't feel anything. My toes are numb, and I slip across the carpet, struggling like a newborn colt in åthe X-ray contraption. In the mirror, I see Mother's head down. She's clutching her handkerchief while grandmotherly faces stare at me. The peasant blouse, hair ribbons, broomstick skirt don't go with the unyielding black leather now encasing my bobby socks.

"Wear just one pair the first year—leave the others in their box," Mother says as we reach our back stoop, and I struggle with my awkward bundle of shoeboxes tied together with flimsy wartime string. The whole way home on the crowded bus, Mother held a trance-like silence. "Your feet will change," she did say. "You're still growing. I can always exchange the second pair for you. You never know what will happen once you get there. You'll grow, fill out. When I was your age, I kept growing for a long time. You're awfully young, Betty."

I feel as though there's an ugly weight in my chest, and I wonder, but cannot ask, at what age did *you* go to the convent? Did you fill this kind of trunk? Get shoes like these? "Remember, Betty I can exchange all those other things."

She means the piles of long underwear and the thick black cotton stockings piled on Tom's old bed. As each received its own hand-sewn name tape, I've put it carefully in the trunk. "You may never need any of this," she says as I follow her upstairs into their bedroom where she takes off her hat. Is that what she wants? I wonder. That I fail as she did? Watching her face in the dresser's mirror, I can see she's still vexed. "Promise me, Betty, don't ever worry about changing your mind. Girls must do it all the time, change their minds about the convent."

Did she worry about changing *her* mind? How long did it take her to know it wasn't for her? Was she happy or sad to give up her dream? Why can't we talk about what happened back then? As she turns to close her bedroom door, I think she's going to tell me her secret. But instead it's an order. "For heaven's sake, if you ever want to quit, just do it. Don't worry about what people will say. Or how we feel. Promise me? Just come home." Her lips begin to twitch and her eyes water, but she closes them tight and squeezes my hand the same way she did on that awful Pearl Harbor Sunday when we all knew Tom would have to go to war. Yet in a moment, she's again composed. "Everything will be all right for you, I know that. Everything will be all right. But, if you do quit, we can always use these blankets and linens right here. We never have enough, the way you and Suzy invite people to sleep over. Besides, she'll need such things herself for college."

Right now, though, we're reminded of how far off Suzy is from college. Screeches of laughter from Tom's room tell us that Suzy and her girlfriends are up to no good. Ever since helping me move the trunk from the Lindell house, they've been pestering me about the inner secrets of a nun's wardrobe. Now, I discover, they're exploring for themselves. Those little twerps! They've gone through everything! There they are, the three of them, sprawled on the floor, poring over pages of the nun's outfitting catalog—poking fun at the corsets, camisoles, knee warmers and bloomers, giggling over whether chamber pots and cheesecloth "personal napkins" are part of their fifth-grade teacher's life. Suzy holds up the page filled with pictures of hair clippers, her freckled face beaming with discovery. "I knew it! They shave their heads!"

Mother shoos them out of the room and lowers the lid over the disheveled mess. Then she hesitates, caught by the sight of Dad's handiwork underneath the new isinglass cover on the nameplate. Her fingers move over his elegant printing. "Your father loves you very much, Betty." She speaks quietly, reminding me that sign painting was one of his many occupations during those early Depression years, right after he got out of the hospital. "You can't, of course, remember that lovely sign he made and decorated when I was pregnant with you. There were tiny roses all around— and lettering just like this." She fingers the isinglass. "Only it was pale pink and said BABY ELIZABETH. We never had a crib for either you or Tom. And we never called you Baby Elizabeth either. That was his idea. I wanted something to dress up that old wreck of a bed we used for you. The sign was his idea, too."

Quickly she covers her face with both hands. I sit beside her and would like to put my arm around her but, with my awkward bundle, I am even more clumsy than usual. Finally, she turns and we hug as the four black submarines spill out of their boxes and onto the floor. "Betty, my baby," she keeps repeating, and I think that "baby" seems to go with "Betty" better than it does with "Elizabeth" (and would have fit better on that sign). Then suddenly I feel sorry for Mother, aware of some very deep sadness and insecurity. I wish she could share it with me. Does it have to do with her own convent experience? It's perplexing to feel older and more secure than your mother. But I do.

May 1946

It's a Friday. "This is the day the Lord has made," the choir sings, as we postulants, all thirty-two of us, move solemnly down the aisle of our motherhouse chapel dressed as brides. We call this big day Reception Day, because each of us will receive the "holy habit" and, with the donning of the habit, we will also receive a new name. We will then be officially received into the order, though still "novices" until a year from now when we make our bridal vows to our Lord and Master, Jesus Christ. A major celebration for all involved.

Yet as words of the glorious hymn keep reminding us about what "glories the Lord has made," I find myself distracted more by what I've made than by what God has made: my own habit up there on a table in the sanctuary, all neatly folded, along with those of my classmates. We've been struggling with them in sewing class these past ten months; the umpteen parts folded into one of those dark bundles up there with my name on it. And now this prelate of the Church is giving it to me as if he (or God?) has made it! Some, maybe most, Catholics refer to this ceremony of becoming a nun as

"Taking the veil." Yet making the veil was the most impossible of our efforts. While each of us managed to complete, in varying degrees, all the other parts of the habit—coif, band, tunic, scapular, inner and outer sleeves, cincture, rosary (yes, we even mastered the stringing of beads into the rosary that will hang from our cinctures), to a person we flunked out when it came to the veil. All that was needed was a hem at the top and bottom of a seventy-two-by-fifty-four-inch rectangular piece of silk, since the selvages on the fifty-four-inch sides didn't need hemming. The trick was the hand-rolled hem, which none of us could master. So old nuns in the infirmary—our sisters now, though we've yet to speak with any of them—were recruited to hem our veils. Only then could the makings of each girl's future habit get bundled together with that white satin ribbon up there for the bishop to bless.

Right now, though, we are brides, brides of Christ, as the choir reminds us over and over, as our slow procession makes its way down the chapel aisle: *"Veni Sponsa Christi,"* in Latin, then English, "Come Bride of Christ." We carry no flowers, though our simple white dress with its short veil is held in place with a ring of simple garden blossoms—providing a stark, but rather lovely contrast with the super-decorated convent chapel. An abundance of spring flowers fills every possible niche, tied onto pews and prie-dieux, in baskets on the high altar and nosegays on side altars.

To my friends and family who have come to witness the ceremony, the table with its weight of black serge may look like an ugly mistake, as Mother says. Dad is more concerned that no one, family or girls, gets sick, considering the heat and length of the ceremonies and our empty stomachs. Not to speak of the heavy floral scents mingled with incense challenging his asthma. Yet he remains his usual unflappable self, enjoying and joking about some of the odd names for girls he previously knew as my friends Patty, Judy, and

Mary Jean.

I, though, am oblivious of any humor. All is a beautiful blur, as the swoosh of a fan ruffles slightly the light tulle veil falling over my forehead, tickling my nose. I feel pretty and girlish and grown-up all at the same time, and there are smiles of love everywhere. More nuns are crammed into this chapel than I've ever seen in one place. My sisters, all of them! I float with pride at my decision to join them. Being the tallest of our postulant class, though the youngest, I am the last to reach my place at the far end of the curved altar rail as the choir is concluding its long *Veni Sponsa Christi*.

Mother Pauline takes her place behind us, ready to introduce our class to the bishop sitting high up on the altar in an elaborate chair brought out only for such solemn ceremonies. In a high clear voice, she repeats the prescribed formula from canon law, concluding: "Therefore I humbly petition Your Excellency to allow these postulants to commence their novitiate." Meaning, that after our ten months as postulants, or "seekers," Mother Pauline and her council have determined that we are, each of us, of sound mind and body and sincere in our desire to continue with the next phase of our formal testing time, the Novice Year, before the making of vows.

She moves over to the girl at the start of the line and gently taps her on her shoulder. Judy rises to face the bishop with eyes "modestly cast down"—a convent discipline we're already practicing. As the bishop comes down from the altar toward her, he takes one of the dark bundles, mumbles a Latin blessing over it, and sprinkles it with holy water. When he hands Judy her bundle, he raises his voice so all of us can hear: "Judith, my child, you have been known in the world as Judith Marie Flynn, but henceforth"—the congregation hushes to hear every word—"you shall be known in religion as Sister Francis Assisi." A sudden intake of breath is audible: Nuns and families alike are surprised by her new name. The bishop continues his formula, in normal tones. "My dear Sister, you are now beginning your novitiate. May God give you the grace to learn the meaning of the vows you intend to make at the conclusion of this year as a novice." He offers his hand for her to kiss his ring and moves on, repeating the same ritual with the next postulant. Meanwhile, two older nuns materialize next to Judy and whisk her out the side entrance and through the doors marked CLOISTER to "dress" her.

Everyone strains to hear the next name, and the next, as one after the other of my classmates gets a new name and disappears into the cloister to be clothed with the contents of her dark bundle. The chapel remains hushed as the bishop stumbles a bit over some of the stranger names, like Sister Anastasia, Sister Marie Hedwig, and Sister Mary Didacus.

We were asked to submit three names. There were no guarantees, of course. I chose "Mary Clare" after my mother, "Mary John" after my father and grandfather, and the theological savvy "Maria Theotokas." So I was surprised, and slightly let down—yet somehow relieved—when the bishop gets to me at the end of the line and calls me "Sister Elizabeth Mary." It's my real name, my birth name. What Dad asked for, so he must be pleased. With Mother, the whole thing is more complicated. I don't think she had been too happy with how her second baby was named in the first place, at my baptism, after Mimi—who also had been Elizabeth Mary.

My dressers are Sisters Stella and Aloysius, neither of whom I've met before but instantly identify as "Mutt and Jeff." Tall, slim Sister Jeff immediately locks herself onto my elbow and guides me out of the chapel through the cloister doors, while little Sister Mutt holds my precious dark bundle tight to her ample bosom as she bustles down the hallway ahead of us toward the refectory. As we walk, Sister Jeff plucks the tulle off my head with one hand and finds a candle for that trip back down that aisle. We must hurry, she says quietly. Except for two other postulants and myself, everyone else was ready to head back to the chapel when we arrive in the dining room. It won't do to keep the bishop waiting any longer, Jeff declares. We must skip the ritual haircut for me.

For this special day, our cavernous dining room serves as the dressing area for our transformation from bride to nun. Silence, ordinarily prescribed for mealtime, technically still prevails, yet the atmosphere was unmistakably giggly and joyful. Tables and chairs, rearranged into separate dressing areas for each girl and her dressers, are littered with the discarded bridal paraphernalia from the other brides preceding me.

In seconds, Jeff manages to hoist the heavy robe over my head, add the inner and outer sleeves, while Mutt works the stiff leather of the cincture so the rosary can hang properly from my waist. Then as Jeff secures my long hair in a tight ponytail, Mutt fusses with some recalcitrant wisps of stray hair. Together they arrange the stiffly starched coif and band over my head, adjust the scapular on my shoulders, and finish with some final pins for the veil. All in less than five minutes!

I can hear the *Veni Sponsa Christi* starting up again in the chapel, so we know the others are poised to start the procession back. Hurriedly, I tie up my stiff new shoes while Sister Mutt scrambles to locate a match for my plain white candle. Then, despite unfamiliar skirts and heavy shoes, I run—veil flying and rosary swinging—out of the refectory down the hall to the chapel door. I reach my place at the end of the line just as the novice at the head of the line starts back into the chapel for Mass.

That's when the discomfort begins. Gone is that queenly sense of floating. I feel encased like a mummy in clothes I've never imagined could be so heavy—throughout all our sewing we never tried on all the parts at once. We should have.

Now with every movement of my head, this starched coif cuts into my forehead and neck. And the heavy veil, on top of my mass of hair, makes everything itch, especially my ears. Of course, there's no way to scratch, even if such an indecorous act were permitted. I feel trapped in this very habit I've loved making. Yet an entirely different sort of discomfort wiggles even deeper inside me now, distracting me no end. It penetrates my now starched-in ears as the bishop repeats the words of Jesus himself: "You have not chosen me, but I have chosen *you.*" We are Brides of Christ, chosen by Him, this Prince of the Church keeps reminding us. It is God's choice for me to be here, not mine.

But it *is* my choice! Everything about this day reminds me: It is my choice. Can this bishop possibly grasp the drama surrounding this word for me? No one's forced me—or even encouraged this step—quite the contrary. I want to yell out to him: It's *my* choice. Been *my* choice all the way! Even in these months since I've joined the order, with each stage in the long sewing process, I've felt a renewed sense of embarking on a great adventure, one that I've chosen for myself. Now at last I am wearing the habit I've longed to wear, even if it feels awful. I hear again our neighbor Mrs. Hughes yelling at me over our back fence: "You're crazy! You're going to kill your mother. You're only a child!" And she wasn't the only one to say such horrible things. Mother told me to just swallow it and think about the nice things Mrs. Hughes has to say about me.

Again, I try to swallow feelings certainly not suitable for this great day, to switch to the nicer things this old bishop is saying. Like how we are being initiated into this family of sisters, he says. And I think that it's like those young braves in Indian tribes; to initiate them into the tribe, their elders put them through all manner of difficult challenges. The comparison helps. The bishop may say that it's God choosing me, but I know I've been doing the choosing—including this coif I've made that's now making my ears itch. It's not queenly or bride-like, but it's *mine*. Definitely. What I chose that day back in Gaby's English class. My choice, yes.

Chapter 4

1947

Fall Semester, 1947

After finishing two years of novitiate and finally making first vows, I've started teaching. Six of us live in the convent of St. Patrick's parish in a run-down section of north St. Louis—five teachers and infirm Sister Anna. Our convent is the nicest home in the neighborhood. Twice as many nuns lived here when the school was established in the 1920s, with less than two-thirds the number of children enrolled now. That, of course, was long before the war, before defense industries blanketed the neighborhood, back when the children of prosperous white families took music lessons and art classes from nuns who taught only music or art, a time when housewife mothers picked up their kids promptly at three o'clock.

Not now, though. Since the war, everything's different. Yard duty lasts until six o'clock, when working mothers—many of them single mothers, an unknown phrase for me before now—rush to pick up their kids before the gate is locked. By doubling up grades and cutting such "frills" as kindergarten, art and music—five of us teach all eight grades, a total of over 330 children. Seventy-three of them make up my third and fourth grades, and each has a place to sit, except me. My desk and chair have been moved to the cloakroom in the rear, replaced by a dozen kindergarten stools up front—giving me slim yet sufficient access to the blackboard. My first classroom.

We also cook and keep house in our small convent while performing parish duties considered too important to be entrusted to laywomen: chores like ironing the sacred altar linens for the church; making hosts for communion; and counting the Sunday collection. On Saturdays, Sister Julie Anne and I—the only ones in our convent without college degrees—trek across the city to classes at the Jesuit university near our motherhouse.

The school day begins with all the children in the yard lined up by grade—girls first, then boys, "arm-distance apart." Sister Mercedes, our principal as well as our sister superior in the convent, stations herself up front, in charge. The other four of us guard the rear. We salute the cross, then the flag, and struggle through the "Star-Spangled Banner." As we all file into the schoolhouse, "Stars and Stripes Forever" blasts over the loudspeaker while Sister Mercedes keeps a keen eye on us all, registering the details of every student's and every nun's posture, carriage, shoes, and socks. The kids call her "Sister Sergeant." She's both my mentor and monitor, because, as a sister of temporary vows, I'm still "in formation." She trails my students into our classroom during the "Stars and Stripes," then stands in the rear while I lead morning prayers. These few minutes, along with the outdoor rituals, are the only truly orderly moments of my day.

After she leaves, peace disintegrates. My classroom becomes a mass of wiggly kids filling in the reams of dittoed workbook pages I pass out every morning. I struggle to teach, aware all the time of not knowing how. The lowly crayon has become my best teaching aid as I switch back and forth, alternating between third and fourth grades. Baskets of these crayons—broken or discarded, scavenged from other classrooms—sit at the back of each row. It's more fun for me, I tell them, if their spelling and arithmetic pages are decorated. So they color away, with things growing steadily noisier until the three o'clock bell. Only with the closing prayer does order return, and then we all march out into the yard, joining Sister Sergeant on the PA singing with gusto "Faith of Our

Fathers, living still, in spite of dungeon, fire and sword."

But it's my own dungeon I collapse into when the kids are all gone. Exhausted, I slump into the large desk chair in the cloakroom. Turning to my daily paperwork duties, I once again attack the daily attendance record. How can I be sure who among the seventy-two wiggly little people were here today and who weren't? At the beginning of the year, I tried calling roll, but all hell broke out, with Dickie not answering to Richard and William not recognizing he was Billy. So I've been relying on memory. Yet the darling little devils keep switching places. So every afternoon it's the same quandary enveloping me: Was he or wasn't he here today? Sister Mercedes has drummed into me that completing the roll book, in permanent ink, is one of the most serious of our obligations as teachers. It's a legal document, she says, apt to be called into court as evidence. Guessing at attendance could be criminal, yet guessing is all I can manage. In confession every Friday, Father Fogarty doesn't know what to make of my sin.

Worst of all, though, no one is learning much, including me. That's the real crime. The kids who didn't read in September still don't. I'm simply babysitting. Each morning I wake up exhausted, and each night I go to bed more so. My voice is perpetually hoarse from trying all day long to keep order, and my legs never stop throbbing, even in bed. It's a losing battle. I am neither a good teacher nor a good nun, yet Sister Mercedes seems none the wiser. She calls me "Sister Mary Joy"—because of my pink cheeks and ready smile, I suppose. Yet this is only the outside me, the one who every recess slathers peanut butter on leftover toast and gulps down milk and has been steadily "filling out"—a sign to my superior that everything is okay. "High color and good appetite are the signs of a true vocation," she chortles.

I'm not so sure. Shouldn't I be happy, or at least at peace, if I am doing exactly what my superiors—and, therefore,

God—want of me? Or does "becoming truly spiritual"—a goal still elusive even after those novitiate years when "spiritual formation" was the whole point—mean that life for a nun is destined to be one long penitential trial? Miserable, though holy? This dark thought plagues me during each night's Examination of Conscience: I feel myself further away than ever from what I came to the convent to be.

When I can finally admit this, I seek out Mother Alicia, my beloved Novice Mistress, up at the motherhouse. She knows me better than anyone. So I worked up the courage to ask her—in confidence, of course—if maybe I should leave this order and transfer to a cloistered community? I wouldn't have to teach, and the surroundings might foster the "spirituality" still eluding me. Perhaps I'd fit in better there, I said. She listened patiently, smiling sweetly, but told me I'd never last in a monastic setting. Better I should pray to the Blessed Mother, then ask my principal for help.

When I go to Sister Mercedes, I hear only that I should "offer up" my troubles and ask God to make me more spiritual. She then delivers long-winded accounts of *her* laments: how her once lovely school bulges beyond capacity, fewer teachers for so many more children, no repairs since the war, and on and on. It's all God's will, she sighs, then turns to her large wall calendar and dramatically draws a diagonal through that day. "You've got to tie a knot and hang on, Sister dear. In no time, it will be Friday." She flips the pages of her huge calendar, one after another, faster and faster: "Soon it will be next Friday, then the Friday after, then next month. And soon it will be June!"

Tie a knot. Hang on. She doesn't expect anything more of me. But I do.

Chapter 5

1948

March 13, 1948

I'm still miserable, and ashamed of it, both in the convent and in the classroom. I feel out of joint with my own life. Except on Saturdays, which are fun. On this Saturday, I leave St. Pat's early in the morning for the university, where I'm taking Calculus 1 and Western Civ, both hard subjects forcing my brain to work the way I love: intricately in calculus, dramatically when studying the sweep of civilizations.

I feel alive, inside and out, these few hours every week. Even the weather seems better and the smog less thick on Saturdays. Most of all I get to exchange ideas with professors and classmates, and to mingle with my BNCs (convent lingo for beloved novitiate companions). We giggle like the schoolgirls we really are but are forced to forget during the week, swapping horror stories and laughing at our blunders as beginners in the classroom.

I relate things I never tell any sisters at St. Pat's, like the time my petticoat was falling and I ordered the kids to put heads down for a nap, but little Jerry looked up and saw it all: the underskirt falling to the floor and me stepping out of it. He smirked at me for the rest of that day, letting me know he had something on me. Or when I gagged while inspecting scalps for lice and could barely keep from throwing up. Or lost my voice when some kid asked me how to spell Stuyvesant. Or froze in terror one night in the kitchen as I watched the entire evening meal, a meal I had prepared, going up in flames while the other five sisters sat silently in the refectory, waiting to be fed. But I've never shared with anyone those deeper, dark thoughts boiling up in the middle of the night, nor mentioned the tears that come over me in the silence of meditation or my struggles to keep my inside self from showing on the outside, or how I asked to switch to a cloistered order. Not even with my good friend and special BNC, Sister Madeleine. I'm just too ashamed.

I think I could tell Sister Marie Gabrielle, my wonderful high school English teacher, except she is away at Fordham getting her graduate degree in English lit. Of course I'd feel ashamed and humiliated to have Gaby know how impossible it is to hold on to that wonderful insight I got from her English class, about the real meaning of "religion" and how her poets can help us understand its place in our lives. Yet somehow it wouldn't be as bad. I miss her.

I'm silent around Sister Augusta as well; she might as well be out of town, too. In the three years since she was my high school civics teacher and helped me with my application to join the order, she's become a brand-new assistant professor of political science at the university. Some Saturdays I get a chance for a quick visit with her, in the refectory at the motherhouse, or in the hallway near her office at the university. I chat easily about the small, easy-to-retell dramas of my weekday life. She listens and laughs with me, yet I say nothing of my dark inner self. There's no way to express that. Right now I'd like her help choosing a topic for my very first term paper in Western Civ. Its due date is uncomfortably close, so I'm here outside her closed office door going over how I should pose my request.

When I step into her office, I'm so startled I almost forget what I rehearsed. Her tiny office has the same high ceilings, old-fashion windows, and creaking wood floor as my calculus professor's a few doors down. Yet it's worlds apart. His is as spare as any monk's cell—despite his being a youngish, very handsome, layman. Augusta's is unlike any nun's space I've ever seen, either office or convent cell. Not at all what I would expect from someone whose rule of life, the same one I'm trying to live by, cautions us to "shun the superfluous." When she answers her phone, I get a moment to drink it all in. A sprouting avocado pit balances in a water glass on her windowsill; odd-shaped rocks act as bookends and paper-weights; seashells lie scattered on the edge of bookshelves. A play of lovely colors shimmers across the otherwise drab wall, catching my attention. She covers the mouthpiece and whispers: "Chartres," pointing with her phone elbow to a transparency taped high on her windowpane. Nothing contrary to our vow of poverty, I think, because nothing's of monetary value. Yet for Sister Sergeant, all of it would be contrary to the Holy Rule's maxim to "avoid whatever fosters individuality." Everything here is so unmistakably Augusta's.

"Congratulations! I'm so glad you've come by," she says, bidding me to close the door behind me, then whispering, "I was hoping you would. We need to celebrate a birthday, don't we?" How does she know I turned twenty last Sunday? Birthdays aren't noted in the convent, not officially. Certainly none of the sisters at St. Pat's was any the wiser, although a number of cards were stuffed into my drawer in the refectory. Mother and Dad must have got all their living relatives to mail me birthday cards. Suddenly the bleakness of this Lenten time lifts. Turning to her file cabinet, she removes a large thermos and some brown lunch sacks. Can she mean celebrating—with *food?*—in Lent? "So how are things going?" She speaks casually.

My usual "Oh, fine!" doesn't come out. Instead, I blurt out, "It's awful, all wrong. It should be more like them," I practically shout, pointing to the avocado sprouts and the shimmering colors. "But it isn't—not even remotely." I stop short of mentioning my frequent stomach upsets, nose-bleeds, or black despair. "I'm a lousy teacher, Sister. And a lousy nun. My life's all wrong." Sister Augusta signals for me to close the door and sit down.

My outburst mortifies me, almost as much as my rising tears. But I pull in my chin, take a deep breath, and they're checked. I've retrieved my composure, and she seems none the wiser. I watch in amazement as an extravagant—by convent standards—spread of goodies materializes on her desk: a couple of red apples, a banana, a fist full of licorice ropes, a couple of Mars bars, a few slices of Velveeta, and, most improbable, a slab of brownies. I'm astonished at the loot. But also perplexed. How can this be? Our Holy Rule states, "Sisters shall not take their meals outside the refectory, unless ill, traveling, or otherwise unable to join their sisters at table." Besides, it's Lent. Catholics don't eat between meals in Lent.

Sister Augusta reads my confusion and quotes the rule back at me: "'For charity or necessity, *any* rule can be mitigated.' Even in Lent. Besides, 'Pilgrims en route must take nourishment wherever it can be found.' Remember that one?" Her sly look reminds me of when she was my teacher explaining how a talent for rationalizing helps politicians. "You are en route, so...." How clever. From the many rules regulating our lives, she uses one to dispense us from another. She's right of course: I am a pilgrim on this earth. Just never thought about my life, or our Holy Rule, this way.

When her phone again occupies her attention, I take a closer look around at the journals and books everywhere: stacked on the floor, atop a locker-like cabinet, wedged every which way in bookcases reaching the ceiling. The titles are mostly political science, but there are also sociology, philosophy, and literature books, and all sorts of novels. Even a Pogo. What would Sister Sergeant say about all this? She scolds me about the library books I bring home from college on Saturdays, inspecting the titles, making sure they relate to my courses, and then tells me to store them in the closet, out of sight. "Your cell's for prayer and sleep, Sister. This isn't a college dorm."

"You enjoy it, don't you?" The words shoot out of me the instant Sister Augusta hangs up the phone. "Teaching, I mean." My tone startles her—and me—yet I don't give her a chance to reply. "Teaching's just another chore at St. Pat's, like cleaning the johns, or scrubbing floors. A duty—a penance to be 'offered up.' Our superior actually says that!" I'm aware, but don't care, that complaining is positively forbidden by our Holy Rule: "It rarely happens that a sister complains without sin," our rule says. Yet the complaints tumble out: "I tell my superior I'm so inept I fear that I'm harming the kids, and she tells me any exposure to nuns is good for the children, and to take that 'on faith.' She says, 'The habit itself teaches them, Sister,' and reminds me that praying for my students will be 'more helpful for them in the long run.' I should see my teaching as sandpaper 'smoothing out the rough spots' of my soul. Like incense, she reminds me, it has to be burned before it can give off its sweet odor and rise up to God." The mix of metaphors amuses Sister Augusta, and I demur. "Maybe I exaggerate," I mumble.

"You probably do," she replies, peering over her glasses to hand me a licorice rope. "Even so, I'd be slow, if I were you, to follow that sandpaper theory of spirituality. Or that burning business. Could be dangerous." If she smiled any more, or differently, I might feel laughed at, but as it is, I feel only that I've been heard, really heard. "But you're right. I do like teaching. Love it, in fact. Everything about it—the students, the study, the research."

She removes her glasses, slowly massaging both eyes and her brow. I hope she doesn't have a headache. Maybe those creases around her small eyes suggest too much study. Is that what it takes to love teaching? "Not that it's always fun," she says. "Sometimes, yes. Lots of times, though not always. Always it's *work*. Hard work. Still, I don't look at my teaching the way your superior does, never have. Though, sad to say, some sisters do." With a sigh, she adds: "In time you'll also enjoy your work—I'm sure of that." Just hearing her say these words makes me feel better. "But right now, your situation is tough, and also quite different from anything I ever experienced. Seventy-three kids, two grades. Egads! If you were *not* upset I'd be worried."

With her glasses back on, her funny flat glasses reflecting light every which way, she again speaks to me like my assignment-giving high school teacher. "Come by here next Saturday, same time. I'll ask my friend Sister Carla if she can help you. Give you some ideas, maybe. She's very inventive. You'll like her. During her years with the little ones, she was a real genius. Let her help you till things smooth out. Promise me?" She clears the student papers off her desk, stacking them on the floor to make room for our lunch, and I think how tired she looks, and old—a lot older than when I had her a mere three years ago. Was it all that study to become a professor? Then I recall: She's got to be well over forty by now, maybe even forty-five. Then again, she may never have looked exactly youthful. She resembles our nun aunt in Denver that Tom and I used to think was ancient, "but only because she's plain," Dad would say in defense of his beloved baby sister. "Nuns aren't trying to look Hollywood, you know. She's really quite handsome, just rather large-boned." Like Augusta, I think.

"There's more to what disturbs you," Augusta says, pouring us coffee from her thermos. "More than a tough assignment, or your newness." I warm my hands, sniffing the hot brew, while she spreads paper towels on the desk between us and starts cutting the Mars bars and brownies into small pieces. "Dessert first," she says mischievously, while I'm wondering what else she thinks is wrong with me. "As I see it, your concerns are not so much a matter of self-discipline, or following our Holy Rule, or even growing up—as your superior seems to imply." She speaks deliberately, choosing her words cautiously, as if pulling them out of her head. "First, some reality: You have a terribly overcrowded classroom. And you are undertrained. Both not good. They need to be addressed by those running things." She clears a couple of large volumes away from the middle of her desk and draws a deep breath. "But also, it's a matter of how you, Betty Byrne, see things—your faith and your reason. This, you can do something about." I try to grasp the significance of what she obviously thinks is important for me.

"How you relate these—your *believing* and your *thinking*—is basic. There's more than one way, you know." She stops to break off a piece of brownie and dunks it into her coffee before continuing. "It's how you connect your two professions: nun and teacher. For someone like you, especially. You're still Betty Byrne, remember; no veil can cover up that questioning head of yours."

More silence. Augusta's brownie hovers over the coffee, and I put down the licorice to listen. Far from stinging, her words feel comfortable. "Think how often, even in your brief time in the order, you've heard talk about 'the natural' and 'the supernatural' or 'nature and grace.' The language is woven into our lives—references to 'the physical' and 'the spiritual,' or 'the secular' and 'the religious.' But how to connect them?" Her look is intense, as if she's trying to pour her ideas directly into me. "All depends on how *you* relate your faith and your reason."

After an uncomfortable moment of silence, she resumes her dunking and her steady professor voice. "People have had vastly different notions throughout history, great thinkers, some of them saints—ancient and modern. We've got several versions right here, within our own order. Sometimes in the heads of sisters kneeling next to each other in chapel."

We've worked our way through the brownies and are crunching away at the apples before she tells me more.

"Look, attitudes don't change for everybody the same way. Or at the same time. Just like in the big world. Remember prohibition and women's suffrage?" Are we both remembering the same boisterous debate in her classroom three years ago? During her life in community, she tells me, she's experienced both the hostility toward secular pursuits I hear at St. Pat's and the excitement about learning I witnessed in her and Sister Marie Gabrielle at the academy.

"Some people still wonder why the order put out so much money to have me educated in, of all things, political science. Can't get more secular than that—at a secular university, to boot! More than once I heard: 'What's that got to do with the Gospel?'" Augusta's brownies and chewy Mars bars are gone, but not her Milwaukee twang, reminding me how much I loved her class at St. Mary's Academy. I'm beginning to think she may have forgotten about my term-paper request, when she stands and starts pulling from her bookshelves first one, then another, slim volume tucked in among the larger ones, finally locating the book she's after. She thrusts it toward me. "This will help with that term paper."

The slender red volume is *Reason and Revelation in the Middle Ages* by Etienne Gilson. "It's quite suitable for beginners," she claims, and proceeds to describe the portly mustached Frenchman she once went to hear at the University of Toronto. "He's made a career of studying the different approaches to this issue within Western civilization," she tells me. "You'll discover his challenge was much like yours." Augusta sits back down and looks directly at me. "He may also help with your life. Ideas make a difference, you know. They have consequences."

While I'm still puzzled by how any ideas from the Middle Ages can possibly make a difference in the disaster that is my life from Monday to Friday, she abruptly turns to the practical. "You'll like Carla—she's been a good friend to me since our novitiate days. Right now she's in the midst of grad work at the Art Institute. But she started out—also at nineteen—assigned to our 'foreign' mission down in New Mexico, responsible for throngs of children, all ages, under quite primitive circumstances. Worse even than yours. It was tough for her, very tough. But the artist in her turned it around. I'm sure she can help you do the same. Surely more than I can. So don't forget: next Saturday, same time. Come by and I'll take you down to her studio in the boiler room. Okay?"

March 20, 1948

Augusta is waiting for me when I show up at her office following my weekly Saturday excursion through Western Civ. She'll travel back with me to the motherhouse, she says, if we hurry. And we do, making the six-block trek in record time and then hurriedly locating her good friend, Sister Carla, in the remote bowels of the motherhouse.

She's hovering over a large kiln when we arrive, her white coverall splattered with colorful remnants of the clay I see stacked in bags throughout the vast basement room. Augusta tells me how her good friend has single-handedly repurposed this unused storage area as her "studio." Sister Carla's wide sleeves are pushed into two white puffs at either shoulder, and her veil is tucked into a snood-like cap. She reminds me of one of those stiffly posed army nurses in Dad's old World War I album. Yet there's nothing stiff or posed about this tiny woman who is hugging Augusta goodbye. When she turns her attention to me, her lightheartedness becomes all business. "So, you're Mother Brendan's niece."

"Grand-niece, actually." I'm startled to hear this stranger connect me with Auntie Brendan, the longest resident of the infirmary wing and, sadly, senile for some years now. How can this youthful nun know anything of that sweet old lady who so many years ago fished candies for me out of her big pocket until Mimi stopped her?

"Now, about your teaching: What troubles you most?"

"Everything," I mumble.

"Well then," she says matter-of-factly, "you'll need some clay." She leads me across the room to a workspace that appears to be recently cleared and indicates that the fresh bag of clay is for me. "Next Saturday you can bring me two dollars. Or maybe four; you'll be needing a second bag shortly." What's happening?! What am I getting into? How do I tell her—but she continues calmly, "Here, you can use this." It's a white apron like hers.

Does she think art is my main problem? Could it have slipped out during that emotional outpouring with Augusta: that I never quite get around to art? Or that I've let the kids use those old pieces of crayon to scribble away for hours when I don't know how to teach what I'm supposed to be teaching? No, art is not the biggest problem for me or for my seventy-two. Yet how can I say this to Augusta's good friend, her *artist* friend?! Who's taking all this time to help me? Let her know how dismissive I am about something so obviously central in her life? How can I not go along with this little nun, so serious about her art and so clearly seeing it as a way to help me?

Besides, there's no time for questioning or for any small talk as she leads me around this large room that's been transformed into a cool gray world of wet clay. She calls the half dozen or so mounds covered in gray canvas "works in progress" but gives me no more information about them. Or indeed about those brightly colored tile strips that have caught my eye. She remains all business, indicating now which stool is mine, which hers.

Finally we sit before the portion of the counter that has been cleared for our work. Without further enlightenment about this mysterious haven of hers, Sister Carla begins methodically laying out plans for the weeks of work ahead. Each Saturday, I'm to pack a lunch before leaving St. Pat's and then drop it off down here before taking off for my university classes. She points to a cool, safe spot off in a far corner away from the clay. "But most important, add your lesson plans from the week you've just completed. Then when you come back from the university for lunch, we'll work on your plans for the week coming up. Is that clear?"

I want to say, not really—but I'm desperate. I'll try anything, even art. So I move with her around her studio, transformed now as a taller version of herself, with pinned-up sleeves, covered in nurse-like white, and listen as her lessons begin: how to open the bag, use a wire to cut off a piece of clay, knead it into a ball, and slam it into one of the plaster slabs on the counter to use. Her confident "Now you do it" follows each concise direction. None of that sing-songy baby talk so many adults use with little kids—and older nuns so often use when introducing us rookies to the ways of convent life. That's not Sister Carla; she speaks with an authority that belies her age—just ten years older than I am. She's all smart eyes and deliberate words, as if she were letting me in on a secret. Which is what starts to happen this very afternoon as I begin discovering the secret of my own hands.

For the next hour or so, in a deep silence, we work in the cool air of this basement—I with this strange-smelling gray stuff squishing through my fingers, she with her bright strips of tile. Just how all this fits into the mess of my weekday classroom life remains a mystery, even as I'm fascinated by how naturally I take to working with this clay. Am I returning to the days of mud pies at Mimi and Grandpa's? Perhaps. Seemingly they're designed for just this, my amazing hands, surprising me by how much they can do: the knuckles, fingertips, heels, palms—flattened or cupped—and my amazing thumbs, maybe most of all, my thumbs. How could I have taken them for granted these past twenty years? How they can push, pull, poke, shape, mold. At first timidly, then boldly, they are gradually transforming a slab of watery clay into a smooth ball, rid of its air bubbles. All in this cool, quiet basement where a gentle breeze plays across my bare arms, ruffling that abundant black hair I was so ashamed of when last my arms were bare like this.

I've never paid much attention to my hands after fumbling with nail polish when I was thirteen. I wondered then whether Byrne hands might be better off not decorated. It's what, my mother told me, she had decided for herself. Not our best feature, she said then. Best not call attention to them with bright colors. And I followed suit, unaware till now of this entirely different kind of beauty in my hands.

The discoveries continue the next Saturday—beyond the magic of my hands and arms and clay. When I return to Carla in her basement studio, I'm as eager to get back to my messy clay as I am hungry for her reactions to my lesson plans, or the lunch I deposited here hours earlier. As I munch my peanut butter and jelly, I am awed at how much she has absorbed from my sketchy lesson plans: the *feel* of my classroom, disasters as well as those rare moments when things worked. Just as when she inspected my first ever effort with the clay: the same knowing eyes, same direct manner, practical, specific.

Carla seems gentler, somehow, with her observations about my teaching. My lesson plans unlock memories of her own that must have been particularly painful or funny— or both. Especially bits and pieces from her own first year teaching, in New Mexico. Sometimes in surprising ways. Like that Saturday shortly after we started when, out of the blue, she asks, "You have an even number across, in your classroom?"

"I do. Six rows across, twelve kids down." A pattern etched indelibly in my mind after watching our janitor last September squeezing in an extra row of small chairs and stools.

"Alphabetically arranged?"

"Of course," I say, remembering Sister Sergeant's demand once she discovered my problem with the attendance record. Easier for memorizing names, she said. That was in the fall and I'm still struggling, this time with memorizing all the nicknames.

"Great, a cross section. Not all the smarties in a row. So you can set up a buddy system." She explains how I should pair off kids sitting beside each other, three pairs across the width of the room, thirty-six pairs in all. After presenting a lesson, I give a specific assignment to everyone. They work on it in pairs, one as teacher, the other as student. Then they switch roles. The assignment, with several examples and any rules, go up on the board for all to see. In some cases, answers are up there, too. I am the referee, squeezing myself up and down aisles to settle disputes, clarify rules, etc. Sometimes I use a kitchen timer, making it like a contest: so many minutes for each child before switching. But no points or prizes or grades. Knowing how to do it "by myself" becomes reward enough. "Trust me," she says. "They catch on fast."

The logistics worry me though. All the desks are nailed to wood strips, I tell her, which in turn, are nailed to the floor. That's a challenge, she admits, yet assures me that their bodies are much more flexible than ours. "They love to twist about—and do so easily. It becomes a game."

My first try with her buddy system brings complete mayhem, yet I have to admit I sort of enjoyed it, and the kids definitely did. But did it work? Only time will tell, I guess, along with those dreaded end-of-year tests, a threat Sister Sergeant never lets us forget. At one point, the noise level in my classroom brings her storming down the hall. She throws open the classroom door, intending to stop whatever I'm up to. Instead, she ends up sending the janitor to close the transoms. That night she tells me how taken she was by the number of kids absorbed in the "story problems" up on the board. She promises to have that huge commercial fan from the parish hall brought over to my classroom "to cover some of that noise."

None of this surprises Carla. "Things get messy when you're learning to master the tools of a craft." We both chuckle, knowing how awkward and sloppy I've been with her tools for clay, chafing at times under her disciplines of sharpening and cleaning and storage, especially that special knife and spatula she lent me. I'm always impatient to finish up, especially when I must rush to catch the last bus back to St. Pat's. Yet I must admit her disciplines work. Even in the chaos of trying out her "buddy system," the kids who were at the ready with their tools were not only up to the challenge of those twisting story problems but instinctively took on teaching their buddies. They were eager and hungry to share. They were having fun.

As will be true with their other tools, Carla promises, whether letters and sounds, or the rules for phonics or grammar or math. When they have them at the ready, there's no limit to what these kids can teach themselves, in your classroom and in the rest of their lives. Call it mathematics, composition, or science, when kids can put numbers and sounds and images together like this, she promises, "they are *creating their own art.* And that's what we're after," she says. "That's the prize." Her intense focus relaxes into a kind of blissful glow, and I am astonished at how truly beautiful her face is when she abandons, even for a moment, that piercing look of hers.

Our lunchtime talk time has gone on longer than usual, so I bundle away what remains of my lunch to follow Carla back to work—she to her shards of tile, I to my carefully packed away clay from last Saturday. We are as industrious as those white-clad monks in our refectory murals, silently working away on their manuscripts in some remote monastery. I'm well into my weekly struggle, reacquainting hands and clay, when I notice Carla off to the side removing the drape over a towering mass of gray concrete.

What's been a ghost-like mystery these last weeks I now recognize as an unfinished human form, clearly female, though faceless. A statue? Probably. But who? Not the Blessed Mother? Yet I see an M carved in its base. However, this large, stocky, tower of a woman—much taller than I am—is completely different from the statues of Mary that have been in my life since childhood. They've been commonplace, in church, classrooms, homes—my uncle even has a small one on his dashboard! Each one is a lithe, gracious creature, rendered in colors sweetly soft and delicate, always womanly, even girlish. None remotely resemble that looming female that Carla is decorating with her bright colors. How could those strangely angled tiles ever create a face as beautiful as Mary's?

I ride back to St. Patrick's that afternoon, and the following Saturdays until the end of the school year, next to Sister Julie Anne, wondering if her labors all afternoon in the chemistry lab could possibly have been as exciting and strange and fatiguing as mine. I'm actually relieved by our Holy Rule's discipline about "silence when traveling on a public conveyance." The practice allows us to remain sleepily mute as we travel home, side by side, on a smelly old prewar bus. Yet increasingly I appreciate that silence since I haven't a clue about how to explain, to Julie or anyone else, my afternoon's "research" in the motherhouse basement with Carla.

As Saturdays come and go, the stocky tower of a woman gets more brightly colored and my own muscles strengthen from the strenuous disciplines of throwing and centering and using the wheel. I discover that Carla's slated to teach geginning ceramics in the fall—for the first time—and I feel better about all her time and energy mentoring me: I've been providing a chance for her to hone her skills. I'm her very own guinea pig! I've stopped questioning how such work relates to my classroom troubles. Or asking Carla about her increasingly strange sculpture.

I'm still uncertain about accomplishing any of what Sister Augusta hoped for me when she introduced me to Sister Carla. My students' test results are still weeks away; then I'll discover if all this mayhem has actually helped them learn anything. But in my bones I feel sure that both the kids and I are better off having fun while learning how to learn (despite Sister Sergeant's caution that "feelings don't count"). Certainly the kids are more lively, if more noisy. They seem much more connected to what we've been doing these last weeks, which I interpret as being more aware of their own responsibility to learn, to sharpen their tools, perfect their craft. Calling it "art" may be a bit too elegant; however, it does reflect exactly what I hope is true about my own Saturday struggle to create truly centered pots.

What I am sure of—both in my bones and in my brain— is that I've changed. I've become more savvy about several things: how to draw up lesson plans that work, at least some of the time; how to connect with what I've called my "mystery kids" (Tommy, who used to mix up "saw" and "was," and Jane, who wouldn't ever look at me, and even super-smart but strange Frankie, who muttered to himself but who now, at times, speaks directly to me).

Each one has been helped by Carla's suggestions, as I personally have benefitted from her various suggestions for "regeneration" (her word): a hard-boiled egg or cheese slice instead of extra toast at breakfast; the peanut butter and jelly boost ("more peanut butter, less jelly") before class rather than gorging after; the quick ten-minute nap before afternoon meditation. All helpful with the fatigue that had been crushing me, especially with the "nodding off" problem at prayer I found myself telling her about. A quick nap is possible, even in full habit, if you learn the "corpse pose." She demonstrates for me right there on the floor of her basement studio, including tricks for not mussing habit or veil in the process. Her ideas have definitely made a difference.

Most of all, though, these last Saturdays away from St. Pat's have given me feelings of being at home with at least some of the grown-ups in my new family of nuns. First with Sister Augusta and now with Sister Carla, I feel something like what my cousin Sally confided about her sorority sisters at the university. Though in many ways it could not be more different, with each group of sorors there's rushing, then pledging, and finally being initiated. That's what Augusta and her dear friend Carla have done for me: They've "vetted" me as Mother Alicia never could have, nor surely Sister Mercedes—or even dear Aunt Maggie. All this without any mention of God, or His will, or any suggestions about "tying a knot and hanging on" or viewing my labors "in the light of the death candle." Until I met Carla, I'd come away from my weekly lesson plan session with Sister Mercedes feeling at best empty and sad, wanting her to do something, though I never knew quite what. Now I know, and I feel only sadness for Sister Mercedes.

May 7, 1948
This is the first "free day" since I've come to St. Pat's. In convent parlance, this means a day free of obligations except Mass, an hour later than usual. So an hour more of sleep, silence dispensed all over the house, no obligations in common, not even prayers or meals: a perfect free day!

And it's all because yesterday, Ascension Thursday, after our annual school picnic, the pastor surprised us by declaring today a school holiday—and not just for the children. The "good sisters" are to be as free from toil as our superior can arrange, our pastor said. No manual labor in our classrooms or in the convent. Meals picked up from the picnic leftovers whenever we wish. Sister Mercedes suggests that we either study, sleep, or take a walk—the decision is ours.

Finally, my chance to tackle that term paper that's due in a couple of weeks. Since my visit with Sister Augusta last March, I've had little time to think about the civilization of the western world. I've been so busy with the challenge of civilizing my lively little buddies in the classroom. But first some more of that German chocolate cake the ladies of the parish provided "just for the sisters," a great way to start this glorious May morning after a night of thunder and lightning. With the bowls of fresh berries, also from the parishioners, and hot coffee, it's the best breakfast I've had since joining the order.

I plan to take all three of Sister Superior's suggestions, with plenty of time in between for more of the picnic goodies. But then I pick up Augusta's little red book—I'd almost forgotten about it and am again surprised by the title: *Reason and Revelation in the Middle Ages,* by Etienne Gilson. Immediately I'm deep in the world of arching medieval cloisters, with Gregorian chant soaring in the background. It's a world I've often imagined, since I once had the job of dusting art tomes in the novitiate library. Now, in fantasy, Gilson escorts me through the ages, pointing out first one, then another, of the great "doctors" or teachers of the medieval church—each in his distinctive setting. There's Augustine, the scholar-convert from North Africa; Ambrose, the bishop in Milan; Anselm, the Archbishop of Canterbury; and the solitary poet Bernard, in stark white robes on his mountaintop. Then, down in Paris in his brown habit and bare feet, the Franciscan Bonaventure; near him, the "angelic" yet rotund Aquinas; and Albert the Great, who taught them both. Far off, separate from the rest in his cave, I spot the emaciated, darkly angry Jerome.

Soon I begin to imagine Gilson taunting me, "Just because they're all saints, you presume they felt the same about the world they left behind? Or about faith? Or reason? Or about how a Christian ought to look at the Bible? Or study things not found in the Bible? Or even care about what happens in this 'vale of tears'?"

"Far from it!" I hear him answering his own challenge. "They—or their disciples—have been arguing for centuries about the same questions that vex you. These fellows were actual people, remember: Frenchmen, Italians, Africans. Like you, they struggled to make sense of their Christian lives. And like you, they asked questions all the time, of themselves and of everyone else. Separated by centuries and cultures, they all left home and family for monastic cloisters and ended up asking even more questions."

I stop to take some deep breaths. No wonder Augusta thinks this will help me, and not just with the term paper, but with my life. The cloister, a place for fostering questions! Exactly how it's turning out for me. And the author sees that as normal. Even good! "Don't think for a moment these guys end up agreeing about how faith and reason fit together," my fantasy Gilson insists, with the roguish nod Augusta described. "Some of the greatest fell into extremes: relying solely on faith, or solely on reason."

It soon becomes clear that Gilson's hero in this long controversy is Thomas Aquinas, who was able to harmonize faith and reason. For him, reasoning and believing are not alternatives he has to choose between. Reason complements revelation, and vice versa. And to think he is my very own patron saint, this Thomas guy, because I was born on his feast day, March 7. At least that's what Mimi always told me.

As I slowly turn the pages of the little red book, I recognize in Aquinas, via Gilson, the spirit I've admired in Augusta, Marie Gabrielle, and now in my new friend Carla. It's a spirit that loves this world, even though removed from it.

That delights in exploring the wonders of this world, whether of literature, sociology, politics, or clay—and delights in opening up these wonders to others. A spirit that's been reaching for life inside me since I stepped into the classroom in September. At last.

The long afternoon shadows tell me I've lost track of time, forgotten about the pantry stocked with picnic fare, the cokes, even the German chocolate cake. And when I stretch out on my bed, it's not to nap. Every part of me is awake to the hot afternoon sun. I am part of an ancient, honorable tradition in Christianity—despite its being virtually unknown in and around St. Pat's. I see exactly why I'm on this bed, in this particular cell of this convent, teaching these children, studying these books. Not because it's my assignment or God's will for me, though I believe it is. Nor because I am being obedient, though that also is true, I hope. No, it's because I'm part of something much grander than myself. Educating these kids—or attempting to—has something to do with the natural order of things; something understood deep inside of me yet infinitely beyond me.

My notepad and pen lie untouched. I cannot write, nor do I need notes about the lesson I've learned from Augusta's book. It's already part of me, spreading throughout my entire body like a wonderful stream of clear mountain water. It's lit up the whole of creation for me, and I understand now—because God became man, the entire natural world is holy. There are no separations between what is godly and what isn't.

I shudder to remember the dire words of the *Imitation of Christ* we listen to each morning with our breakfast—about "despising this world," and "turning away from the mundane" to "fasten exclusively on heavenly realities." Is this the cause of the stomachache I so often have at breakfast? Well, no more. That kind of Christianity is not for me. There are other, just as good, ways to "imitate Christ." Gilson is showing me.

I should have known from Aquinas's hymn *Adoro te devote, latens Deitas*. Mimi had me memorize the English of that hymn for my First Communion. She told me it was her favorite after communion prayer, and over the years I've come to agree with her. Now, though, his simple words of worship carry a meaning for me far beyond the Eucharist: "Devoutly I adore you, hidden God, who lies within these forms before me." Forms I can now see include this entire world of matter and motion, of life—far more than the simple water and wine of Holy Communion. These are not the words of one who hates this material world or turns from it in disgust. Gilson knew this, and now so do I.

The consequences are momentous: The whole of creation is to be explored, not avoided for fear that it will take me from God. All study, all teaching, even the difference between saw and was, or the truth of a truly centered pot, or a mathematical equation. Any of these can be part of that great reach toward the Truth that is God. Today it's a message from Gilson, tomorrow it may be the calculus—they are of a piece with each day's Mass and meditation. I am back with Hopkins and Gaby: "Nature is never spent; there lives the dearest freshness deep down things...it flames out like shining from shook foil."

As I emerge from my Gilson trance, a lovely cool breeze tells me it's evening, while the balmy weight of that breeze reminds me that summer is around the corner. With summer, more college classes, then a new teaching mission for the fall, maybe another convent, or a return to St. Pat's. I'm ready. In fact, I'm eager. Wherever I am, I will search for "truth." Though I'd be completely embarrassed for anyone, even Augusta, to hear me say this. It sounds so pretentious.

※

Summer School, July 1948
"So...she's finished?"

I'm gazing at Carla's large, still draped woman standing in the midst of several projects in an unlit section of her large basement studio.

"Not quite. We're just taking a break." Carla's over at the counter, lettering a banner, which is in fact just a long piece of shelf paper. She looks more flushed than usual—even this cool retreat can't protect her from a St. Louis July. I approach, to see up close some remarkable calligraphy:

TELL ME AND I FORGET. SHOW ME AND I REMEMBER. LET ME DO IT AND I UNDERSTAND.

The words are in spare, angular script, meant for her upcoming ceramics class in the fall, she tells me. "Suitable, don't you think, for beginning potters?"

I nod in agreement, thinking it's exactly how she worked with me those last months of the school year. "Especially if you are the teacher," I add, and watch intently as she adds in smaller script CHINESE PROVERB beneath the quote and remember her words about growing familiar with the tools of our trade. She certainly has—her pen seems an extension of her fingers, a part of her hand and arm. Something I don't think I can ever achieve, at least not with the fingers of my hand. Though maybe with the fingers of my brain.

This summer these "fingers" are becoming more comfortable with the tools I first took up, awkwardly, last September, in my university Saturday class, Beginning Calculus. Now, just two short weeks into Advanced Calculus and already I'm discovering just how magical this intricate invention can be. Perhaps because I'm luxuriating in the single-mindedness of this abstract world, without the "distraction" of the classroom and community life at St. Pat's. For along with all my novitiate classmates I've returned to the motherhouse to be immersed in summer session at the university. This developing confidence in my studies emboldens me to blurt out to Carla, "Who is she, Sister?" It's been bothering me for months now, just who this woman under the gray drape is.

"Oh, I thought you knew. Sorry." She moves over to the shaded area, switches on the light and dramatically pulls away the drape, gesturing as if to introduce a celebrity: "Sister, meet Mother. Mother, this is Sister Elizabeth Mary."

I can see no clue in the brightly colored mosaic about who or which mother she is. "You mean Mary? The Blessed Mother?" The endless titles of Mary as mother flash before me: Mother of Good Counsel, Mother Most Pure, Mother of Perpetual Help, Mother of Sorrows.

"Well, yes. Yes, of course," she answers, somewhat reluctantly. "But not just Mary, not only Mary. Others, too."

"Other mothers, you mean?"

Off the top of my head, I can't think of any saint who was a mother. The official book of saints seems, in fact, limited to virgins, virgin martyrs in particular. Though possibly she could be one of those strong female saints, often called "spiritual mothers": Saint Gertrude or Saint Teresa—or that fierce contrarian, Saint Catherine of Sienna. Big mamas, all of them. These women could scold and preach to popes and princes alike. As they did!

But then, after another moment or two of her silence, I realize it doesn't have to be a saint just because it's a statue...

"I discover more about her all the time," Carla says, only adding to my puzzlement. "Sometimes she seems to be speaking to me."

"Scolding? Or instructing? Or what?"

"Well, sometimes, and sometimes both. But other things as well." Carla's faraway, impish look returns, and for a moment, her whole body seems to loosen up, shedding its intensity, and glows. "She's always helpful, though, always motherly."

The confidence that has allowed me to question her now

tells me to shut up, or I will insult her creation, maybe even Carla herself. I'll learn more when she wants me to. What I am surprised to discover, though, is that it doesn't much matter to me anymore whether she's pretty or not. Whoever's mother she is.

Chapter 6

1960

August 1960

For nuns and their trunks, the first week of August is moving time. This allows both to get settled into their new "missions" in time to celebrate "with all possible splendor" the feast of Mary's Assumption into Heaven on August 15. And so Mimi's old Irish trunk, having come to the convent with me on August 15, 1945, is here with me now, fifteen years later, at St. Catherine's House of Studies at the Catholic University of America in Washington, DC.

The two of us have made a number of moves in the intervening years. After those first two novice years in the motherhouse, it was on to four different parish convents in as many years, where I taught a different grade each year. Then, during the last nine years, we were back at the motherhouse, where I taught high school math at St. Mary's Academy.

And now that good old trunk of Mimi's is with me here at St. Cat's while I work toward a doctoral degree. If and when that happens, we will both return to the motherhouse, where I hope to teach college courses to our junior sisters.

Before this, no sister from our order ever took an advanced degree in philosophy, the field selected for me. The subject, like theology, was considered a man's field, most often a priest's field. But then in the mid-1950s some new ideas about educating nuns floated through the cloisters of America. It was called the Sister Formation Movement, a massive attempt by nuns across the United States to pull themselves up by their bootstraps. It was started by a handful of mothers general and a select group of sister-scholars and educators, among them my old friend Sister Augusta. Their dream was to upgrade their education and that of other nuns—for the eventual benefit of every sister-staffed institution in the United States, schools and hospitals. It would be an enormous undertaking.

In their audacity, these leaders planned for young sisters to get the same sort of intellectual grounding as young men training for the priesthood. Thus, instead of being assigned, as I was, to one of the order's missions immediately after their novitiate, young nuns in the future were to first get a bachelor's degree, as seminarians do, before being assigned a mission. And, as it was for young men, this basic intellectual training was to be grounded in the liberal arts, especially philosophy and theology. Even more revolutionary, this foundation was to be provided not by imported clergy, but by "one of our own." This was the plan. To get it going meant finding a sufficient number of sister-professors for the task.

Thus was generated a need for more advanced degrees within every order of sisters, bringing a record number of nuns to universities in the late '50s. We were to become the professors for a younger generation of nuns—a goal that was itself revolutionary. What no one could foresee at the time, however, was just how this deepening and broadening of intellectual life among American nuns would, a decade later, blossom and affect the entire Church.

Perhaps because my own early training was so pathetic, I had followed closely the thinking of this Sister Formation initiative from its beginnings, offering opinions whenever asked. And asked I was—particularly by Sister Augusta. Our mentor-student relationship had evolved as I grew up and grew into my teaching life. By the time I was in my late twenties, I had shared the wonders of algebra and geometry with hordes of high school adolescents, enlivened largely by that beautiful blending of "faith and reason" I continued to witness in Sister Augusta.

But my stimulating influences didn't end with her. Just living in the motherhouse meant a daily contact with the oldest, the youngest, and the top leaders in the order, a total of more than two hundred women. During most of those "math years," I had refectory duty either at breakfast or dinner or both—serving, clearing, or scrubbing up afterward, as every young sister did.

The subgroup that probably influenced me the most, however, was the group I chose to sit with on those special "talk at table" days. They were the SS people to me—a name inspired by their listing on the posted community roll call: Sister-Scholars and Sister-Students. The handful of "scholars" were faculty at various local institutions—like Sister Augusta at the local Jesuit university. The "students" were in advanced study at these same places, some for nursing degrees and others for academic degrees. I found myself socializing more and more with both of these groups as the Sister Formation program was developing.

Like me, most of these sisters were acutely aware of the problems the SF was attempting to address, having ourselves suffered through the traditional lack of training, a process variously called the "twenty-year plan"—which was how long it took many sisters to get a BA—or the "sink-and-swim plan"—for the way young nuns were tossed into the classroom or hospital ward directly from the novitiate—or, for obvious reasons, the "survival of the fittest."

I was keenly aware of having survived because of the friendships and mentoring of older sisters like Sisters Carla, Marie Gabrielle, and, of course, Augusta. My BA had been earned "on the side" in Saturday, summer, and evening classes, most of those years teaching in grade school classrooms. During those difficult years, I lost thirty pounds, then gained forty, lost my pink cheeks, and acquired ever darker circles under my eyes. But I also got the answer I had posed to Reverend Mother Pauline on Reception Day: How do I know if

God wants me to be a nun?

"By living the life," she had said. "If you are able to live the life and still want to stay with us after your period of testing, and—more to the point—if the community still wants you at that time, then God and His Church want you. It's that simple." And so I discovered: God had indeed chosen me to be a member of the Sisters of Mary.

So here I am, chosen by my order, or by God, or both, to study at Catholic University, with sisters from all across the country, and across the world, studying all sorts of subjects. Nuns from many different orders, with different traditions and different cultures, are assigned to one or other of various houses of study here at CU, called collectively Sisters' College. Together we eat and recreate, sleep and study—in habits, mostly black, among a scattering of blue and gray and even some white habits.

However, my companions in the philosophy department are something else. They are foreign in a way none of my sister housemates are, even the sister students from Europe and Africa and Asia. They are men.

September 2, 1960

"Hi, there!" I'm looking away when someone clutches my arm, catching the corner of my veil in the process. "Didn't I see you in the philosophy office?" asks this person, whose face seems lost in a mass of black curly hair and heavy glasses.

Without allowing me to answer, she congratulates me on being the "other woman" among this year's grad students in the philosophy department. "We're the outsiders, the two of us, among all these priests." She tosses her head toward the throngs of long-skirted individuals in lines to register for the new term. She can't be Catholic, or she'd know that not all the skirted are priests. Most are either brothers, or seminarians, or those like me with veils on our heads who will never be priests.

"What are you taking?" she asks, peering over to inspect the class list I'm clutching. "Good choices; same as mine...." She continues to chatter on about the professors and offerings in the philosophy department, pressing so close I flinch, causing me to bump into the person in line behind me. People don't normally get that close to, let alone *touch*, nuns. Besides, she's cutting into the line—which snakes behind us the entire length of the gym—embarrassing me.

All the same, her hand is comforting, something I sort of welcome at the moment, after that dreary orientation session this morning. I've never felt so much the outsider. As we shuffle ahead in the seemingly endless line, she makes me laugh at her take on the various professors, each with his own peculiar foibles and set of sacred insights. Her humor is "orienting" me far better than that bleak session this morning.

When her welcoming remarks switch to the topic of DC, with all its opportunities for grad students, she mentions her own interests in the social ramifications of studying philosophy. For a non-Catholic, she seems remarkably informed about the Church's social justice concerns.

"That's why you chose CU, right?" She tightens the hold on my arm, turning to look me in the eye.

How can I explain that I haven't chosen anything—I was *assigned* here. She remains uncomfortably close to me, breathing out the smell of stale cigarettes with each of her tales. While I'm flattered by her interest, fascinated by her stories, I'm also put off by a familiarity I don't expect from seculars, especially strangers. I bend slightly to one side, to look at her carefully.

Despite her plumpish arms, she's diminutive and, as my brother Tom would say, well put together. Like those beautifully rounded bathing women so favored by Impressionist painters, I think—perhaps because of those traces of French I hear in her voice. With a kick of her foot, she nudges ahead her cumbersome satchel on the floor as we progress slowly up the line. She tells me her name is Sophie Arnault, she has spent an impressive stretch of time studying philosophy at the College de France, and she's now in her second year at CU. She hopes to combine philosophy with social concerns, and she will probably go to law school later on. She says she definitely feels older than twenty-seven.

"So how old are *you*?" Again, she leans in close. "And where are you from? Your family, I mean." Now she's fingering my registration form to see my name. "Sister Elizabeth Mary Byrne. That's way too long for me. The nuns I knew in France had regular names—there was even a Sophie." She's caught me off guard. Before I can answer, she announces: "I'll call you Liza, okay?"

By convent custom, no one except our own ever omits the title "Sister" or calls us by a nickname, except behind our backs. The words are on my lips, "You can call me Sister," but I can't get them out. It sounds prissy, even to me, yet I resent that she elicits such a response. Suddenly I'm remembering how, both as a youngster and as a young teacher in parochial schools, "Sister says" was enough to command compliance. Am I expecting respect like that from this young woman? So accustomed to the teacher mode that I'm treating her as my student? And why am I put off by her questions about my age, family connections, etc.? It's true that by custom we don't talk about our age or celebrate birthdays—recognition of our saint's day replaces that—nor talk about our lives, including our families, up to the time we entered. But of course we don't need to. The drawn-out process of becoming a sister is so lengthy, with the whole order celebrating along with our families each step up to final vows, that everyone in the order pretty much knows these basic facts about everyone else. Come to think of it, I know such facts about all my novitiate friends without ever having asked.

Maybe that's why this meeting feels so peculiar. I'm learning so much about someone who doesn't know anything about me. So I tell her I am thirty-three, and she tells me she thought me much younger. "But then, with all that—" she gestures at my headgear, "there's not much to see. All that white around your face hides any nasty stuff." Then, with alarm, she adds, "Are you okay? You look pale."

In fact, I have been feeling a bit light-headed and weak-kneed, offering less and less resistance to the pushing and shoving bodies that are inching me forward toward those registration tables. It's three o'clock, and I've had no food since a light breakfast at seven. "Just hungry, I guess."

"I'll get us both some food. Keep my place, okay?"

She darts off for the vending machines, asking me to guard her satchel. I am chagrined to have to rely on the kindness of strangers like this, but I must. There is no money in the pocket hanging by my side, as I have not yet taken on the independent ways of "a sister residing outside the community." After she darts off, I scribble a reminder to pay her back and tuck it into my pocket. The last thing I want is to take this new friend for granted. I have ugly memories of what my dad once called "trading on the cloth"—when priests and nuns take for granted the generosity of loyal Catholic layfolk to provide for them. Even worse if the provider is non-Catholic, as I've figured Sophie must be.

When she returns, I fumble with apologies about not having any money. "That's okay, we Jews are all rich. You must know that. But we're not *necessarily* stingy." Her tone is light, but I feel a jab. Is this how she sees me—with stereotypes so ingrained they just pop up casually? I devour the cheese and crackers, candy bar, and Coke she brings me, feeling like I have seriously insulted this person who seems to want to be my friend. Though she certainly is different from every other friend I have.

November 1960

For the past few weeks, my mind's not been on Sophie or how and why she is different from me, even though we sit across from each other in our three seminars. In struggling to keep up with the newness of everything around me, I have perhaps been more formal and aloof than usual. She's not put off, however, persisting with requests—for the loan of a book, a pencil, a Kleenex. She's fascinated by the seemingly endless number of things I can carry in my huge pocket.

Today, though, as I drowsily ponder the "possibility of real plurality in the pre-Socratics," I awake to how different she appears to me now, sitting across the seminar room, alert and poised, as if she's a runner about to sprint forward. With her hair drawn back in a ponytail, her dark eyes signal her special presence in the room. It isn't simply that she's quick and agile with the arguments defining our discipline, or that she cuts through to the heart of each argument. It's that she is so at home, so confident, and at the same time so thoroughly gracious and poised. She never seems to be "asking permission" to be heard, as I always feel I am. It has become obvious to me that Sophie is hungry to learn and loves being smart. She contributes in class like the men do—confident, direct, and taking for granted that she belongs here.

I try to convey these impressions to my friend Sister Christine over our nightly mug of hot chocolate, particularly how generous Sophie is in sharing her insights. I finish with a quick add-on, "But there's absolutely nothing aggressive about her...." I seize up in midthought: another ugly stereotype of Jews, out of my own mouth!

Vague and uncomfortable thoughts from these past weeks have been surfacing, keeping me from sleep. Sophie's own words, "We Jews..." started it, this dredging up of old memories about the word. Grandpa's anger over losing out to "that smart little Jew," bringing Mimi's instant disapproval: "You mean that Jewish gentleman." And years later, the same sort of rapid reprimand from Mimi when a friend mentioned that my aunt's neighbor was a Jew. "Mrs. Weeger is only *part* Jewish." Both Mimi and my aunt were quick to convey that this word "Jew" was far too crude for proper speech.

But wasn't their propriety itself insulting? As if calling someone a "Jew" had to be softened or recast. Or apologized for! Am I doing the same thing? Using this old stereotype to assure Christine that Sophie is okay?

December 31, 1960
It's the year-end retreat here in our small chapel at St. Catherine's. The priest conducting the service urges us to examine our consciences on how faithful we have been to the traditions of our order. Living apart from the rest of our own communities of sisters can bring many temptations, he reminds us, especially about the details of how our rule is lived back home.

"Being graduate students, some of you may fancy yourselves intellectuals, and all too easily succumb to the sin of pride, judging yourselves wiser than your founders who wrote your rule. So take heed! *Keep the Rule, and the Rule will keep you.*" It's an exhortation that I'm sure has been drilled into each of us listening, in every order. And in the long stretch of meditation that follows, I dutifully attempt to follow his direction, mildly distracted by the irreverent thought that it's the devil, not God, who's in the details.

And, indeed, I must admit that ever since that first day with Sophie at registration when I borrowed money and ate outside the refectory, I have been exempting myself from many details of a rule I've found easy to keep for the last fifteen years while living "in community" back in St. Louis. Yet that same rule tells me such customs can be laid aside "for the demands of charity or necessity." So the real question is, have I been using charity as an excuse for my own comfort or convenience? As the good father says, have I rationalized that I know better than my rule what the demands of charity are? Was it charity—or just plain hunger—that led me to borrow money from Sophie? Probably not, yet the word "charity" trips up my train of thought. *Ubi caritas et amor, Deus ibi est*: Where charity and love are, there is God. Probings from meditations past bubble up to remind me how charity is the very heart of Christian life. Or it should be. Jesus was fierce in his condemnation of those who put the minutiae of the Jewish law above the love of one's brethren. So should I.

But how do those old prejudices about Jews figure in all this? What's that saying about the elephant in the room? Here I am fretting about exempting myself from the lights-out rule, a mere detail I know, while the *sin* of anti-Semitism stares me in the face. It's sin of an entirely different order, and it is the challenge confronting me now: How to love Sophie without the distorting lens of this hateful prejudice?

Not that it's new for me to be pondering seriously my personal involvement with this sin. Back at the motherhouse, when I was teaching at St. Mary's, Sister Augusta loaned me *The Diary of a Young Girl*. I was horrified at what the young Anne Frank, practically my same age, suffered during the same years I was moving happily through Catholic schools and into the order. So I joined Sister Augusta and some other sisters in a Jewish-Catholic dialogue, where we read and discussed not only Frank's volume but the great *Last of the Just* by André Schwarz-Bart.

What a shock to realize I was a part of a heinous crime, which, until then, had always seemed foreign to me. One by one, during those months in the dialogue, we identified, and then deplored, our own stereotypes. We studied how these judgments develop into prejudice. After each session right there in a parlor adorned with a statue of Mary, we joined our Jewish women friends to pray the Psalms. We asked God to forgive this centuries-old sin of which we sisters were a part. With the grace of God—the God of Abraham and Jesus, I believed—I could grow past some nasty prejudices of my genteel Gentile upbringing. All that was before I knew personally, as a friend, any Jew. But now I do. And those awful stereotypes are still alive in me, more real now because they're more personal. If I want to be Sophie's friend, I must do more than deplore the biases of my Christian birth. But how?

Chapter 7

1961

November 1961

Sophie stops me as I am leaving Kant's Copernican Revolution, the seminar we're sharing this semester. "Hey, Liza, I need your help." Over a year now, and her forward ways still unsettle me, though more by the guilt I feel in noticing them than by any real discomfort. She explains the project pushing her: She and some friends have volunteered in a tutoring project at an inner-city housing project and need help. "We've discovered a sizable group of adults without any schooling. They're basically illiterate." She's wide-eyed in disbelief. "We have to teach them the basics. From scratch. I need you, Liza, and I need you to recruit some other nuns for us, a bunch of them. All nuns know about this basic stuff, don't they?"

I try to tell her that I've absolutely no experience with the really "basic stuff"—beginners, learning to read and write. I tell her what a miserable failure I was my first year with the young students at St. Pat's. That I didn't feel like I was really teaching till I got to the upper grades and finally to high school math. But she can't hear me—her enthusiasm doesn't let her. I find myself drawn to her high-minded commitment, despite her bossy manner. Besides, I'm flattered. She presumes I am as generous as her friends are. So I compromise: I'll find some nun volunteers, but count me out for teaching that beginning stuff. I can't do it.

By the time we reach the library steps, I am anxious to go in to discover more about this amazing Immanuel Kant I've met in the seminar, but Sophie persists with her pleas.

"Come on, Liza, come with me now. I want you to meet the others. You'll like them, get some sense of our project. It'll help you recruit other sisters. I promise I'll get you back in time for dinner." She's picked up on the inflexible schedule at St. Catherine's, as well as my predictably insistent appetite. "We need your input, Liza."

With that last remark, a light goes off inside me. This is the first time, over the many months I've known Sophie, that my position *as a nun* has been valued by her. I like that, though I'm uncomfortable knowing she presumes me as socially conscious as those nuns she met in France, or as she herself is. So when she persists to "come get the feel of the place," I once again exempt myself from the rule about not traveling without a sister companion. Though she could, from a distance, and with a little myopia, pass for my sister companion with that long black raincoat, ankle-length denim skirt, and thick dark hair...just another nun's habit, you might think. Except, of course, for her usual halo of smoke.

We set off across campus, the blustery air billowing both our skirts. She walks briskly with a stride that seems impossible for someone so short. "I have to hurry. I don't have all your layers of wool keeping me warm," she reminds me. True enough, but having those layers makes this kind of rapid walk difficult, I want to say, as I struggle to keep up. We march on, though, in an almost military silence, bringing a calm I've not experienced around her before. Eventually I find confidence enough to pose the question I've wondered about ever since she startled me with "We Jews...." "Sophie, however did you get here, to a *Catholic* university?"

She stops abruptly to set me straight about her Jewishness. It's not a religious thing at all for her, she says, more like her political identity. Like her mother, she's a "secular Jew"—a curious and new term for me. When we start up again, at a more conversational pace, I learn that she was born in the United States to French parents who returned with her to Paris after the war. "My father was Catholic, though lapsed. Very lapsed. And they were both great readers and talkers, great debaters—about everything, including their own religious backgrounds. So I heard about both cultures at home, regularly. Same at the university. I seem always to have been surrounded by Jews and Catholics thrashing it out."

Just hearing her talk about those years in Paris leaves me envious. She's rubbed elbows (and brains) with those giants of the "new philosophy" at College de France. But beyond that, and beyond even the cafés and bistros she and her friends inhabited, there was a certain spirit in her crowd (their elan, she calls it). They were socialists or communists, mostly, fired by a common hope of changing, not just the lives of the poor but also of the institutions oppressing them. "That's how I met those 'worker-priests.' You must know about them?" Her eyes light up like a little kid remembering a favorite fairy tale. "They work in factories and dockyards, anonymously; no one knows they're priests. They don't preach or conduct public services. They're not really very religious. They speak of being 'evangelized by the poor' rather than the other way round." That's also how she met some radical nuns—Little Sisters, they were called.

I do indeed know about both groups, though not firsthand. When we were young sisters in the 1950s, my friend Sister Madeleine and I used to check out Dorothy Day's *Catholic Worker* when we went over to the university for Saturday classes—along with other "liberal" Catholic periodicals, like *CrossCurrents, Commonweal*, or, especially *Jubilee*, a sort of Catholic *Look* magazine with stunning photography. We had heard these journals were "unsuitable" for our motherhouse library, but why? Too upsetting, too communist, too European? So we tried to find out, and in the process devoured stories about those worker-priests and the Little Sisters in France, along with that monk down in Kentucky, Thomas

Merton, and his *The Seven Storey Mountain*, and the young Jesuit poet Daniel Berrigan in New York—all of whom were, like us, religious (the noun) yet living and thinking so differently. Were they the sisters and priests of the future? Clearly Sophie thinks they are or should be. That's why she came to DC, or at least part of her reason: The Little Sisters are planning to start a mission here.

When we arrive at the housing project, Sophie's three friends are waiting in the large meeting room, now a storage area stuffed with detritus of all kinds. They rescue an extra chair for me from the clutter when, in the midst of introductions, a Black man, a laborer, it appears, pokes his head in the doorway. He seems to be looking for something or someone not here. After some hesitation, he walks directly up to me, demanding in a high-pitched voice something I can't understand. A foreign language, perhaps? I'm chagrined by my own awkwardness and look to Sophie for help, even though he clearly wants me. When finally I grasp the word "school," I start to explain how classes—"school"—won't start until next Sunday. But he doesn't seem to understand, or accept, what I am trying to say, growing more insistent, even angry. I'm relieved when Sophie intervenes and takes him aside. After some quiet words in the corner, she returns to introduce me to him as his teacher.

"Sister will teach you what you need," she says firmly. And just as confidently to me, "This is your new student, Sister." I hope the poor man can't see her *I told you so* wink to me. Her friends dig out another chair for my pupil. A crate, cleared of its debris, becomes his desk. A large roll of shelf paper materializes, and Sophie tears off a swath. "Here, use this. He needs to learn how to write his name. So teach him, okay?"

Again, Sophie stuns me. Even my superiors don't give

orders like that. They ask politely, say please and thank you. Besides, I don't know how to do what she wants.

She reads my reaction. "Look, Liza, he's a truck driver. As of tomorrow he'll lose his job if he can't sign those bills of lading. You've gotta do this for us. We can't. WE AREN'T NUNS. We don't look like you!" I swallow my protests, and with a reassuring hand on my arm, she calmly whispers how she needs to go plan with the others, and says, "Besides, you're the only one he'll let teach him." She smiles her wonderful supportive smile, while grabbing my arm again. "You've got a pen in your pocket, right, Liza? But just his name. Okay?"

My slender ballpoint is hardly the instrument for the task, though. I know this as soon as I look at his fingers: huge, thick, and callused. I ask him to tell me his name, slowly. From his indistinct jumble I must now choose the letters and syllables to create the name I think I hear. I take up the task with authority, hoping he doesn't notice my flicker of indecision as I try to figure out whether his first name should be written Pommley, or Pomlee, or Pomley, or none of the above. "So, Pomlee," I announce decisively, printing it in large letters as he looks on proudly. His last name is easier. If it weren't Irish before, it is now: "Pomlie Connor." Together we admire the string of letters I've printed on the paper in front of us, and he giggles.

He seems never to have held a writing instrument and drops my ballpoint repeatedly, his spirits falling each time as well. So I stand over him, put my hand over his, and together we struggle to trace over my printing. Over and over we work—with absolutely no sign of progress. I print the letters again, larger, and then again still larger, grateful that the roll of paper is huge. It's a hopeless task for one afternoon, I finally conclude, and I beg Sophie to convince him to return next week. Besides, I've got to get back to St. Catherine's by six o'clock. It's late—and I'm starving.

She doesn't seem to hear me but manages to find a lead pencil in her friend's purse for me. "Don't worry about getting back to St. Catherine's," she tells me. "You've got to finish with him today. He won't come back. It's now or never."

So I grasp the pencil like a talisman, letting the memory buried in my fingers move again in their once familiar Palmer Method routines from my own childhood. Together we begin the rhythmic push-pull of the tall, straight slants, moving on to the long, looping strings of e's and l's and o's and the softly rolling m's and n's. (I'm grateful there's nothing as complicated as an "f" or "g" or "y" in his name, and hope that his fingers will be nimble enough for the challenge of "r" when we get to his last name.)

He's hunching way over the crate. Does he need glasses? No time to think about that. He attacks the rote exercises with zest, over and over, eventually shaking off my hand. His fingers are getting used to the pencil, and he progresses from tracing to writing on this own. He's slow, and his squiggles barely legible, but he's working on his own. I give an occasional compliment, but otherwise shut up. The others have finished their meeting and seem to be killing time, waiting for me. Gradually my student straightens up. He's got the hang of it, though I can still barely decipher his name amid his scratchings. With a burst of industry, he signs his name for Sophie, smiling proudly at his work. Then, putting down the pencil, he stands to shake her hand and mine. He can write his name. It's what he came for, and so he leaves.

By the time we clear up and lock the place, it's dark outside and much colder, and Sophie decides on the bus. She promises to get me back to the campus at a "decent hour" if only I come to her place for pizza with the four of them. "What did I tell you, Liza? You're a natural. That guy knew it. He knew you were the boss." She nudges me with her elbow as we sit side by side in the back of the bus, her voluminous raincoat spread over us both.

"It's my habit, not me personally." I speak from a conviction reinforced by the afternoon's work.

"Well, okay, so it's your habit. You'll still be wearing it next week, I presume?" Her group, their spirit, and their compassion draw me in even though I'm more aware than ever of my incompetence as a primary teacher. "What's it going to be then, Liza? Are you with us?"

As we bounce over these dingy streets, I think that a two- or three-hour stint down here on Sunday afternoons might be just what I need to relax my brain cells, maybe even straighten out some of their kinks. So, yes, I tell Sophie. I'll recruit some sisters and, yes, I will join them. Maybe I can redeem those long-ago failures with the kids at St. Pat's that I'd like to forget.

"We're like secular nuns, don't you think?" Sophie tells me as we leave her place for the short walk back to St. Catherine's, she in her long coat and I like an Indian chief wrapped in a large brown blanket off her bed.

"If you only knew!" I say, laughing when remembering, among other things, their earthy language over pizza at her place. I surely felt at home, but I was terribly aware of being different and slightly physically uncomfortable, sitting there on her floor. I haven't done that since I left home. Yet I easily dismissed their offer of a chair. I didn't want to put myself "above" Sophie or her friends, nor emphasize any more my obvious differentness from them when they spoke about men and money problems with words my mother would have washed out of Tom's mouth for using. I was glad they didn't cast any shamefaced glances toward me, as if I were some avenging angel, when they spoke this way. I didn't know much about their friends Pete Seeger and Woody Guthrie, but as we sang those folk songs about peace and poverty and war, that's when I first felt truly one of them.

NEW ART

Sophie interrupts my ruminations to say she's glad we're walking back to St. Catherine's. She's been wanting to ask about my hometown. "What are your nuns doing about the racial situation out in St. Louis? I've heard your inner city's a mess."

She'd be shocked that our motherhouse, my beloved island of peace, is surrounded by, yet seems to be largely unaware of, that mess. She'd admire us more, I imagine, if we were still like our Irish foundress, Anne Gallagher, who left her home in County Down to live among the poor in the slums of Liverpool. I can easily imagine Anne and her first sisters treating one another and the poor the way Sophie treated Pomlie, or the way her friends were with me just now at her place—caring and welcoming, yet concerned little about being polite or proper. Could they be closer to the ideal of "detachment" preached at nuns than present-day nuns are themselves? Our passion for rules and propriety (and house cleaning!) don't seem to bother Sophie and friends at all. Yet these "preoccupations" have become so much a part of our lives that I don't think Anne, any more than Sophie, would feel at home with us these days.

We stop for a light at the intersection and she returns to her startling claim about her group as secular nuns. "We're socialists, too, just like you. We protest individualism wherever we can. That's what you're doing, right? Isn't that what your vows, your community life are all about?"

It's never dawned on me to think of our life or our vows that way, but then Sophie's got me thinking in entirely different ways about many things. What she admires about those French nuns seems very different from the respect so many Catholics show us, what we in fact expect from them. We're seen, I think, as pious, innocent, and self-effacing but hardly relevant in "the real world."

Sophie, by contrast, understands that the whole point of the Little Sisters life among the poor is to protest how our

contemporary world works. For her they are revolution-
aries. They work for radical change in society. I've never
heard any of my sisters explain our vows that way. Or any of
the priest retreat masters preach to us that way. We pretty
much accept the world as we find it.

"You probably think 'socialist' is a dirty word, don't you?"
Sophie asks after my silent spell. "But wasn't that what Jesus was all about? Jesus, the revolutionary?"

The truth in her challenge makes me uncomfortable
even as I'm aware of how she distorts and even glamorizes
our life. What I still want to understand, though, are her own
political convictions, which I am convinced lie behind her
perception of us. "I'm curious, Sophie, you described your
Jewishness as more political than religious. So what are
you? Socialist? Marxist? Communist?"

"I was born a socialist. My parents and all their friends
were. So I took socialism for granted. It wasn't really personal until I read Marx. I was barely seventeen! Was it like
that for you, the first time you encountered Jesus? Marx
blew my mind! He spoke directly to me. To me, personally. I
converted, you might say, on the spot. I had discovered 'true
socialism,' true humanism. So I upped and joined the Communist Party. It was so clear for me, so certain. I was joining
the elite of the elite. Together we could save the world! Probably how you felt?"

Yes and no, I want to say. Some comparisons are obvious. My parents and their take-it-for-granted Catholicism,
and I am doing them one better by joining the order. But
I'm ashamed to admit that saving the world was not part of
my idealism at seventeen. Nor did the Gospels ever really
"speak to me" personally. And I certainly never had an "encounter" with Jesus like hers with Marx. As for "convert-
ing," I suppose what I discovered around Gaby and her poets
could be called that. But I'm not up for telling her any of this,
despite these last hours of Sisterly sharing. Instead, I quiz

her, "What became of all that certainty?"

"It lasted until my twenties, all the time as a heart and soul party member. Not because of my parents or their world, but because *I* was choosing it!" Her voice has a hint of nostalgia, something I also feel about that early period of my life. "I bought it all, yet I imagined myself open to other views. But of course I wasn't. I was always firmly tethered to the system. The Party had answers for everything. Like your catechism, maybe. I loved it, loved being so certain! But then, came my *crise de foi* when I got to the university. *Everyone* was a socialist. Yet they understood socialism so differently. Some were straight-out Marxists, some Leninists, others Stalinists, and still others Trotskyites. Most were dyed-in-the-wool atheists, though not all. There were Christian Socialists. Even a few Catholic Socialists. The effect on me? My oh-so-secure faith was shattered. I've never believed the same way since." She turns to me. "Anything like this for you? Attitudes toward Church or convent changed much?"

Can she tell? Does it show? Ever since my first semester of grad school, I've been grappling with the variety of views about what it means to be a nun, which has led to questions about Catholicism, about Christianity, about faith itself. Yet even earlier there was a time—hard to date—when the "answers" filling my Catholic consciousness no longer answered my own big questions. That wake-up call during my first year teaching, when I met all those characters in Augusta's little red book? All Catholic, great Catholics, some saints, yet all *so* different.

Still, though, there's a huge difference from Sophie and her relation to the Communist Party. I've never really questioned that I belong with my "party," the Sisters of Mary, though I certainly have questioned, in many ways, the Church itself. Exactly what this means has definitely become more complicated as the years add up. Whatever else it means, though, I don't think of us as "the elite of the elite," though I may once have.

Yet I am very far from being able to share any of these ruminations with Sophie. Besides, St. Catherine's is in sight, so I resort to lame humor, echoing McCarthy's witch hunts of the 1950s: "Sophie, are you now or have you ever been...."

She bursts out laughing in her wonderfully hearty way, grabbing my arm the way Dad used to when he was intent on having me hear him. "Yes, of course I am a Communist. About the same way those worker-priests are Catholic. Tell me something, Liza, are you afraid of associating with a 'fellow traveler'?"

Fall 1961

Sophie points out one of the new grad students at our department picnic prior to the start of classes. "Father Aloysius. He's a monk! Can you believe it?"

I know what she means. After a year on the CU campus I consider myself adept at spotting clerical mufti. And he definitely does not look like one: that tall, skinny, left-handed redhead off in the distance shooting baskets. No shiny black pants, no nondescript sport shirt. Just ragged, very secular-looking Levi's and a weathered sweatshirt.

When classes start, I discover this same Father Aloysius in the Kant seminar, in which Sophie and I are both members. Yet I don't really meet him until almost the end of the semester. From the first, however, he has piqued my curiosity. My image of monks—since being smitten early in convent life by many things monastic—is of patient, kindly old souls fairly oozing wisdom. Often quite rotund and jolly. Not sharp and angled like Father Aloysius, who brims with zest and impatience and sometimes, a piercing anger for the seminar to begin, for it to end, for another cigarette, for Professor Schneider to keep things moving.

His routine, though, is predictable. No mingling or small

talk or gradual shuffling up to the seminar table. His maneuver is last minute, quick and sure, like that graceful basketball player I've spied. Moments after the professor arrives, he appears in the rear doorway, tall and slim, his monk's habit draped from his shoulders as from a clothes hanger, caught only by a low-slung cincture. A kind of clerical cowboy, I think. He hesitates for an instant, nodding ever so slightly toward the professor, then swoops over to pluck an ashtray from the table before settling into his corner chair. He's separate from the rest of us around the table, and as far from Schneider as possible. After seminar, he snuffs out his cigarette, slings the book bag over his shoulder, and darts across the back of the room, through the crowd at the door, without a word to anyone. Hardly the asceticism of otherworldly monks, devoted to solitude and silence. More just a bad-mannered jerk?

Then one day there's no chair in the corner. He's forced to sit further up in the room, though still not at the table like the rest of us. He's pulled a chair away from the table and dragged it over next to the wall, angling it a bit so he faces Schneider, and I get a better look at his face. Were it not for the pug nose and freckles, his lean and angular face could seem ascetic. Sophie sees him a bit differently, "More arresting than handsome."

From across the table, I notice two books balanced on the leg crossed over his lap—a large well-worn library volume alongside the Modern Library paperback the rest of us are using. He seems to be making line-by-line comparisons between the paperback's English and the Old German on his lap. More scholar, less cowboy or street tough, this Father Aloysius. (From where I sit, I can also observe the frayed, torn hem of his monk's habit, held together with staples, testimony to his "life without a wife," as my priest-cousin Bill says.)

∿

December 1961

"Enjoy your nap? You should do like me, Sister, sit in the back. Then no one sees you, except old Schneider." He stands over me, handing me some of my papers. Apparently they slid to the floor during my unplanned snooze. After everyone else in the seminar leaves, he plops his book bag on the table by me and empties one ashtray into another. "He deserves the insult, don't you think?" It's never occurred to me that boring old Dr. Schneider might deserve an insult. When he asks if I mind that he smokes—in that gentlemanly fashion presuming compliance—I smile an okay, wondering if I would respond so sweetly were Sophie ever to ask.

With that, he turns around the chair in front of me, raises one leg on to it, and slowly lights his cigarette. As he stands there, staring out the window, he inveighs against Professor Schneider, the translation of Kant we're using, and the lousy DC weather. I listen and take in details the late afternoon sun reveals—hair a darker red than I remember from the picnic, huge hands, freckled and roughened with calluses. Not like a priest's hands, I think, as I watch him pick a speck of tobacco from his lip. More like those old pictures of Grandpa's nephews—weather-beaten, angry-looking "lads" longing, so I was told, to get out of Ireland and come to America.

Cigarette finished, he folds himself into the still twisted-around chair and leans his arms across the back as if to interrogate me. In fact we interrogate each other, discovering much in common about our lives before Kant, including our departure from "the world" in the summer of 1945, our stint teaching high school math in the '50s, and grandparents from the north of Ireland. In the middle of this exchange, he reaches over to take back one of the papers he had earlier retrieved for me. It's a reprint of an article from the *Sister Formation Bulletin.* "'Femininity and Sprituality.' Any good?"

"Some sisters think so. There are reprints all over the

place at St. Catherine's."

"Is this *the* Father Gallen, Jesuit, 'noted canon lawyer'?" I nod in agreement. "Who says he's an expert on women?"

"He does." He gets my sarcasm, I can tell.

"Really?" His inquisitive frown makes those bushy eyebrows merge somewhere over his nose.

"Because he knows all the legal stuff governing nuns' lives, he has the right to claim he knows all about women, especially nuns." I've never spoken like this in front of a priest before.

"And spirituality?" he says, with what seems like genuine curiosity.

As our exchange continues, I feel the color rising in my cheeks and my normal reticence around priests slipping away. My negative reactions to Gallen's article are scribbled everywhere, bringing first quizzical, then amused, expressions to his face. He fingers the pages carefully, almost delicately, twisting his head to read my marginal notes. He seems both more friendly and more serious than I had imagined him to be, watching him dart in and out of seminar. If he were a sister friend, I would by now have launched into a full-scale critique of an article I feel is seriously wrongheaded. Instead, I hold my tongue to see how he reacts.

"Hey, what's this? This is your writing, isn't it?" I nod and he shoves his glasses up over his close-cropped hair, drawing the pages closer to read the tiny script of my longer comments. "Wow. 'STUPID! WRONG! NO!!!' " He abruptly stops. "Sorry. I didn't realize this was so personal. Do you mind?" He's asking with a slightly crooked grin lighting up his face. "Not that I can decipher it all. Doesn't look like a nun's penmanship to me. But then, I don't consider myself an expert on nuns, like he does. Certainly not around one who knows more about Kant than I do."

He seems embarrassed to be complimenting me and picks up the article again. "Look, I've got to give a retreat to

some nuns this summer. First time, and I'm scared shitless."
He tries to swallow this last choice of word. But he doesn't
apologize. "This would really help—your remarks as well as
the article itself. Mind if I borrow it?" I am astonished how
much more vulnerable and less confident he looks without
his heavy glasses. "Scout's honor, Sister. I promise to give it
back. Your nasty cracks are safe with me."

Chapter 8

1962

April 1962

Spring is glorious. Through the dusty windows of our seminar room we watch the gardens of CU flower into new life, and past that, our youthful White House, and beyond that, a Vatican at last thawing from years of frozen thinking. JFK promises to put a man on the moon. And the new pope says the Church needs to "open wide the windows, let fresh air in."

The language itself is different. Instead of the usual clerical Latin, the pope is using his Italian *aggiornamento*. The word not only tickles the tongue, it's agitating minds all over the Church. And his words that follow go beyond anything I or anyone I know has ever heard from the top authority in our Church. He speaks of a thorough revision of canon law, something that will affect how every Catholic lives! And that's just the beginning. The pope in Rome and the president right here in DC! Whoever linked these two before? Yet each now pushes onward, outward to new frontiers, new life. Together these two great men are firing up every grad student I know with hope for new life, in our country, in our church, and in the whole world.

And all the while Father Aloysius and I, along with eight other grad students, are digging more deeply into Aristotle's *Metaphysics*, the focus of the seminar we share this term. A most relevant philosopher for these times, we agree. Because for Aristotle, change in the world is a *good*, not a *defect*—a dramatic departure from what we've each been taught, even by those claiming to follow the great Aristotelian, Thomas Aquinas.

Our tradition—the scholastic one of our Catholic up-bringing—was fearful of change, especially in philosophical or religious matters. We've been cautioned to fear novelty, to embrace the status quo, and, if necessary, to resign ourselves to what seems meaningless in our heritage. Now Aristotle reminds us of a more dynamic strain in our intellectual tradition, one that actually supports many of the initiatives for change floating through the Church. I'm lucky to have had Sister Augusta, and then her friend Gilson, as mentors who challenged this assumption that change is not good. Unfortunately, my new friend Father A had no such luck.

"This was great, thanks, a real eye-opener. A huge help for that retreat coming up." Father A is returning the issue of the *Sister Formation Bulletin* with its discussion about femininity and spirituality. "And your scribbled reactions. A huge help! I had no idea nuns were thinking such thoughts. A helluva lot more interesting than most monks I know. Talk about a hidden brain trust."

How nice to be appreciated for my intelligence. I start to open the large envelope he's handed me, but he stops me. "Please, open it later." He then launches into a harangue about the intellectual apathy among the monks in his monastery.

As I breathe in the sights and smells of the warm April afternoon, I decide to skip the bus and walk back to St. Catherine's. In such moments lately I am filled with an awe for which I have no words. I've taken to letting Gaby's friend, the poet Hopkins, speak for me silently as I thank my Creator God for a world "where lives the dearest freshness deep down things." And deep down, *people*, I add, thanking God for my new friend Father A and marveling again at the world of people discovered here in this live-away-from-home world. I was prepared to be excited by all the philosophers

I'd be meeting when I arrived here at CU almost two years ago, but never could I have anticipated the thrill of those tiny glimpses into the exciting worlds of the people I now call my friends. Worlds inhabited by sisters from different orders, from as far away as Africa and China or as close as Kansas City or Chicago, immersed in fields as foreign to me as microbiology, or Sister Helen's psychology, or maybe most of all, Sister Regina's sociology. And now, of course, those fascinatingly foreign worlds of Sophie and Father A. Again, the poet Hopkins helps me refer all these glories of creation back to the Creator: "Christ plays in ten thousand places, lovely in limbs, and lovely in eyes not his. To the Father through the features of men's faces." And women's as well, I add.

Outside my door, all wrapped in brown paper and carefully tied, sits a box of special cookies that my friend Sister Madeleine has mailed me—another reminder, and a tasty one, of grace playing in ten thousand faces. Maddy, as only I call her, was my BNC (beloved novitiate companion) and is now a parochial school principal in St. Louis. Every few weeks she sends me homemade cookies. Usually I ask Christine or Helen to bring mugs and join me, but this afternoon I want to open Father A's envelope by myself.

What stares out at me is an eight-and-a-half-by-eleven-inch print of President Kennedy's inauguration last year. Marian Anderson is singing the "Star-Spangled Banner," and cold bites into the faces of Eisenhower and Nixon and the Kennedys. On the reverse side of the photo, I recognize the back-slanted script of Father Aloysius:

"The energy, the faith, the devotion which we bring
to this endeavor will light our country...And the glow
from that fire can truly light the world."
— January 1961

To which he'd added: *and light up our Church, we hope!*

I'm startled. This same scene, in a much smaller newspaper clipping, all yellowed and wrinkled, has been taped inside my closet door since I moved to St. Catherine's, right next to a quote from James Joyce in Sister Carla's elegant calligraphy. I've never quite understood the angry Irishman's words about "forging in the smithy of my soul the uncreated conscience of my race," even though I love his other words about *welcoming life* and encountering *the reality of experience.* To my ear they complement those words from Kennedy about *asking not what my country can do for me, but what I can do for my country,* especially when I substitute *community* for *country,* meaning my Sisters of Mary.

I've been dressing each morning since I moved to DC with these words and this picture staring at me, reminding me of a commitment I was inspired to make on the long train ride from St. Louis here to Washington, DC. I vowed then to use these years away from the pressures of the classroom to make my own, in whatever way open to me, the enormous project of renewing our community life. Just how this would happen, or what shape it would take, given my primary obligation of getting the degree, I didn't know then, nor do I yet. But I vowed, at the very least, to use the required hour of meditation each day, plus my daily "spiritual reading," to focus on the subject. Somehow or other I trust these efforts will affect my community, possibly the Church, maybe even my country.

I'd be embarrassed to say this to anyone. It sounds so grandiose, even to me. But here now is this new friend, Father A, who seems to feel as I do, that each of us can truly make a difference in the world and in the Church. A new excitement burning inside me cancels out any need for those cookies and coffee, and I almost miss the index card still stuck inside his large envelope. I recognize his backhand and feel his message pressed forcefully into the card:

Gallen may know a lot about canon law, but he's dead

wrong about men, at least this man—that we don't need to be "appreciated, encouraged, and dealt with as individuals!" Bullshit. Of course we need it. Plenty of it. And you, my friend, provide it.
Thanks, Dan

Dan?! Just Dan? That's his name? It fits him, I guess. Certainly better than Aloysius. I stare at his funny printing, going every which way, with ink splotches at the tail of each letter and the aroma of his cigarettes penetrating it all. Running my finger under and over this scrawl, I discover he has pressed so hard I can feel it on the reverse.

Dan. Just plain Dan. Dan Doherty. I like it. Ever Danny? I wonder.

The chocolate bits have melted into my coffee. Time to stop the dunking and drink up.

May 1962
"An emergency call, Sister. Your brother Dan," whispers tiny, bent-over Sister Pascal. I gave my seminar presentation this afternoon and turned in early after too many late nights preparing for it. But "Pascal the rascal," as we call her, is not the person to tell that I have no brother named Dan. She's already irked by a call after nine, the beginning of the nightlong Grand Silence at St. Catherine's, as it is in most convents.

The phone available to us student sisters is downstairs in a phone booth inside the area reserved for visitors. So down the stairs I pad, in slippers and robe, along the drafty halls into the "parlors," convent parlance for where nuns can "visit with externs." Visitors aren't supposed to stay past eight o'clock, nor are we to make calls after nine, so outlier that I've suddenly become, I have the empty, drafty place all to myself.

"Well, now, Sister, aren't we all brothers and sisters in Christ?" His speech is much less cautious than his careful contributions in seminar. "You don't think I'm going to tell that old crone I'm a priest, do you?" he adds over a noisy background. I ask where he is, and he identifies a phone booth at Villa Italia, a local bistro I've heard other grad students mention. "Listen, your report was terrific! Definitely a bright spot in that dull class. So much for 'women being too emotional to handle the abstract.' Father Gallen should have been there. What am I saying? *You* should be here, now, with all of us. Kevin, Sophie, Basil, we're all here. We want to toast you."

I hear him opening the door for a well-wishing clink of glass. "Congratulations, Sister!" Brother Basil's unmistakable Brooklyn voice soars above the rest. "Hey, Sista, ciao! From Chianti!"

I ask who that is, and a slightly frivolous conversation ensues.

September 1962

A new term at the university, and Dan's after-nine calls are coming more frequently. When he hears from his younger sister Martha, a parochial school nun in Minneapolis, he sounds frantic. "Help me answer the kid. She's all tied up in knots."

His retreat for nuns in the summer was successful, bringing more invitations for next summer. This is making Dan even more curious about "how sisters think." And now his own sister Martha's problems are intensifying his quest, especially about the changes we sisters anticipate with the opening next year of the Vatican council. I'm flattered he thinks I can help.

The issue of possible reform in sisters' lives is not new for me. Back in the late 1950s, when I was teaching high school, our whole community, prompted principally by the Sister Formation Movement, was busy imagining how the customs and rules of our order could be tailored to better fit our twentieth-century lives. For some time there had been a growing awareness that many of the accepted, sometimes venerated, attitudes and practices in our convent might actually impede the original mission of our order.

So the new pope's announcement in 1959 about "updating" the whole Church, his *aggiornamento*—was a blast of very welcomed fresh air for us, at least everyone I know. It's given us a heightened sense of purpose that's perceptible: We want to open not just the windows but also the doors and walls and whatever else separates us in our own convent ghetto. Imaginations fire. How best to go about changing age-old—some say, medieval—ways? Bundles of these imaginings find their way into the *SF Bulletin*.

Yet even three years after this blast, there still isn't much written by nuns themselves to provide a theological basis for this new attitude toward "the world." This is because nuns, or any other females, are barred from the advanced study of either canon law or theology, and consequently lack the rudimentary tools that priests get at least a smattering of during their seminary education—tools necessary to be heard by Roman ears.

Luckily, though, I have found a backdoor entry to some of this because of Dan. He's started sharing with me the writings of "foreign" theologians: de Lubac, Rahner, Congar, Kung, and Schillebeeckx, among them. He even translates portions for me at times, letting me eavesdrop on the thinking of men already named *periti* (experts) for the upcoming council. I've got the feeling of being sneaked into the boys' locker room.

Our excitement over all this theorizing is dampened, however, by disturbing news for us as Americans, right in our own South as well as in a place called Vietnam. Sophie is adamant that the two are connected. With little interest in our Church life, she shames the lot of us into speaking out in protest, if only by writing our elected officials. Her passion is contagious, prompting both Dan and Basil to join her in taking their anger to the halls of government.

I stick to letter writing, but I also start leaving my door ajar after nine so I can answer the phone before Sister Pascal stirs herself to action, which usually isn't until after the fifth ring. Dan alternately anguishes over these two American tragedies and enthuses over his latest European article on churchly reform. I get used to strong drafts shooting under the French doors, hissing across the polished linoleum of the parlors and into the phone booth, tickling my bare ankles.

As fall progresses into winter, Dan's language becomes more salty, the effects of liquor more obvious, and I take to wearing wool socks with a shawl over my bathrobe. He speaks heatedly about the indifference or even apathy among his brother monks when it comes to Church reform, how he needs to talk to someone who cares about what he cares about. And when he starts hearing confessions in a suburban parish during Advent, his calls often come from bars. I worry how his anguish seems to be outweighing his enthusiasm.

He doesn't discuss anyone's confession with me, of course. But the travails of young married parishioners bewilder him and, increasingly, anger him. He fumes about the Church's continued rigidity on sexual morality and his obligation as a priest to uphold a policy he judges morally wrong. His anger saddens me, even scares me a bit, so I'm relieved when he tells me he's seeing a psychiatrist, Dr. Brunner. About then, Sister Pascal says my brother Dan should call earlier.

I cannot yet call him Dan, but I also can no longer call him Father Aloysius, nor sign myself Sister Elizabeth Mary.

Yet unsigned and unaddressed, a steady stream of materials moves back and forth between us—European articles from him, often as not returned with my personalized annotations. Sometimes I even rewrite portions of the words of his esteemed authors, tailoring their thoughts, as I understand them, to fit convent life. I hope these will be helpful for planning his retreats for nuns, I say, and for dealing with Sister Martha—and for him to understand more about me, I come to see.

Never do I see this more clearly than when I instinctively retrieve a long-cherished, dog-eared card from my life before CU to share with him. It had been among a number of sample Christmas cards my artist friend Sister Carla had prepared to submit to our superiors for sending benefactors at Christmas. Yet as we studied it, we both knew it would never pass muster, either with our superiors or our benefactors, despite finding it extremely appropriate for us that Christmas:

Another December, and again we look to Bethlehem, at the tiny new light emerging from the darkness. No matter how Jesus's followers may have garbled his message, it is still a light to be discovered and nourished, by each of us every Christmas. A lifetime work: No institution can do it for us; we alone are responsible for our faith. We need to feed and cherish the fragile child bringing light into the dark December night, crying for food and love. We fear Decembers, but we need Decembers.

My hope is that it may speak to Dan, as it does to me, still. Help maybe to lighten a bit of the darkness I increasingly hear in him. Maybe even let him know about the darkness in me, which I've been careful to keep out of our talks. It's easier to write it this way, not as personal. When I don't get the immediate response from him that I've come to expect, I wonder if the priest in him may be put off by the unorthodoxy of my message. With this cowboy-scholar-street tough it's easy to forget he is also a priest, another Christ, we say. The Church is officially "his business" the way it never has been mine. Beneath the surface, though, a deeper worry grows: Why am I so anxious to reveal myself to this increasingly dark man?

‒‒‒‒

December 28, 1962

Feast of the Holy Innocents. A gloom hangs over me, starting almost two weeks ago when St. Catherine's virtually emptied for the holidays. Not only have I not heard from Dan, I'm struggling to listen to those very words I sent him about nourishing the light in this dark December. Without having much luck.

I chose to stay here in DC, in these empty halls of St. Cat's, even though Mother Augusta, as well as my own mother, urged me to come back to St. Louis for the holidays. I am lonely, of course, but I've put up with a lot of that these past two years. And this lousy head cold is nothing new. Nor, sadly, is this miserable, dark, and drizzly weather. So what is it? Some subterranean guilt? Have I rationalized my need to stay here, telling myself I can't afford two weeks of "vacation" with three research papers due in January? Avoiding the always-frenzied lead-up to Christmas at the motherhouse?

It does mean, though, that I'm free to venture out with my friend Sister Christine, who also didn't go home to Los Angeles for the holidays. Each of us knows the same trick for relieving the blues: bring cheer to someone worse off than yourself.

‒‒‒‒

St. Joseph's Home for Retired Priests. Each time I've taken a bus this way, I've noticed this sign in front of the old stone building filling the corner lot. It looks as sad and neglected, as forgotten and worn by time, as I imagine its inhabitants to be. And as the bus moves on, I think how lonely it must be for an old or sick priest, without children or a spouse, or the kind of community surrounding elderly nuns or monks. Especially at the holidays.

So on this empty after-holiday week, why not share with these lonely old men some of the goodies piling up on our "takeaway table" in the basement of St. Cat's? Sister Christine agrees. The stash of cookies and candies left behind by the nuns who went home for the holidays is much more than the handful of us rattling around here can possibly consume. Why not bundle it all up and deliver it to these dear old souls?

No answer comes when we ring the doorbell. The air is frigid and our bundles heavy, but we ring again, wait, then ring again and wait again, listening for any signs of life inside. I have images of a house full of dead bodies, remembering a story about such a place, where escaping gas trapped inmates and staff alike and were only discovered when some innocent bell ringer had the nerve to barge in. Perhaps we should just be bold and....

But Sister Christine, ever the practical scientist, is more Nancy Drew than I am. She prowls around the big ugly building and discovers muffled sounds emerging from a barely open transom on a basement window in the back. We make out moving figures in white who seem to be giggling—or is it crying? When we manage to make ourselves known, we are quickly welcomed by a group of white-habited nuns into their basement refectory. There must be at least a dozen of them, all short and stocky and of indeterminate age, though clearly older than we are. And all of them "foreign."

We're answered with broad smiles and childish giggles when we attempt to introduce ourselves and our mission. Only one sister, presumably the superior, speaks, haltingly, and in heavily accented English. This is their one day of holiday celebration, she says. The "good fathers" who live above ground in private apartments are off at some sort of grand celebration with their friends at a country club.

Gradually it dawns on us: These sisters are the priests' housekeepers, their maids! Nuns brought over to this land of the free and home of the brave to wait on priests? To be their servants? They clean and scrub the priests' quarters, while their own community life is confined to this dreary basement. Yes, they cooked and cleaned up all day Christmas for the priests and their guests. No, they haven't seen any of DC, nor met any American nuns before us, let alone received any language or other education. They're bubbly, like little children, excited to be "free" for a whole day, with cakes and cookies, bottles of champagne and boxes of candies left by the "good fathers." Many, already a bit tipsy, urge us to join them. We beg off—must get back before dark, etc.— and make our farewell, offering them our bundles of holiday sweets. (More to lighten our return trip than to treat them, I'm afraid.) So much for our good deed and attempt to dispel our gloom.

Half frozen from waiting for the bus, we sit sad and silent most of the way back. But by the time we're ready for mugs of hot chocolate—this time in Christine's room—my simmering insides have reached a boil, with personal pique exploding into a global fury. "How can such a place exist? What does this have to do with God?"

Christine busies herself with mugs as I rant on. "Is this what these women gave up marriage and family for? To be maids? How does it differ from white slavery?" I regale her with some of Sophie's horror stories about this particularly awful form of immigrant exploitation. "And this? This is a million times worse. It's done in God's name!"

December 31, 1962
On this closing night of the year, while much of the world celebrates with food and drink, most nuns, surely the ones

here in St. Catherine's House of Studies, spend the night in prayer. This follows an entire day of austerity: fasting and silence extending into night, with the chapel left open so we can pray "in reparation for our own and others' sins this past year."

Try as I might, though, I'm simply not up for much introspection. I'm unable to empty my mind of those images from that old-priests' home. Of the sins being committed at that place. And of my own sin now of being so judgmental! They're uncomfortable enough, those images, to make me leave the stuffy chapel for some fresh air, only to find Sister Christine with apparently the same goal.

We move back up to her room, where I contribute my current stash of Maddy's cookies to match her reliable supply of instant coffee. Necessary rescue aids, we both agree, though slightly guilt-producing. Like me, she's still overwhelmed by images conjured up by that old-priests' place— and from her own Los Angeles Church history as well.

While we share the sweets, our common memories are anything but sweet: Out in California as a twenty-year-old beginning teacher, Christine spent her "free time" laundering and mending the parish altar linens, while her sister friend, also new to the classroom, stayed up a couple of nights a week making altar breads. And both had jam-packed classrooms. Not to be outdone, I tell her of those seventy-two kids at St. Pat's and how our whole household of seven nuns spent our "free time" on Sunday afternoons counting the parish collections. She then reminds me of those other jobs: training altar boys, conducting the choir, playing the organ. Jobs for "the good nuns" in every parish either of us ever knew. Yet neither of us can remember anyone questioning the propriety—either in LA or in St. Louis—of these arrangements or of the habitual neglect of lesson plans.

But now we both wonder, Why didn't our superiors prioritize classroom preparation? Why didn't they insist that the pastor hire laypeople to perform the parish duties? Was it that the pastors judged these chores more sacred than our classroom obligations? Too sacred for anyone other than "the good nuns"? Just as cleaning up after those elderly priests at St. Joseph's Home is too sacred? I tell Christine we should stop; this is making me crazy.

"You've forgotten the golf?" she adds. We both—she in LA and I in St. Louis—remember those Wednesdays when no priest was available at the school. The poor fellows had worked overtime all weekend, so like their medical doctor buddies, they needed time off for some golf. "Can you imagine anyone even suggesting that 'the good nuns' take a day off? Or get out to a country club for some fresh air? Or golf?"

Together we laugh at the notion of a nun golfer—but not at the reality of how differently priests' and nuns' labors are valued. "And not just by the priests! By us too—we buy into it all," Christine remarks with an air of sadness unusual for her. It's no surprise that she is less sanguine than I about ever really changing this particular component of our Catholic culture. Her group out in LA is feeling the heavy hand of clerical authority right now. And it's no joke.

Chapter 9

1963

January 1, 1963

"Happy New Year!" Dan's voice seems almost peppy—as he struggles to be heard over the noise and bustle of wherever he is. Union Station, maybe? He's more energetic, more "up" than I've heard him in many months—more himself. Cigarettes can do that, Sophie tells me. Sounds of his exhaling tell me he's gone back to them.

I slide down to the floor of the phone booth, forced by the tiny space to pull my knees up close to my chest—a very comfortable position, actually! It's more than his voice though. Something about Dan himself relaxes and warms me. "Listen. Thanks for that thing you gave me about the December darkness and all..." an inhaling lull, and then a softer, gentler tone, "...it helped, helped a lot, over a pretty bad patch. What about you? How was Christmas in your cloistered cell?"

Like a lot of people, Dan assumes our life is more secluded and monastic than it is. Even though I have been pretty solitary lately, that's not what my own December darkness is about. Yet I haven't a clue how to share the amorphous mix of gloomy feelings that have enveloped me these last days. So I toss his question back: What was so bad about your bad patch?

"Those nuns Martha belongs to. What bitches. Tried to see her yesterday and they wouldn't let me! I'm her brother, for God's sake!" His switch of tone is troubling. I hope he wasn't shouting like this when he asked to see Martha, or using such language. Sounds like he's been dipping into Salinger again. How well I remember my own first exposure to *The Catcher in the Rye* soon after I got back here. I read it straight through, couldn't put it down, but then, for the first time in my life, "goddamn" came unbidden to my lips.

"Get this," he continues, "a ghost-like recorded voice comes out of a little grill by the front door: 'Sister is on retreat.' That's all, a goddamn mechanical voice. Not even face to face. Frigid as the weather. I hate 'em."

My impulse is to defend these nuns; our nuns do the same thing sometimes when we're on retreat. But I check myself, suspecting his anger actually lies deeper. He's told me how he and his younger siblings were "put with the nuns" in an orphanage after his mother died giving birth to Martha. He was just ten years old. Now though, his shrink, Dr. Brunner, is helping him see how he's still furious with these sisters for taking his mother's place, and for separating him from baby Martha. "So I got the hell out of there when I turned fourteen, escaped to high school, away from those witches." Has he been drinking? I noticed that drink brings out what I've come to call his inner Salinger. "Then Martha ups and joins them, for God's sake. How could she?"

During a lull, I wonder if he could be crying, until I hear sounds that tell me he is indeed imbibing right there in the phone booth. Should I be doing or saying something to help him? I remember Mother letting her older brother Pat go on and on when he sounded this way. I just hope Dan's taken off his Roman collar.

The "Irish curse" runs in his family, he tells me, as it does in mine, both sides. My mother never used, or let us use, the term "drunk" when Uncle Pat sounded the way Dan does now. She'd say he was "sick," while Dad said he was "high" or "tight." Yet Mother's special sadness when Pat was "sick" like this seeped into all of us. Is this what's happening with Dan? I wonder if Martha has seen him like this. It must make her sad, the way Mother was around her brother. Are Martha's superiors trying to shield her from her big brother,

I wonder?

"They were on my case all the time when I was a kid, those nuns, telling me to shape up. They were only 'sanding off the rough edges for my own good!' Because I was 'made for higher things.' Why they beat the hell out of me—they loved me so much!"

"Beat you? I can't believe that—no nun ever touched me in school." If he's really drunk, it's better not to argue, I know, but I can't seem to help myself. He's hit a sensitive nerve. People claiming to have been abused by nuns always get a rise out of me. It's so contrary to my experience. Especially now, after seeing those poor nuns out at the old-priests' home. More oppressed than oppressing, I feel. Still, I should let it drop, remembering how Mother avoided arguing with Uncle Pat. Just change the subject, she'd say. "Have you tried phoning her?"

"Good God, how I've tried. They tell me in that icy nun voice: 'We don't talk on the phone, unless it is an emergency.'"

"So tell them it is an emergency!" I demand, turning bossy, just like Mother when she'd finally had enough of Uncle Pat's complaining.

"I'm not so sure she *wants* to talk to me. She gives me these little sermons, about how I should act more like a priest. As if I didn't carry all that shit around inside myself." More of Dr. Brunner, I surmise, and wonder if I could be interfering with his therapy by letting him go on like this. "You probably have that same pious crap tucked away just waiting to dump on me."

"What do you think?"

"That you're different." A slight pause, and then he speaks more soberly. "I know you're different. Do *you* know that?"

"Our order is—"

"I'm not talking about your order, for God's sake." For a moment, his gentle voice has turned harsh and cold. And the cold of the linoleum floor has finally penetrated the layers of my habit, so I struggle to my feet, saying it's time to go, when again he speaks, ever so softly. "What does your family call you? I can't call you 'Sister' anymore, damn it."

I hesitate, remembering how differently I answered this same question from Sophie. "Elizabeth...Betty, sometimes."

"That's your real name? I've called you that all along. Never thought it was your real name. Martha says that never happens, gets furious when I call her Martha." He continues in a mocking tone, "Now she's 'Sister Vincent,' for God's sake." Another long silence, and I wonder if he's weeping. "As if that whole crew isn't de-sexed enough, they give her a goddamn man's name. What the hell was wrong with her own name?"

During another awful lull, I worry that he might fall asleep, as Uncle Pat used to. I imagine him slumping over in the booth, then sprawling out like a homeless person right there in Union Station. I could go out, catch a bus, and rescue him. The fantasy vanishes instantly with rustling sounds, things crashing onto the metal floor, and finally his whispering voice. "Elizabeth...call me Dan, okay? Please? Elizabeth?"

I'm much too wound up to go back to that piece of my "research" still up in my typewriter. Or to that remnant of holiday lunch crowd whose laughter still drifts down here. Probably even to pray, devoid as I am right now of that calm needed for "lifting mind and heart to God." Even so, I head back to chapel.

Maybe I can salvage something of that year-end spiritual accounting that I dodged last night. At the very least I can take old Mother Alicia's advice: Thank God for the good things of the year past. Make a prayer out of what's distracting you. Bring the cares of your heart and lay them on the altar of the Lord. Right now the cares of my heart are firing off in all directions, but most directly toward Dan.

It frightens me to connect him with my Uncle Pat. I loved my uncle but was puzzled by him: one day bouncing me on his lap and gayly singing that I was his "pretty little girl from Omagh, in the county of Tyrone." (No other man in our family ever sang, even in church or at ball games, so I loved it, fake brogue and all.) Other times, though, he seemed mad at everyone, including me, and once I even saw him cry—which I didn't think grown-up men could. That prompted me to ask Mother if it was something I did, and she said, "No, no. Your Uncle Pat is an unhappy man. You should say a prayer for him."

That never quite satisfied my five-year-old mind, but then he was gone from our lives for good, something about a war injury. A terrible look came over Mother whenever I asked about him. She prayed her rosary for him every night, and from the way she looked, kneeling by her bed, head bowed, a picture of the Mater Dolorosa above her on the wall, I thought she might be crying, too.

I used to imagine "Danny Boy" playing through her mind when I saw her like that. It was her favorite, the song she always begged Uncle Pat to sing—this unhappy brother, lost to a secret war destroying him from the inside. Is that like my unhappy friend, Dan? I take the rosary hanging from my side and kneel to say the *Aves* now for him.

January 3, 1963
I learn about Dan's war in the letter he dropped off in our mailbox this morning. He is profoundly contrite for his drinking and angry words during our long conversation. He had planned to use my "Dark Decembers" piece to say some difficult things he's been wanting to tell me. But Demon Rum interfered, for which he repeatedly begs my forgiveness. His

backhanded script, all in one paragraph, fills the page of yellow foolscap. Over Christmas, he tells me, he requested a dispensation from his vows as a monk. He will continue as a priest, of course, but not within his monastic community—a decision he had wanted to share with Martha and then with me. It has been building ever since he arrived here in DC a year and a half ago—why he was assigned to graduate study in the first place. Why he's sought the help of Dr. Brunner. Living here at CU was to be a kind of "sabbatical" from the monastery, a leave of absence allowing him to settle once and for all his problems with his abbot and the order itself.

He'd wanted to be a priest ever since he was a kid. He vaguely knew, as every Catholic does, that there are many ways to be a priest, many different orders along with the basic "secular," or diocesan, priest. But all the priests in his young life were monks, so when he decided to be a priest, he headed for the monastery. It was another reason for hating "Martha's nuns": They never acquainted him with other ways to be a priest. So in his youthful mind, being a priest and being a monk were bundled together.

Over his years in the monastery, he's been disruptive, he writes, a "young Turk"—not enough to be dismissed from the order, but also never quite fitting in. Alternately show-off bad-boy, dark humorist, anti-establishment agitator—he's been "a regular jackass," he writes. Only now—with the distance CU provides and the help of Dr. Brunner—is he able to see the anger and frustration fueling this behavior. "The monastery has been an enormous detour in my priestly life. I've been the square peg always fighting to fit into the round hole."

My piece I sent him on "Dark Decembers" arrived just before Christmas, as he was leaving DC, he tells me. "It says exactly what I've finally come to see: No monastery can take responsibility for my faith. For years I've bitched about 'them.' It doesn't help that the abbot himself is a neurotic jackass. Yet I am the one handing over the decisions of my life. I was the petulant adolescent, griping about what I was told to do, but not having the guts to take charge of my own life. But no more." Now he is separating what has been "bundled" together in his life. He needs to concentrate on what is, and always has been, dearest to his heart—being a priest.

The yellow page, ragged at the top, appears to have been roughly ripped from its tablet. I stare at his pointy letters on the quivering paper I'm holding and am stunned—so shocked I don't exactly know how I feel. For some time I've been aware that we feel very differently about our religious families. And I've also known how he cherishes his calling as a priest. But to leave his order to be a secular priest, just an ordinary diocesan priest, seems...what? Too drastic? Misplaced? Disappointing? Sad? No doubt I'm reacting to how I would feel were I forced to give up what I've imagined his monastic life to be—a remote life of solitude and silence, physical labor and erudition, all wrapped in an aura of otherworldly contemplation. A fantasy I've shared with Maddy for years. Yet more than once Dan's called this image of the monastery "romantic."

Still, how can he do this? Quit in the middle of the game? Scads of stuff in the Church need to change. Everybody knows that, including the pope—it's his reason for calling the Vatican council. Lots of our customs are out of date, some even crazy-making. But to leave your order, your family *now*? What about that "reforming, updating, reimagining" we've all been talking about? Or the "revolution" that so inspires you? The council's just getting going, Dan! Everything's up for grabs. Stupid customs will change. Orders will change—even monastic orders. Even yours! So why now, Dan? Why? Why abandon the rest of us?

As I stuff the yellow page into my pocket, I can taste a fiery rage rising. I grab cape and shawl, and head out to the library. Walking against the cold wind like this, decisive steps leading in a clear direction, may quiet the upheaval in me. But it only gets nastier and meaner. How can he go from a higher calling to lower? Monk to parish priest? Like a doctor turning chiropractor, or a judge becoming a cop, or a professor peddling encyclopedias door to door. How can he?

I hate such nasty thoughts churning inside me. Even more, the snobbery behind them. Yet the strenuous walk hasn't rid me of the bitterness I feel even when I reach the library and check out some volumes from the reserve shelf. In a quiet corner of the main reading room, I carefully fold my cape and shawl, arranging them and the huge volumes resting on them in an arc on the table out in front of me. It's as if I need some neatly arranged bulwark to fend off a threatening tide as I attempt to submerge myself in one of the more challenging of our graduate reading assignments.

Then it hits me: My violent reaction is more about me than it is about Dan. The truth emerges through shifting layers of memory, and when the young girl from the reserve counter politely asks, "Are you finished with the books, Sister? Your reserve time is up, others are waiting," I realize I've been sitting here in reverie for over an hour, staring at the unopened books and blank yellow pad, pen and pencil untouched. I've been reliving a dark day in December 1947—the most momentous of my short convent life. It was the start of Christmas vacation in that first, miserable year of teaching at St. Pat's when I'd come to the motherhouse with the express purpose of consulting with Mother Alicia, who had been my novice mistress. I'd found her out in the laundry yard, where a group of novices had just completed their duties and gone back inside. I hadn't spoken to her since the previous May, my Profession Day. She knew me better than anyone in the order, having been responsible for my "formation" during the twenty-two months of novitiate. So I had blurted it out. Instead of renewing my vows in the spring, I told her I wanted to transfer to a cloistered order. How would I go about such a move?

It had been an awful decision, reluctantly and painfully made—and terrible to have to tell her. She's been my guide and confidant from my first day in the convent. Her title "Mother" was exactly right, and I wept to tell her all this. She must have heard from St. Pat's what a lousy teacher I'd turned out to be. Yet that was nothing like my failure at "the spiritual life." I'd never really gotten the hang of it, even in the novitiate, which she well knew, but whatever I did learn about spirituality had washed right out of me during this horrible attempt to be a teacher.

As she guided me over to a bench by the clotheslines, I started pouring out some of the stuff I'd discovered in my research into what canon law says about a person in my situation.

"Betty dear," she interrupted, planting her hand firmly on my lap and stopping the words spilling out of me. "The monastery is not for you." She pulled a huge linen handkerchief from her pocket and wiped the mess my face had become. A mother, indeed. And then told me ever so gently that I'd never last in a cloistered convent. "You ask too many questions, my dear. Your mind's too busy for a monastery. No amount of silence or manual work or beautiful Gregorian chant will change that. Besides, my dear, your mind is a gift from God and should be used—for Him and for others—not avoided."

To my amazement, she then put her arm around me, gently squeezing, and with her sweet choir-mistress voice began a whispery imitation of Bing Crosby: *"You've got to ac-cent-tchu-ate the positive, e-lim-in-nate the negative...."* Those sharp blue eyes, which I'd found a bit cold and distant as a novice, were warm and loving. I knew then that she understood me more than my own mother ever had. "And Sister, dear—as you live the life, you can discover how to train your mind so that it becomes a tool for you."

Those long-ago feelings of failing utterly, of wishing to

give up and start again, of dreaming for the unattainable, have been safely buried for years. Maybe I'm more like Dan than I've recognized. By the time I was twenty-two and ready for final vows, I had discovered I could teach, and I loved it, thanks largely to the help of friends like Maddy and Gaby and mentors like Augusta and Carla. I understood those dreams of my nineteen-year-old self for what they were, the romance of an early love.

Yet even now, these many years later, knowing Mother Alicia was correct in her assessment of me doesn't keep that old romance from pulling at my heart. It was, I see now, of a piece with my early decision in that home economics lab with Sister Marie Gabrielle and her clay and poems.

When the librarian interrupts my reveries, I understand immediately: I've been transferring onto Dan this same romance, even though he's given me no cause to think he ever shared my sentiments. Could my accusing him of choosing second best be a loathing of the "lower" path I resigned myself to years ago? Are my current energies for reform—my heightened "political consciousness" of the past few years— so many attempts to displace earlier hankerings for the monastery? To defend how long ago I settled for what I must still judge to be "second best"?

I now realize my true feelings of admiration and support for my friend Dan and his big choice. He's in a tough war, and he's fighting it. He's not surrendering, not being taken prisoner. He's probably still an "unhappy man" with a lot of buried demons. But he is not a defeated man as—sad to say—I fear Uncle Pat was.

Spring Term, 1963
"Have a moment, Sister?" Brother Basil lingers after Dan dashes off for late afternoon Mass over at the student center. The three of us have been meeting on Wednesday afternoons

in a remote office in ancient Cantwell Hall that's serving as Dan's current parking place. "First, though, I must ask you something." He speaks with a hesitancy, something I've never noticed in him before. "The other day, when you were lecturing us, Dan and me, about teaching young women. I began to wonder...."

For some weeks now, we've been sitting around what's probably an old kitchen table, from the look of its worn oilcloth covering. Dan is always very casual, in his outside-the-classroom, no-longer-a-monk attire. And Basil, like his mood, is unchanged: black clerical suit plus Roman collar, only slightly loosened in this sweltering heat. A solitary fan, perched at the head of the table, moves back and forth in an arc, fluttering my veil while sending a hot breeze to the three of us clustered at the far end.

These Wednesday get-togethers started after Easter break. We had each received similar assignments for the coming summer—teaching Introduction to Phil at one of the start-up Sister Formation programs. Brother Basil, close by in Virginia, Dan back in Michigan, while I'm going to Marie du Lac, a college in Baton Rouge, Louisiana. Proof that this upstart movement for nuns is catching on.

It will be my first crack at teaching philosophy, while both Dan and Basil have taught this beginning course before. But the "first" that scares me most is teaching Negro students, of any age, men or women. And these guys are no help—neither has ever taught Negroes either. And women frighten them both. Neither has ever taught women, let alone nuns, which is why they look to me as some kind of expert. "Women think differently," Dan tells me, which usually is bait for a fierce argument.

Today, though, I resist the bait. "Stop! Please!" The vehemence in my voice surprises even me. Yet I've got to change the subject. "Whether we're women or men, we hear the phrase 'Christian philosophy' for what we're studying and teaching. Sounds like religion! You don't think that way, either of you. I know. So how do you deal with it? Especially when you're introducing young people to it? Young *nuns!*"

Dan's ignited, says that kind of talk "prostitutes Lady Philosophy"—often from folks who speak about philosophy as being in the service of our Christian faith. "It's just the opposite, dammit! Philosophy *challenges* faith, simple-minded faith, and thereby allows faith to be richer. I try to be clear from the outset: Philosophy is a secular subject. That's how I deal with it."

Basil, being mostly silent till now, sits solid and steady, with beads of sweat accumulating on bald spots above his forehead: "I just stress that 'Christian' is an adjective—plural, descriptive, historical. The way we speak of Islamic or Jewish philosophers." With that he removes his plastic collar and drops it on the table, a finishing touch to his statement, it seems.

Dan checks his watch, seeing, I presume, how long he has before evening Mass. He then moves quickly to the corner of his office, to a fairly well-disguised beer cooler. "Look, if we solve everything today, we won't have any good reason to meet again—which would be too bad."

My question's made him uncomfortable, I can tell, yet he is all pleasantness, as he hands me a Coke and sits down with Basil to open their Budweisers.

"I hope this isn't too personal." With Dan gone, Basil sits fiddling with his collar in front of him on the table, seeming more than a little flustered. Basil from Brooklyn, or BB as we call him, is a large, placid-faced man with an even disposition and enormous quiet energy, the wit of our department. His awkwardness now surprises me. I move the fan away from our faces and signal him to go on. "That 'Christian philosophy' business—so glad you brought it up, though you got really red in the face, Sister. Made me wonder: Is this personal for you, like it is for me? Maybe? Am I even remotely on target?"

My face flushes even more, as I nod for him to go on. "When I first joined the brothers—way back in 1950—I very quickly came to dread any talk of 'the spiritual life' or those exhortations about becoming 'more spiritual, shunning the things of this world.'" He looks up, suddenly embarrassed—maybe about to cry?—while I'm suppressing a smile. He's *younger* than I am! That receding hairline's fooled me. He's not my wise older friend!

"It was crazy-making," he continues—a confession that sounds ripped from his heart. "At least for me. I'd entered the order because I loved science, wanted to teach it. I wanted to be a brother so I could help young kids explore our wonderful natural world, especially poor kids who may never get to know much beyond those slums. I wasn't trying to shun this world. Yet all those exhortations—about the supernatural and becoming more spiritual—made me feel like a failure, right from the start. I even thought about leaving."

"But you didn't."

He mutters something, shaking his head.

"Because you still wanted to teach those kids?"

"Yeah. So I guess you know what I'm talking about? Did you get this same kind of shit—excuse my language—dumped on you?"

I want to hug him, yell at him that yes, yes, I do know what you're talking about! But where to begin.? Besides, clearly he's not finished, so I nod for him to go on.

"Then last summer, when I got this job to teach the intro class, I was so excited. I can help these kids. Keep them from going through what I did! I felt downright missionary, Sister. I'll show them that there's more than one way to look at all this religious stuff! Philosophy can help you, show you different ways, different mindsets, different ways of thinking about everything, including your religious lives."

I'd never seen Basil so worked up about anything. His cool, measured approach to most topics is nowhere in sight. Obviously, he was on a mission last summer.

"These kids shouldn't have to go through what I had to," he concludes, lowering his tone as he rummages through his briefcase on the floor beside him, finally extracting two sheets of typing paper. He places them carefully side by side, facing me. "So that's why I made these for them." He looks at his drawings with a gentle smile as he might when gazing at a newborn. "I thought maybe you could use these, when you're teaching those young sisters. They were a huge help for me last summer, Sister, helped me get my message across to those kids."

They're what he calls his "cartoons"—like the nun on the donkey he gave me last year. Each pictures a monk-like figure, one labeled AUGUSTINE, one AQUINAS. Augustine is gaunt and ascetic, hovers over a dark, dismal world with his eyes heavenward and his hands clasped in prayer: "My heart is restless until it rests in thee, O Lord." The other monk, rotund and smiling, is identified as AQUINAS. He's sitting cross-legged in a patch of sunny garden, gazing lovingly at the clod of fresh soil in his hands with its tiny sprouts of new grass, and prays: "I adore thee, O God, hidden within these works of your creation."

"He saved me, Sister, Aquinas did. He saved me from all that crap thrown at me in my novitiate." His finger rests on the tubby, smiling monk, but his own words sound more like tears. "I met him in my first philosophy class right after that awful novitiate year. It was titled Cosmology, I think. But in that class I came to see where all that crap dumped on me in the novitiate—where it all came from. And, most of all, I also found an alternative." His face fairly sparkles with joy as he reminds me what we have both come to know so well from our study of philosophy's history. "There have always been very different ways of thinking—different philosophies—through which believers have expressed their Christian faith."

"Or Jewish or Muslim faith," I add. Exactly what Gilson's little red book showed me!

"Right. They're all using some philosophy, some intellectual tradition to express their faith. Some like Augustine followed Plato, clearly valuing spirit above matter. Their ideal was to become 'more spiritual.' Yet others followed Aristotle, his pupil, and focused on the natural world. And my man, Aquinas."

"My man, too!" I chime in, remembering Gilson again—and Augusta who gave it to me. "Each called a doctor, or teacher, of the Church," I add.

"Indeed. But they didn't *teach* the same way! Aquinas tells us that nature, the natural, all the world around me, is *good*! Spirit and matter intermingle in God's creation! To enjoy the world, to study it, is not to turn away from 'the spiritual' or from God. You can worship God in those tiny blades of grass! That was Aquinas!" His voice drops. "Sorry, Sister, didn't mean to shout. But for me that class was an honest-to-God epiphany, changed my life—meaning how I think about my life."

The peace that seems to engulf him lights up his face, and he murmurs, "That's what I wanted for those kids last summer." Hence the sketches. "Augustine longs to escape his earthly home and all things material. A real Platonist! But not Aquinas! He delights in the world around him, as Aristotle does. Same religion, different philosophies."

"'Ideas make a difference,'" I say, offering him Augusta's words.

"Indeed. So maybe 'Christian Philosophy,' for what we do, is not too far off?"

"Or 'faith seeking understanding,'" I add.

"So, what about you, Sister? You seem to be nodding when I spilled my guts."

"As a novice I wasn't nearly as aware as you were of wanting to teach kids about the beauty of our world. In fact, I loved the novitiate, though I never really understood all the talk about becoming spiritual either. I even wondered if I should switch to a cloistered order so I could learn how to become *really* spiritual. I didn't feel your kind of angst until I moved out of the cloister-like surroundings of the novitiate and started teaching. That's when everything fell apart for me."

And then it all spills out. Somehow I know Basil will understand my tale—that horrid first year at St. Pat's with that superior who was forever urging me to become "more spiritual," to "offer up" the distasteful "chore" of teaching, and that our "spiritual life" was what being a nun was all about. All problems could be solved by bringing them to the chapel, to the Blessed Sacrament. "Yet that chapel was the worst part of my day," I tell him. "For a half hour every afternoon just before dinner, I'd sit silently, trying to meditate, only to have all the disasters from my classroom day play and replay in my mind. Often, my appetite vanished. It was awful. Though I did get skinny!"

"Wow, you had it much worse than I did—and with seventy kids in the classroom."

"Seventy-two!" Even this long after, it still pulls at my insides to say that. "So why did we stay, Brother, if it was so crazy-making?"

"Because we knew, somehow, that wasn't the whole of it."

"Yeah, I guess," I say, as my memory lights up with Augusta in her office, her mind filled with wonderful thoughts; Sister Marie Gabrielle reciting her beloved poets; Carla leaning into that potter's wheel; dear old Rosie putting her seedlings to bed; or way back, old Auntie Brendan putting my baby hands on those lavender stems in the motherhouse garden, making me rub and then smell them to see that beauty was as much in those plain green stems as in the tiny little purple flowers. My sisters, all of them. None of them believing "the natural" was all that bad. "We could sense that wasn't how other nuns were living, people all around us, people we loved."

In the silence enveloping us, I hope he's feeling as I do—the wonder and warmth, the comfort of sharing these gems of community life.

"I'm glad I had the guts to ask you, Sister," he says, handing over his cartoons to me, looking more relaxed than I've ever seen him. "And I'm glad these were a help."

In a few short weeks, I must face the drama of teaching. So for now I feel the panic rising in me—the racing heart and weak knees—the *fright* of teaching. Every radical change, every time I've been challenged with a harder assignment, that same panic has descended on me, from that move right after St. Pat's out into the county to a sixth grade, then a year later when I had to move up to an eighth grade, then back to the motherhouse with an assignment of algebra and geometry at St. Mary's Academy. Possibly the scariest was my assignment to teach twelfth-grade religion a few years back—a course with a required text titled *16 Steps to the Catholic Church—Reason's Path to Faith*. Then, by the time trigonometry was added to my plate a couple of years later, I had learned to inoculate myself against this "August angst" before it engulfed me. It's what I must do now.

These students I'm soon to meet are like beginning potters learning how to sharpen their tools so they can carefully craft their own pots, their new art. I need to focus: What is the art I hope they will create when I introduce them to

Lady Philosophy? I know my answer, or at least what it is *not*: It is not their ability to spout names and dates and quotations from different thinkers. There are encyclopedias for that. Nor do I expect them to have developed "their own philosophy" after six short weeks. That's a joke. But neither do I want to have them spouting anyone else's predigested thoughts, catechism-like. Not even my personally preferred insight about the faith/reason conundrum I learned from Aquinas. So what, then, do I want for them?

First and foremost, I hope to start building with them a habit of critical thinking about the sort of claims typical of those we call "philosophers." This means giving my students a taste of how certain issues have been argued by a number of different thinkers—just enough to let them experience that "no one way fits all." I will choose selections for them from a small group of authors as consequential as they are different—Plato, Kant, and Marx. Or Descartes, Hume, and Sartre, or Hegel, Nietzsche, and Dewey. I want to help make them critical thinkers: What does so and so *mean* by this word or concept?

But how to do it? How do I bring them to understand that a concept in one philosopher's universe cannot be extracted and inserted into another's universe, any more than a chunk of Carla's MOTHER can be cut out and plugged into that MADONNA AND CHILD in our chapel? That "idea" in Plato doesn't function in his philosophy as it does in Kant's universe, let alone Marx's. Nor does the concept of "God" function the same in any of these philosophers.

My tools must be those of a close, careful reading and analysis of a philosopher in his own words, followed by the commentaries of accepted scholars on this philosopher. Only then should their grasp of a philosopher's thought be tested by writing out their understanding and sharing this with other students and with me. Correcting, rewriting, rereading, and reanalyzing must follow—like Carla's reworking the clay—thus they will sharpen their tools, and bit by bit create their own art. Not as tangible as a pot or statue, but every bit as unique. For each young sister her own creation, her *new art.*

We plow ahead, Dan, Basil, and me, with questions about which thinkers to introduce and which problems to choose getting us more tangled. Even Basil has a hard time keeping track of where we are going as I defer more and more to the two of them and their experiences from last summer. Dan wants to structure his class around three big questions: Who are we? Where did we come from? What is morality? Basil would focus on a single question—What is philosophy?— while exploring with his students several widely divergent answers. I am stimulated by one, then the other, easily imagining myself a student in either man's classroom, eating up every challenge they give me.

"Philosophy is not religion, or any blinkety-blank hand-maid," Dan insists, pounding the table. Again I agree with him, as does Basil, completely, since early on when I was rescued from the scholastic approach by Sister Augusta's little red book by Gilson. But then he blurts out, "And calling something 'Christian Philosophy' is a contradiction in terms!" He's beginning to sound like some missionizing preacher.

"That's oversimplifying a bit, don't you think?" I venture.

"Help us out, Sister," Dan says in one of our final meetings before I leave for Louisiana. "We need your experience here about teaching girls. All those years in the trenches. You've gotta know some secrets. C'mon, a few pointers, please."

His "women think differently" notion is one I've long had to battle, both in college and now graduate studies.

"Who in the hell has more authority for young Catholic

girls than a nun, especially a tall nun?" he insists.

"You do!" I spit out. "Look, you ask, 'How do women think?' I can't answer that. We're all different. But these particular students of yours, because they are women who happen to be nuns, fresh from a novitiate, they might hear anything you say as Church doctrine, as absolute, as dogma. Because of who you are—and how you look!"

My own voice has been rising, and I fear I've already gone on too long with what my students at St. Mary's used to call my "Sister says" tone, yet I haven't even gotten to my main point: that the most important thing we have to give these young women next summer is a taste for critical thinking—their own critical thinking. Whatever they possessed of such ability before joining the order could easily have washed out of them.

Now, though, my face is burning—I've turned into the beet I become when I'm worked up. It happens in seminar when my turn comes to report, and I hate it. It's the only time I really miss makeup. But no makeup could help me in this dreadful heat—which I'm feeling now. And Dan, in his loose-fitting cotton shirt that's now sticking to his torso, front and back, is clearly finished for the day and ready to share the contents of his cooler before heading out for the evening Mass he's scheduled at the student center. "It's how *you* think, that's what should worry you. Both of you. Because of how you look and sound, students hear what you say as gospel truth."

My vehemence silences them and surprises me. "Look," I continue, trying to calm my tone, "I'm just trying to remind you that your students are not only the 'second sex'—they're doubly so, being Church women. Girls, Catholic girls, are brought up to be deferential to priests. Young nuns especially, their novitiate experience has intensified this."

When our talk goes well past the dinner hour of our respective refectories, Basil asks if I believe "God will provide" my nourishment that night.

"Of course," I answer, picturing my stash of "study aids."

"God will provide some peanut butter and crackers, lots of peanuts, in their shells, of course. Straight from God, the peanut-maker. Plus some hot chocolate, a little less directly perhaps, but still, I believe, from God. Maybe some dried fruit, possibly even a candy bar or two. God works in mysterious ways, my friend."

⚹

June 3, 1963

Basil's Augustine and Aquinas come with me to Louisiana, along with his Donkey and Train. I tack them up as soon as Sister Jeanne leaves, even before I unpack, right above the phone. "For emergencies only," Sister Jeanne makes clear, when she sees me eyeing the phone. Both are startlingly out of place in a nun's room—cartoons and phone.

Sister Jeanne d'Arc is my boss for this summer job. As soon as the airport taxi delivered me earlier this evening, this imposing, white-clad nun greeted me. "Welcome to Marie du Lac," she said formally, then in silence led me up the stairs of the grand old mansion, across a wide porch, and through its majestic white columns. An imposing presence, this tall, erect woman. Though without the broad-winged headdress, she's probably no taller than I am.

As she moved ahead of me, deliberately, silently, with those voluminous white skirts, she reminded me of an enormous moving statue. Once inside, however, I recognize this laconic woman as quite elderly—though unmistakably in charge. For the next six weeks of summer session, she tells me, I will stay in these guest quarters "normally reserved for the bishop."

Marie du Lac is short for Hôpital de la Charité Sainte Marie du Lac. Until very recently, it was known to me only as the hospital "down South," where sisters from my own order suffering from nervous breakdowns are sent. But then I learned this spacious plantation outside Baton Rouge also houses a new Sister Formation college, where Mother Augusta volunteered me to teach Introduction to Philosophy to their young nuns.

I've never known any sisters from this French-rooted order, having seen them only from afar, and thought of them as foreign, different. Mimi told me about them when I was very young—what she'd picked up from her time in France as a young Irish governess before emigrating to America and marrying Grandpa. They were called "God's Geese" or sometimes just the "Big Bonnets" from the way their huge white bonnets flapped like wings as they spread out across Paris each day, gathering up the hungry and homeless to bring to their convent. No sister ate or slept until everyone had eaten, Mimi said. I was impressed.

God's Geese are still venerated for their dedication to the poor and disenfranchised, especially for their work in the American South with Negroes. But because it is not a teaching order, they must recruit faculty from other orders—priests, brothers, and now nuns—to staff this new college. After explaining the rituals of shutters and fans, Sister Jeanne d'Arc hands me a sketch of this huge estate. The dreaded "insane asylum," as we called it, is far removed from my quarters and from the new college. "This path leads directly to the campus—and to our new chapel," she says, indicating the gravel driveway directly beneath my porch. "This other way through the woods is much longer." Her finger trembles slightly as she points out a wiggly path into an area across the meadow marked simply *les bois*. As she relates the story of this huge estate, she conveys a pride of ownership unusual in nuns of my experience. Her pride, though, does not extend to this new enterprise of a sisters' college, I soon figure out. Nor does Sister Jeanne d'Arc share other "new ideas" about the Church circulating among the young nuns, which becomes clear almost immediately. A startling contrast in this post–Vatican II world. Only a dutiful obedience motivates her to embrace this newfangled "college."

I'm fascinated by her and by her story, though distracted by how little she resembles her patron saint—that youthful Joan of Arc, astride her horse, of either Mimi's statue or Ingrid Bergman's film. More like those hungry men Mimi fed during the Depression, with their utterly weary faces and raw voices. Her own face is leathery and gray, with stubby hairs scattered along her chin. Under her habit, she's probably as skeletal as the hungry men of the Depression; were it not for that white habit and bonnet, I could never imagine her a nurse.

"Now, Sister, about your class—we must talk." I can tell she means now, even though meetings after Grand Silence are not allowed in any order I know of, except in emergencies. So although I'm dying for sleep after this long first day, I follow Sister Jeanne down the long path to her office, where I discover the emergency.

"This will never do, Sister," she says, lifting a page from the slim file folder on her otherwise empty desk. I recognize a list of the books I'd mailed the sister librarian a couple weeks ago—the result of long efforts by Dan and Basil and me—a minimum requirement for students being introduced to philosophy. "Some changes must be made, Sister." I recognize the sheet she now fingers as the *horarium*. "You are expecting far too much; there's no time for your extras."

Extras! My blood boils at hearing this. There's no time for what I came down here to teach. That *philo-sophia*—love of wisdom—most folks see as vital for anyone serious about being educated. Yet she's got a point; from the 5:15 rising bell until lights out at 9:45, minute by minute, convent duties cram each sister's day. So I'm not surprised to see my class—called simply College Instruction—wedged into a forty-five-minute slot in the late afternoon, with no more than a couple of pauses throughout the day. Hardly time for reading anything, let alone the "extras" on my reserve list.

"We've never had a problem like this before, Sister. Never," she says, rubbing her large hands together, as if they hurt. "Before all this business about college credits and becoming modern nuns. There's just no room for what your reforming friends, or you, want."

Must I defend the entire Sister Formation Movement!? In the last five or six years it's become a reality within most orders, or at least all the orders I've met at CU. There are some naysayers, of course, some even in our own order, but not among my friends or anyone I really respect.

When she stands to leave, Sister Jeanne hands me the file folder from her desk. "You can use this to plan something more suitable. Sister Librarian has enough copies for your students." An order, her tone tells me, or as we say, an "obedience." Discussion closed. I feel punched in the stomach.

I walk back up the long path to my fancy room in the dark night, lit only by a diminishing moon. Feeling her folder in my hand, I fret about those young sisters I have yet to meet. In being deprived of access to the library, and the time to read any "extras"—or to read, period!—won't the sisters just reinforce the old prejudice that Negro minds aren't as sharp as white minds? But then Sister Jeanne probably hasn't had such an awakening, either. Have those strange old hands ever held a library book, let alone a philosophy book? Or any book—other than prayer books? Has she ever wondered about other versions of some "truth" she was taught? Perhaps something with troublesome implications? Why she sees my course as an impractical burden for her flock? Or is it, as she said, that "philosophy's not really a woman's subject."

"Nor is this philosophy!" I want to scream back, when

finally I open the folder she gave me. The fans in my fancy room do nothing to cool the heat rising in me as I realize what it is: a syllabus from the seminary priest who was to have taught my class, that very same Scholastic Philosophy Dan and Basil and I so deplore. Judging from its well-thumbed pages, I guess he has repeated the course many times to classes of young seminarians, or to previous classes of these young bonnets. It's an outline of scholastic formulations—clearly much too much to be understood in six short weeks, even if the goal were merely to memorize other peoples' conclusions! So forget Plato. Forget Aristotle—not to speak of Marx or Sartre! Forget arguments, historical context, or critical thinking. Just memorize. It's the catechism all over again!

When I open the elegant shutters, seeking some peace from the still night air, a shaft of moonlight hits the shiny black phone—and my mind explodes. Providential! After writing down his summer schedule for me, good old Basil added his office phone. He'd be there every night, he said, night owl that he was and encouraged me to let him know how things were going. And thus was hatched my revised lesson plan for the summer.

After his unmistakably Bronx "Hiya, Sister," I pour out my tale, my outrage at being given that "scholastic" outline, only to hear his favorite expression of outrage, "Holy Moly!" Then, "Wait, Sister, I'll call you right back." He didn't want me to run up a huge phone tab on top of everything else...and called right back. "No, Sister, no! You can't let this happen. If your Sister Boss wants to keep her young ones down on the farm, doesn't mean you have to go along."

His anger is a comfort, even more his eagerness to help. "I'd hand out that priest's outline—get a nice clean copy for each of them. Show your respect—and then just forget it.

They'll catch on as the weeks go by that you're not too interested in it. But at least they have it. I'd be careful not to criticize it; just neglect it. And start with *your* stories, your cartoons."

"You mean yours! I already have your Augustine and Aquinas one at the ready. Their faith/reason story is a good way to start, don't you think?"

"I do. It's a great start. I'll send you more. Maybe first of all a timeline of great philosophers that I made last summer, right up there above the blackboard, a scroll around the room. It's got a lot of big names on it, including some I've got cartoons for I can send you: Plato and Aristotle you already have, but on up to Descartes, Hume, Kant then Hegel, even Marx."

We joke about how this would look in a classroom with a crucifix and pictures of a number of saints on the wall already. Marx next to St. Joseph—or Jesus!

His tone grows serious. "You've got to compromise, Sister. Hard for us perfectionists. 'Despise not the good for the sake of the best,' remember? There's plenty of good stuff, maybe not the best, but good enough." I glance up at his donkey and speeding train. "Don't waste your energy on that stupid syllabus or get drawn into defending it. You've got to get creative. Tell stories. Improvise. You're the actress, remember?" he says, reminding me of how much fun I found the theater games my friend Sister Stella, from the drama department, had taught some of us. "Take stuff from TV, or the newspaper, help them imagine how—"

"You don't understand!" I interrupt. "All that's verboten here! No TV, radio, newspapers—nothing secular. For *everyone*, including faculty. Besides, there's no time—"

"Okay, okay...I understand. Look, Sister, you've got to put your pride in your pocket."

With that, he explodes, laughing to recall the huge pockets nuns have, "the better to stuff your pride in. But, seriously, the main thing is that your students get some hint of how radically different minds have explored the big questions of life. The Catholic faith doesn't dictate one philosophy over another—no matter how many 'Catholic authorities' say just that."

And so together, Basil and I chose a handful of thinkers suitable for his kind of classroom entertainment. Without books. My "lesson plans" for the summer.

The humidity wakes me well before the alarm. It's sticky and unrelenting, worse than DC, worse even than St. Louis. I must get outside. With more than an hour before Mass, I've got plenty of time, enough to take the long way around to the chapel, watch the Louisiana sunrise, explore a bit of this world I was dropped into last night.

Only minutes into the woods, I stop to loosen my cincture and headdress, letting air circulate a bit beneath my heavy habit. The overgrown path follows a barely flowing marshy stream, strewn about with decaying leaves. It's like some sacred space, a darkened, musty cathedral, long empty of its celebrants. Old oaks arch high above me, with Spanish moss hanging like lace over fern and azaleas, and tiny new lives sprouting out of moist soil. Finally a small hand-lettered sign, *CIMETIÈRE,* points me away from the stream onto a narrower, yet well-worn path. I trudge along until a twist in the path shows daylight in the distance. It lights up a white statue facing away from me with rows of small white stones on either side, and I realize I've been approaching the graveyard from its far side. Moving closer, I recognize the familiar statue of the Sacred Heart of Jesus, whose shoulders and head are speckled with bird droppings. He's gazing out at the college chapel, facing a bright early morning light.

As I walk alongside the tiny tombstones, I stoop to decipher names and dates on the weathered white stones. All nuns, all patients, yet no names from our order, I am relieved to see. Just God's Geese—from Tours and Compiegne, Beauvais and Amiens. I imagine the flock assembling from all over France, then winging its way to this New France.

Many of the death dates are from the summer of 1853—the summer Sister Jeanne told me about last night, when yellow fever peaked in New Orleans and one out of five inhabitants died. That's when a wealthy Frenchman opened his Baton Rouge estate, this gorgeous Marie du Lac, to the fever victims and the nuns tending them, and ended up deeding the whole place to the sisters.

When I do the math of the dates, I'm shocked to see how very young most of the sisters were—a few even in their teens, probably only novices, many in their twenties. It hurts to imagine all these eager young nuns, in a land still so foreign to them, surrounded by voices crying for them in a language they can't understand, living in and breathing in and finally succumbing to that awful plague.

I'm still subtracting dates when the chapel bell pulls me away. Mass in five minutes—I've spent almost an hour with the dead and must now take myself to the living, the thirty-two young women across the way, kneeling in that brand-spanking-new chapel. Are they anticipating—or dreading—our class tomorrow? What do they know of "philosophy"? What have they been told about the course, about me, this white nun from a different order? Suddenly, anxieties safely tucked away for weeks rise in me, and I realize how little I know of Negro life and culture—even of the ongoing racial strife in this part of our county. Except for the likes of Mr. Pomlee Connor, my own contact is almost entirely through books and newspapers. Will these young women even be open to learning about Western philosophy—which, of course, means European philosophy? Will they care?

_\\|/_

A surprisingly modern chapel stops me short. Early sun streams through an enormous stained-glass wall behind the altar, reaching up to the rafters and sprinkling bright colors in geometric shapes across the rows of white bonnets up front. They kneel upright, all seemingly the same shape, these students I've yet to meet, all thirty-two of them, backs rigid, not a slump nor slouch in sight. Like clones, I think, or geese in formation.

Yet it's not what I see that shocks me—it's what I hear. The sounds are from my past, from another time, way back, maybe my first grade, or First Communion? Or even earlier, with Mimi at Mass? The sweet, high-pitched voices are pleading, desperately:

"I need thee precious Jesus, I need a friend like thee,
A friend to soothe and sympathize,
*   a friend to care for me.*
I neeeed thee precious Jeeessusss,
*   I need a friend like thee...."*

Dim memories of that long ago time with Mimi and Grandpa have always been sweet, but now these words in that melody feel like an affront. So sentimental and simplistic, so needy—as old-fashioned as that stained-glass wall is modern. I can't believe I ever sang those words with the least bit of conviction. With all the thinking and writing and discussion these last years about the Church's desperate need for reform, I realize in this instant the enormous changes I've already lived through. Especially in the feel and sound of our worship.

Sometime in the fourth or fifth grade, my classmates and I were introduced to startlingly different sounds at Mass. An energetic young Belgian priest was visiting our parish, maybe in 1935 or '36, and shared with us his enormous enthusiasm for the "liturgical movement" that had burgeoned in Europe in those prewar years. It was all quite simple he said, the Mass is a meal, a reenacting of Jesus's last supper with his apostles. We share this meal when we go to Mass each Sunday, not as onlookers at a performance but as participants, guests in a meal. Sermons and hymns are merely extras, add-ons. But we've let them distract us from the meal itself.

This message was completely new to us. Back in grade school, Mass was an obligation, a weekly chore, a burden, more or less, depending on the priest's speed in mumbling through all that Latin. We needed to get out and go to breakfast! But that's not how it should be, this young priest said. He let us say the words of the Mass along with him—much easier than singing them, we learned. He had "missals" for each of us to use—a new kind of prayer book, one neither Mother and Dad nor Mimi and Grandpa knew anything about—a smaller version of the missal he was using up on the altar. Its divided pages had Latin on one side, English on the other, of the actual words of the Mass. We were literally *saying Mass!*

Eventually everyone will be doing this, he promised—as Catholics did in an earlier time—participating in the meal, with or without fancy music. Plainchant, like the Mass itself, is universal, he told us, *the prayer* of the Church—not just the music accompanying prayer. We didn't need the complications of a fancy choir.

Nor did we need the emotional gratification of the hymns like the ones I'm hearing now. Some people who don't know any better may still like them, though I doubt it.

> *"Jesus Jesus come to me, all my longing is for thee*
> *Of all friends the best thou art...*
> *Comfort my poor soul distressed,*
>   *come and dwell within my breast.*
> *Oh, how oft I long for thee! Jesus, Jesus come to me."*

The old drivel forces itself into my ears. Catholic schlock, my friend Dan calls it. Do Sister Jeanne and her other white nuns presume Negroes can't do any better? Can't learn what I learned in grade school? This needy, childlike yearning seems pathetic to me now. Embarrassing, really, totally lacking the purity, the beauty, of the Mass's own Latin chant.

At communion time, I start slowly up the aisle, trailing the older hospital sisters ahead of me in line. As we inch ahead, I try to block the awful hymns by gazing up at the lovely kaleidoscope of colors behind the altar, splayed out over the white bonnets of the student sisters kneeling now all along the altar rail, waiting to receive the host. Such a contrast with this horrid music!

I beg forgiveness for my critical thoughts, lecturing myself to be grateful for the chance to be in this place at this time, with these particular sisters, able to play a part, however small, in righting the wrongs of our racially divided country. Just thank the good Lord for the chance to be here. This dreadful music is a small price to pay, a penance....

But then every reverie explodes. The first young sister receiving the host rises and turns. She's white! One by one, each receives the host, rises from her knees and turns. They are all white, every one of them. I'm dumbfounded. God's geese, indeed. White as their bonnets. I struggle to remember where I got the notion it would be otherwise.

The recessional with its thundering organ cuts out the childish music and I follow the silent procession making its way toward the refectory. All the while, I'm wondering: Why did I think from the start that this was a college for Negro nuns? That call from Mother Augusta and her talk about the challenges of "our troubled South"? My discussions with Christine and Sophie? Or Basil and Dan? What was I hearing?

I finish my cereal without really tasting it, but when the clink of dishes rises above the monotonous voice at the lectern, I can relax. Finally, something familiar: the wordless routine common in convent life—head of table washes the soiled dishes passed her, then hands them off, dripping with hot soapy water, to the person at her side to dry. It's the same quick, dexterous maneuver I was introduced to that first morning in my novitiate: Wash, dry, put back into the drawers at each of our places, without so much as a drop of water left on the table.

With all the dishes back in the drawers, we can process out of the refectory. I *heard* what I wanted to hear. Or needed to hear. A truth even harder to digest than the cold breakfast.

The tolling bell interrupts my after-lunch nap. The pope is dead, it's telling us—and everything stops. Not only here, but all over the Catholic world—in chapels and churches, monasteries and cathedrals—bells toll and the faithful stop whatever they are doing and pray: "Eternal rest grant unto him, O Lord." While it shocks, the news is not a surprise. The media has been reporting his decline for months.

As the tolling continues, I realize the chattering and laughing off in the distance have stopped. I imagine the novice nuns, standing still in silence, bonnets and skirts still pinned back for volleyball, praying together for our dear dead pope. When the tolling finally ends, they will not take up their game again; instead, they head for the chapel, where they will chant the psalms and litanies, spelling out in graphic detail the day of doom that awaits those on their way to judgment. *"Dies Irae, dies illa...."*

But not for me, this doom and gloom. I'll walk to the chapel, all right, but with a joyful heart. Primarily, of course, for the heavenly rewards awaiting this truly good man. But also for my own good luck, and not just because my first class has been delayed until after his funeral—by which time I should

NEW ART

have Basil's package—but also for the great gifts this pope has given me through my community of sisters.

How can anyone fear for, or be sad about, this great good man's death? He's finally leaving behind that awful cancer, not to speak of the endless challenges, disappointments, and heartaches this new council has brought him. And years ago, when, during that terrible war, with his flock on both sides, and for a long time before that, he chose to work with the "forgotten ones"—especially Jews. If he doesn't get to Heaven, nobody will. He's as close to a saint as anyone I've known of in the long history of the Church. Moreover, in these last years at the council, he was respected by everyone, even those who disagreed with him.

And that's where I'm fearful. Within the council, some of the hierarchy, while respecting this pope personally, have let it be known they'll oppose some of those "worldly" changes he had been willing to discuss. Changes that particularly affect women in the Church, married women with their concerns about family planning, and nuns struggling with centuries-old customs, like their clothing. This good pope was willing to allow discussion and debate on these topics, while others considered them inappropriate for a council. He asked his council to listen to what was going on in the world, especially to the voices of its people, and to bring itself into the modern world, to reform and renew our Church. And that's exactly what's irked some of the "fathers of the council."

This great man's goal for the council to "open wide the windows" was all about reform, and my sisters and I had high hopes because of this. So much hangs on his successor and this successor's priorities.

≈⁄⁄⁄≈

June 5, 1963

These past couple of days have been a mini retreat, waiting for the pope's funeral Mass. Basil's cartoons, notes, and clipping arrived safely, and I've had time to decorate my classroom with them. With the pope gone, I look to Mother Augusta and what she has made available to our community. It is her wide-ranging inquisitiveness—which I first witnessed in that cluttered university office—that has been helping to reform my community of sisters. Even before the good pope started talking about opening windows to the fresh air outside, Mother Augusta had been studying a broad group of contemporary, mainly European, writers who spoke of reforming the Church from within. One of her favorites is the young Belgian canon lawyer and scholar Joseph Suenens, known for his concerns and ideas for improving the situation of women in the Church. When his *The Nun in the World* appeared in English, it was no surprise that Augusta wanted us all to hear and learn from him. How she brought this off, however, was a complete surprise to everyone.

Ever since I entered the order, and for decades prior, a little book called the *Imitation of Christ* has been read over and over, cover to cover, in all of our convents, at breakfast every day of the year. That pious little book from the fifteenth century has been exhorting us each morning to shun the world, keep mind and heart on our heavenly home, and eagerly await our departure from this world—ancient wisdom has been as boring as our oatmeal and canned orange juice, and, as far as I'm concerned, tolerable only because of the hot coffee.

Augusta purchased dozens of Suenens's new *The Nun in the World* and sent one to each of our convents. It was read aloud at breakfast in the refectory at our motherhouse and in all of our parish convents—a prominence usually reserved for scripture or official decrees from the Vatican. Sadly, though, a number of older sisters were quite distressed by the book, I've been told. Feisty ninety-three-year-old Mother Mary Michael, former mother general and latter-day Irish immigrant, was heard muttering in disgust, "Communism, plain and simple...secular, Godless socialism," while making her slow wheelchair exit.

Yet for most of us, Suenens's book is a breath of fresh air, an inspiring call to action, profoundly different from anything addressed to us by any member of the clergy or hierarchy—ever. And because he's a canon lawyer, he knows the law, knows what is and is not workable, what is possible to change. I love how he simultaneously respects what sisters have accomplished in the past and is forceful about the need to rethink our lives, top to bottom. To change, radically, if necessary. Jurist that he is, Suenens knows how to do this, how to change the rules and regulations designed for us in another century, threatening now to hold us in that century. Best of all, being a cardinal, he has a vote at the council. He knows—what many Catholics are unaware of—that decisions from a council can change canon law, not merely those governing individual Catholics, nuns included, but also those governing the pope himself!

Back when I was teaching math at the academy in St. Louis, right in the middle of a lesson on the Pythagorean theorem, I recalled a passage from that morning's reading, admonishing, "Free your lives from the anachronisms which fetter you." I wondered then why we nuns were still wearing huge billowing sleeves that only got in the way of the circles I needed to draw. Suenens questioned whether certain practices were distinctive or just anachronistic. Did those practices help fulfill my mission, or were they a waste of time? He was telling us: "Take your tradition and translate it—rewrite it, update it—for the needs of today."

In having us read *The Nun in the World*, Augusta wanted us to think about how details of our life might change for the better. She scheduled an "extraordinary general chapter" for the following summer—a meeting that will gather a combination of fifty or so sisters elected at large and an equal number of already appointed superiors. Unlike the regular general chapter held every four years to elect the main leaders of our order, this chapter was to focus on the results of a questionnaire she'd distributed throughout our order, which offered each sister the chance to give her opinions and preferences about what the delegates would discuss. I'd been asked to help with reading, evaluating, and compiling data from these questionnaires. To encourage honesty, Augusta had asked that our answers be anonymous. We were requested to give our views about the types of work we were engaged in: Did we want to stay with education, in particular, parochial education? Did we want to remain in nursing, in hospital work? Continue our work within the established Catholic world, or in "the outside world"? Work within the United States or venture abroad? And what of community life? Keep to large groups living in convents, or small groups out with the faithful?

Anyone not acquainted with convent life might not realize just how dramatic a change all this was. That we were being asked to evaluate so many aspects of our community life was remarkable. The vow of obedience is at the very heart of our lives. With it, we chose to unquestioningly accept what was not chosen—rather, what is assigned—to us: our jobs, our training, our clothes, our daily schedule. Why it is said that obedience explains everything about convent life. Which could have been true...until now.

After the solemn funeral Mass, the young sisters are almost giddy as they process—in silence, of course—out of the chapel to breakfast. The ancient custom of celebrating the day of burial must be playing in their imaginations: how much grander the celebration when it's the pope! And so it is. *"Benedicamus Domino,"* Sister Jeanne intones. Her community replies with an eager, full-throated *"Deo Gratias"*—and the convent custom known as a "free day" begins.

As happens wherever we celebrate a nun's funeral, and certainly now when "our Papa has died," silence is lifted in the refectory and elsewhere, and will remain so all day. And there will be special treats all day—games and entertainments, a picnic in the evening, surprises at every meal—starting right now with marvelous breakfast sweets. I can smell them even before seeing them. The incongruity tickles me: celebrating the pope's "entry into Heaven"—by any account a place of otherworldly fulfillment—by indulging in such earthly goodies?

As I dig into a second of the sugary pastries, a large, solid-looking nun comes out from the kitchen area to ask if I'm okay. The wings of her large bonnet are pinned back, and her habit is covered with one of those long gingham wraparound aprons, with its bib pinned up over her ample bosom. "Don't rush," she tells me, "bad for digestion." Last night she saw me with some food still on my plate when Sister Jeanne started the final grace. "Take your time," she cautions me now. "Sister Jeanne eats—how do you say—like a bird? And much too fast. Says grace too soon. I worry for the young ones."

Her face flushes and she stops herself from continuing what could be construed as criticism of her superior, definitely a convent crime. Her voice and her high color remind me of many of our elderly nuns, though with a French, not Irish, touch. I can imagine her a farmer's wife in an earlier era, fretting yet relishing her responsibility to provide meals for a hungry household. When she sits down across from me, I learn that she's Sister Felice, kitchen boss. And yes, she will relax a bit—this is a free day, after all—and have a second cup of coffee with me. I congratulate her on her special pastries and delicious coffee, which are amazing for a crowd this size, I say. Clearly she's pleased, and she explains how she's been working on these special fritters for days.

"I knew the good pope couldn't last much longer," she says, crossing herself. "He was very old." Then a mischievous wink. "But not as old as Sister Jeanne." As if to redeem herself for another indiscretion, Sister Felice launches into a litany of praise for her superior. Sister Jeanne is unusually good, she says, at being the boss, knows how to run things. During the Great War in France, it was a hospital ward full of German prisoners, even after she learned that her own brother had been killed by "the Hun." Then an orphanage for lepers in Indochina, and during the second war, a dispensary in Africa, with its mix of French and German nuns. Sister Felice seems pleased to deliver such inside information and goes off to fetch me another pastry and more coffee for both of us.

I do some arithmetic. Sister Jeanne must be well over ninety, and Sister Felice herself close behind, each of them on this earth more than twice as long as I and four times longer than most of their little French sisters buried up in the woods.

June 6, 1963

I wake with the taste of yesterday's rich food lingering unpleasantly and remember it's Dad's birthday. After a holiday splurge, he could never wait to take his "constitutional" and would be off for a vigorous walk before breakfast. So with a quick prayer of thanks for his sixty-eight great years, I decide to follow his example with a circuit of the meadow before Mass, beating the real heat of the day. Yesterday was too much of a good thing, starting with those fritters, then the barbecue picnic, not to speak of the cookies and candies all day long. Yet a short way around the meadow, I turn back as the sweat is just too much. Even with the luxury of a shower before Mass in my private bath, my habit will stink for the rest of the day—maybe for the rest of the summer. I've got replacements for the underthings, but only one habit and veil. Besides, my legs are about to give up. Three years of full-time study may be developing brain muscles, but no leg muscles!

It's not simply the sweat of an out-of-shape body, though, nor all that rich food. I need to come to terms with a jumble of unpleasant feelings. I think of ancient Sister Felice at breakfast yesterday, standing over me, hand planted on my shoulder, assuring me that I am a "blessing for the young one."

"My class hasn't even begun," I protested.

She knows nothing of what I'm up to in this place nor, I suspect, of what the Sister Formation Movement is all about, and certainly not of the importance of a liberal arts education. I've a hunch she has little formal education. Yet she is so certain I will do great things for all of them here. Is it this, her flattery, that's changing my taste for this place? Or her wonderful strong coffee and sweet rolls—especially those with the dark chocolate inside? I can't float over these feelings as easily as I did during that all-night vigil Monday for the dead pope. So I sit now, Rodin-like, contemplating the small white gravestones, with the long haired Jesus—His heart all aflame—standing over me and his bevy of young, dead brides. I shudder at the childish simplicity of this devotional tradition in my Catholic culture, just as I did at the soupy sentiments in those hymns at Mass.

But now I wonder, Is this sort of romantic fantasy—or "belief"—what people need in order to live, and die, as these young women did? Is this Sister Jeanne's "real philosophy," the one she told me cannot be found in books? When did they know they were doomed? Did any of them want to escape, flee back to their families in France? Did they ever have fun in this new world, real physical fun, like that volleyball game yesterday? Or real friendships—like mine with Sister Madeleine? Or my new friend in DC, Sister Christine? Or men friends, like Dan and Basil, adult friends, not just crushes of childhood? Or any truly private moments—like mine right now—before being trapped by their fate? Could they have been secretly just a tiny bit bitter? Victims of way more than they bargained for when they joined their order? Like Peter when he discovered what his beloved Navy looked like in fiery battle? Did any of them despair when the tedium of their everyday duties suddenly pointed to a gruesome death? Especially the young French nuns. Did they ever doubt the mercy of God? Or did they remain, to the bitter end, eager to "go home," to be at last with Jesus, their one true friend, their Spouse, with a joyful, glad heart? Or were they—like Peter and his shipmates—steadfast in their duty, yet scared witless about what awaited them? With all the same doubts I would have were I in their place—about what was happening and what it all meant? Frightened, probably weeping? The young sisters most likely; Peter maybe.

After a week of failing at imitating Dad's constitutional, I change tactics with some help from my new friend, Sister Felice. I begin a different routine and keep it up all summer: out of bed at 5:15, kitchen aprons tied, one in front and one in back, a dish towel for a "veil," then out to the meadow for my morning meditation/constitutional. The first few days I had to turn back part way around, feeling about to collapse. Far from meditating on union with the universe or God, I was aware only of quivering thighs. Soon, though, new strength came into my legs and I was able to keep it up for a good half hour before showering and Mass. Thanks to Sister Felice, I didn't have to compromise my serge habit—I could sweat my way through her cotton aprons for the entire six weeks.

Gradually, the steady plop-plop on the moist path emptied my mind of its discontents—like those primitives, I thought, who induce sweat to rid themselves of evil spirits.

Without the weight and heat of my habit and veil, and the restraint of the starched coif around my face, I felt I was running naked, though I must have looked absurdly covered up to anyone who might have seen me. Moist air breezed over the top of my head and swished against my face, fluttering through my cropped hair, penetrating my floppy clothes—pleasures I hadn't been aware of missing. The memory of them came back each night before sleep, giving me an entirely new slant to all those questions about our habit.

July 15, 1963
I'm glad to be on this train meandering up through Mississippi, then Tennessee, Kentucky, Illinois, and finally back home to St. Louis and the motherhouse. I'm carrying with me the batch of sister questionnaires I've been entrusted to evaluate, but that's a task for another day. With the solitude and empty time, I hope to discover some strands of meaning beneath the events of these past six weeks. Untangle, I hope, some of the complicated ways I've been challenged to rethink so much—before plunging into the busyness of the motherhouse and the Byrne clan. All too soon it will be August 15, when I will return to DC and once again be engulfed in the cloistered world of a grad student.

Thoughtlessly, I count the train's clickety-clacks, like I did my running feet each morning. The train jerks and, instinctively, I reach over to protect the bundle next to me—the fritters Sister Felice had tucked into my satchel at the last minute. Already, I can smell their greasy deliciousness. When Sister Felice saw how I had relished them that free day after the pope's requiem, she had found a way to deliver a plate of them to my room the next night. It was already Grand Silence, so I couldn't thank her right then, but with some winks and nods, her tasty treat started arriving every few days—and I've had to loosen my cincture a notch after these last six weeks. Now, in her shaky script, she gives me an even more nourishing surprise: "God bless you, dear Sister. We will miss you."

Already, I miss her. She helped turn around this strange summer for me, starting with that volleyball game on the free day. I was sitting on the sidelines next to Sister Jeanne, thinking how different their "pinned-up" habits looked from ours. Was it the thicker wool of their habit, or its more voluminous cut, or heavier underthings? I'd never thought of how we looked during those summer games on the motherhouse courts. Yet thinking about them now, the scene is pretty funny, like those pictures of nineteenth-century ladies with their bustles playing tennis. These student sisters played with fierce determination, their big bonnets clipped back, giving them a look closer to Viking warriors than graceful geese. My readiness to play must have shown; I had never been a passive, bench-warming onlooker. Soon Felice's hand was on my shoulder in such a way that the young nuns knew to invite me in. They liked how I set up the ball, surprised, it seemed, that at my advanced age I could keep up with them. I surprised myself, jumping up to kill a ball or crouching low to return an almost lost one—showing off, I was aware, playing with abandon, glad the free day allowed our game to go on and on. That night I smiled ruefully at my vanity. I had wanted—or did I need?—to establish authority with these sisters before meeting them as students. If not with philosophy, then with volleyball and sore muscles. It worked, at least somewhat.

I lean back into the train's old seat and examine what will sustain me for the next fifteen or so hours. The sweet and savory, I see, the ordinary and the unexpected, not unlike this summer's mix of blessings: friend Basil especially, and even Sister Jeanne d'Arc, in her obstructionist kind of way. And the students themselves, of course, or at least some of them, though I must admit none came close to that *philo* of *sophia* I had hoped to awaken in them. Though in one sister there was at least an awakening of curiosity.

I was thinking of young Sister Angela. After I posted one of Basil's cartoons, the one about Augustine and Thomas, she burst out, "How is that possible!? How can they be so different?" Her cheeks were flaming, her arms thrust out—as if she were still on the volleyball court—decorum be damned. "Aren't they both Catholics? And saints?"

The cartoon from Basil pictured two monk-like figures: one, St. Augustine, gaunt and ascetic, kneeling, hands clasped in prayer, eyes heavenward, his face lit with anticipation. He hovers slightly above a dark, dismal world, at the outer edge of a heavenly radiance, crying out, "My heart is restless until it rests in thee, O Lord." The other monk, Thomas Aquinas, rotund and smiling, sits cross-legged on a patch of sunny garden, reverently staring at the clod of fresh soil with its tiny sprouts of new grass as he prays, "I adore thee, O God, hidden within these works of your creation." Augustine longs to escape his earthly home and all things material; Thomas delights in the world of God's creation. "Same religion," I say, "different philosophies." My long-ago lesson from Mother Augusta, appreciated now again: Ideas make a difference.

The train jerks violently, waking me. How long have I been out? Enough to get this stiff neck and tiny stream of drool running down my chin. And enough to not notice that my satchel has slipped from my lap, scattering the carefully guarded questionnaires every which way. I lean over to hunt in the darkness for the precious pages—the only copies representing many sisters' honest input—attracting the conductor's attention. He insists on taking over the search, addressing me repeatedly as "Sister," irritating the sleeping passengers in front of me. He's a sad, heavyset man, older than Dad, with an even worse wheeze. As he scours with his flashlight all about the floor in front of me and on either side, I pull back, put off by his disgusting body odor that envelopes me while he continues "Sistering" me so deferentially, asking if I know Sister Mary Joseph up in Chicago.

I wished I could say I know this woman from another time, and another order: I might be able to engage feelingly with the poor man and his recollections of a happier time in his life. As it is, I resist, more comfortable being the grand lady with a dutiful servant at her feet. "Princess Elizabeth," Maddy sometimes teases me, and I've always known she's on to something. It's a duplicity I've lived with for years— that beneath these robes of poverty and penance, I am far from what this weary conductor should be able to expect, from what I publicly profess, what the words of our prayers and meditations would have me feel: that I am *Sponsa Christi,* as I say each morning at Mass. Not just friend or follower but *spouse* of one who is "true God, true man," who chose to live among the wretched of this world, who was himself poor and weary (and, very possibly, quite smelly), and who urged those who would be his friend to "go sell what you have, give to the poor and come follow me." A man who is still urging me to follow him.

Yet a deep, dark secret: I've never really felt any desire to be close to Jesus, the way a "follower" is, let alone a spouse. I have wished I *could* feel this way, could want to be among those "least brethren" he gathered around him (while finding relief in the maxim "feelings don't count," which otherwise I reject). Some young sisters represented in these anonymous questionnaires—a very few, but enough that I still feel the prick to my own conscience—asked why our vow of poverty doesn't impel us to live and work amid the squalor of the truly poor, like Dorothy Day and her Catholic

Workers up in Chicago, or those Little Brothers in France that Sophie so admires? Or like Jesus himself?

"Why are so many of our sisters out in comfortable suburbs, teaching rich kids in parish schools? Why can't laypeople do this? The parents themselves, most of them aren't working; some quite possibly are trained as teachers. Shouldn't they be the ones to instruct their own kids in the Catholic faith? Or use some of their wealth to pay teachers for their kids? Leave the poor kids to us, the ones with single or working mothers." I recognize the distinctive handwriting, and sentiment, of young Sister Janet, once my student Suzzie Schmidt at St. Mary's six or so years ago. She's now part of a new breed of young nuns, not afraid to complain, especially on an anonymous questionnaire, in a way I couldn't even have imagined at her stage of convent life. "Is this what we've given up marriage and having a family of our own for?" she continues, "to be the religious nannies for lazy parents? Why aren't parents, or rich grandparents, here every Wednesday night preparing their darling sixteen-year-olds for Confirmation instead of me, after my long day working with fifty-three third-graders?"

Because, I could tell her, many of these parents and grandparents are golfing at the country club on Wednesdays, wining and dining the Right Reverend Monsignor Sweeney, their pastor. I know this from my friend Maddy, who may well share Janet's sentiments. Maddy, however, keeps such misgivings to herself, would never express such feelings, even to me, so fully and wholeheartedly, so successfully and prudently, has she embraced her assignment as principal. From our long friendship I know how thoroughly she believes it is God's will for her.

Chapter 10

1965

"To Basil!" Dan says. "Cheers!"

"Cheers!" we all echo, holding up our wineglasses.

It's almost two years since I set off for Marie du Lac, and we are gathered at Sophie's apartment. She lives alone now, having shed cat, clutter, and roommate. We're celebrating Brother Basil's successful defense of his dissertation. All that remains now between him and the PhD is the university's formal commencement, which takes place in a few days. Right now, though, he's planted Buddha-like in one of Sophie's mammoth corduroy floor pillows, a wall of books behind him, looking exactly the same as he did when I first saw him four years ago. There's the same amount of balding, the same rounded, pleasant face, the same nondescript glasses. And always in his clericals, though at times dispensing with the plastic Roman collar, as he has this beastly hot night.

Basil acknowledges the toast, rising effortlessly from the pillow (those Air Force exercises!) to make a toast of his own. Suddenly, my easy, congratulating words about envying him turn real. I wish I were leaving, over and done with all this study. With a sweep of his glass, he takes in the four of us—Kevin and Dan opposite him at either end of an old couch, a bag of chips between them, and Sophie and me standing by the kitchen counter. "Look, all of you, thanks so much for getting together like this, before I leave. These last years, it's been great being with all of you. You all mean a lot to me. I'm grateful you've come into my life. Thanks!"

An awkward silence follows, during which I notice Dan's huge sandals negotiating for space under the tiny coffee table. In the four years I've known him, Dan has changed in appearance more than any of us. A couple of years into his studies, he abandoned his monk's habit around DC in favor of Roman collar and black clerical suit. These were replaced with windbreaker and turtleneck, while closely cropped tonsure gave way to longer, wavy hair, softened with flecks of gray. Now tonight, another transformation: His beard is neatly trimmed in the manner of Freud's, and his snug jeans look like he's lived in them for weeks. The peace symbol on that leather thong around his neck? It would be a stretch for a stranger to recognize him as a priest, let alone a monk.

Sophie's different, too, I think. Taller, straighter, lighter. Partly it's the flowing caftan and the hair, now off her back and shoulders, puffed into a high new Afro. Even more, though, it's her eyes. Contacts have freed her from those heavy frames. Is there something different about her make-up, as well? Or is it simply that she is relaxed now, with her legal studies almost finished? As I watch her come back and settle into her high-back rocking chair, I think her lovelier than I've ever seen her. Before anyone else arrived this evening, we were teasing each other, and I felt closer to her than ever before. The redo of her apartment is charming: a solitary palm, the bentwood rocker, her sandalwood scented candles. "And your toenails! They're like moving decorations against the bare floor," I say. She actually blushed to have this slight extravagance noticed. When I played with her dangling earrings, she took one off and pestered me to try it on. Me! With ears covered up for almost twenty years!

"You especially, Sis-tuh." Basil puts down his wineglass and reaches out for me, enveloping my hand in both of his. "I hear you organized this spread. Thanks so much!"

With a start, I realize that this crackling "Sis-tuh" is about to leave my life. I think about the months of writing ahead of me without the assurance that Basil is just around some corner. In many ways, I've come to depend on him, more than Sophie or even Dan.

Lately, Dan has been more caught up in reading Freud than he is with his dissertation, and I am learning never to accept a cigar as just a cigar.

"You Catholics!" Sophie sputters as she rises to open the front door wider and turn up the speed on the fans.

Again Kevin speaks up: "You may be right, Sister, about keeping the old along with the new. Take your habits. I noticed the nuns at Selma had the traditional habit on."

"All the ones you *recognized* as nuns, Kevin," I shoot back, hearing this by now familiar comment. Many traditional Catholics were stunned to see nuns joining priests and ministers and rabbis during those heady days last March. "You don't know about the ones not in habit. There were several, I understand."

"But that's my point, Sister! Without habits no one knows which ones are nuns!"

Sophie looks exasperated. She's heard this before. She thinks the habit both a great idea and an anachronism, yet she's riled whenever one of the fellows becomes dogmatic about nuns' garb. "Why should a bunch of men decide what you gals wear," she declares whenever the topic comes up— as it has increasingly of late among both lay and clerical Catholics.

How differently we've all "grown up," I think, in the few short years we've been together. Kevin was the only layman starting PhD studies in 1960, and I the only nun. Because she had been the only layperson in the whole department until we arrived, Sophie immediately latched onto the two of us non-clergy. *We* became the outsiders together. When Dan and Basil showed up the following year, each gravitated toward us rather than their black-skirted male cohorts comprising the bulk of our department.

We're well into the cherries I'd brought when once again the current hot topic for debate in Catholic academic circles comes up: contraception. Tonight the topic takes a decidedly personal, ironic twist. Kevin, liberal on such issues as ecumenism, religious liberty, and liturgical reform, argues the traditional, conservative Catholic position that contraception is "intrinsically immoral," while Dan, the celibate, defends the liberal position: that birth regulation is morally permissible in some situations. It's this familiar scenario that Kevin interrupts when he starts clearing up the dishes.

"Sit down, Kevin! The dishes can wait," Sophie orders.

"I rather like puttering in the kitchen, Sophie."

"Oh, come off it, Kevin." Her rocking stops and she draws her legs up under her, continuing to bellow toward the kitchen. "You don't need to rationalize for us, Kevin. Housework's a bitch. You must know that." Then, in an aside to Dan and Basil and me—with only slightly diminished volume—she says, "It's got to be awful with all those kids." Kevin's back is still toward us, but I can see his long neck and ears flush. He knows we've seen firsthand the confusion that poverty, cramped quarters, and crying babies have brought to his disheveled apartment. Yet he obediently wipes his hands and returns to his spot on the couch. "I just can't see how somebody as smart as you, Kevin, can do that to yourself—or to Rosemarie. I think it's plain cruel." Sophie's eyes are more forgiving than her voice, which is strident.

"Hey, Sophie, take it easy," Dan says softly. He's over by the doorway, standing with his back to us, pressing his face against the screen to watch the rain we've been waiting for.

Sophie, though, is not to be deterred. "A kid every year—Jesus! You're making her into a regular baby factory! No wonder she didn't 'feel too well tonight.' How can she feel anything? I don't think I could get up in the morning if I had three kids and was pregnant again, for Christ's sake." Christ—or what the Church says in His name—has everything to do with Rosemarie's getting up or not in the morning, I want to say to Sophie. But I don't, because I can't complete that way of thinking, even to myself. I'm relieved when Dan takes her on.

"Easy, tiger, you're the one so big on privacy of conscience."

Tiger?

"But this is not *just* a private issue!" she retorts. "Or haven't you heard of the population explosion?"

"You just don't understand, Sophie." Kevin's voice, strong and low, makes me nostalgic for a simpler time when he and his guitar led us in Irish folk songs. For such a slight man he has a big voice, but how gently he uses it! "What you don't understand about us is our faith. Rosemarie and I *believe*— in family life, in the Church, 'Holy Mother Church.' She is our mother, our life. Our children are God's gift to us. The difficulties, our cross to bear." This must be how he speaks to those kids at Central Catholic High, where he teaches religion class part time—measured and reassuring, convincing. He and Rosemarie come from large immigrant Irish families and consider it a privilege to be parents, to pass on the faith, Rosemarie in particular. "She's a true Christian woman, Sophie. She feels deeply that being a mother is her vocation, her reason for being as a woman. That's not your background. I don't think you can understand what it's like to believe this way."

Sophie, with a measured, modulated voice, responds, "What I believe, Kevin, is that the world is overpopulated. No one should be allowed to have as many kids as you will— if you keep up this pace." She includes all of us now in the sweep of her eyes. "What's more, I believe that we've got a hell of a lot in life to do besides reproduce. Your church is preoccupied with sex and procreation." The raised voice and fiery eyes are back; she looks ready for a night of battle when Dan pulls her to her feet and guides her out into the kitchen. "Come on, old girl," he says. "Let's get some coffee for everybody." Old girl? Tiger? What's going on? Basil also seems surprised, even shocked.

Only Kevin remains unflappable. "Sophie, you're like Tertullian: *great but wrong!*" The fiery exchange has brightened him. It's the peace that surpasses understanding, I think, while I watch him thank Sophie and say thanks but he doesn't need any coffee, and he'd better be on his way "back to the factory." This rouses Basil to make his own goodbyes, for he's promised, as usual, to drop off Kevin on his way home.

I am disturbed to see the group break up on a strained note, yet I am at a loss to stop it. What I planned was a warm send-off for Basil. I look around the empty living room and realize it will never again be the same. Gone is the easy camaraderie of our first years—of even a year and a half earlier, when we gathered at Sophie's to watch JFK's funeral. I'm wrong to blame Sophie, yet I feel an old anger toward her for forcing our differences to the surface.

I walk outside with Kevin and Basil, clutching each by the arm and promising to keep in contact. Of course, I'll see them next Easter—the ACPA (American Catholic Philosophical Association) will be here in DC! After that at Notre Dame, then possibly New Orleans, someday in San Francisco. By then we should all be rooted enough in our own colleges to get our way paid. Give papers even. We promise a reunion lunch or dinner whenever our conventions meet, and in the meantime to send each other papers to critique. We'll stay in touch. They drive off, and for a moment I stand at the curb, soothed by the rain-cooled air with its hint of a gentle breeze. What a relief after those heated exchanges and that stuffy apartment! I could leave right now, but this has been my party, too. At the very least, I should stay to help Sophie straighten up.

When I get back to the apartment, she's arguing with Dan about cigarettes, so I duck into the bathroom. There, the mirror surprises me. I look better than I thought possible, considering the turmoil of the last few minutes. More rested and healthier than when I started out. Younger looking than Sophie, as she so often reminds me, even the improved Sophie. And, truth to tell, younger even than poor Rosemarie, who's at least ten years my junior. Maybe tension agrees with me? Or wine? Or not having kids? I feel ashamed somehow, at thirty-seven, for what Dan calls my "girlish glow." As if I'm not working hard enough. For all its challenges, the life of study hasn't been nearly as strenuous for me as teaching, when I had to juggle a dozen different responsibilities with a lot less sleep. And certainly not nearly as wearing as Rosemarie's life. Maybe before I finish the degree, my lucky streak will end. I've seen the effects of writer's block and the dreaded dissertation depression all around me. Even Basil grew perceptibly more strained in the process. But for now this silly vanity from Sophie's looking glass perks up my spirit, and I set about washing the taste of wine out of my mouth.

I lower my head to the sink and see specks of black beard. Looking up, I see a shaving mug next to Sophie's douche bag, plus a worn copy of *The Moviegoer* that I know Dan's been reading. Of course, he could have given it to her the way he passes on books and articles to me. But who other than a monk uses a shaving mug? And what about the empty box of Trojan Extra Strength? What am I supposed to think? Hasn't Dan himself—or Freud through Dan—made me question such chance occurrences?

The door slams, and I hear Sophie yell after him to get her more cigarettes. Instantly, details from earlier in the evening flashback: How he knew exactly where the Scotch was and how to manage the quirks of her stereo. And before the others came, the two of them were so domestic—she ordering him around, he taking out the trash, knowing where the extra bags were kept. Dan's out getting more than cigarettes, I figure—and coming back for more than the dishes. I'm furious with Sophie, sad for Dan.

I'm hardly out of the bathroom when she attacks, "Why didn't you back me up? You let all that romantic shit about family, motherhood, and being a real woman just go by! You left me alone!"

I'm flabbergasted. I want to strike out at her to say how she's got things twisted, and that I'm fed up with her for manipulating all of us, ridiculing our way of life. She's still yelling about responsible parenthood when I start screaming back, "Talk about cruelty! You're cruel, Sophie—saying those things to Kevin. You don't have a clue about the love Christians try to live."

"Oh, no! Now I'm going to get a lecture about true Christian love and how we Jews care only about money."

"Don't tell me what I'm going to tell you!" My voice is as strident as hers has ever been. "I don't care what the Jews did back then. Or the Christians. I'm concerned with now, with what you do. To all of us. To me." I'm trembling, sick of her intelligence, her conscience, her world awareness. Why must she be so invariably right! More controlled, I continue, "You use that legal head of yours to argue away anything you can't figure out. You've trapped me into defending stuff I don't even care about: the Inquisition, the flagellants, the Virgin Birth, indulgences. But I'm not going to get pushed into attacking Kevin and Rosemarie. Or watch you attack them. That's their tradition; it's in their blood."

"And in yours, kid," she says calmly. Anger doesn't upset her as it does me. "You're plenty mad about it, that's why you're shouting at last." She smiles benevolently.

"I'm shouting because I'm mad at you."

"You're mad there's no place for you in that romantic shit about motherhood and the 'real Catholic woman.' Where do you fit into all that? I don't see nuns turning out babies each year."

"That's a cheap shot, Sophie," I add.

"What I know about you, Liza, old girl, is that you're

afraid of *any* talk that's not 'nice.' You don't believe that bullshit any more than I do; yet you let me be the nasty one." I want to say she is nasty, but I hold my tongue. She adds, "You're just jealous of me, sweetie, and you can't even see it." After all of Sophie's talk about the importance of anger, she now answers my remark with a condescending smile. Has she noticed my trembling? I'd like to snatch the bottle of brandy still on the counter between us and smash it all over her tiny kitchen.

She must have seen my eye fix on it, because she picks it up and says, "Here, take it, Liza. It's good stuff; Basil brought it as 'a gift for the hostess.' And you were the hostess as much as I." She turns back to the sink. "Besides, he's sweet on you, you know. It would've pleased him to know you planned a party for him. Or do you have a hard time with those feelings as well?"

"Thanks, I will take it," I say and grab the small bottle. I turn abruptly and bolt out the screen door. In my rage, I try to slam the door in her face. But its slow spring resists my thrust. Instead, I twist my wrist, causing Sophie to burst out laughing. "That bitch," I spit into the night, surprised at my own words but hoping, if anyone hears me, it'll be Dan. But I don't meet anyone as I walk with determined step to the end of her block and cross over one street to the bus stop. What did she say about Basil? That he's sweet on me?

Over the years, I've carried a vast assortment of objects in the large pocket hanging at my side, but never a bottle of brandy. And never before have I stepped out of an apartment in the Capitol Hill area of DC after dark, nor stood at the bus station, nor sloshed my habit through a rain puddle because in my fury I didn't see the pools of water all around me. Inside the bus, I am vigilant to keep the weighted pouch from swinging and smashing against the posts. This steadies me. I find the bubbling rage in my head forming itself into a nest of disquieting questions: How can she do that to Dan? Take advantage of him that way? Can't she see how vulnerable and defenseless he is? Just because he looks so—well, sexy is the right term—doesn't mean he isn't still a priest.

A note with a phone number is stuck on my door when I get back to St. Catherine's. I recognize Dan's number at his new place. The time tells me he must have left Sophie's shortly after I did. Good! Whatever his news, it can wait until morning; the celebration of Sister Christine's qualifying exams cannot. So I slip through the silent halls to her room, the party long over.

"A medical emergency! Come quickly," I whisper at her door. With a couple of mugs snatched from the dining room, we make our way up the darkened stairs to my third-floor room. Together we savor the brandy from Brother Basil— the best I've ever tasted. "Just like Jesus," I say. "The best saved for last."

Chapter 11

1966

January 1966

I know Dan can bluff, just how well I discover shortly after New Year's. With my dissertation nearly finished, this will be my last year in Washington, DC. Dan, though, is stuck on chapter one of his. He hasn't written anything for weeks. Throughout last summer and fall, he listened to my moans— jollying me through the dark hours preceding each chapter. He brushed off my inquiries about his own work, saying he preferred to wait until his first draft was complete before letting me see it. With the confidence of one who at last sees the end of her own tunnel, I persuade him it's time for me to help. Maybe I can get him back on track.

And so, on this bleak winter afternoon, I've come here to his office on the third floor of Cantwell Hall, filled with plans for his project. As I take off my snow boots and great cape, he turns up the knob on the small electric heater and checks the hot water in his ancient percolator.

"What about a tad of the old St. Bernard's stuff?" he asks, pulling a flask from the desk drawer. "I give you a monk's guarantee: It'll warm you like nothing else."

"Not for me, thanks. I'd rather get right down to work." Some monk, I think, as I eye his bulky Irish turtleneck. We stand across from each other at his desk while I unpack his pages I've been working on. As I busy myself assembling them, I feel slightly uncomfortable in his silent presence. I almost wish I had agreed to share some of the brandy. "Look, this is very finishable," I say, breaking the tension. "Maybe not by the March deadline, but surely by next fall. What you've amassed is truly impressive."

I render my suggestions with authority. Recast here, cut back there, focus, rearrange, tighten, develop, give examples—enough for a first draft, I tell him, moving away from his desk and the mass of notes. Sitting a few feet away at the typing table, I can at last look directly at him. "What do you think?"

"I think it's cheating," he replies, a broad grin spreading over his face, "but I also think it's wonderful." He spreads out this last word, then adds softly, "I think you're wonderful!"

"It's all yours, Dan, with just a little help from your friend."

"My friend, yes." He pauses, as if savoring the term. "You are a real friend, Elizabeth." It's the tender voice of our phone conversations. Of one conversation in particular last fall, shortly after the start of that academic year, I came right out and asked him if he was "sweet on Sophie" as I suspected that night last spring in her bathroom. "Are you serious? No, Elizabeth. That's not for me. Never. Besides she's got a guy. Someone I really like, by the way. But you're my woman friend, Elizabeth. I go over there to see her and Tony and to cop cigarettes and booze. That's all. Believe me."

That tone, more than his words, has bound up this assurance in my heart these last few months of lonely dissertation writing. They comforted me during the dark days of Christmas vacation when St. Catherine's was virtually empty and Dan was out of town. But now in his office, without the buffer of the phone box, his voice unsettles me, and I find myself stiffening against the typing chair, chattering on about the complexities of his various arguments. Although I sense he's staring at me, I am unable to look directly at him. Instead, I roll back in the typing chair and let my eyes roam around the room.

Frayed cords stretch dangerously across the floor to a decrepit heater buzzing on and off, to a coffeepot burping irregularly, to an old file cabinet up against the typing table with a not-quite-closing drawer. The single window shade is ripped, while stacks of old blue books, copies of the CU NEWS and a half dozen or so dusty beer bottles are heaped against the baseboard of the wall on either side of the door. Over it all hangs a molded wood crucifix, the kind that can be found in practically every Catholic classroom in the country.

When finally we move into serious talk on the dissertation, my anxiety dissipates. Once again he's the old Dan, sparking with insight. I twist back to the typewriter to bang out the sentences and half thoughts streaming out of him. Dan at his best. We work for two more hours this way.

Then I stand up, stretch, and move over to the window. "Now I'll take some coffee—if you're still offering."

"I want to offer you more than coffee, Elizabeth."

It's that voice again. Though he's behind me, I again sense his gaze. Again, I am uncomfortable, only this time I'm also stiff and heavy, unable to move away. I sense his closeness even before his hands rest on my shoulders. Their weight anchors me to that very spot on the fifth floor of Cantwell—a statue frozen in its stare out across the gray snow. But then slowly, gingerly, he turns me around to face him, and his look rapidly melts away my frozen weight.

We stand there for I don't know how long: He holding me by the shoulders at arm's length in front of him, gently brushing back the veil that drapes over my shoulders, repeating my name, while I look at his face, speechless. "Elizabeth," he murmurs, over and over. In some abstracted way, I am horrified at what is happening, yet I am also aching to yield. Then as surely and naturally as the heat pulsing through me, we collapse toward one another, as I let out a piercing screech that's loud enough "to raise the dead," he later tells me. His huge, cleated snow boot had landed squarely on my stockinged foot! As I bend toward my injury, I manage to throw us both off balance. And we both topple to the floor. I hunch over my drawn-up knee to grasp my hurt foot. As I rock back and forth in pain, he quizzes me about my arch and my ankle and is the skin broken and can I move my toes and is there feeling here there and elsewhere.

"I'm okay. How about you?" Sheepishly, he reaches for my good foot, apologizing over and over, and starts stroking it gently. But when he attempts to bring it to his lips, he manages to twist my leg so that I end up kicking him in the face, sending his glasses skittering across the room. It's my turn to apologize, as he starts crawling about on all fours, searching for his glasses. Giddiness overcomes me. There he is: specs missing, hair tousled, face feverishly flushed, plopped down in the midst of blue books and empty beer bottles, while Jesus on the crucifix agonizes overhead! I must look as silly: my coif and band at an angle—like a drunken sailor, he tells me—rosary beads tangle in my skirts; my habit twists impossibly under me. There's a moment's uneasy pause before we both explode with laughter.

Eventually, we wear ourselves out laughing and he crawls over to help me work my swollen foot into my snow boot. We don't speak, but he offers me his hand, helps me up, and adjusts the heavy cloak over my shoulders. For a few awkward moments, we stand at the door, each searching for a way to end this bizarre episode. "Elizabeth," be begins—yet nothing follows. And I am as mute, able only to mumble his name. Finally, he looks at me directly, which he hasn't done since we tumbled onto the floor, and says, "Elizabeth, never in the world did I want to, in any way, involve you in my—"

"Foot fetish?"

"You're impossible!"

"And you're not?"

On the bus returning to Sisters College, the buzz of talk feels intrusive, so I move to the rear to be alone. I open my office book—a message every nun understands: Leave me alone, I'm praying. The red ribbon marks the day: January 21, feast of St. Agnes, Virgin Martyr, and I recall that morning's lesson in the liturgy about how little Agnes took Jesus as her spouse when she was ten. By thirteen, she was dead for resisting marriage to a pagan. "The one to whom I am betrothed is Christ, whom the angels serve," she is supposed to have said and, while awaiting the executioner's ax, pleaded for him to "strike without fear, for the bride does her spouse an injury if she makes him wait." Three days ago, it was St. Prisca, also thirteen, with virtually the same story. Next month it will be St. Dorothy, who sent roses and apples to her executioners, with thanks, for dispatching her so young to her bridegroom. Then those other martyred maidens in the Church's calendar—Catherine, Margaret, Cecilia, and beautiful Agatha who, for Christ's sake, was roasted over live coals.

And so, on this ordinary gray Friday afternoon, I wonder, Just why is virginity so highly prized? I'm not sure I ever truly believed that the purity of innocence is holier or better than the complications of maturity, but I surely don't think so now. Facts long familiar to me now raise troubling questions: Why are there no strong women saints in the canon of the Mass? And in the whole liturgical year, where are the stories about valiant woman who were passionate brides or loving mothers? Women who prized their sexuality? Who loved their bodies for responding as mine did to Dan's this afternoon? Isn't *love* what the message of Christ is all about? Why have we believed that the absence of sexual feelings is more saintly than experiencing them? Or why have women who saw their sex as base and contemptible been put in the highest place of honor?

They have surrounded me from childhood, these tales of "holy virgins," as indeed those about the preeminence of Mary, the Blessed Virgin Mary, "tainted nature's solitary boast." I have accepted this without question as part of my faith. But now as the bus struggles homeward, I am angered by this tradition that glorifies girlish immaturity. Besides, I simply do not believe it anymore. Maybe I never have.

Now, in the solitude of this backseat on the bus, I pray my thanks to God for the awakening of my own sexual feelings. Like the rosebud placed on the altar long ago, it has become a more precious gift, a more fitting sacrifice for having blossomed more fully. I open my eyes and take in, one by one, each of the distinctive veiled heads in front of me, and wonder: Have any of these sisters ever felt that overwhelming fullness, or that pulsing warmth and excitement, that I felt this afternoon in Dan's office? Or the dizziness of those wonderful man odors from his hair, his cigarettes, his coffee? Or the pressure of his beard against my veil, or his strong hands massaging my foot? I hope so.

With a jolt, the bus stops at the path leading up to St. Catherine's. Suddenly I'm aware of chatter all around me. It's TGIF for this group of cold and weary nuns, yet I find it hard to join in the banter with pain shooting up my leg at every step. Dan's boot inflicted more damage than I realized. Sister Clare, a nursing sister from Chicago, notices my slight limp. She insists on inspecting my foot, and by the time we reach my third-floor room, I welcome her ministrations, as much for my soul as for my wounded foot. Obediently, I take to my bed, elevating the foot so she can bathe and dress it properly, savoring only too readily her pamperings: first an ice bag, then a dinner tray, and finally the pill that allows me to relinquish—for that night at least—my soul's struggle to fit together the pieces of my life.

But now it's morning and I spend the meditation period before Mass pacing slowly back and forth in the long cloistered corridor alongside the chapel. Sister Clare's pill has left me slightly groggy, so I welcome the chill from the courtyard outside, which penetrates the tall, slender slices of window flanking the corridor. I need to be thoroughly awake before taking my place in the overheated chapel, for I have only this half hour before Mass to reach an important decision.

Our rule considers any deliberate entertaining of a "thought, word, act, desire, or satisfaction contrary to the virtue of chastity as a sin against the vow of chastity." So my ingrained Catholic response system would have me confess the way I enjoyed my feeling around Dan yesterday and be shriven before approaching communion. The logistics are easy enough, since the chaplain waits for customers in the confessional box each morning during the half hour before Mass. The problem is, I do not believe my encounter with Dan yesterday was a sin. It seems the very opposite—a grace, a mitzvah, as Sophie would say. Calling it *sin*, out of some habitual conditioning, would be a worse sin. Still, doubt haunts me: Could my pride be rationalizing away the admission of personal sin?

I no longer believe what was unquestioned when I entered the order: that our lives as nuns is "more perfect" or "higher" than the single or married life. Or that holiness has much to do with the innocence of undeveloped sexuality. But now I must move past the clarity of what I do *not* believe any more to focus on what I *do* believe—without any doubt. The answer easily emerges: I believe in the Sisters of Mary, in the works they perform. And I believe in them for me. We can accomplish what, by myself, I cannot. This bedrock belief implies other commitments, however: to live publicly as a Church person and to remain celibate. Not because these are better than other ways to live, but because they are necessary for remaining with the group I want to be part of. For me, group action is better than solitary effort.

Group thinking is another matter, however. Never again

can I substitute it for individual conscience, which is exactly the issue for me this morning. The light's on in the box indicating that the priest is free. Yet going into that confessional to say the things any priest would expect me to say—were he a fly on the wall in Cantwell Hall yesterday—is no longer possible for me. I no longer want the security in his "Go in peace, my child." To confess penitence, even to myself, would be a lie.

Oh that I could confess the truth! That I love Dan, body and soul; that I cherish his love for me; that I see each as a gift from God; that I take responsibility to keep things from going physically any further. Unfortunately, the confessional is not set up for confessing one's faith in this way. So, gazing out across the cold beauty of the courtyard, I confess all this directly to God. Finally, then, I'm ready to proceed to Mass, "unto the altar of God, the God who gives joy to my youth." I feel blithely youthful, but at the same time more mature. For what I am bringing to the altar of sacrifice are womanly gifts, more glorious by far than those of childlike innocence.

"Elizabeth?"

His voice sounds different, though I do recognize him. All morning I expected his call and worried that Sister Pascal wouldn't be able to find me down in the laundry.

"Are you okay?" His voice sounds jittery.

"More than okay!" I say brightly. "What about you?"

"It's been rough on me, real rough." Oh no! It's the heavy, leaden, voice I hear after his sessions with Dr. Brunner. I also hear the quick draw on his cigarette and the force of his rapid exhaling, followed by a deep breath. All is not well. "Elizabeth, I need to apologize. I'm sorry, really sorry for what happened yesterday. Can you forgive me?"

At first I think the apology is for my injured foot, but then quickly sense a different drift. "Forgive?" I ask.

"Can you?"

"Of course, but..." I search for how to explain what became so clear in that early hour this morning. It doesn't fit with talk of apologies and forgiveness. I'm frowning, confused.

"Wait a minute, Dan. Yesterday, we discovered—"

"We discovered what we both really want!" he says severely. "Want but cannot have. At least, not now. That old language about the 'treachery' of the body and its 'frailty.' It's all true, isn't it?"

How to respond to such an impossible tangle of truth and half-truth? How differently we perceive yesterday! Even though I'm securely closeted in this phone booth, I'm uncomfortable talking about yesterday this way. "You've shaken up my world, made me rethink my whole life," he says.

"I've done some rethinking as well, rethinking my faith— what I truly believe." I want to share with him how everything came together this morning, how my intellectual quarrels with the faith suddenly became extremely personal.

"And I've been thinking about you, where you fit into my life. You are the nicest temptation I've ever had, Elizabeth!"

"I hope I'm more than that!"

"Of course, you are, m'dear. You're my very best friend." At last, it's the voice from his office. It cancels, somewhat, the feistiness I was feeling at being called his temptation. "Listen, Elizabeth. I love you. You know that, don't you? But for now, well, for now I think we need to cool it." The same conclusion as mine—but for such very different reasons.

Spring 1966

A certain coolness has come into our phone conversations this term. Though I sense it's never far from either of our minds, we don't refer to that afternoon in January for quite some time. Yet that experience in his office gives me a comfortable new warmth: knowing that he loves me for exactly who I am, the way I am, and not because I happen to be someone's teacher or pupil, daughter or granddaughter— or sister. The memory of his "I love you" words nestles inside me during the next weeks, not as a distraction but as a support. We take for granted we are each other's ally in the struggles that fill our days.

For Dan, it's the struggle to enlist others in resisting the war in Vietnam and the war in our streets between the races. For me, it's primarily the same, plus the challenge of negotiating a smooth finish to my degree. A couple of my committee members not only do not favor the pragmatist cast of my dissertation, they are also on record for disapproving of sisters who demonstrate against the war. Though we never speak of it, I am aware—I feel Dan is as well—that we each seize every opportunity to contact the other.

One such occasion is the "Lenten underground" Mass that our Peace Group is sponsoring. Dan—with his left-leaning politics and monk's liturgical training—is a favorite among groups eager to explore liturgies not yet formally approved by Rome. He has translated portions of the Mass into English, then composed additional prayers to convey the mood he wants. There are vestments appliquéd with PEACE NOT WAR, a guitar group and folk songs for everyone. It's my job to prepare text for the Mass booklets from Dan's scribbled notes. In the process, I find myself editing some of his compositions, saddened at how his versions exemplify the mind/body split thinking I abhor. So, one evening, just before Ash Wednesday, I call him to read to him how I've recast one of his compositions. "Okay, here goes. First, what you wrote:

"Heavenly Father,
We your children gather here

In celebration and thanksgiving,
Take from our hearts every trace of greed and hate;
Remove the violence in us and in our communities;
Bestow on us those gifts of tolerance and love
That will make of us, your children, for our time,
A new creation for our time. Amen."

"What's the problem?" he asks, warily.

I question the edicts *take* from us, *remove, bestow, make* us. But what I say to him is, "It's beautiful, Dan, captures the sentiments of our group and the spirit of the day. However, you stress God's power, okay, but I think you slight our responsibility, make our role passive. And since the whole point of this celebration is to urge us to get involved in changing the world, my rewrite is an attempt to highlight human power while not denying God's power. Like thus:

"Oh God, we gather here
To celebrate and to give thanks:
For the power you have given us
To work for peace and justice in our world.
Bless our every effort to forge
Within ourselves and our communities
A new creation—of tolerance and love. Amen."

"What do you think?"

After a long pause, he answers, "Gee, Elizabeth, you have enough work without trying to rewrite the whole thing."

"Which means—you don't like it?"

"Well, no, to be perfectly honest, I don't. The rhythm seems off. Remember, this has to be recited by a whole bunch of people."

"I can fix that. It's the theology I care about."

"Elizabeth m'dear, the theology is nil. Read it to me again." I read it a second time, disturbingly aware of nervous inhaling and exhaling at the other end of the phone. "You've cut out God—completely."

"Only God the puppeteer."

"Oh, for Christ's sake, Elizabeth! No one's gonna notice your philosophic niceties."

"But do you?" I hear desperation in my desire that he agree, as he did months ago, when I told him how I rejected the duality in so much of Catholic piety.

"Sure, I do. But I still think you've gone too far this time. Besides, I'm in enough hot water now without adding heresy!"

"You're calling me a heretic?"

"Materially...if not formally." It's Father Aloysius, the authority, speaking. A voice I haven't heard for a long time.

"Of course, priests can tell?" I say, surprised at my sarcasm.

"With something that easy, sure."

Has he forgotten how we both struggled for an entire semester in that seminar on human freedom and divine causality? Struggled to find arguments to uphold human agency without compromising God's power? It was a bore for him, I recall. Tonight, however, I don't pursue the point with Dan, whether because of tact, or fear of his increasingly black moods, or simply because I'm tired.

When Ash Wednesday comes, Dan's version of the prayers is recited with gusto by the two hundred-plus gathered for Mass. If anyone else shares my problem with his wording, I'm none the wiser. Dan's ecstatic. Why haven't I noticed it before? He's cut out to be an evangelist, much more than a monk. Then, I catch myself. That's *his* language, "cut out to be." Why not just say it: He *chooses* to be this new kind of priest. Whichever style, though, he's still very much the priest—mediating between God and man—even in this stuffy basement, under a too-low ceiling with too-bright lights.

I wish I could share his happiness, not be so put off by

his theology—or the aesthetics of this basement. My intellect tells me Dan's changes in the Mass are good: The liturgy should be available for everyone, and, for most, English is much more understandable than Latin. Yet for me, Mass today is less available—whether because of those atrocious banners hanging from the ceiling, or the lack of ventilation, or the dreadful music. I long for the cool, dark caverns of the Immaculate Conception Shrine right here on campus. Whether for private devotions or grand liturgies, the vastness and majesty of its space and the foreignness of its pageantry promote in me a meditative state. Flickering candles allow me to follow the simple Latin of the ancient liturgy enough to weave over it my own reflections.

Not so this wretched basement. Huddled here around Dan, our clerical cheerleader, I find any sort of contemplation impossible. His modern, almost too "relevant," translations blast over the microphone, assaulting exactly that part of my mind that is the most argumentative and literal. I wish I could abandon myself wholeheartedly to the moment, but I cannot. I'm plagued by the memory of a Dan anguishing about what God *really* wants from him, while here in front of me is someone doing exactly what *he* wants, yet calling it God's choice.

I think of how often we fall to arguing over the question of ordaining women to the priesthood. He's uncomprehending and annoyed at my indifference, calling me difficult. "I can't for the life of me figure you out, Elizabeth. Why don't you want to be a priest? You're smart enough." The only answer that satisfies him is his own: I'm anti-clerical, old-fashioned, just contrarian.

In fact, I do prefer much of the old to some of the new—the old stiff-armed "kiss of peace," for example. In the traditional Mass, the congregation watched from afar this exchange of "Pax Christi" among the celebrants. That was better than what I'm subjected to in this stifling basement:

a flurry of hugs and kisses, chitchat with people around me, strangers most of them, telling me how much they love me as they tangle in my veil and scapular. It's embarrassing. Worse, it trivializes, distracts from the truly awesome mystery of God's power. A power so great that it allows us to choose whether or not we wish to acknowledge it—far more wondrous, for me, than a magical God who plucks us from troubles and fills in for us when we fail.

As Mass winds down, I think how old-fashioned Dan himself is, despite these modern trappings. When he speaks about the priestly "call" that he's so sure he "has," he says it comes from "the divine reality in the Church," while the foibles of his monastery are part of "the human aspect of the Church." Like his "frailty" that afternoon in January, I suppose?

With his "Go in peace" at Mass's end, Dan beams his priestly benediction to all assembled, then turns to bearhug his student helpers. The crowd mills about, waiting to shake his hand. Their squealing reminds me of the home team after a basketball victory. Quite a different Dan from that ludicrous clown scrambling about on the floor of his office last January.

Late May 1966
When the day finally comes to leave DC for good and return to St. Louis, I'm joined by Sister Johanna. She's that hospital sister, friend of my dad, who came here to DC for a meeting and stayed over for my graduation. It's a bright morning, feeling already like full summer, when the two of us wait with our bags in the driveway of St. Cat's. Dan's offered to take us to the station in the car that comes with his new parish job.

As he helps us with our belongings, he manages to squeeze my hand in a way that so unnerves me that I feign piety, asking him to stop at the Shrine for a last visit before leaving DC. Once enveloped by the darkness of the cool shrine, I kneel with my hot face in my hands, hoping to quiet a racing heart. The send-off this morning had taken me by surprise. I'd no idea old Mother Loretto could display such emotion, nor little Sister Pascal, always so vexed by my late phone calls, nor, God help us, cranky Sister Pancratia. Whoever started the tears I don't know, but I'd felt like a blubbering mess by the time Dan arrived.

It didn't help that I had packed most of the night after a party for me up on our third floor. Often enough, I've been on the other side of these tearful farewells, knowing I'll most likely never see the graduating nun again, let alone live with the Sisterly closeness of graduate student life. Now, I'm the one sailing forth, my newly minted degree in hand, and leaving others behind to struggle on. Every minute after my final oral exam until this very moment at the shrine has been jam-packed with the emotions of leave-taking. There's been no room left for feeling my imminent separation from Dan—or so I thought. But now, kneeling in the quiet darkness, I know that with every sister's hug and kiss and promise of staying in touch, I've been imagining how I could ever say goodbye to Dan.

This thought calms the tumult within me, and I move over to the flickering candles, surprised at my impulse to light some. Never since I was a toddler with Mimi have I done such a thing—considering it altogether too superstitious a practice for me. Though I've had money in my pocket "for necessary expenses" after that first meeting with Sophie, it's never occurred to me until this moment that the quaint Catholic custom of lighting votive candles might become a necessity for me.

Yet here I am, about to return to the motherhouse—when I'll have to return the coin purse—deciding with a flurry to empty its contents into the donation box. I gather up some tapers, first one, then several, for this intention and that, this person and that. As I light each one, placing it before the altar of Our Lady, I thank her and the good Lord for the many people crowding my heart at this moment: the nuns with whom I have lived, my professors and fellow grad students, Sophie, Basil, sweet young Ed, Kevin and Rosemarie—who is, alas, pregnant again. The last candle is for Dan. By this time I'm sniffling away tears, savoring for the umpteenth time the words of Hopkins: "There lives the dearest freshness deep down things." Yes, indeed, especially deep down some particular people.

Minutes later, I'm again composed, and head out toward the waiting car, where Sister Johanna and Dan are getting acquainted. With eyes not yet adapted to the bright daylight, I am startled by an old woman grasping my arm and imploring, "Sister, will you pray for me?"

"Of course, of course," I reply, clutching her hands the way I wish I could take Dan's. Then I look into her sad, weathered face and ask her to please pray for me as well.

At the station, Dan carries our bags, takes us to our seats, and waits in the coach with us for the train to start. By the time ours finally starts moving, Sister Johanna has fallen asleep, and our hovering conductor is so absorbed in his ticket punching that he misses what passes between the two of us. Which is nothing to cause the conductor or other passengers to see anything amiss. In this Washington, DC of 1966, it's not uncommon to see a youngish priest helping an older nun and her traveling companion with their bags. But what this priest says as he prepares to part from them is that he loves the younger companion and always will, and that it doesn't matter if she's a heretic. God loves her and so does he. And, if it is God's will, they will get together sometime before the Last Judgment. This leaves her stunned, as she follows him back through the coach to the platform.

Then, as matter-of-factly as telling her the time of day,

he says he is not sure he can live without her and touches his hand to her face. In that instant, she feels like Venus on her pink shell with the breezes of Firenze blowing through her hair. Then he jokes, she laughs, and once again she feels like the hot and sticky nun she is, swathed in starch and yards of heavy cloth, whose veil is getting sooty from the grime of the wheezing train.

⁂

Sister Johanna and I go back a long way, which probably is why she got permission to stay in DC for my graduation. Besides being the procurator general, third in line for Augusta's job, she's a great friend of my parents, especially of Dad's. He's been her chief fundraiser since they first met in August 1945, right after I was accepted by the order. Back then, Mother grumbled when she heard of our privilege—to be visited by the "good sisters." She fretted about the sticky weather, about tidying up the house, about what to serve, but mostly she was concerned about what she would say to the reverend mother. She was not at home with nuns the way Dad was, because of course she didn't have nun relatives as he did. Besides, these nuns were about to snatch her daughter away.

Dad, though, was all energy, sprucing up the yard, updating the scrapbook of his major construction projects. Any nun smart enough to be a reverend mother, he was sure, would find his accomplishments fascinating. Also, he was flattered by the news, still secret, that our Aunt Lucy—Sister Immaculata—had leaked to him: Dad was about to be asked to head a committee of laymen to raise funds for the order's new hospital.

With Reverend Mother Pauline that afternoon in 1945 was young Sister Johanna, who would be shouldering the order's responsibility for this immense project. I thought her beautiful and mysterious, quite like Ingrid Bergman in *The Bells of St. Mary's*, even though the teachers at my own St. Mary's assured me the movie bore no resemblance to actual life in the convent. Yet there she was: tall, poised, seemingly aloof from the busy exchange between Dad and Reverend Mother. Eventually, she and Mother and I left Dad with Reverend Mother and moved to the dining room to peruse Tom's war scrapbook. Mother and I both knew better than to bring up Sister Johanna's "past," what we had heard from Aunt Lucy, that is. It seems she'd come as a thirty-year-old "late vocation," a convert from Lutheranism, who had given up a promising nursing career and an engagement ring in Chicago to join the sisters.

Instead, we answered this striking young nun's questions about my plans to enter the order and about Tom's serviceman's star in our living room window. Mother relaxed. She was in her element. Eventually, she brought out the rest of our family albums. I remained forever grateful to Sister Johanna for the way things turned around in my home after that visit. I could tell Mother and Dad felt assured: If that's the way young sisters turn out, it can't be all that bad to let Betty go.

Thus began the charmed relationship between my parents and Sister Johanna. Every visiting Sunday during my novitiate—when novices were completely cut off from the rest of the order—Mother and Dad would regale me with tales of this remarkable woman. She became for them, especially for Dad, the ideal modern nun. I felt he was counting on me to turn out like her: cheerful, professionally competent, with a sense of humor, yet still—as much as all the old-fashioned aunts—unquestionably "spiritual." When at last I joined the ranks of the professed sisters, I discovered that the worlds of hospital and school seldom intersected, so for years, I rarely saw Sister Johanna. With Vatican II, though, there was a great mingling of ages and occupations throughout the order. So once again we met—in a study group on "training" in the fall of 1964. My work on the questionnaires distributed throughout the order the previous summer had drawn me to this group. Sister Johanna, a senior nun now, supervisor of all hospital sisters and a member of our general council, was determined to have her say in how nuns are recruited and educated.

Over and over during those months of working together on the questionnaires, I came to appreciate in Sister Johanna the qualities my parents admired. I observed, though, something else as well: a disciplined single-mindedness that easily turned dogmatic about churchly matters. She was among that small minority of sisters who not only did not embrace the idea of reform but also were convinced we should bolster the status quo instead. "There's too much change all around us—in the world and in the Church. We should be a sign of contradiction to such fashions and fads, not succumb to them."

This amazed me. How could anyone as professionally competent, as worldly-wise and well-liked, sound so much like that crowd at Marie du Lac? Yet I was not about to give up on her as my more liberal friends were. In fact, I hoped to change her views. By the time she'd arrived in DC last week, I was still trying, however cautiously, to help her see the need for reform. So I planned some outings and hoped that the experiences would get across my message. I wanted to avoid the snarled and overly abstract discussions of our community meetings.

I took her to the obligatory tourist stops—the White House, the Lincoln Memorial, the Capitol—at times when I knew the civil rights prayer demonstrations would include nuns and priests. But Johanna was oblivious to the demonstrators, gliding past them with the cool assurance of one who has no interest in protests of any kind. We stood beneath the huge Lincoln and together read his Gettysburg Address—without its influencing one whit her conviction about "the proper place for Negroes."

Another of my bright ideas was a concert by a trio of nuns. Two were getting degrees in musicology, but the third, a violinist, was a hospital lab technician now studying microbiology. I hoped Johanna might think differently about including the arts, which she dismissed as "frills," in the curriculum for our student nuns, including those going into nursing. Yet throughout Brahms, Schubert, and Beethoven, she dozed. As she did during the *A Doll's House* performance at the university's drama school, where my friend Sister Christine had arranged for us to watch a dress rehearsal. I had a double motive. Not only was Ibsen's message—that paternalism, even kindly paternalism, infantilizes people— particularly apt, but also, I hoped as I had with the sister musicians, that Johanna would see the importance of a liberal education for all nuns, even those in hospital work.

But, alas, as far as I can tell, all my clever plans fizzled. Maybe on the long train ride back to St. Louis, maybe then there'll be a chance to open some windows, as good Pope John said, and let Johanna see why basic reform is needed in the lives of nuns, whether teachers or nurses.

May 25, 1966

During the stop-and-start trip up through Baltimore, around the faceless towns skirting industrial Philadelphia, and then west toward Ohio, we pray, read, doze. It's late afternoon by the time we break our retreat silence to decide on dinner plans. After a skimpy breakfast and a skipped lunch, I'm relieved that Johanna favors a "proper meal in the diner" over the cart that's beginning to make its way down our aisle. She stops the conductor with the flushed face who tips his hat each time he passes. "Would you be so kind as to inform us when there is an empty table?" Johanna asks him, presuming that he knows it is unseemly for us to wait in line like everyone else. He seems flattered to be asked.

My stomach rumbles, and I remember the dining car on that trip thirty-plus years ago with Mimi to Kansas City. My reveries of draped linen and heavy silver and tiny bud vases are abruptly halted, however, by a cart clumsily rolling down the aisle next to me. Mothers with clinging children begin choosing plastic-wrapped sandwiches and dividing fruit they've brought along, and once again I am embarrassed. I see with Sophie's eyes the privilege of our supposedly humble life.

We are settling into our table in the diner when a man and wife lean across the aisle, offering to "buy you ladies a drink." Sister Johanna's gracious refusal—friendly yet remote—discourages further conviviality. She takes over the ordering, which is fine with me, as my only experience eating out in the last twenty-one years has been with her in DC this last week, and then only a couple of other times. She frowns as she reads the short menu. "The only real choice for us is the Salisbury steak, I'm afraid." After some pleasantries, she orders for us both. She then surprises me by bringing up our afternoon at *A Doll's House.* "I thought it unseemly for them to carry on that way."

She meant not the character of Nora, I quickly realize, but my friend Sister Christine and her crew, whom we visited backstage. "What way?" I ask.

"I would have thought they were seculars, the way she was giving orders—the tall one—raising her voice. I thought her more aggressive than womanly. And those other two— they looked like novices at recreation, not mature nuns."

"You mean because they were obviously loving it, having fun?" I can hear my defensive tone rising.

"Well, yes, dear, that's part of it."

"Surely you enjoy your work?" I say, still feeling the need to defend Christine.

"Not that way," she says, jaw firmly set—but then

instantly softened into a polite smile. A waiter approaches with our salad, his face as expressionless as an altar boy's at Mass.

"How then do you enjoy your work? It must be pretty pleasant to work with people like my father."

"Yes, of course, dear, but that's not the point." The polite smile is gone, as I listen to the firm, sure tones of a sister superior explaining to me about the "spirit of simplicity" that's won through detachment and resignation. "We should work at tasks, simply and solely because they're assigned us by those who represent God for us."

How does her spirit of simplicity justify the extravagant hotel dinner in celebration of my graduation the other night when there were plenty of simpler places? I can't imagine how to phrase my remark without seeming impertinent. "You're famous for going the extra mile, Sister Johanna. Seems to me that means your work must be enjoyable." It's a polite way of referring to her well-known stubbornness in championing anything pertaining to health care. "I'd imagine anybody who works as wholeheartedly for as many years as you—and been as successful as you—would love your work, or at least enjoy it."

"Not necessarily. Many sisters work against the grain their whole lives," she says. "The saints, for example." She lowers her voice. "It often happens, for someone truly detached, that the more distasteful, the greater penance a task becomes, the more energy and enthusiasm is summoned to do the job well." With this pronouncement she straightens back into the banquette.

"So that's why you've been so successful? Because it's all been so distasteful?"

I'm relieved at her laugh. I've been toying with the sugar spoon, which I'm surprised to see is the old, heavy silver plate. "How would you feel if I pocket this—as a memento of our trip?"

"You tease like your Dad! Good thing you're not always serious." She reaches over, squeezing my arm with her strong grasp. "Sometimes you can be so literal, Sister; I guess that comes from your studies. I'm talking about an ideal we should strive for."

She continues by telling me that she's enjoyed most of her assignments, especially those early years working with professionals like my Dad getting the hospital built. But that's because it was God's will for her. "Peace comes from that kind of enjoyment. And true joy. But frivolity—what I saw with those nuns at the theater—is quite another matter. Their 'fun' epitomizes the worldliness I fear is creeping into our community. I worry about nuns like that."

"Worry about me?" I venture.

"Not in the least, my dear. You're too much a Byrne to go off the deep end with any of these current fads. Oh, we have our differences—you and I—but I think that's only because of these years you've been away studying. When you're back home, I think you'll see things a bit differently." She plants a firm hand on my arm. "You'll always be Dan Byrne's daughter for me."

My hunch is that her regard for me—besides being my father's daughter—stems less from principle than from the fact that, like her, I have a certain conservatism about my bearing. I have not, for example, taken part in various plans to modernize the habit that have tentatively begun in some parts of the order this spring. However, her reasons and mine for keeping to the old ways of dressing are quite different. I have nothing against the plans. It's simply that during my last months in Washington, DC I felt it would have distracted from my final push on the dissertation, not to speak of complicating my leave-taking. I know how different I felt in my makeshift running togs at Marie du Lac. I wasn't prepared to introduce that person to anyone in DC, least of all to Dan or Sophie.

As the last diners prepare to leave, I watch the waiters begin their breakfast preparations. Against the white background of the empty tables, the assembled salt and pepper shakers and sugar bowls gathered together on one table remind me of the way I used to clean up after meals when I was refectorian that awful first year of my professed life. The struggles of that year are the chief reason I'm sure I will not see things differently when again we meet to discuss the training of young nuns. From my own painful experience, I believe young sisters need to finish college before entering the classroom, or the hospital. It's the *person* in the nun who needs what a liberal arts education can give. Technical training in either education or nursing should come later. After they grow up a little more.

"There's no reason teaching nuns can't be trained the same way nurses are," Johanna says. "On the job. At least in the grade schools, where everyone should start out anyway. Later on, for those going into high school work, I can see a few specialized courses at the university. By then, they would have final vows so that we—and they—would be sure of their vocation. No use wasting tuition money on people who are not going to stay with us. Education, even at Catholic colleges, is not cheap, you know."

She's hit a raw nerve with me. Once again I feel like a child in the presence of my provider: There wasn't a day during my drawn-out studies in Washington, DC when I wasn't aware of the cost of my full-time study to the order. No matter the strains of research and writing, I knew how much harder it was for those at home whose labors were paying my tuition.

"I am not, as you may think, against change," she announces. "But there are some very important practical issues that concern me."

"You're famous for what Dad calls your 'good business sense,' Sister. You must know he's got a low opinion of most nuns on that score."

"Well, thank you, dear." She thrusts her chin forward and tips her head back to focus her bifocaled eyes on the menu's small print. "So we're not going to pass up the dessert. It's included." Then she pulls her chin back, peers over the top of her glasses at me, and says with authority, "Our finances indicate we should do exactly the opposite of what you want."

"*I* want? I'm not alone in my views, you know."

"Oh, I know. But I don't believe you sisters with higher degrees realize how we need to cut back, not expand, our dependence on universities. Education is expensive, even with the discounts for nuns. "Our personnel costs, in the hospitals alone, have been affected by the minor changes already started in the order. When young nuns are off reading poetry or going to concerts in the park, someone has to mind the store. So far, they're only studying part time. If it turns full time, we could be crippled financially."

"But the proposal is to phase in a college program gradually. Tell pastors and hospital administrators there's a moratorium on enlarging staff for four or five years, and then start sending sisters right from the novitiate to college. After a while we'd have a new crop of nuns with BAs in hand at the end of every summer session." How I've envied Dan the years spent studying and traveling before setting foot in a classroom. "Religious order priests spend longer than that before they begin to teach."

"But they teach only in their own schools. They are not, like our parochial nuns, employees of a diocese." I've never thought of us in these labor/management terms, yet I know she knows what she's talking about. "When was the last time you met with a pastor and tried to tell him anything about 'his' nuns?" she asks, eyebrow arched. A rhetorical point, for she well knows that I haven't any working contact with the clergy. I was assigned to our academy at the motherhouse after only four years in parish schools.

"Never, but I've heard stories." Augusta had confided in me that the biggest shock in her new job was to see what petty tyrants some pastors are when it comes to "their" sister staff.

"What most concerns me," Johanna continues, "is whether or not we are doing God's work in this rush for degrees. I fear we are getting *means* and *ends* confused. The Holy Rule tells us that our main work is prayer and penance. Everything else—teaching, nursing, what have you—is supposed to be only a means for achieving that goal. Changing our prayers to English may help a bit, so I can go along with that. And possibly the Mass itself has to be updated. Though I doubt it. And maybe—God forbid—those new hymns and guitars help some people to pray. Though I suspect they're a hindrance to many more."

"I'm with you on that." It feels good to be able to agree with her about something.

"But tell me now: How do movies and novels renew the spirit? Or playing in a band? Or directing plays? Or shortening skirts or veils, for heaven's sake?" With that she leans across the table, exasperated. "If you ask me, most of us are far more spiritual with a lot of that covered up. Can't you just imagine what a fool I'd look like with my gray hair and fat legs on display?"

We're still chuckling at the image when our chocolate sundaes and metal pots of hot water, with tea bags on the side, are set before us. Johanna continues about the dreadful aesthetics of most attempts to update the habit. And I must admit I feel as she does about the habit; that I am comfortable wearing it and think the suggested modernizations look atrocious. What I don't say, however, is that I see the vanity of my attitude, and that, along with most of my friends, I feel we should examine very critically the long tradition of using the habit to so dramatically set ourselves apart.

"I don't like the taste of the discussions on change that

have been going on in the community," she says. "Two years of it, and already we're seeing a new breed of nun. They're energetic, well meaning, but so opinionated! And critical! Very un-nunlike! Many of the young nuns are not good team players, Sister. I'm tempted to say a couple in the last batch were just plain lazy, certainly undisciplined. I don't see that spirit of prayer and dedication, or that simplicity of heart a young sister needs to blend into community life."

My goal of affecting Johanna's attitude about the order's renewal efforts is slipping away. I've been gazing at the cup I'm holding as she spoke. It could be from any one of our convents: thick, unbreakable, reliable. Like the habit: uniform, durable, and utterly lacking individuality. The way sisters used to think they should be. But sisters are changing, because the world we're in is different. We are asking different questions, for which the answers of yesteryear won't work. Like the railroads, they made sense for another day and age, a more rational time maybe, surely a more orderly and simpler time. Dan may be more right than I want to admit.

⁂

September 1966

I awoke this morning, chilled. Our Indian summer has turned into fall—weather befitting this glorious Ember Day, when the liturgy bids us rejoice in the harvest. It's great to be home again, back in the Midwest again, and teaching again.

I know nothing about farming, let alone those Middle Eastern harvests celebrated in today's Mass. Yet I'm acutely aware of an amazing harvest taking place all around me. With Vatican II, the whole Church is reaping the fruits from years of arduous preparation: the plowing and planting, the prayer and study for a new, renewed—dare we say *reformed?*—church. Nowhere is the sense of long labors coming to fruition more tangible than here in the motherhouse.

Less than a month ago, sisters from every convent in our

order, totaling almost 650, assembled at the motherhouse for a unique moment in our history. Reverend Mother Augusta formally promulgated a long-awaited instruction from Rome called a *Motu Proprio* on "The Norms for Implementing the Council Decree on the Appropriate Renewal of Religious Life." Behind this dull title is the exciting issue of renewal. Seeds for revitalizing sisters' lives were sown back in the 1950s, when the Sister Formation Movement pushed to upgrade the professional training of young nuns. Then three years ago, in 1963, Pope John XXIII and Vatican II challenged the entire Catholic world with *aggiornamento*—updating. Mother Augusta had responded immediately by encouraging every sister to put both her ideals and her discontents into an anonymous questionnaire, a process I'd been part of. Now, three years later, the new pope commands us to finish what we have, only too eagerly, already begun. So it's hard for me—or for any of my close friends here in St. Louis—to imagine anyone still questioning the need for reform. Yet some still do.

The majority of sisters, though, seems more than eager to follow Mother Augusta's lead. She's sent us each a packet of council documents and asked us to study them, use them in our meditations, discuss them among ourselves. The effect is explosive, mobilizing everyone who has been stewing about the need for reform since the late '50s. This *Motu Proprio* has quickly become our *Magna Carta*. Groups have sprung up overnight: commissions, task forces, ad hoc committees of every sort. Last month, in every convent of our order, sisters worked overtime, scrutinizing every conceivable detail of our lives. Surveys were drawn up, generating reams of findings and making instant sociologists out of us. Proposals—at first timid, but then bolder—began appearing in mailboxes. Some are carefully worded and scholarly, others, often anonymous, sketch in broad stroke what would have been unthinkable only five years ago. From the trivial to the profound, anything is fair game. Next summer, delegates from each convent will deliberate and decide on all these proposals. I'm thrilled to be one of those elected delegates.

Nothing generates as much passion as questions about our work. Who does what, how much say a sister has in what she does, and how they are trained for it. This last involves me directly, since I'm now mistress of juniors at the mother-house—along with my teaching job at the university. Technically, I'm supposed to coordinate the professional and personal development of sixty-some junior sisters during their three years of temporary vows. Practically, however, it's mostly a Saturday and summertime job for me, since junior sisters are not yet free to pursue college studies full time. As I was nearly twenty years ago, they are being missioned to parochial convents or hospitals right after their two-year novitiate, completing college on Saturdays and summers. So for most of the year I see them only on Saturdays, when they come to the motherhouse after college classes. Only in summer do they live here full time. Tonight, in this cell (for that is still what we call our room, irrespective of size), I slouch into one of the chairs, putting my feet up on the other. I am past weary—too many classes, too many students, too many late hours.

"Your goddamned pope's a liar!"

I've just begun to compose the exam for my Intro class when Dan calls. I'm not thrilled to be interrupted or challenged in so surly a fashion "*My* pope?"

"You make excuses for him."

"Oh, c'mon!" I say, exasperated. Lately I've heard myself turn defensive when Dan criticizes poor Pope Paul. "It's just his bad luck to follow someone as popular as Pope John." Dan and I could not be more different on our feelings about Church reform, though tonight his anger is sparked by an item in today's *Washington Post*. "The pope's reported as saying—to some Italian gynecologists—'There is no doubt about the Church's teaching on birth control. There cannot be any doubt!' Now that, my dear Elizabeth, is a flat-out lie!"

And, indeed, I am baffled. It's an open secret, at least since the close of the council almost a year ago, that theologians disagree among themselves about the Church's long-standing prohibitions of birth control. Major theologians, respected leaders. Dan and his priest buddies have been acutely aware of these differing opinions—both here and abroad—for years. Many clergy are saying in the confessional, and some publicly, that *doubtful rules don't apply.* That in forming their consciences (as the catechism says we must), Catholics must consider both the traditions of the past and current theological teaching, then act according to an "informed" conscience. So how has this changed? I want to ask him but decide to hear him out.

"He's a clever bastard," Dan blasts into the phone. "He knows the entire Catholic world is waiting and listening to his every word on this issue. He knows most Catholics believe the moral thing is to limit family size. So he drops this bombshell in the midst of some pious crap to a bunch of Italian medics. No, he says, there's no doubt among theologians. The old teaching still stands."

"But that meeting sounds like a minor event—hardly the setting for making a definitive statement on such a major issue," I say.

"It may be a minor event, Elizabeth, but it's an omen."

Our preoccupation with Vatican II, especially the debate on birth control, is reforming our minds and hearts as Catholics, much as the debates on Vietnam are reforming us as Americans. But it's also reminding us of our reality as man and woman. For while it's fashionable among us Vatican watchers to say that the debate over birth control isn't so much about sex as it is about the power of Vatican authority, it is also, of course, about sex. In the midst of scholarly articles urging the Church once and for all to rid itself of its age-old bias against things bodily, words fly about that have never before been uttered in mixed company.

Dan translates for me from journals with unpronounceable titles the thoughts of Dutch and German scholars about the relevance of a woman's estrogen count, her libido and her fertile periods, about the relative merits of *anovulants, abortifacients, condoms,* and *diaphragms.* Could it be, what one writer calls our "celibate psychosis," that all of us intellectuals are examining—with the care we once took in dissecting the intricate syntax of Augustine's Latin—such topics as *coitus interruptus, frigidity, masturbation,* and *premature ejaculation?* No matter. Both Dan and I know this intellectual ferment grows from a collective sense that somehow the Church has got it all wrong. When it comes to the reality of our bodily being, it's well past time to set things right. The true Christian figures out how to love, not how to *keep from* loving.

"We don't need *Time* magazine or *The New York Times* to tell us what's going on," he continues. "For Christ's sake, of course there's doubt! And disagreement! Nobody can square 'sex only for procreation' with what good Pope John taught about marriage and family life!" Dan's on a roll, so I kick off my shoes and curl into the dilapidated but comfortable old chair.

"This new pope thinks he can mandate away doubts and disagreement, force us to accept a sun that moves around the Earth. Fuck the scientists, he's saying. And most of all, fuck the theologians!"

"Oh, come on, Dan!" I answer, exasperated by more than his vulgarity. "You're overreacting. It's just Vatican boilerplate, not a formal pronouncement. Even the pope can't dismiss work commissioned by a council or toss aside years of study and discussion."

"He sure as hell can! And he will! Just watch. He's taking us right back to the nineteenth century, back to Pius IX and his infallibility crap!" He pauses, and I'm aware of his inhaling. Smoking again? Not good. "You might as well forget about Good Pope John's promise of shared authority. That died with him, I'm afraid." Then his voice comes down a few decibels. "This guy's telling us *he* is the Church. He and his band of old Italian farts. They're not about to share one iota of power listening to us. 'Shut up!' he's saying. 'Get back in line!' *That's* his message, Elizabeth."

Dan's increasing negativity unnerves me—just when I am filled with hope. Does his fury blind him to the truly good things happening in the Church? Or am I being naive?

"Listen, my friend," he continues. "Bishops don't want to jeopardize the good thing they've got going: armies of docile nuns the world over making their vestments and their altar breads, running their schools and hospitals, laundering and cooking and cleaning for them. How else could the legions of seminarians and priests and bishops do without wives? Thinkers like Suenens *threaten* all this, can't you see? Nuns are one of the last systems of slavery in the modern world! Why would anyone listen to a guy who wants to change all that?"

I resist being pulled into his negative spiral, so I shift to one of my own fears about change in the Church. "We need to change the way we train young nuns. We need to recruit a different kind of woman for the convents of the future, young women not so prone to the docility, the slavery as you call it."

"I like the kind of woman you already are, Elizabeth. I miss you." It's his gentle voice again, and it makes me smile, warming me all over as it did that cold January afternoon in his office at Catholic University.

"And I miss you. But you know what I mean, Dan. You probably had the same junk in your training as we did.

'Novices should be like putty in the hands of the master builder, indifferent to whatever obedience comes to them out of the divine lottery...' "

"...and above all, they should be 'blindly obedient'—willing to plant cabbages upside down, if that's what the abbot wants."

"We can laugh at that stuff now. Yet it was the ideal put before us both."

"Ah, yes," he sighs.

In the brief silence, I remember how just last Saturday, young Sister Janet poured out a tale not that different from mine at St. Pat's so long ago, one of conflict, even contradiction, between her novitiate training and her present life as seventh-grade teacher, baseball coach, and sociology major struggling to complete her BA. Just the memory of her words raises my dander and I end up shouting at Dan, "Why should being a nun and being a teacher be so much at odds?"

"Elizabeth, Calm down! Listen to yourself. It's me, Dan, your old pal. I believe you. You don't need to convince me. Okay?"

"Yes, of course." I sigh. "I do understand." Slowly I simmer down and feel how wintry the autumn evening has turned. I struggle out of the old chair and shiver as I cross the linoleum floor in stockinged feet to close the window. For a moment, I am back at CU, in his office, with Dan wrapping my heavy cloak around my shoulders.

"I'm afraid for you, m'dear, that's all. I'm not the enemy."

Advent 1966

"You're all alone?" Maddy discovers me in the home ec lab of the academy, where more than twenty Christmases ago I enjoyed brownies with Sister Marie Gabrielle, my English teacher. Maddy's startled to see me up to my elbows in Christmas cookies. "What on earth?" she says, eyeing my gingham work apron and surrounding clutter. For years she's teased me about my distaste for, and ineptitude around, the kitchen.

"For the infirmary," I explain. "Gifts for the doctors—great guys!—they come all this way to care for the nuns in the infirmary." I'm surrounded by the various stages of production, from dry ingredients to cellophane wrappings, as Maddy approaches and wipes flour from my chin.

"No helpers?" She finds a spot to put down her large plastic bag, brimming with Christmas gifts.

My dear longtime friend is now the sister superior of eight nuns at St. Raymond's parish convent, about a half-hour drive from the motherhouse. Every Christmas, after school is out, she comes to the motherhouse infirmary to play Santa. It was her idea, years ago, at holiday time, to bring our infirmary sisters the best of the classroom goodies from her parish school. And not only decorations but also the children's gifts for their teachers (following strictly, as she does, our rule about not keeping personal gifts). Whenever she can, she adds her own cookies—which I see she's done today. "With your new job, I should think you'd have no dearth of juniors helping you," she says, removing mittens and winter cloak and putting them safely away from my splatters.

"That's what I hoped for, but everyone was booked," I reply. "It's a bad time for them—graduate record exams, senior theses and all. You remember."

"Do I!" she answers brusquely, startling me, for Madeleine is a gentle soul. "I remember when helping the superior, doing what the *community* needed, what your *superior* judged important, was far more important than what you wanted, including your college work! Last night, I let it be known I was coming in here today, that I'd be gathering up decorations and gifts right after breakfast. But nobody came to help!" She simmers for a moment; I know she's not finished. "Sister Janet even had the nerve to ask for a ride in here, then takes off as soon as we get here! Can you imagine, when we were juniors, ever acting like that? When our superior needed help?"

"Never," I say truthfully. I don't mention that Janet had stopped by here earlier and hadn't offered to help me either. Instead, she'd offered a well-known critique of the cookies-for-doctors custom, our longtime way of "paying" medical doctors for their help.

So why doesn't the archdiocese just get health insurance for all of its nun-teachers? We are their employees, after all. Then the doctors could be paid properly. Though I might have at another time, I hold back now from sharing this bit of wisdom with Maddy. She's already begun the deft routines signifying a sister's readiness for manual labor: removing inner sleeves, rolling up outer sleeves, pinning back the veil, donning the coverall gingham apron. She has a couple of hours before she has to head back to her convent, she explains. She'll help out, she's indicating, the way younger sisters should.

Madeleine was my first friend in the convent, someone to whom I was drawn on our entrance day in 1945. She was Noreen Becker, one of the prettiest girls I had ever seen, tall and slender, with gobs of strawberry-colored hair. A real Breck girl, we could have said back then. Her pale blue eyes could turn from wistful to merry in an instant, even as those lovely white eyelashes disappeared. She was kind, generous almost to a fault, our novice mistress once said, when she turned up with yet another stray cat to feed. Though we've never lived in the same convent after those first two novitiate years, I've often visited her in the various parish convents where she taught and where, very early on, she was appointed principal or superior. Now at St. Raymond's she is both: school principal and convent superior.

"I wonder, at times, if some of the old ways weren't

better," she begins, still testy. "Maybe in the good old days we did go a bit overboard on housekeeping, maybe we didn't take 'our professional lives' seriously enough. But these young nuns! They want to spend every bit of free time off in the library or out there being Miss Social Worker. That's no way to build community spirit!"

"It may be that what we've meant by 'community spirit' will be very different going forward," I venture, only to be interrupted as she turns to face me, hands on hips.

"What I know, my friend, is that you are a college professor who hasn't had to run a community of nine sisters—when the young ones vanish during the weekend! *I* am the community today. I'm it! And I don't like it—not one bit!"

Her angry words, so unusual for her, settle uncomfortably in me, and keep me from sharing my own growing concern about what some call a climate of busyness, and how some are saying it is so destructive of our community spirit, and how this may or may not be the result of "all those newfangled notions" linked with the Sister Formation Movement. Others, of course, say that the SF training enriches the life of the spirit, which is the essence of a nun's life. Either way, I think, we need to take a good look at what we understand by "community" and "community spirit." I'd love to hear what Maddy thinks about this, but I realize now is not the time when I glance over at her tidy cubicle, with her beautiful rows of uniformly browned stars, Santas, and Christmas trees. A silent rebuke to my production of ill-defined, lumpy Christmas shapes that are leaving flour all over me and the floor. No matter how gingerly I handle them, the pack breaks off Santa's back almost every time. Maddy will be shocked when she see what I've created.

A blast of the intercom brings my friend Sophie into our midst via the telephone. "Liza, goddamn it! What a horrible switchboard! I thought they'd never find you! Where in the hell are you?" As I move over to grasp the receiver, I see Maddy staring, shocked at what she's heard. More shocked, it seems, than with the display of wasted frosting and sprinkles. "Listen, Liza, Dan's got some really bad news. A Vatican guy, Davis something, has abandoned ship, shaking up Dan, big time. So call him, okay? He's completely bummed. He needs you, Liza. I can't handle this Catholic crap!" With that she slams down the phone, leaving me breathless, wondering if she meant Davis? Father Charles Davis? But that just can't be.

"*Liza?*" Maddy asks, looking completely perplexed. "Liza? Is that you? Your new name? I like it! Liza."

"I was hoping it would be you," Carla says, when I peek into her room. She's huddled in the old wicker armchair wedged into the corner of her tiny cell—a chair she rescued from the trash years ago and covered with a brightly striped Indian bedspread—dispiritedly making Christmas chains from shiny paper scraps saved by old Sister Zita. Now though, even the bright Indian colors fail to lighten my somber-looking friend, who bids me to sit on her iron bed.

"I need your help," I blurt out.

"And I need yours," she answers, setting aside her chain. We each need help with the same gut-punching news, still hot on the wires: Charles Davis—priest, theologian, ace reporter/New York Times columnist throughout the six years of Vatican II, esteemed interpreter of Church matters for a majority of English-speaking Catholics the world over—has left the Church!

"Reliable, clear-headed Father Davis. What's happened? He was a true insider all through the council's six years. Now he's left the Church?" Carla repeats to herself, as if I were not in the room. "Why?"

Why not? pops into my mind, shocking even me, yet I hold back and remind us both: "He's seen the hierarchy and its machinations up close for years. Maybe he's come to see the Church—Holy Mother the Church—as just too top-heavy to change?"

Carla is silent for a few moments, then speaks as if recalling a long time past. "Those words always bring for me the image of a tired, worn-out working mother with throngs of needy kids, all very special-needs children. Her day never ends, her tasks are never finished. She's both changing all the time and never really changing at all. Same old, same old."

"And I imagine a wise old papa, listening patiently to his kids as they tell him what's going on out in the big world, falling asleep even in the midst of their tales. Of course he already knows what's going on, what it really means, and soon enough will let us all know the 'real truth.' "

"Which reminds me of your friend Camus saying that he wants to be able to love his country and still love justice," Carla says. "Davis wants to be able to love his church and still love truth."

"Or maybe the reverse," I offer. "He wants to be able to love the truth and still love his church. What he sees now, though, is his church opting for 'authority first, truth second.' Just the reverse. He can't have both. So he's choosing truth."

"And abandoning the Church, abandoning us," adds Carla. "What an odd thing, to feel abandoned by someone I've never met, never seen or heard. Know what I mean? You feel that way?"

"Yes and no. Though I haven't met him face to face, I have *heard* him—and so have you—in the columns we read at the library every week. And now he's turning away, taking another path. Still, *abandonment* is the right word—a feeling of being out there, all alone...a very strange feeling." We sit silently, as the thought sinks in, bringing me to the verge of tears.

"So why haven't you called him yet?" Carla asks. I'm sitting with her in her studio again, helping with the paper chains. She knows I have phone access because of my new job with the junior sisters, so why haven't I called Dan? She gives me her furrowed-brow look. Without hearing too many details, Carla has discovered how close we are and how angry he is. "Even before this Davis thing was announced?" she asks.

"Oh, yes. He is terribly angry about a lot, but it's this current pope's delay on contraception. It's central." I pause, plunk down the stapler to let my hands rest. "Oh Carla—he and I are so different! It's beginning to matter—a lot."

"Like?"

"Like how we feel about the Church. He takes the Church much more seriously than I do. Yet he's angry with it all the time, cynical about the possibility of change. He has none of the hope and excitement we have." I struggle with not quite right words for how I feel. "I'm not nearly as connected to the Church as he is, Sister. I'm more...." I can't finish.

"Is that why you haven't called him about this Davis thing? Just too uncomfortable?"

"Exactly!" I say. "The Church doesn't figure in my life the way it does in his. It's not the one fact that explains everything else in my life."

"Well, you aren't a priest."

"No, thank God! And, until now, that's how I've seen our difference: He's a priest, I'm not; he's on the firing line, has to speak for the Church, especially in the confessional, something I've never had to do. He believes that, as a priest, he's linked up with the truth. God reveals the truth in Christ, Christ entrusts it to the Church, and the Church authorizes him to be its minister. So even when he's angry with the Church, he still believes the Church is, or should be, a conduit of truth. The authentic link with the right answers."

"No wonder he's so worried about the contraception thing," Carla says. "Maybe it's that for Davis as well?"

"Could be. Both of them needing the pope to be the pope of right answers."

"Sounds to me like Dan is more emotionally tied to the Church than you. And to his order?"

"Oh, he's finished with the monks—he's been exclaustrated since Easter. The other day, he said something about his choice of the monastery as 'a wrong turn' on his road toward God."

"Is that the way you feel?"

"Not at all," I answer. "I've told him going into the convent was the best choice I ever made. He worries, though, that the Church won't allow nuns to change in the way we all know we need to change."

"He's got a point." Carla stops stapling, leans back, and stretches her arms up toward the ceiling, and then brings them down to look directly at me. "Until recently I felt that way, Sister. But as I travel around, I pick up resistance, even among some sisters, and some clergy—certainly some hierarchy, and quite surprisingly, a number of lay groups—to the changes we're planning. It's given me pause."

"Dan thinks Rome will only approve superficial changes, that orders of nuns will slide back, or be forced back, to where they were before the council. You don't feel this way, do you?"

After drawing a deep breath, she answers. "I worry for the Church if things don't change." She stands up stiffly and stretches. I begin gathering up the heap of glittering chain around us on the floor. Together, we measure it, by looping it back and forth against the far wall. "This chain makes me think about what people will and won't accept in the way of 'art' or 'the new.' And how much we should or shouldn't listen to them."

She recalls a time almost twenty years ago, when, as a junior sister, I was part of a decorating crew at Christmas. We had persuaded Carla to let us display her *Mater* statue, that wonderful, ever-changing mosaic monster she had just begun when she was mentoring me. *Mater* had come to embrace poor women from all over the world and was widely acclaimed by many who've come to see her artwork at the motherhouse. Despite that, nobody was surprised when it wasn't appreciated by our own—particularly our older nuns. Though we were all shocked when Reverend Mother Pauline was heard directing someone to "Get that wretched-looking woman out of here!" The tale is usually told at the expense of Mother Pauline for not appreciating modern art, for being oblivious to Carla's popularity as an artist. These many years later, though, Carla tells me how the episode taught her about the need to listen to those who disagree with her, and about the importance of tradition, even the tradition of Christmas chains.

"So?" I ask.

"So, Merry Christmas!" she says, tossing up a piece of sparkly chain. She moves to the window. "We need Decembers," she says, "these dark days before the light." For a few seconds, we both stand, gazing out into the night, until the bell for Vespers.

"Yes."

Chapter 12

1967

Mid-October 1967

Our order's experiments—which I presume will become reforms—have affected the parents of our students far more dramatically than any of us could have anticipated. Nowhere is this more true than at St. Raymond's parish, where Monsignor Sweeney is pastor and Sister Madeleine, the superior and principal.

A tragic series of events in a slum area of St. Louis could well have gone unnoticed by the affluent parishioners of St. Raymond's if their Sister Janet hadn't popped onto TV screens between segments of a football game one lazy Sunday afternoon. She was part of a protest outside the dilapidated Olympia Village housing project in downtown St. Louis. During the early hours of that fall morning, two men were wounded and a fire was set. In the aftermath, local TV captured the confusion of police cars, fire trucks, and angry tenants protesting their landlord's neglect. There amid all the turmoil was Sister Janet and other SSA—Students for Social Action—tutors shouting into the cameras: "RATS OUT NOW! RATS OUT NOW!" And, yes, she says proudly to TV viewers, she is a nun and teaches at St. Raymond's parish. By evening, complaints had reached both the rectory and the convent of quiet and peaceful St. Raymond's, a largely affluent suburban parish. The news was quickly relayed to the motherhouse. And to me.

"What could I do? I was *there* when it happened!" Janet blurts out. She's come by my university office on her way to an evening class. "You wouldn't want me to keep my mouth shut, would you?" I'm tempted to repeat what I've had to say before: that she needs to learn when to hold her tongue. That a bit of patience won't turn her into the "nunny nun" she so scorns. Instead, I tell her to close the door, take a seat, and tell me the facts.

She had boarded the bus heading downtown yesterday with no plans other than how to use most effectively the contents of her book bag. "Sister Angela lent me some of her primary pencils. I'm helping teach a father of two kids to read and write. His name's Joey. And Sister Ignatia gave me flash cards." She drops her jacket on the floor, folding herself cross-legged into the large armchair opposite my desk.

How different, I think, from the way I appeared at the door of Augusta's office in these same halls twenty years ago. Twenty-four-year-old Janet is experimenting with one of our alternatives to the traditional habit. She's chosen to wear street clothes, the most secular option of the experiments in dress that are open to us. The goal is to dress in a way that is "at once simple and modest, yet poor and becoming."

That's exactly how Janet looks now, in a denim jumper and woolly turtleneck sweater. Her abundant curly hair has grown out without proper styling, giving her a slightly wild look. Even so, she's attractive in that unselfconsciously intense way of so many of my other, secular, students. She is confident (some would say cocky) about the nobility of her cause. And about what a nun's life should mean.

"Joey, and the rest of them down there, they know real poverty and real humiliation," she says indignantly. "Unlike us. We vow poverty, but we live comfortable middle-class lives."

I've gotten used to waiting for Janet to simmer down, so I sit back and listen. I suppose she feels her friends are seeing for the first time the social ills of our city. Even so, I'm proud of her—and proud that our order has attracted someone as generous, impetuous, and bright as she. Not many young women like Janet are entering religious orders these days. Indeed, it's far more common to see her cohorts across the land attacking institutions of every kind. She continues to pour out the details of her work at Olympia Village.

Finally I interrupt. "Those readers and flash cards, were they in your bag? The bag Monsignor was told you swung at a policeman!?"

"That's a lot of bull! I didn't swing at anybody. I was just holding it up in front of me, to shield me from those police clubs. It makes me so mad, the way people twist and exaggerate! Most of all, Monsignor Sweeney."

She's calming down now, occupied with picking at the little balls of wool on her dark knee socks. The rust shades of her sweater set off lovely highlights in her wild auburn hair, once hidden by our elaborate headgear. Gone with the headgear are hours of scrubbing, starching, and ironing, then pleating, folding, and pinning. Hours that now can be spent down at Olympia Village, I think, recalling our admonition to make "our daily schedule reflect the priorities of our life."

Finally, Janet says, "It's probably unrealistic to imagine that people outside the order—like Monsignor or the parents of our kids—will be happy about our changes. But to be so angry? So unwilling to listen? I don't understand. It's our life, after all—not theirs!" She looks up through glasses thick as coke bottles with an intensity that hurts.

Apparently St. Raymond's parishioners haven't had the changes from our summer's chapter properly explained to them. We had asked pastors to use materials we sent to show how our reforms (or "experiments") fit in with the worldwide renewal in the Church. We wanted parents of the children we teach to know ahead of time about the changes that would affect them and their children. Monsignor Sweeney, however, did not see fit to share our news with his flock.

Because I was one of the writers among the forty elected delegates at last summer's chapter, I was asked to attend a parents meeting in the school hall of St. Raymond's to explain the rationale behind our changes, Mother Augusta was certain I could allay any concerns.

⁂

October 30, 1967

My challenge tonight is to convince the parents that changes in our convent life mean a higher quality of teaching for their children. I will emphasize the positives—smaller classes, fully credentialed teachers (eventually), full-time principals, more flexible curricula—before springing the negative: The sister faculty of eight will have to be reduced to six by the spring term. That means hiring two lay teachers at a salary considerably more than the stipend the pastor now pays the motherhouse for each sister.

Sister Janet is one of the three junior sisters from St. Raymond's who's come to fetch me. She knows why so many parents are upset. "They're totally unprepared for any change because Sweeney hasn't given us any support. None at all!" She drives with her window rolled down, enjoying the blast of autumn air through her bushy hair, unaware that the two of us in the backseat must struggle to keep veils on our heads.

"I don't think Monsignor Sweeney himself understands what's going on," adds Sister Angela, in the front seat. "It's for him as much as the parents that you're coming." She fiddles with a wayward bang slipping out from under the short veil of her "modified habit"—another option available in this time of experimentation. "He probably hasn't had time to read our decrees."

"You mean he hasn't *taken* the time," Janet snaps.

"Whatever. I just know he was shocked to see some of us without our regular habits."

"Why must everyone focus on what we wear!" I say. "I can only hope this crowd can get past the issue of clothes and hear what we're doing to upgrade teaching. That's the issue: to improve the education of *their* children!"

Even as I burst with righteous indignation about the fuss over our clothing, I must admit that the contrasts in this car are startling. Like me, Sister Jeanne Marie is still garbed in the traditional habit. The two in the front seat, however, looked a good deal more professional and competent before they chose to participate in our experiment with clothing. Janet, in her Goodwill outfit, looks downright scruffy this evening. And Angela resembles nothing so much as a dumpy prison matron, instead of the truly committed seventh-grade teacher she is.

I worry about Sister Angela, who like Janet and Jeanne Marie, is a third-year junior, set to make final vows next summer. Everyone loves sweet, good-natured Angela, including the kids in her class. Yet she can't organize herself or her class. The result is four moves in her first two years. When last I checked, this fifth switch, to St. Raymond's, seems to be working—though barely. Is her "modified habit" helping or hindering her situation? Or does it matter? Do her second-graders notice, as I do, that their dimple-cheeked, dark-eyed friend no longer looks so angelic in shortened skirts? For Sister Angela is now simply another plumpish young woman whose bandana veil can never quite hide her squat neck.

Statuesque Sister Jeanne Marie, on the other hand, has the composure of a veteran teacher. She looks exactly like the ethereal, slightly removed nun from Central Casting. "Sister Superior's done her best, with letters to the parents, talks at the Mothers Club," she says. "But Sister Janet, on TV! With those people, and all that shouting. It was just too much." She turns to look out the window and I glimpse her set jaw and cool air of detachment. With an equally cool eye, Janet also watches, in her rearview mirror.

⋆

"Since when do nuns get to choose what they will or won't do?" The interrupting question comes at me from a spot about halfway back in the auditorium by the side aisle. So I explain how, come February, two of their faculty will be assigned elsewhere: Sister Charlotte will become the director of the Diocesan Retreat House, and Sister Mary Paul will work with Catholic Social Services. I want to show how these departures from the faculty of St. Raymond's are linked with the general upgrading of our order's work. What I don't tell them is that Sister Mary Paul is a wreck. At forty-four, after twenty-five years of elementary teaching in a half dozen parishes, she has only this past summer managed to get her BA.

Explaining Sister Charlotte's switch from classroom to retreat work is easier. She is more feared than liked around St. Raymond's. Her rigidity makes her ill-suited for the classroom and plagues her with psychosomatic problems that Augusta and Madeleine both hope will disappear once she pursues a different line of work. I don't divulge the common opinion of those who have taught with her that Charlotte should never have entered a classroom, or that the order has too often tolerated a "good nun but lousy teacher." Instead, I say that this finely tuned, deeply spiritual woman is inaugurating a new ministry for our community by moving into retreat work. It will benefit everyone in the archdiocese, including the parishioners of St. Raymond's.

Both these moves, as well as Sister Janet's volunteer work in the inner city, I emphasize, are in direct response to the pope's directive to nuns the world over to explore new ways to share our Christian life with the modern world. With norms from Rome about what can and what cannot be changed, we have at last begun a few carefully planned changes in the way we live our lives.

I'm still explaining these moves when a distinguished older man toward the front signals that he wishes to speak.

I acknowledge him but indicate that I'll be finished in a moment. This irks him, apparently, for he rises abruptly to interrupt me.

"Allow me, Sister. *Please.*" He pauses to button his jacket and adjust his tie to fall inside the jacket. "Perhaps I can focus things a bit for you." The room is hushed as he steps sideways to the end of his row and stands in the aisle against the wall. "I feel sure I speak for most people here tonight when I say we have no argument with your desire to renew your *spiritual* lives. Far from it." He pauses to look over the group, and then fastens his eyes on me. He's at home with this group, and they seem comfortable with his authority. "Our concern is with something else, Sister. I refer to the issue of individual conscience. We heard your young sister in that outrageous display Sunday before last on television say that she was following her conscience."

I wonder if Janet has discovered, as I have, that Olympia Village is managed by the realty firm owned by one of Monsignor Sweeney's golfing buddies. And has the pastor discovered that Janet and her friends are the ones responsible for a quote in the *Post Dispatch* about the "morally indefensible" position of any property owner who can tolerate "Olympia's scandalous conditions"?

"What alarms us, Sister," he continues, "is that our youngsters have started using this same language—about 'following conscience'—to justify all manner of things. In a way that doesn't sound one bit Catholic to many of us." He pauses dramatically, yet I know better than to reply. "I understand, Sister, that you teach at the university, so I trust you know the basic Church history most of us learned long ago: about Luther, the Reformation, the Modernist heresy. About how individual conscience can go awry. About the sin of pride that disregards the authority of the Church or dismisses tradition. So, I'm confident you must know that other lesson from this sad history: Truth can only come from Holy

Mother the Church."

As I stand listening to this graceful oratory, I'm aware of stretching myself up to my full five-eight. All eyes are turned on him, including those of my sisters in the front row. All but Janet's. She sits bolt upright, arms folded over her chest, staring straight ahead, while old Sister Ignatia dozes.

"What concerns us, Sister," he goes on, "is that nuns with their vow of obedience should be exemplars for the rest of us. Models of Christian humility. A true Catholic puts the teaching authority of the Church first, before the whims of private conscience. With all due respect, Sister, I want to remind you that without authority everything falls apart. We stop being Catholics."

"Rest assured, Mr.—?"

"*Doctor* Haggerty."

"Rest assured, Doctor Haggerty, we agree completely with you about the importance of history and tradition for any discussion of conscience." My voice slows to indicate a confidence and competence I wish I felt. "However, let us for the moment start further back, with the Biblical tradition, of both Old and New Testaments." As I speak, my admonisher moves back to his seat, shaking his head, and shrugging his shoulders. Communication with me is hopeless, his gestures say as I continue. "Jesus teaches, as do *all* Biblical religions, that one must follow one's conscience. Informed conscience, to be sure. Which certainly is not the same as the 'mere whim' you speak of." I'm sounding teacherish, but I don't care.

"Our Catholic tradition helps tremendously in forming conscience—especially the new teachings of Vatican II and the directives of Popes John and Paul. This is exactly how we came to the decisions contained in our Decrees of Renewal. How Sisters Charlotte and Mary Paul—in consultation with our superiors—came to their decisions. How Sister Janet came to hers. Of this I want to assure you, *Doctor* Haggerty."

He waves me off and shakes his head to indicate he does not wish to be addressed any longer. So I shift my attention to the group as a whole. "Let me assure you—nothing in the decrees of our general chapter translates the following of one's conscience to mean 'I can do whatever I feel like.' Or 'Anything goes.' That is *not* the understanding of conscience among the Sisters of Mary of Missouri. Nor is it what we teach your children!"

In a momentary hush, I'm drawn to the questioning face of an unsmiling but intelligent-looking woman who asks about changes she's noted in the school over the past year: modular class divisions, sociometric grouping, ungraded work, "Protestant hymns" and a "different catechism." "Are any of these approved by the Church? Or are these just more of the sisters going modern?"

I turn the answering over to Sister Madeleine, who doesn't let on that she's felt the woman's sting. She's direct and gracious, explaining that none of these innovations is specifically associated with our order's reforms, yet each is fueled by the spirit of Vatican II. For the most part, she says proudly, they have succeeded handsomely. Then, she calls on one after another of her sisters to explain these various classroom experiments.

Good for Madeleine. Her very presentation illustrates two of the practices our reforms want to encourage: delegating authority and fostering individual responsibility. Eventually, even old Sister Ignatia speaks up—in the rough manner many knew from being her pupils years earlier—to explain that while she supports the need for change, and is wholeheartedly behind "these young ones" and the order's reforms as a whole, she has personally resisted any of the newfangled classroom ideas mentioned. "Too late to teach this old dog new tricks," she chortles. Our audience applauds.

"If stewardesses and nurses wear uniforms, why shouldn't nuns?" asks a woman with a clump of jangling bracelets. "If there's no more authority, why even *have* nuns? You might just as well be regular people." My mind flashes back to my talks with Dan about how much I'd like to be just a "regular person." But what I say to my questioner is that we must not confuse altering a few details of convent discipline with abandoning a belief in God's authority.

She replies with anger, "But that's the whole point of a Catholic school, Sister, instilling obedience to the God-given authorities of our Church. That's not just a detail! If the nuns can't discipline themselves, how can you expect the rest of us to obey the rules!"

So that's it. No wonder this focus on our clothes—we're changing the rules! Which must be what religion's all about for her. She's kept her rules, however grudgingly, it appears. So she resents that we are allowed to change ours.

Others take up the issue of our dress in a series of tedious questions that liken us repeatedly to military and airline personnel, and I smile to myself. How few of us could qualify for these professions either by disposition, age, or weight. Though none of my questioners is as colorful as the bracelet lady, their words are laced with similar hostility. I am growing increasingly annoyed and feel my enthusiasm for attempting to communicate with them draining away.

Their message is now clear. They want us to stay as they have always perceived nuns to be: uniform, reliable, and completely at their service! They haven't a clue about our need as mature women to test the usefulness of the various disciplines that make up our lives—let alone to explore a new, more adult role for sisters that the Vatican council has inspired. "Perhaps we need to set this clothes thing in perspective," I say, my cool voice belying the heat rising in me. "The women who started most orders of nuns, including our group, dressed in the garb of their time. They certainly did not start out as distinctively or elaborately dressed as we are today. Our order began when the young widow Anne Conway

O'Neil left her native Ireland to work among the poor in the slums of Liverpool. Nuns of her day were not allowed to go there. So Anne and her followers decided to dress simply, like the people they served, so they could work inconspicuously. But now, more than a hundred years later, our dress is *conspicuous*."

A bustling in one of the front rows directly below me distracts me; I pause momentarily. A broad-faced older woman is being urged to rise by the elegantly dressed couple on either side of her. Clutching a large handbag tight below her bosom, she seems reluctant to participate, so I extend my hand. "Please," I say. I see beneath her coat the light green of a domestic's uniform. Their housekeeper, I imagine: this stocky woman with an accent, maybe Polish or Lithuanian.

"Nuns are special," she says. "Your habit—special. It protects you, because you're God's bride." There's a hush in the hall as this stolid woman continues her measured statements. "Let me tell you this, Sister. A lot of us don't get to Mass very often, the way you can—right in your own house! We're too tired to pray very good. But you don't have no kids, no husbands, no jobs. You're lucky." A rumble of low-toned laughter runs through the crowd. "You've got that beautiful convent, that beautiful chapel. So why leave it and go down to that bad part of town—so you can get on TV?"

Every eye is on her. Faces light up with broad smiles of approval. The elegantly dressed couple beams, like parents of a child successfully launched into her first recital. The wife whispers something to her; and she continues with a new confidence in her voice. "In the old country, when I was a little girl, I worked in a convent laundry. The nuns go off to chapel five, six times a day. It was their work, they said. Nice kind of work, I said to myself." This brings a quick laugh from the crowd. They like her. They're on her side. "You should thank God every day for your nice convent. Forget about getting on the TV!"

The room erupts with applause, and she sits down between the proud couple. The husband shakes her hand then pats her on the back while his wife pulls her over in an awkward hug. Her simple eloquence has set off a flurry of friendly chatter throughout the room, with many of those near her reaching over to congratulate her or the couple with her.

How to meet this well-intentioned admonition? Explain that even at our inception we weren't like the cloistered nuns who ran the laundry in her old country? Or that the smooth running of our parish schools leaves little time for retreating to chapel during the day? Or that the nuns in her native country could never have known our peculiarly American push for self-determination?

My quandary is settled by a commotion at the door nearest the stage, where the imposing figure of Monsignor Sweeney materializes. He's followed by a layman, also of substantial bearing. They are chuckling as they enter the school hall.

At the outset, the audience was told by the young assistant, Father Gerken, that the pastor had been called away by an emergency, but that he would join us soon. So here he is, mounting the stage, shaking my hand, and insisting with great charm in a brogue mixed with whiskey, "Go right on now, Sister dear. Oh, please now. I don't want to be interruptin'!"

I've never met Monsignor, although I've heard much about his financial acumen in both the diocese and his own "parish plant." For some reason, I'm surprised to see—for all his abundant white hair—how athletic and youthful he seems. I can just imagine an earlier version of his rugged face smiling down from the mantelpieces in his native Donegal. "My son, the monsignor in America," or "My nephew, the Yank: looks like a fil-lim star, doesn't he now?" What they might call a "fine-looking lad" I see as one of those square-jawed, curly-headed Irishmen cast as a Boston fireman or a New York cop in the films of the 1940s. An Irish import much better known to Catholics across America than the poetry of Yeats or the novels of Joyce.

While the monsignor fusses about finding a chair off to one side, so as not to interrupt me, Doctor Haggerty stands up and, once again, the crowd quiets. "Monsignor, I think we probably should not proceed as we have been. Your time is precious. So may I suggest you repeat the gist of your sermon yesterday for the good sister here, who, I trust, will relay it to the proper authority at her motherhouse. We've not been too successful, I'm sorry to say, getting your message across to her." An interesting maneuver. Was it rehearsed earlier?

Monsignor gushes with praise for our sisters: "One of the truly outstanding groups of sisters in America, which I'm proud to say had its roots in Ireland." With care, he reviews our decades-long relationship with St. Raymond's. How it was one of the first parishes "out in the county" to have our sisters. How he and old Sister Bridget, God rest her soul, were pioneers together. And though, God bless them, nuns are far less expensive than lay teachers, it's still a struggle for his always growing parish to provide for the good sisters. Yet it's a sacrifice they're only too happy to make. He's proud to report that with the check he sends the motherhouse each month, he's able, most times, God willing, to add "a little something extra." And more: He encourages parishioners as well to give the nuns a break at the gas station, grocery store, or pharmacy. Most of all, he reminds us, Doctor Haggerty himself—God bless him—and a number of other physicians in the parish, provide unpaid services to the sisters in the motherhouse infirmary. All of which makes St. Raymond's a great supporter of the Sisters of Mary—and, I say to myself, has allowed St. Raymond's to develop that proprietary mentality that allows you to imagine you can control "your nuns," the way you have resisted hiring lay teachers long after other, poorer, parishes have!

He continues, emphasizing the parish's loyalty to the sisters, listing the various motherhouse ventures from the last twenty years that he has supported: the drive for the infirmary wing, the novitiate wing, our bazaar and raffle every year, and on and on. "This, however, is only the financial side of things, Sister. We've also been sending girls to your academy over the years—with some even joining the order. In a word, Sister, I think you'll find us very well represented among your friends. In fact, I see a number of St. Mary's girls here tonight. In all honesty, Sister, I wonder if some of your sisters could be too caught up with this council business."

He is indeed elegant—tall, handsome, with the relaxed face of the outdoorsman. Yet I find the gold cuff links, the highly polished gentleman's boots, and the finely tailored black suit odd trappings for this boyishly open-faced Irishman.

He speaks solemnly now. "Rejecting this world must be at the heart of every Catholic's life, clergy and laity, but most of all in *your lives*, dear Sisters. We were reminded in yesterday's Mass, on the Feast of Christ the King, that 'My Kingdom is not of this world.' a message no Church council can obscure. Our Savior wants us to keep our minds and hearts fixed on heavenly realities."

He pauses and looks directly down at the sisters sitting before him. "His message is for all Christians, but for you especially, Sisters. It is your vocation. More important than your teaching or any of your good works, which, after all, will pass away in time.

"The council and the news it generates distract us from these basics. The secular press, as well as the liberal Catholic press, had a field day. They took a purely natural, even political, view of the goings-on in Rome. In some this fostered the unsettling mentality of 'reform,' some might say *revolution!*"

He lets the dangerous word hang in the air while he sips water from the crystal glass next to the lectern. Then, forcefully, but deliberately, he continues: "This is *not* the way God works. The Spirit brings peace and humility—not discord and unrest."

Another protracted pause. Then, he relaxes into his jolly manner and thickened brogue. "You know now, this council over in Rome is nothin' to get yourselves all riled up about. Not a'tall!" His handsome smile turns impish. "You sisters, being women, may be a wee bit too literal. Maybe you have complicated things too much. This council is no great song and dance. Nothing to threaten the good things we've got here at St. Raymond's. I'm sure the Reverend Mother will understand, when you tell her we want things to stay *just as they are* here at St. Raymond's." Another sip from the sparkling crystal. "And now, my good sisters, it's time to bring this meeting to a close. So good night now, and God bless."

He thanks the parents for coming, assuring them that "the good sisters" are grateful for their input. I feel riveted to my chair as everyone stands, clapping approval. Monsignor turns to shake my hand, bending toward me. I manage to rise slowly, and from habits long ingrained, smile and say, "Thank you, Father!" Then, with a flourish he turns and leaves the stage.

I'm embarrassed, then ashamed, then furious for letting the thank-you slip so automatically from my mouth. But when I realize I've also used the ordinary "Father" instead of the honorific "Monsignor," I feel a slight smile of vengeance rising. Still, I have to concentrate on getting down the stairs without stumbling, feeling slightly dislocated from my wooden body. Certainly, I have none of that peace or humility he urged upon us.

Once the monsignor is off the stage, engulfed in conversation with his flock, the young assistant Father Gerken crosses over to Sister Madeleine and her group. As I join them, the young priest with the ashen face is doing his best to convince Madeleine that the group in the hall tonight does *not* represent the entire parish, that most here tonight no longer have children in the school, that he understands and supports what we're up to, as do many of his cohorts among the younger clergy. But, alas, none of them is free to speak publicly in support of the sisters. "You're lucky to have a community behind you, Sister," he says shaking my hand. "I envy you." His breath is foul. I hope his unhappiness has not made him ill. "I hope you pray for the rest of us. Just think of guys like me, in this wasteland. Count your blessings, Sisters." The tears I have been tasting are suddenly for him.

Madeleine takes his hand, comforting the one who came to encourage her. "Count on my prayers," he says to her. "You're taking flak because you're at the head of the line. But we're right there behind you, trailing but following. Courage, Sisters!"

I could kiss the guy. Then the parishioners really would have something to talk about!

The crowd empties by every door except the one we're standing near. I feel keenly the awkwardness of knowing we're being shunned. Eventually the ten of us file out of the auditorium and, more from sadness than piety, enclose ourselves in the ancient monastic ritual of the Grand Silence as we process in single file across the schoolyard to the convent.

Maddy and I kneel side by side in the rear of the small dark chapel at St. Raymond's convent, a space barely large enough for its ten prie-dieux and tiny altar. My evening prayer is being overtaken by images from the parish meeting tonight. Finally, I give in to the distraction, and closing my prayer book, gaze up at the large crucifix over the altar. None of the images is as distressing as how I remember myself at the meeting, standing stiff and self-righteous, a real Miss Know-It-All. Even that obnoxious Haggerty man, so self-importantly straightening his tie, is not as depressing. Nor the pink-cheeked monsignor with his glittering cuff links and whiffs of alcohol. Is there something about me that made the whole thing go bad? After other meetings like this in other parish halls filled with parents eager to hear about what's going on in their convents, I've walked away feeling proud about my small part in the order's process of renewing itself. But not tonight.

"Thanks for your help tonight, Sister," Maddy whispers.

"Some help!" I whisper back, grimacing.

As I continue to gaze in the dark upon the figure on the cross, a painful truth emerges: I have so identified with our order's renewal efforts that I cannot bear to see them—to see myself—not taken seriously. I should be thanking God for this occasion to imitate Jesus in His humiliation. But I cannot, any more than I can get the image of that monsignor out of my head.

Again, Madeleine leans toward me. "I've got something we could celebrate with. Okay?"

I'm startled. It seems hardly an occasion to celebrate. Especially not now—after Grand Silence—nor here, at St. Raymond's, where Madeleine's strict observance of the Holy Rule is well known. She's never before suggested visiting after the Grand Silence bell.

"You're the boss," I say, happy to move away from images of Monsignor Sweeney and his flock.

We were the youngest two in our novitiate class, with birthdays the same month. Now we are within six months of turning forty, caught up in complications we could never have imagined in those simple, well-ordered days of our novitiate. Back then, I'd complicate things that she, just by listening, could simplify. She once teased that I could turn a sneeze into a three-act play! Our habit of falling into deep conversation after long gaps away from each other grows from our first years teaching. Then we'd lunch together at the motherhouse on Saturdays after our college classes, swapping books, ideas, insights—anything to help us better understand our still-new way of life. Exactly what did it mean to "renounce the secular" when in both our studies and our teaching we were so thoroughly immersed in secular concerns? Thus we managed, in those growing-up years, to steep ourselves in what we later discovered was called "radical Catholic critique."

My liberation from traditional pious literature had already begun with Augusta's early gift of that volume by Etienne Gilson. Madeleine's largesse continued throughout my college years and, with Madeleine, I went on to explore even more "modern" and "foreign" Catholic writers, from Francois Mauriac and Gabriel Marcel to Graham Greene and Evelyn Waugh. (We managed to stretch the meaning of "Catholic" to include Anglo-Catholics T.S. Eliot and C.S. Lewis.) What we took from these writers was not so much their rejection of clericalism, though there was plenty of that. Rather, it was their radical Christian vision that captured our imaginations and raised our sights above the humdrum routines of the middle-class Catholic culture of our families. We felt we were at what Greene called "the heart of the matter" of Christianity, devoid of the sentimental piety found in most things written for nuns.

Not long after final vows in 1950, Madeleine and I found ourselves scheduled for the same week of vacation at old Doc Moore's compound of cabins up in the mountains. One afternoon, as we walked up the path to Lookout Point, we began to frame questions that would occupy us for months. What would an American version of these radical authors look like? An urban, Midwest version? An American-nun version? When we reached the lookout, we stopped to gaze over the lake and low mountain range to its west, and swapped fantasies about our still new nun-life.

Often, I told her, when I sat in the chapel for meditation, instead of closing my eyes to "dwell within," as we had been taught, I would instead undertake to mentally "clean up the chapel." One by one, I'd remove the superfluous adornments—the Infant of Prague with his jewels and kingly garments first, then the stations of the cross, then the statues of the saints, even the longhaired Sacred Heart of Jesus and sad-eyed old St. Joseph. The flowers and flickering votive candles, the heavily embroidered altar cloths all vanished. In my fantasy, only a single length of linen covered the altar, and on it stood a simple wood tabernacle. There was no jeweled missal stand. No painted clouds behind the altar—only whitewashed walls, maybe a cross, just not a crucifix.

Madeleine understood perfectly, for she had similar fantasies about the sound filling our chapel. In her cleanup, the soupy, sentimental hymns of our parochial upbringing were replaced by the purity of Gregorian plainchant. Also, she admitted somewhat shamefacedly, for some time she had avoided dipping her hand in the holy water font—a standard practice of Catholics coming and going from church. "Pure superstition," she scoffed. "And very unhygienic!"

On the last day of that vacation, she came dashing out to the volleyball game set up behind the cabins. She could hardly wait for it to finish so she could show me what she'd discovered browsing through Doctor Moore's library in the main house. There, in an art book on classic American architecture, she'd found "my chapel." It was white with a single tall spire and could be found in every New England town. But it was Protestant! "We're just a couple of Protestant nuns," we concluded that day—without a glimmer of just how "protesting" we would become.

It's hard to say exactly when or how Madeleine and I began to think differently about what it meant to "reject the world," but I've always connected it with some *Jubilee* magazine photographs she discovered. We pored over the breathtakingly beautiful pictures of monasteries perched on mountain peaks, filled with the austere art of Byzantine Christianity. Around these pictures we started the last shared fantasy of our youth. We asked ourselves, what if, by some catastrophe, one of those always expected and feared Missouri tornadoes wiped out all our order's convents. What then? Join another teaching order similar to ours? (Absolutely not.) Go back to our families? (Never.) Find a monastery? (This we'd do!) But which monastery?

That became the question for our ongoing fantasy. Maddy unequivocally favored Thomas Merton's austere and silent Trappists, saying if there were no American female branch, she'd start one. I settled on the regular Benedictines. They were teachers as well as monastics, with a rhythm of *ora et labora* that powerfully drew me. And just up the river in Nauvoo, Illinois, was a Benedictine monastery of nuns. That's where I'd go.

"If it's not wiped out," she quipped.

We were not yet twenty-five then. Madeleine was already an able administrator of a parochial grade school, and I was well into what I thought would be my life's work teaching math at St. Mary's Academy. Every visit to her convent revealed a cell more spare than the time before, whereas mine grew progressively more cluttered as I became, in her words, more "political." Eventually my fascination with the monastic developed into an interest in the social Gospel, leading me to nibble at the edges of social and political philosophy.

That was how I came to attend a lecture by Dorothy Day, the great lady of the Catholic Socialist Movement. I was so moved by her that I sought out copies of her *Catholic Worker* paper and whatever else of hers I could find. This "radical" news soon led me to tales of the priest-workers in France who worked anonymously in factories and dockyards. The lives of these new heroes of mine preached a Christianity that sought to change the world, not flee from it. They were on another planet from my family's and the order's middle-class Catholicism, and they were definitely not monastic. Yet their message had the ring of truth that nothing in my Catholic life till then could approach.

This was heady stuff for me. With talk of the "cell technique" and "critiquing the established order of things," I knew I was exploring, however furtively, the fringes of Marxist thought. It was this flirting with socialism that most of all disturbed Madeleine. So at that point I began to censor my thoughts around her. Of course, I wanted to share with her what I was reading, especially from the Jewish/Catholic dialogue among the academy faculty that had been sparked by the publication of Anne Frank's diary. But I held back, sensing her discomfort around my enthusiasm she considered "political." Now, however, these many years later, with that fiasco tonight in the parish hall, there is no escaping "the political." For that's what our renewal—and the parishioners' reaction tonight—are all about.

Tonight, she presents an odd sight at my guest room door—dressed for bed with the night headdress coif, robe and slippers, but carrying the oversized black briefcase that principals as well as lawyers take to work. After setting it on the desk, she extracts a lumpy bundle wrapped in a linen tea towel sprinkled with shamrocks. " 'Tis Waterford, no less," she says, unwrapping the towel gingerly to reveal a delicate pair of small sherry glasses. "Nothin' but the best for my sisters!" She's got Monsignor's brogue down pat. A musician's ear makes her a good mimic. Out comes a bottle of amber-colored sherry with a caped black figure on its label; then an oblong tin box of English biscuits; and small linen napkins embroidered with tiny green harps. "He's really a very thoughtful guy," she says, slumping down into one of the rounded chairs. "Especially when he's stuck in Shannon airport. All of this—even the biscuits—he gets at their airport shops on his yearly trip home to see his mother. He's very generous, Sister."

"But not generous enough to find time for our chapter decisions?"

"Oh, he's read them, I'm sure. That's an act—what you saw tonight—how he plays uninformed."

Madeleine still has that wonderful bathrobe she brought to the novitiate. We were supposed to have dark blue or black, but the war was on when we were assembling our convent "trousseaux." So her mother cut up a lovely wool blanket from her hope chest and Madeleine was allowed to keep the robe made from it. These twenty-plus years later, its creamy off-white has darkened into a light beige, just as her red hair, or at least what I can glimpse of it from the wisps not quite captured by her night coif, has deepened into auburn. But her skin is still unwrinkled, still milky white. Only her pale eyes give hint of the toll taken by two uninterrupted decades of grade-school teaching and principaling—eyes lately more often weary than merry or wistful.

"So. Here's to dear Annie from Armagh!" she says raising her glass to meet mine. "I liked the way you spoke of her tonight." She hunches over, elbows on her knees, clutching her glass in both hands. Slowly she twirls the glass, letting the wine come just to the edge but never letting it spill over. "She probably had crystal like this before she chucked it all." It's her wistful look once again. But then straightening up, she speaks with authority, "She'd be proud of you tonight."

"I hope so." I feel anything but proud of myself.

"I'm afraid it was a waste of your time, though." Her eyes tell me she's concerned for me the way she was for Father Gerken. Typical Madeleine. Everyone else comes first.

"Madeleine," I say, deciding not to beat around the bush, "How do you feel about tonight?"

She bristles. "Ah, feelings! The new way to examine your

conscience! Please, don't you start that wretched sensitivity stuff."

The craze has apparently touched her convent. But I do want to know how she feels. Increasingly, as my years in Washington, DC dragged on, I heard less and less about her feelings. Although it's almost a year since our cookie-making afternoon at the motherhouse, her prickly attitude then still concerns me. Does she think me out of touch with sisters who work in parish schools? She's silent for a spell while I concentrate on the tin of English biscuits, finally picking one to dunk in my sherry. "What a wicked, wonderful idea!" she says. "You really did learn something practical in graduate school after all!"

"This I learned from my Irish grandpa. Each time he did it, Mimi would scold him! Then he died, and she started doing it herself!"

She follows my example, and waiting for the cookie to soak up the sweet wine, says, "So, how do I feel? Puzzled, I guess. About Monsignor. I didn't expect such, well, what do you call it?"

"Disloyalty?" I suggest. "Siding with them against us—against you."

Madeleine frowns, skeptically, but then continues as if to convince herself along with me. "He's got to keep on the good side of those folks—his country-club friends, I call them. Without them, there would be no parish plant, surely not one like this."

St. Raymond's is the ritziest of the suburban convents where our sisters teach, built in the '50s, in the flush of postwar prosperity. Both pastor and parishioners wanted the very best for the "good sisters." The time had long passed when a pastor or his flock, especially in wealthy parishes, honored the order's request that each parish convent resemble the simplicity and austerity of the motherhouse. It's their convent, they own it; they want it nice. At least some of them do. Some sisters appreciate these Hiltonizing touches, but not Madeleine—nor I. We love the drafty expanses of the old motherhouse—for what she once called its Andrew Wyeth look—where generations of varnished browns and blacks stand stark against ubiquitous white.

"And these lovely glasses?" I ask

"Ah, these are his personal gifts. His own money, not the parish's." Her hand sweeps past the bottle, the crystal, the linens, the tin of cookies. "Don't get the wrong idea. Despite what you may think, he's a good man. Very generous to us." She sinks back into the deep chair. "In fact, a constant, though minor, problem has been resisting his generosity. He'd like to take us all to Ireland to meet his mother! Can you imagine? He's serious! Over and over, I've had to explain to him about our vow of poverty. He never quite gets it. Despite the fact that his sister in Ireland is a nun."

More of my black thoughts about the pastor as proprietor almost spill out, but I manage to hold my tongue. "So, that's why I'm puzzled. He's always been on the side of trying to help us 'relax, take the day off.' He gives us the keys to his car so we can have a day in the mountains. Arranges for us to have the use of his friends' vacation homes."

"How we got Doc Moore's place?" I ask.

"Exactly. That was his doing, years ago. Before I ever heard of him."

"Here's to those wonderful walks—and talks," I say, and our Waterford crystal again sings out. I'm wondering if she remembers our doomsday post-tornado fantasy.

"Even now, after the school play, or at end of term—and always on St. Patrick's Day—he has his housekeeper pack a wonderful picnic, rents us a station wagon. Well, you get the idea."

"Yet when it's something you *need*," I say, "like changes in our convent life that would truly help *all* of us do a better job, he seems to have turned against you."

"That's too strong. I can't say he is against us. He's just, well, different lately. His interest in us and in the school has changed. Before this, he's never shown any interest in our private nun-life—our convent's rule and all that. And when it comes to running the school, he's always just followed the script I give him."

"As well he should!" I know Madeleine has put St. Raymond's on the map as a model of achievement and innovation, with test scores repeatedly topping the archdiocesan charts.

"He's always backed me when I've had a difficult call with either parents or kids. Especially with the altar boys, he's very involved. That's hard to criticize, with picnics and prizes and, for his favorites, cash gifts."

More of the proprietor, I think to myself, but say only, "which these kids need about as much as I need another one of these." I search for a broken cookie as if to somehow to justify my indulgence.

"You didn't eat much at supper," Madeleine says solicitously. But when I offer her another one, she shows me her swollen ankles and tells me of her need to lose weight.

"That's not just overweight," I say, but stop myself before suggesting that she see a doctor. She was decidedly cool to my last such suggestion.

"But Monsignor has never, in the six years I've been here, challenged what we are doing in the convent—or in the classroom, I might add. Until now."

"He challenges you?" I ask, disbelieving. Besides her teaching credential, Madeleine has a couple of master's degrees, far beyond the seminary education of the monsignor.

"Does he! He wants to know what lectures we attend at the university. What books we are reading. What I deal with in my conferences with the nuns!"

"Can't you tell him it's none of his business?!"

"But he has informed me that it *is* his business! Listen

to this: He got after me for inviting some mothers to those study groups at the university—where we were discussing the documents of Vatican II. I thought he'd be happy. Figured it was just an oversight not to include the announcement I gave him in the parish bulletin. So I sent a note home with the kids and gave a little talk at the Mothers Club. Turns out he deliberately kept it out of the bulletin. He didn't want them getting 'all riled up about this council stuff.' What he said tonight. It was quite a dressing-down he gave me, Sister. I haven't been scolded like that ever." She shrugs her shoulders as if this is entirely too large an issue for her to handle. "Lately, he's all over the place about our teaching of religion. About anything other than reciting the catechism! He's questioning things we've been doing for years."

"That's none of his business either," I repeat.

"But it is! Literally. According to canon law, he tells me, every pastor is the official principal of his parochial school. Nuns are only the acting principals, stand-ins for the pastor!"

"*What?*"

"That's what he says. He should know. He's got a degree in canon law."

"That is news! Does Augusta know about this?" I ask, thinking it's no wonder even stoic Madeleine looks beaten.

"Oh, heavens no. She's got enough to worry about. I shouldn't even be complaining about this with you." A deep sigh, and she adds, "This is our cross to bear, until this renewal stuff is settled. Besides, he's not about to tell the parents or kids that I'm not 'the real' principal."

"Mighty big of him," I grunt.

"He's worried that the Vatican council will be used to seduce the unwary into a kind of secular humanism. He's constantly reminding us that 'the Church is not a democracy!' "

"Ever the Irishman," I groan. "Do you worry he might be right?"

"I do," she says softly. "In these matters I respect him. He knows more about all this than any of us. For sure!"

I'm stunned, yet somehow not altogether surprised. She respects him! Like she did her authoritarian father. I pour myself more sherry and begin Madeleine's twirling trick with the glass. I wanted to know how she felt. Now I know. Or do I?

As if she were reading my thoughts, she breaks in. "Don't get me wrong. I'm one hundred percent for our education reforms. But I do wonder sometimes about the rest." She gestures toward the folder with our chapter decrees that lies between us. "I've been thinking. If we could manage to get classroom size down and the nuns credentialed, then the results will speak for themselves. Everyone will be happy. Then—with parents and pastors on our side again—we can get more adventuresome about all the rest."

All the rest! Where do I start to respond? I'm baffled. And sad.

"You know, Sister," she begins tentatively, "what most got to me tonight was when Monsignor spoke Christ's own words—about His kingdom not being of this world. How rejection of the world should be at the heart of every Christian life! He's right, you know. We do need to be reminded of this. Don't you agree?"

The pleas of that Polish woman—or was she Lithuanian?— haunt me as I begin my nightly ritual of undressing. On the right of the dresser goes my watch, and with it the many minutes of today, never to return. To the left, the cincture coils, its black leather worn through to a frayed brown around three holes, marking my expanding girth over the years. Then in the center, my crucifix with its sturdy chain: "Sweet the nails, sweet the wood, *dulce pondus*." A weight around my neck all day, it has lodged between my breasts.

Now it shocks me with the hard, cold fact of my own death, and I pray with Him, "Into thy hands I commend my spirit."

Lately, I've felt especially vulnerable during this interlude before sleep. In my light cotton nightgown, free from the habit's weighty serge and without the starched coif across my forehead, and the sturdy leather buckled around me, a certain dread comes over me. Until this moment, I can busy myself with all manner of argument for changing or eliminating the habit. Yet each night, I am haunted by the truth of the dressing prayer I say each morning: The habit is indeed my "comfort," the coif and veil my "shield of love." Not because they arm me against worldly love—as that housekeeper believes—but because they wrap around me the loving presence of my sisters and their good works. Stripped of these armors, I am alone. Nothing, no one, stands between me and my own death and the judgment of a God I hardly know. The soft simplicity of nightgown and night coif only intensify the reality. Like the fresh folds of linen wrapping Christ's body or the altar cloth cradling the host, this is my shroud, how I'll be in that last moment when neither the extreme unctions of holy oil nor the sweet blessings of incense can hide the loathsome reality of dying flesh.

"The bride prepared for her bridegroom," our rule says of this final moment, for which the holy habit is a constant reminder. I am pulled back to that spring morning in 1946 when old Reverend Mother Pauline welcomed us, her new white-veiled novices. She came over to me to straighten my skewed coif and I blurted out that I didn't feel much like a bride. She responded with an arm around my shoulder, an affectionate squeeze, and soft whispers into my eighteen-year-old ear: "My child, feelings don't count! It's *faith* that matters. Faith tells us we are special to Christ. Your emotions will follow. Give yourself time."

It's a long time now since those words mingled with the lush scents of beeswax and orange blossoms, and still the bishop's words eat at me: "Christ will be your sweet solace, your love above all others. You need no other. You are His beloved, His chosen one." Truth is, those words have never become real for me. I don't feel any "intimacy with Jesus"—which is what the foundation of a nun's life is supposed to be. God is not my consolation "above all others." I no longer even expect to feel this way.

Over the years, I've learned I'm not the "emotional type." I've even mocked sentimental piety. My faith has been more like that blind faith of the Apostle Thomas who prayed, "Lord help thou my unbelief." God—the Creator of the universe, the Lord before whom all creation is beholden—is for me more awesome than comforting. I well understand the creature's need to bow down in adoration before her Creator. That's why I entered the convent in the first place, why I've persevered this far: I wanted to offer back to this God of creation certain creaturely gifts in sacrifice. But is this enough? To keep a nun's life going maybe she needs to feel a deeply personal—dare I say romantic—relation with Christ. Yet not only do I not have this feeling, it's also an attitude I've always scorned.

But I don't know about Madeleine, and sometimes I wonder if she does experience a "personal relation with Jesus." Strong enough to see God's will in that awful monsignor?

For all our discussion of the life we share, Madeleine and I never venture into this most personal of topics. Only with Dan have I been able to reveal my "Old Testament mentality," how I feel not fully Christian. The priests who write "that spiritual crap" for nuns are simply ignorant, he assures me, presuming it's a "woman's nature" to be sentimental about Christ. Had more priests a chance to hear from nuns, as he has from me, they'd know we are not that different from them. We also grope through darkness to God, and experience God's love in the human love around us.

I move on to shower and, groping through the dark

hallway, think again how the love of friends has lit up my life. Augusta, Madeleine, Carla, my nun friends at CU, Basil and Sophie—and, of course, Dan. Maybe especially Dan. I step under the cleansing rush of water to let it slap my pate, soothe my knotted neck, and wash down my back. Then, turning, I lift my face to be splashed and kissed and roused with the memory of those friends whose love I offer back to God each night.

⁂

Late Fall 1967
An ecclesiastical drama brewing out in California may explain some of Monsignor Sweeney's changed behavior toward my friend Maddy over at St. Raymond's. Some weeks back, the cardinal out there, James Francis McIntyre, became locked in combat with a group of sisters in his diocese because of their reforms. Or more correctly, "possible reforms," because they are in a period of "experimenting"— same as we are—which the Vatican council has decreed must precede any reform. They are the IHM (Immaculate Heart of Mary) sisters, the order of my good friend from grad school, Sister Christine.

On the surface, it seems high comedy, fitting for these "Hollywood nuns" whose motherhouse and college, in the hills above Hollywood Boulevard, are surrounded by palm trees and bright flowers: A mighty cardinal, decked out in red, rages against this group of nuns, threatens to expel them from "his" schools, and forbids them to talk to the press or the laity, even to the parents of their students! All because they're daring to carry out the same sorts of reform we're after—that is, getting credentials for their teachers, shrinking classroom size, simplifying their dress, and so on. All labor issues, really. And all pro-tem experiments for possible reforms later, though what reaches the press is just that their skirts are short and their hair showing.

Beneath this news-grabbing drama, however, is a turf war. The IHM sisters did not seek McIntyre's guidance or advice before embarking on their renewal program, any more than we have from our local cardinal to begin ours. Vatican II directives do not require such approval—even when the local bishop happens to be a cardinal. In fact, we've been told Rome wants to hear from sisters themselves about what needs changing. For this task, we are taking at least a year of study and trial before seeking final approval for changes in our Holy Rule. Then, the okay (or otherwise) will come from church authorities in Rome, not from the local bishop.

Yet, when this Cardinal McIntyre discovered that the IHM sisters wanted to withdraw a number of sisters from "his" schools to finish college, and to limit class size to forty, he flew into a rage. It doesn't help that they, like we, are "experimenting" with what many think makes nuns to be nuns: the veil and the habit, the cloister and a uniform daily schedule. Never mind that the highest authorities in the Church have urged sisters to rethink these very details *for themselves*. Rome understands, as McIntyre and Sweeney apparently do not, that for too long the minutiae of sisters' lives have been legislated from on high.

What makes this clash so threatening for us here in St. Louis is the immense power Cardinal McIntyre wields outside Los Angeles. Throughout the United States, he is feared, if not respected, by lesser-ranked hierarchy, being second only to New York's ailing Cardinal Spellman, in both clerical standing and financial contributions to the Vatican. Many clergy—especially of Monsignor Sweeney's ilk—are attentive to this mighty cardinal in LA who warns his fellow American bishops about the danger of "progressive nuns" and their "so-called reforms." The Church, after all, is not a democracy, pronounces McIntyre, emphasizing that the spirit of Vatican II is not supposed to create a "scandal to the faithful," the way "his" sisters are.

At first, this seems humorous. Isn't this the same cardinal who provided comic relief throughout Vatican II by voting (on the losing side) with archconservatives from Spain and Ireland against the use of vernacular languages in the Mass? And against the participation of the laity at Mass? Who resisted exploring ecumenism or revising the catechism? Hadn't he, still earlier, embarrassed everyone by proclaiming, on the eve of those terrible Watts riots, "We don't have a race problem in Los Angeles."

Humor fades quickly, though, when Sister Christine educates me further about the churchly realities of LA: It is the wealthiest diocese of the wealthiest nation supporting the Vatican. Thus, Cardinal McIntyre gets the attention of authorities in Rome, among whom are those who ultimately control the fate of nuns throughout the world. The brouhaha at St. Raymond's begins to make sense. As the holidays approach, the local media report that Catholic parents are fearful that a certain "progressive element" among "reform-minded nuns" threatens the future of parochial education. Suddenly, Dan's prediction comes back to me—that "those guys in Rome" will never allow nuns any real change. If I had room for worry right now, I might grow despondent. But I don't. My brain is busy well past not only the prescribed lights-out time but my personal midnight hour as well.

The new trimester policy at our local Jesuit university is the cause for much of it. Everything has to be wrapped up before the Christmas holiday: junior sisters cramming for finals while also carrying the burden for the Christmas "extras" in their parochial schools, Christmas plays. etc.; I also am cramming to tie up my three courses before the Christmas break, while also visiting several parish groups like St. Raymond's to explain our planned changes, how they will or won't affect their children. I call it my PR job. So there's little time for taking in Dan's foreboding message. But not so in my dreams, those terrifying "baby dreams" that start to plague me toward the end of this fall term.

The first dream, during Thanksgiving night, is the most harrowing. In it, I'm at the Shrine of the Immaculate Conception in DC, in full habit, cloaked in the winter cape I wore when visiting there before leaving DC. In my arms I am proudly holding a warm, cuddly baby. As we approach the communion rail, she starts crying, so I begin nursing her. But when I kneel at the altar rail, the priest distributing communion is horrified at my exposed breasts, then scornful. Finally, with a flourish, he passes me by, refusing me communion. I am overcome with embarrassed confusion, retreating awkwardly from the communion rail, gradually sinking back into the shadows of the enormous church.

As I draw my heavy cloak close around me and the baby, I gradually become aware that the bundle I'm clasping is growing lighter. To my horror, the infant is shrinking. Her chubby pink cheeks wither into the gruesome gray wrinkles of those large-eyed, tiny, emaciated victims of famine pictured in the missionary magazines littering the Byrne household all through my growing up. When her frail skeleton shrinks further into something about the size of Mimi's tiny French thimble, I start to weep. When the thimble collapses into fine dust, my breathing quickly scatters this darling child into the drafty reaches of the Church. And I wake up, utterly disconsolate at my loss, heavy with a sense of responsibility for this ghastly atrocity, though only a fantasy of my dreams. Even the chatty friendliness of this "free day" following Thanksgiving can't blot out these nighttime memories.

If I could hold in my arms a real baby, a healthy baby, maybe I could lick this oppression. So I decide to take advantage of the extra Thanksgiving free-day plus our newly relaxed regulations about visiting our families, and visit my parents. They often babysit Kate, their newest grandchild, especially on a holiday like today. So I'll drop in on them.

But there is no Katie, just the two of them at the kitchen table when I arrive—Mother fussing about being found in her robe at ten o'clock and Dad wishing I had let them know I was coming. He would have canceled his golf date.

"She wanted you here with us yesterday for Thanksgiving dinner," he says as soon as Mother takes off for the shower. He's pouring us both coffee when he looks up at me with his pale gray eyes. "Now that your rules are relaxing, Betty, I should think you'd have been here yesterday with the rest of us. She needed you."

The same gentle reproach I knew so well as a teenager but haven't heard for the past twenty-some years of visiting with them in convent parlors, when he's called me "Sister" and spoken mostly about "the family business" and how Suzy and Tom and their respective families were doing. So even with his rebuke, being called Betty feels warm and welcoming. He's dapper for his seventy-two years, I think. Still handsome, with thick white hair much softer than when he was called "Black Dan" Byrne. Perhaps it's the light blue golf shirt and blousy sweater, revealing swirls of white hair on his chest.

"C'mon, Dad, you know why I wasn't here yesterday." Will it make any difference to yet again explain our changes? How they are for the sake of improving community life, not weakening it? "Thanksgiving's a family day for us, too, Dad. That hasn't changed—thank goodness."

But he doesn't seem to hear me. "These big holidays are getting to be too much for your mother. I told her we should take the whole brood over to the club, but she wanted them here, wanted to do it herself. 'Then get Emma to help you,' I told her. But she says Emma has her own family. So now we've got all this," he says gesturing to the piles of dishes and trays of glasses and linen heaped on the breakfast table. "You could have been a big help around here, Betty."

"I still can be," I say, starting toward the sink, abandoning hope of defending what our order's doing. But he beckons me back; he isn't finished.

"She's worried about you, Betty. All this talk about you sisters upsets her. Those old biddies she plays bridge with have nothing else to do but gossip about 'those modernizing nuns.' You need to tell her what to say to them when she hears tall tales about nuns quitting the schools, drinking liquor, turning, you know, queer, or marrying priests."

"Not the same ones, I hope!" I say, counting on his good humor.

"You know what I mean, Betty. You need to talk to her."

I promise to do what he wants, as I hunt for an apron. Maybe this time I'll be able to get through to her, to them, about our reforms. When I tie on a brightly flowered pinafore apron with ruffles and a bib, Dad smiles broadly. "Now that's an improvement I'd vote for. But then, you're not asking me for advice, are you?"

"That hasn't stopped others from giving theirs!" I say, as I begin removing inner sleeves and pinning back my veil, aware that he is scrutinizing my every move.

"Now, it's plain crazy to have to go through that rigmarole just to wash dishes! I agree with that much: Those outfits of yours do need an update. I've said as much to Monsignor Hickey when he asks me what you're up to." And I'll bet you've said a whole lot more, I think to myself.

He remembers his Polaroids from their Thanksgiving feast and fetches them for me. They turn out, not surprisingly, to feature mostly baby Kate, the newest Byrne. Instantly, I'm drawn back into the world of my dream, mixed now with the recent memories of little Kate's baptism, when I cuddled her close and felt her downy cheek on mine. Like those first moments of my dream. But what of those awful other images, of the wasted, dying child?

Dad announces he must leave but pulls back from a hug to ask about the circles under my eyes, the ones Johanna predicted would clear up when I returned to the mother-house. He's concerned I'm not getting enough sleep. I'd like to tell him about my dream last night, have him listen to my worries the way he did when I was a kid. But that's impossible, I know. He'd think me frustrated because I have no children of my own, which so worried him before I joined the order.

Mother must have heard the back door slam as he left. "Betty, dear, come on up—I need help with the zipper." I climb the stairs in my flowered apron pinafore, once again the obedient twelve-year-old in pigtails off to help Mother, but wishing I was still with Dad or almost anyone else. An old story, not wanting to be around her more, wanting to flee—then feeling guilty for feeling this way.

As I coax the zipper up the back of her shift, I notice how crooked her back is and remember her stoically borne pain these last years. I want to hug her, ask forgiveness for affection I'm unable to demonstrate. We're looking at each other in the bathroom mirror. She fingers my veil, pulls it back, away from my face, as she often does, to see more of me. "You're hiding from me in there," she once said. She pats my habit, gingerly. When she locates my rib cage, she gasps. "Oh, Betty, you're downright bony! Are you sure you're eating enough?"

She doesn't wait for an answer. I want to tell her about my baby dream, or rather, I wish I wanted to, wishing I had that kind of intimacy, the kind I had with Mother Alicia, my novice mistress to whom I could tell anything. But my own mother was always too busy, as she is now, rooting around in one of the bathroom drawers, producing, finally, a pink stick of blush. "Here put some on, it'll make your Father feel better. He's worried about you, you know that, Betty, don't you? He thinks that maybe your reverend mother has gone too far in trying to modernize your convent."

I laugh, telling her we may be modernizing, but we're not

yet into makeup. I'm back in my childhood, when the closest we ever came to girl talk was in the bathroom, when she spoke her concerns by saying they were Dad's. I felt then I could never share with her what was inside of me, not really. I had to protect her, especially when she had that little-girl-sad look I'd sometimes glimpse as she put on her makeup. Before she turned on that wonderful company smile for her guests, the smile all their friends compliment her for.

I leave her, promising to ask permission to see their doctor, which, shortly thereafter, I do, only to hear him say what I suspect they think as well—what they probably told him ahead of my visit: that my dark circles and weight loss have more to do with our convent reforms than anything else. "You sisters ought to concentrate on your work and leave running the Church to the priests."

December 1967
The darkening December days bring little relief. I have to force myself through the paces of preparing and teaching class and correcting final essays. On Christmas Eve, I take to my bed without supper, knowing I'm ill. During the night, my temperature soars. Bright yellow clumps in my throat bring me to the emergency room. After some days of antibiotics and ice packs, my fever breaks, and, shortly after, I'm released with a diagnosis of mononucleosis plus an FUO, which is another way of saying a fever they don't know much about. Back at the motherhouse, I seem at first to improve, but then one morning at Mass, I collapse with what turns out to be pneumonia.

"You must turn off your mind for a while," Maddy says, when she comes to visit me in the infirmary, always the sister superior. "Listen to what your body is saying."

I am indeed listening to my body. What it says is tired! After three days of complete bed rest, I am more drained than ever. A trip to the toilet leaves me shaky and clammy. It's the jumble of noises in the infirmary that keep me from "resting and relaxing" as the doctor ordered. Or turning off my mind, as Maddy tells me. All day the life and times of the old ladies sequestered around me come drifting over the transom and into my silent room. What these snatches of conversation stir up in me can't be quelled by the Sister Infirmarian's regular "shushing" of her elderly, and mostly deaf, charges.

"The young ones in here," I hear one day, along with the opinion that my fever comes from too much study. Only they would consider me young, I think. In fact, I am alarmingly close to the dreaded forty mark—"as you are, too," I remind Maddy—"when we'll leave our youth behind forever." She says "not necessarily" and we are into one of our goodwill fights again.

"I've never pictured myself old or ill, but lying here in this antiseptically clean sick room, without the clutter of the junior sisters, old age has become terrifying. And they don't help," I say, directing Maddy's attention to the pious faces staring down at me from either wall: Jesus with clipped beard and sharp features, a look of icy anger about him as he points to his bleeding heart, and sorrowful Mary, framed in shades of blue, revealing a heart stabbed by seven swords. Each reminds me of the awful "sacred art" in the classrooms of my childhood; I can't believe such sentimental junk still hangs on the walls of our progressive order. But here it is, and here I lie, unable to avoid their accusing gazes.

Or the voices. Some I can associate with the squeak of a wheelchair or the hesitant scraping of a walker, others with the poking of a cane followed by a wayward foot dragging along the terrazzo hallway. All are amplified by their own deafness, forcing me to hear more than I wish of the details of some sad and lonely lives. Is this my future, I ask: a life narrowed to such pettiness? Is this me in thirty years?

One morning, a pair of old nuns approaches from opposite ends of the hallway and meet in front of my door. "Can't you read, Sister?" I recognize Sister Ancilla from her wheelchair and that sharp, bossy voice of a person accustomed to keeping throngs of small children orderly. "It says: 'Do Not Disturb!'"

Just as sharply—in a defiant tone never allowed schoolchildren, but well practiced among their teachers—Sister Stanislaus replies, "This is urgent, Sister!"

I groan. Several times a day Stanislaus finds some urgent reason to exempt herself from the notice hanging on my door. This time, as she and her walker nudge into my room, her message for me is only too clear: My illness is a sign of God's displeasure, an opportunity for me, and others like me leading the "rebellion" within our community, to mend our ways. To heed the message of Fatima about living lives of penance and suffering in reparation for the sins of the world. Specifically, the sin of world communism.

She chatters on and I feel only disgust at how she intrudes, filling the room with the sounds and smells of old age and the sentimental claptrap of childish piety, today a miracle-working Fatima novena, yesterday Lourdes water, earlier holy cards from La Salette. After so long in the order she's still peddling this superstitious, spiritual bribery! Does convent life breed such childish craziness?

Before this, Sister Stanislaus has always seemed to me a bit crabby but harmless—a nun who, after scores of years laboring in the vineyard, has finally been moved to this motherhouse infirmary. During my years as a regular tray-taker, I often glimpsed her, parked at the infirmary entrance. There was the aura of mothballs about her as she handed out holy cards of Our Lady of Fatima, that sad statue of Mary with a tear rolling down her cheek. Only on special feast days did I linger long enough to accept her gift of hard candies wadded up in a paper napkin. I've never really heard what she was saying. Nor eaten her candies.

Now, though, I can't avoid her or her message: The trouble with these changes in the order, she says, is that we've lost sight of the main calling of a nun, which is to suffer for the sins of this world. We are trying to make religious life easy! To take the suffering out of it. This is a big mistake. God is showing His displeasure by striking me down with pneumonia.

I moan to Maddy that, in a better state of mind, I might have empathy for this sad woman. She has been, after all, one of the workhorses of the order in the days before degrees or credentials, when piety substituted for maturity as a requirement for taking vows. But instead, I stew over what revolts me—her whiny voice, her childish thinking, the oppressive whiff of mothballs that envelopes her. I try telling myself it's unlikely that I or any of my friends will turn out thus, that whatever form our old-age diminishments take, they'll never be of this sort. But it doesn't work. I feel trapped in this hallway forever. The bug is having its way with me.

⁓⁓

"Need a little disturbing?" Carla asks, poking her head through the doorway.

"Do I!" Suddenly the energy I did not have for responding to Sister Stanislaus returns. I pour out to Carla my feelings of anger toward the old crone—and how guilty and shamefaced I feel after each encounter.

"A fever's not the best time to examine your conscience," she advises. She then brings me up to date on Sister Zita, who always makes us both smile. Carla has been visiting her old friend, who is about to turn ninety-eight and is now quite frail, bedridden, and not so cheerful anymore, Carla tells me. "She can't cut those shiny strips for the Christmas chains anymore. She worries about who will take over her chains when she's gone. She wants to be sure the tradition is in good hands before she dies."

So I agree to help, and Carla leaves, only to return dragging two large bags brimming with colorful metallic papers. Apparently she's recruited a handful of the infirmary nuns to cut the strips for Sister Zita. In short order, we settle into the simple rhythm of stapling together the tiny papers, and I find myself describing my baby dreams to Carla, who has taught me to pay attention to dreams, claiming they are artistic creations assembled without the critical judgment of our daytime mind. She's fascinated by them, from the first long one at Thanksgiving to the muddled bits and pieces churned out of my fitful sleep in the infirmary, where I continue to dream about "my baby." Often, I'm racing around searching for a bed for her. One time, I wander about, lost in the motherhouse grounds, ending up cold and naked out in the courtyard. Another time, I'm in the refectory, attempting to hide the baby with my habit. I'm never successful, and I often lose my habit or the baby or both.

"What do you make of them?" she asks me. "Who's the baby?"

"I've been thinking, maybe the baby is us, the reborn nun, how we imagine we'll be after all the reforms, our refashioned selves."

"You mean the 'new nun'—the 'nun in the modern world'?"

"Yes—the Vatican II nun—that's *our* baby. We're bringing it to birth, Carla!"

"A virgin birth, I might add."

"Exactly! We've done it on our own. Pulled ourselves up by our own bootstraps—to switch the metaphor."

"Yet when you take your baby up to the altar to present it to the powers that be, they turn away in disgust?"

"Worse, they're indifferent—and scornful!"

"You fear that's what the hierarchy will do in real life—with us, and our reforms?"

"In my gloomiest moments I do. Our bishop here in St. Louis, and the hierarchy above him in Rome, they could follow that guy out in LA."

"What a horrible thought!"

"Yes. It could happen here—to us." I slump back against the pillow; the chain forming on my bed snaps. I'm utterly spent.

"Even here in the motherhouse, your baby can't find rest," Carla continues, as if automated in her chain-making. By now, it's spilling out of her lap and onto the floor, snaking under the bed. For a long time, she says nothing until her hands stop. "Your dreams aren't just about not finding a place for your baby, or having it dismissed by the priest at the altar. They're also about *killing*." She looks directly at me and with great tenderness asks, "You think they have the power to *kill* your baby?"

"I do." I'm surprised at the taste of tears in my throat. "Damn them!" Lately, I get suddenly angry and then weepy this way—sometimes watching the evening news, with its pictures of Vietnam, often after listening to one of Dan's tapes or hearing from Sister Christine about her group in California. Or, more recently, after Sister Stanislaus's harangues.

"I've just heard from Christine again," I say, reaching over to the nightstand for my latest letter from California. I toss into Carla's lap a bunch of yellow foolscap. "Here, read for yourself. It's final: McIntyre is firing all IHMs teaching in the LA archdiocese. That's more than three hundred–plus nuns who will be rootless at the end of the school year."

"You must be kidding. That'll mean hundreds—no, thousands—of kids without teachers?"

"Oh, the classrooms won't be empty. He can always import some nuns. Irish, maybe. It's the IHM sisters that will be ousted from their LA classrooms who will be without jobs! Do you suppose that cardinal will pay them unemployment benefits?"

We both chuckle at the absurdity of this idea, and Carla stops stapling to read the letter. I lean back into the pillows, trying to steady my breathing; once again, tears feel imminent.

After only a few minutes she gasps. "An inquisitor? From Rome? This sounds like the Middle Ages. Wait till the press gets ahold of this!"

"Exactly what he wants probably: publicity! Get the word out. For any other sisters bold enough to try the same thing. Like us. Can you imagine the effect this is having on our own junior sisters, especially the ones coming up for final vows in August? They'll wonder if it can happen here."

Carla gently reaches over to quiet my hands that have clumsily tried to resume work on the chain. "Stop," she says softly. "Let's forget for a moment the juniors, and the IHMs, and the chains. Let's stay with your dream, with you. Because those baby dreams are about you."

I'm stymied by her suggestion to focus on myself. Isn't that exactly what's so frightening about my encounters with Stanislaus. They leave me with a vague disquiet about myself. For I know enough psychology to recognize anger at someone else's foibles is a clue to one's own unacknowledged problems. What am I not acknowledging?

"Could it be with you, as it is with me?" Carla begins softly. "I've let myself become solely identified with the collective, with its struggle. With our group—but also all sisters. I've become so intent that nuns' lives make sense, so determined that the institution of religious life renew itself, that I've somehow lost myself. Does that make sense?"

"Oh, yes," I mutter." Great sense, though I'm not sure why."

"Your dreams make me think: Maybe you need to focus

for the moment on yourself, aside from the group. You as a woman." Her words hang in midair for a moment while I try to move my mind around them. "Could you be avoiding the obvious? About wanting your own child? Feeling the Church has taken it from you? There's still time. I hope you're not forgetting that."

"I haven't," I reply, momentarily distracted by the fact that Carla herself may indeed be beyond childbearing years.

"There's something curious in the way you described Sister Stanislaus—as 'childish.' You used that term several times, each time with a lot of negative feeling. D'you suppose that has anything to do with the child of your dreams?"

"I'm not sure." I let her words sink in, and for some time we both are silent. Finally I reach for the notebook on my nightstand and fish through it for a folded note, something I gave Dan years ago, using some of Carla's own words about "needing Decembers."

"Hope you don't mind how I've borrowed your words? This isn't exactly what you're asking for, but for me it is personal. Very personal."

"No matter how Jesus's followers may have garbled his message, it's still there waiting to be rediscovered by each person—a lifetime work, the work we celebrate each December: How to bring to birth a new December child. No institution can do this for us, bring light out of darkness. We are responsible for our faith."

Carla sits silently, staring at the paper. "Yes," she whispers. She's with me in the same struggle. "Yes," she repeats, folding the paper and placing it on the nightstand.

"In defending our reforms," I finally say, "I often find myself telling parish groups that 'We are not rethinking the faith, only how we wish to live out our faith.' Why can't I be honest, Carla? For years I have been rethinking the faith. My faith. Can the Church allow nuns to do that? Imagine, nuns with doubts about the faith! That's a real scandal. More than shortened skirts or curly hair."

"How true. So many twist up how our faith and our reason relate. Right up your alley, no?"

With her wan smile she let's me know that my words have not been lost in those hours of visiting down in her art department. Hours when I've tried to tell her about some insight, hours when I knew I've been heard about how faith is not the opposite of doubt; faith is because of doubt, how we leap to affirm the truth of something we can't argue to *fides quaerens intellectum*—faith seeking understanding. "Maybe that's what the McIntyres of this world have known all along. 'You can't keep them down on the farm once they've—'"

"How scary for the likes of him! A great growing-up of sisters—all over the world!"

"That will never do!" she quips mockingly, "those cute little nuns growing up into real women? Thinking, questioning women? Never!"

Each visit from Sister Stanislaus pulls me back to Carla's question about the child of my dreams and the childishness I so abhor. But back in my own room in time for the new spring semester, free of fever—and Sister Stanislaus—surrounded by junior sisters and the familiar trappings of my adult life, I see the connection. The day before the new term, it comes to me, an instant after awakening, the words of St. Paul: "When I was a child, I spoke as a child, thought as a child, reasoned as a child. But when I became an adult, I put childish ways aside." This is what my dreams are saying! The child I wrap in my cloak is my own childishness, a childhood I'm still attached to, still cherishing—however ambivalently. One moment I hug my child, delighting in her warmth. The next, I let her shrivel and die. Not good.

Chapter 13

1968

March 7, 1968

I've yet to join those of our sisters wearing civilian garb—despite my enthusiasm for experimenting with every aspect of our life. I rationalize, tell myself it helps those sisters fearful of change to see me, an identified "liberal," still wearing the habit. This is true, and politically helpful, but if I am being really honest, there's an added truth: I *like* wearing the habit, the uncomplicated, loose feel of it, billowing skirts warming me when I'm cold and cooling me when I'm hot. Plus it's easy! Ready for any occasion. Good reasons all—and truthful.

However, I'm less than honest about a deeper reason for my personal procrastinating on the habit issue: I just can't imagine wearing any of the "experiments" I see around me—whether one of the modified habits like Madeleine's, or outfits put together from thrift shops like Janet's. They may conform to my ideals about the spirit of poverty and the ideals of simplicity, but they are so ugly. If I really want to follow Jesus, who was poor and probably pretty poorly dressed, why am I so reluctant to look as he did? This procrastination has put me in a fix. Because during these past few busy weeks, I've been putting off my mother's eagerness to have me try a few things from her own closet, a "perfect fit," she predicts. Now that it's my birthday, and with the little family party at my parents' house, I'll be put upon to try things from her closet. Things she thinks appropriate for a modern nun, a fashion show of sorts for my brother and sister and their families.

"Thank God, at last, he's gone!" Mother's company smile melts into a look of exasperation. She's irked to think that Dad would include his old pal Father Hickey at our family gathering—especially because it's for my fortieth, the first birthday I've celebrated with my family since I was seventeen. Worse yet, this clerical buddy of Dad's is very conservative, apt to disapprove of the new ways our sisters are behaving. Already he's noticed and remarked with a snarky comment that I am here without a sister companion, out past dark, and with no illness or death in the family!

So I'm relieved now, as Mother is, that he's gone, without a scene. She can get on with the business of the evening. She gathers up gifts from the hall closet, returning to the living room with a stack of boxes. It's then I understand that she's not giving me her clothes, as I had presumed. These are new clothes, or as she said in those Depression years, "store-bought clothes!"

My conscience's flickering struggle about receiving expensive clothes is replaced by the embarrassment at being surrounded with a half dozen or more boxes in the distinctive wrappings of Saks Fifth Avenue. Mother's taken care to label each box she has prepared as if from a different family member: from Dad, a delicate gold cross and chain; from Suzy and her husband, Al, pantyhose, a slip, and underwear; from Tom and Mary Kay, shoes and a purse. So many accompaniments, apparently, for whatever's in the large suit box with her own tag. In that box, which I open last, are two outfits, both Kimberly Knits, one long-sleeved, navy wool, the other, a short-sleeved pale blue linen knit. Their simple, elegant styling tells me they're expensive. Things have got terribly twisted; this isn't at all what our changes are about. I'm moving closer to *Vogue* magazine than to Dorothy Day.

"Better than my old lady's hand-me-downs, don't you think, Betty?" Mother says hesitantly, almost apologetically, as she sits on the edge of her chair.

Tom finally breaks the awkward silence. "So how long do we have to wait for the fashion show?"

Dad, fiddling with his camera, chimes in, "Hurry up, girls, we don't have all night!"

"Listen to himself, would you?" Mother says to me as we climb upstairs, toting the boxes. "He's a pushover for every priest with his hand out, yet he tells us to hurry!" Once in her bedroom she hands me a small package wrapped in tissue paper. "Just a little personal something," she whispers softly. In the beautiful little bag, there's a tiny comb and brush, and an even tinier hairspray, blush stick, and lip gloss. "You don't want to look made-up, I know, but these things will help you look just a bit healthier. Knits are practical because the wrinkles hang out," she says, carefully arranging each item on one of the fancy quilted hangers from her closet. Her back is to me; I sense she's deliberately not looking at me. "With care, you should be able to manage on these two until later. Maybe then we can get something cooler."

I'm standing speechless here in the middle of her bedroom, not knowing where to begin with the array of items in front of me, when she says, "You can use the bathroom to change if you wish." She's being offhand, yet I can sniff that natural reticence of the layperson around the mysterious nun. Even my own mother! "Let me know if I can help."

Better to be offhand as well, I decide, trying my best to squelch a rumble of emotion just below the surface. Being so caught up in the political issue of the habit, I've never quite focused on what it would be like to face my family without it. I've called it my "shield of love," my "sweet armor and comfort" when I've put it on each day since 1945. Literally true, maybe? Now I tell myself to keep moving, as I place each item I remove next to the things Mother has chosen for me. She has her own complicated emotions, and though I've wished for years we could share feelings, this is hardly the time to start.

I continue in a thoroughly businesslike manner to undress. Out of the corner of my eye, I glimpse Mother sitting with her back to me at her dressing table, fiddling with its array of bottles and jars. First I remove my veil, then the scapular, cincture, and finally the habit, coif, and headband. There's a faint gasp, as she spies me in her vanity's mirror removing the last of the headgear. I hear the tears in her voice before she resumes a much more familiar tone. "Your hair's really not bad at all, Betty! I thought you'd look like one of those war...."

"Collaborators?" I say. The same newsreel images from the war must be going through her head as they went through my own when I first saw my shaved head. For many years afterward, whenever I'd catch a glimpse of my head in the chrome trim on the shower door, I'd think of those newsreel women in France being paraded through their villages with heads shaved, punished for "fraternizing" with German soldiers during the occupation. In fact, my hair is now almost shoulder length. I'm relieved to release the rubber band and let it fall free.

"I've a scarf all ready for you." She opens a drawer of her bureau, where I notice among her bright assortment of scarves a somber black silk one—with the store's tag still attached.

As she hands it over to me, I start to resist, thinking I'm finished with veils! But her stricken look reminds me of her enormous thoughtfulness. "You're being too generous."

I hug her, and she whispers, "I'm glad for you, Betty." And for just an instant, a feel of Sisterliness binds us. But then she pulls loose, sits me down on her bench before the mirror, and starts fussing with my hair. She pulls it back from my face, trying to puff up the wavy, limp strands with hair spray. I am, again, the little kid forced to sit through having my hair braided, complaining that it hurts, being told I should be grateful, yet wanting to do it myself.

Fortunately, Suzy interrupts with a knock on the door. "Any way I can help? They've just poured themselves another round of drinks down there," she says as she approaches the bed and picks up the bag of new pantyhose. "C'mere, Betty. Let me show you a trick. To avoid snagging pantyhose, you must first clench your hand into a fist." She has a broad, wonderful smile and is so matter of fact that I'm instantly at ease, despite my half-naked state. The three of us decide on the navy knit, the more sedate of the two suits.

When I slip on the pumps, I feel anything but sedate. To my surprise, these objects I had imagined to be instruments of torture are actually comfortable! Though plain navy, with only a moderate heel, they make me feel stylish. In them, I have an energy that gives authority and decisiveness to my bearing. Several times, I catch myself taking sidelong glances at the mirror, smiling with satisfaction.

Mother fastens the tiny gold cross and chain around my neck, claiming Dad picked it out himself. They'd heard from Sister Johanna that sisters choosing secular garb must still wear some "sign of Christian dedication." Recalling the rough peace symbol around my friend Janet's neck, I think how much more a reminder of the Christian message hers is than this tiny, elegant gold cross. The irony distracts me: The kids in my classes—like kids around the world right now— are challenging accepted conventions of all sorts, most noticeably in their clothing. Yet I, who have pledged myself to become a sign of contradiction to this world, am walking straight into a thicket of middle-class consumerism.

Mother notices my detached silence and, as she often does, thinks I disapprove. "If you don't like any of this, Betty, you can return them for something else." I protest my appreciation, thinking, however, that's what I should do. Get something more like Janet's or her ilk. Yet I shrink from the effort—and the embarrassment. Because I can't imagine any of the stores Mother uses having clothes remotely like Janet's. So I simply surrender to the opulence: the silky underwear, the sheer stockings, the rippling skirt. I have forgotten how heavy and cumbersome and rough the habit felt at first. When I step out toward the stairway, there's a sudden rush of air on my legs, and other, more girlish, memories wash over me: playing grown-up in this very house in Mimi's soft gray party shoes with pearly buttons on the side. At the stairs, she'd take my hand, and I'd be the princess descending her palace staircase. And dancing with Dad, he as Fred Astaire, me as Shirley Temple.

However, tonight at the stairs, when Mother takes my hand, I feel churlish impatience. She frets that maybe I'll stumble because I haven't worn heels for so long. Instead I feel strong and confident, with a slight pang of sorrow that Mimi isn't here, in her house, on her own stairwell. Dad's camera is rolling as I come down the stairs. He spouts directions to move toward the fireplace, then away, not too close to any lamp, look this way, then that. We bump into each other and finally freeze. Then, all at once, I hear a jumble of reactions.

"Not bad, not bad," Tom offers.

Mary Kay compliments Mother with, "Good taste. Very good taste. Not like the concoctions I've seen on some of your 'modern nuns.'"

Dad hugs me. "Betty m'girl! You look wonderful!" He straightens his arms, pushing me out in front of him, with his firm grasp on my shoulders. Slowly looking me up and down, he concludes, "It's the real you, all right! Real shoulders, real neck, real hair! No more starch!" Then another tight hug. I'm amazed how strong he is, my tall, still handsome, white-haired father.

"This calls for another drink," Tom announces, as Suzy whispers in my ear to call on her if I need help in the next few days. But Tom drowns her out. "I gotta say, Betty, for your age, you're really quite well preserved." He laughs more than anyone else at his own humor. "So here's to you, kid! Life begins at forty! Happy birthday!"

⁂

I lose no time in taking Suzy up on her offer of help, and by Saturday morning I'm ensconced at her hairdresser's while she braves the credit department at Saks. With the cash she gets by returning the second Kimberly—"Who needs two of those?" she says—she assures me we can get enough practical clothes at one or another of her discount haunts.

Nothing from my preconvent shopping experience prepares me for the nondescript, one-story building we enter on the outskirts of town. Certainly not with Mimi, at her beloved Stix, Baer & Fuller Dry Goods store or, later, with Mother in the ready-to-wear section at Saks Fifth Avenue. Those were the elegant, hushed, and carpeted worlds with a well-understood decorum. Mirrors were reserved for the dressing room. No one dared be so vulgar as to try on a jacket or scarf "out front." Old ladies in dark dresses waited on us, carrying clothes to us. They made it clear their judgments mattered. But that was a quarter of a century ago—or more. Here, shoppers are on their own in one huge room resembling, down to the linoleum floor, a public institution. Mirrors are everywhere. The store's help are stationed around the perimeter, like guards watching a yard full of prisoners. They wait on no one, staring blankly at milling shoppers, completely indifferent, so it seems, to style or color or size. But Suzy isn't. She plunges immediately into the buzzing mass of shoppers like a fierce animal on the scent of its prey. Her easy smile is gone; she's all business. I follow the curly redhead of this tall, slender kid sister, once the scrawny ten-year-old I had to lean over to hug when I left home. I'm stopped by glimpses of my own new haircut in the mirrors. I like what I see.

Suzy gives terse orders: Stick to solid colors and plain designs, look for generous seams ("Still haven't gained back your normal weight, have you?"), don't be put off by funny buttons ("You can replace them"). After working over the racks of dresses, skirts, and tops, she dispatches me to the dressing room, a large, communal affair with mirrors lining the walls and a dozen or more women in various stages of undress. The sight stops me in my tracks until the woman behind pokes into my back with her huge bundle of clothes and their protruding hangers, nudging me farther into the room. Do only fat ladies shop at this place, I wonder, as I make my way to the spot indicated by the matron on guard? Why don't they at least wear slips to cover some of that overflowing flesh?

I can hear Mimi admonishing me not to stare, and my novice mistress pointing out my failure to practice modesty of the eyes. But no matter how much I try to concentrate on my own image in the mirror right in front of me, I can't stop noticing the strange transformations taking place around me. More than twenty years living in an all-woman world and never have I seen anything like this! What an argument for the habit, for keeping some things covered.

Suzy joins me, weighed down with sweaters and jackets. "Makes you feel like Miss America in here, doesn't it? Maybe that's why I shop here." She giggles softly. "Bolsters my ego!" Not that she needs bolstering, I think, admiring more than ever the athlete in her, thinking how little I have known this woman next to me, now all grown up. How little I know any of my family, really.

I'm trying to decide between a bulky salmon-colored cardigan and a lightweight blue one when I abruptly turn to her. "Wait a minute, Suzy. Do you realize this is the first time I've been alone with you—since 1945!"

She gestures not to interrupt, as she's preoccupied adding up prices in her head. "Okay, you can manage both of these," she finally concludes. "You'll need them with that khaki skirt. This one, too," she says, checking the ticket of the long, lacy cardigan she's holding up against the "electric blue" dress—an A-line, synthetic, and stands out like a bell—we've settled on. I think it's too short, but not Suzy. "Nonsense. It's longer than Jackie Kennedy's, and great for you!"

Even with exposed legs, I'm beginning to find my Kimberly Knit too warm, and I decide to change into one of the new outfits. When, moments later, I emerge from the ladies' room, clad in electric blue, Suzy presents me with her personal gift: a scarf of bold red, white, and blue geometric design that she artfully drapes around my neck. "There," she says standing back with a broad smile, "you're ready for the Fourth of July!"

"Hardly," I reply, startled at the chalky whiteness of my arms.

By the time we're seated at Louise's Kitchen, awaiting our tuna salads, I've grown more accustomed to the bare arms and uncovered knees.

"You're a bit heavy on polyester, but it is practical—and cheap," Suzy says. Closer to what other sisters are acquiring, I think, as well as to the "simple and modest, at once poor and becoming" of our guidelines.

"You're a different person without that habit." She looks across the tiny lunch table at me with eyes that look so like Dad's, only greener. "I wanted to tell you the other night, when we were at Mom and Dad's, but you changed back into your habit so fast. Then I couldn't even call you Betty. Weird, isn't it? It's just clothes, yet everything about you is different now: your walk, your posture, your demeanor—even your voice."

Suzy knows what she's talking about. She teaches developmentally disabled kids and knows about body language. And I know now, too. These pumps, this haircut, the unaccustomed drafts tickling my neck and ears, and brushing over my arms, awaken a new confidence in me. I am different.

"I wanted to drive you back to the convent the other night so we could talk," she says. "But once you put your habit on again, I felt like I was back in parochial school with that awful Sister Mary Grace." She sits back in her chair with her eyes fastened on the paper place mat in front of her. "You probably don't know, she never taught you, but she was really mean. Really Irish. Maybe the two go together?" She smirks, then turns confessional. "Before college, I never talked to a nun about *anything* that mattered."

"So what matters now?" I ask, still distracted by how light and free my tousled hair feels. The stylist discovered what he called "my natural wave," which I'm delighted to find out needs neither the spraying or teasing Mother tried to foist on me.

"Things I never thought nuns cared about until I got to college and met nuns like Sister Madeleva and Sister Charles Borromeo. They were terrific." She's remembering the nuns she knew at St. Mary's College, the women's college across the road from Notre Dame. It was my parents' compromise to send her there when confronted with Suzy's insistence on a coed campus. "I've been reading the remarks of your boss, Sister Augusta, in the *Post Dispatch*, about women in the Church, about how we need to make our own decisions. And about those nuns in LA! To think some old cardinal—an inhabitant of Wall Street before his seminary days, I'm told—is telling a bunch of classroom teachers how to run a school!"

As I sit looking at her young face, still dotted with freckles, I'm sad to have missed out on her growing-up years. Sad, in fact, to have been so distant and formal with my entire family. Knowing that I was following our Holy Rule doesn't help me from feeling cheated. But I'm proud as well. This thirty-two-year-old has transformed herself from an indulged youngest child into a beautifully independent woman—without any help from her big sister.

"To think they're actually doing something about their lives! I didn't think nuns had that kind of guts." She leans over the table and lowers her voice, again speaking confidentially. "This may shock you, Betty, but I used to hate nuns before I went away to college. I was embarrassed to be the sister of a nun. I didn't want the other kids to know about you. Al has aunts and cousins who are nuns. When he was a kid, one of them said his father would go to hell for skipping Mass on Sunday." She pauses, looking uncomfortable. "Now we're the ones going to hell."

"Because you've taken your kids out of the parochial school?"

"That, and lots more," she says, elbows on the table. She secures her unruly hair behind each ear, looking worn beyond her years. I think of Dan's tales about his married penitents, how burdened most of them are because in good conscience they cannot agree with their church. It's more than birth control, although that's their crushing, central concern. It's the faith itself that troubles many, especially the better educated, like Suzy, with her graduate degree. They long to help their kids through the literalism and legalism of the catechism, but they get little help or encouragement from any Church person.

"Like the line from that hymn, 'Eat His body, drink His blood,' they used to sing at our parish," Suzy continues. "How d'you explain that to an inquisitive eight-year-old just as you're plunking a hunk of bloody beef into your shopping cart? Or any other time? How do you explain it to yourself? I think I could live with my own questions about God and religion and the Catholic Church if I didn't have to answer so many of the kids' questions." She sighs. "Lately, I just tell them to go ask their father because he's smarter than I am."

"Is he?"

"In many ways, yes. Being an Italian Catholic is different,

Betty. Stuff doesn't get to him the way it does me. He can take it or leave it much more than I can. There's something very rigid in the Byrne Catholicism, don't you think? Maybe because we're Irish. It's as if a curtain comes down on certain issues. Some things are simply beyond discussion with us."

"Like the school issue?" I say, again sad for the way I remained emotionally abstracted from my family and its affairs for so long. Both Mother and Mary Kay hint at Suzy's "difference" from typical Catholics, noting that she has *only* two kids, who are in *public* school!

"It would have helped to be able to talk with you about it. But you were away at grad school."

"I'm afraid I've always been away."

"Maybe you would at least have argued with me. Nobody else would! Just stony silence!" I'm reminded of Sophie's cracks about my "niceness" and am happy to think Suzy has escaped this family curse. "We Byrnes just don't argue, do we? Mother sure doesn't. Or Dad. They just keep it in—even when I know they disagree. Tom and Mary Kay are the same way. Even our Byrne cousins. No one approves of Al and me. I'm a working mom, we only have two kids, and they're not in the parish school. Three strikes and we're OUT! Still, no one says anything." She draws a very deep breath, then spills more of her anguish. "I am furious whenever Tom makes cracks about our not having more kids. Yet I think his Mary Kay, and those other stalwart Catholic wives over at that fancy country club, hate the Church for making them have so many kids. Not consciously, of course, any more than they're conscious of how they envy you nuns. Even as they gossip about you. You're changing the rules. Ye gads! In midstream. The way they can't! They're mad at you because they can't get mad at the Church!"

She's quiet for a moment, but I know she's not finished. "It's such a paradox: So many mothers in the parochial school we took the kids out of griped about 'the nuns going modern.' Yet they've been griping for years about the Church not listening to women. Now that you gals are doing something about it, they're up in arms. It drives me nuts!"

"But we're not doing anything for them."

"Oh, yes, you are!" she fires back at me. "That's my point! What I've been wanting to say to you. I really admire you and your sisters. Progressive nuns are giving women like me hope. So much is needed, so many changes. You've started. You're sticking your neck out—for all of us." Finally, she slows down, appearing self-conscious. "We need so much for the Church to hear women, especially about birth control and stuff. About everything, in fact."

She's pulled back in her chair now and is sitting upright, unsmiling, looking every bit the determined yet angry Catholic schoolgirl. What my little sister says about the sisters makes me proud. Yet that pride is mixed with a sickening sadness for the harm so many sisters—though not just sisters—have done in the name of God and religion to so many students over the years.

Holy Thursday, 1968

Easter time comes late enough that Sister Marie's roses are just perfect for the altar by Holy Thursday. During the long ceremony, I sit staring at the lovely arrangement, from time to time closing my eyes to breathe in their heavy scent. It's great to feel fit again, to have left behind those dark dreams of winter, to be surrounded by such roses!

In the lushness of their first bloom, these velvety whites, deep pinks, and rich golden yellows are spectacular. And they carry a deep personal nostalgia, for roses like these were on this same altar at every important turning point in my life as a nun: the August day I entered, the spring day I received the habit, then again on summer's Vow Day. Always in the same white wicker baskets, placed on the same richly embroidered altar cloth. They are as familiar to me as this ceremony unfolding before me is not.

Tonight there are twelve laymen up in the sanctuary where previously only priests were allowed. They are the men in our lives: the gardeners, cooks, and maintenance men for the motherhouse, plus a couple of fellows from the local gas station who service our cars. They sit on low stools just inside the sanctuary, self-consciously removing their shoes and socks, while the chaplain removes his ornate outer vestments. Then, standing in front of the altar—which now faces us, thanks as well to Vatican II—our chaplain sings with authority: *"Mandatum novum do vobis...."*

"A new commandment I give unto you," we repeat, our English only awkwardly accommodating the ancient Gregorian chant: "That you love one another as I have loved you." Then, kneeling, the priest begins to wash and dry each man's feet, while we in the congregation chant the story of Christ's last Passover meal with his apostles: "The Lord rose from supper, poured water into a basin, and began to wash the feet of the disciples, saying, 'This is an example I give you that you do as I have done for you.'"

For centuries, this ritual, in Latin, was reserved for the bishop and twelve of his chosen clerics in a Cathedral ceremony completely separate from the laity, not part of the Mass. Now, though, the Mandatum has been restored to its ancient, prominent, spot within the Mass, immediately after the Gospel, where the sermon normally is. It *is* the sermon, with a message hard to miss: Service to our brethren is part of the Eucharist, part of what it means to follow Christ. With all the old trappings gone, the Mandatum now has the gritty power of reality: Christ's simple lesson told with rumpled socks and well-worn shoes, an overfed priest, sweating and red-faced in his unaccustomed role as servant, and laboring men embarrassed at being waited on by him.

Gone as well is the exquisitely embroidered banner,

delicately woven in threads of gold, which had hung in the motherhouse chapel since long before I came to St. Mary's in the ninth grade. In its place now is a simple length of white felt with symbols of the day's feast stuck on. The most that can be said is that it's functional, like the motley arrangement of "street clothes" and "modern habits" on the sisters surrounding me, or the cumbersome English of our plainchant. In no sense is this new felt banner "beautiful," nor does it fit with the muted tones of the windows or the dark wood carvings of the chapel's interior. But it fits us. Like everything else tonight, it speaks of a group in transition, a group startled by its own emerging diversity.

Fewer than half the men have their feet washed by the time we finish chanting the story of the Last Supper. So until the priest catches up with us, we repeat over and over again the concluding antiphon, St. John's *Ubi caritas*: "Where charity and love are, there is God." Most of us know the Latin by heart, but now we stumble with our awkward English phrasing, and what should be a seamless flow becomes a jagged struggle to keep together.

Yet again, aesthetic loss is reality's gain, for having to repeat endlessly the line about "rejoicing and being glad" allows me to dwell gratefully on my own joy. Except for one wrinkle, things seem finally to be smoothing out for me and for the world. I've emerged from that spell of illness feeling in top form, and my teaching, while far from routine, has settled into a rhythm that complements rather than compromises my work with the junior sisters and our efforts at reform.

In the big, wide world, reforms are also going forward fairly smoothly. In Czechoslovakia, ordinary citizens are peacefully ridding themselves of their Stalinist oppressors. Students all over the world press for democracy. Closer to home, more and more people oppose the war in Southeast Asia. One of my heroes, Robert Kennedy, is taking on the presidential race; President Johnson has withdrawn, agreeing, finally, to seek a negotiated settlement in Vietnam. Also, at long last, the civil rights bill has become law—though sadly only after the martyrdom of Martin Luther King Jr. Droll Senator Dirksen, so long opposed to the bill, now calls it an idea whose time has come, which is exactly what Pope John's *aggiornamento* promised back in 1962.

To be in the midst of a changing world, knowing I've had a hand in the changes closest to me, makes it easy for me to sing "rejoice and be glad." Except that we are also singing "let us take heed, that we be not divided in mind; let malicious quarrels and contentions cease." That's the wrinkle. For the order has become divided in mind, resulting in quarrels and contentions the likes of which I've never experienced during my time in community. And my young friend Janet is right smack in the middle of one quarrel.

By a cruel irony, the greater freedom to speak one's mind, which the decrees from last year encourage, also allows us to criticize these decrees in unprecedented ways. Encouraging sisters to "experiment"—with, for instance, times of prayer—makes for so much diversity in smaller convents that at times it's difficult to assemble the quorum needed to chant the office. "Chaos" is how my friend Sister Madeleine describes it, and she doesn't mean simple scheduling or other practical problems. In the six months since the episode with the parents at St. Raymond's, Madeleine has grown increasingly tense over the details of our renewal program. I'm sympathetic, but I'm also concerned at what I sense in her as a growing rigidity in the face of inevitable change.

What distracts me tonight is that I've not yet received Madeleine's recommendation for Janet, who is scheduled to make her final vows in August. This is an important document, because Madeleine's been her superior for all three of her years in temporary vows. Most of the other letters are already in, including Madeleine's for Sister Angela and Sister

Jeanne Marie. But I have a hunch about what's holding up Janet's. A while back, a call to support the IHM sisters out in Los Angeles appeared in the *National Catholic Reporter.* The project was eagerly received by many who had been casting about for some way to protest what was happening to these nuns we respect. Here in our motherhouse, as well as in many parish convents, petitions were posted on bulletin boards, but not in every convent. Our experiment with decentralizing authority allows for more autonomy in parish convents. Hence, superiors stronger on orderliness and discipline than on participatory decision-making could squelch such a project—exactly what Sister Madeleine did at St. Raymond's. My good old friend, Maddy! The petition wasn't even posted, much less discussed.

Knowing nothing about Madeleine's decision, Janet saw our list of signatures when she came to the motherhouse and promptly added her name. In the confrontation that ensued, Madeleine shared her reason for having to thwart Janet's plan: Monsignor Sweeney did not want "his" sisters signing such a petition. I learned about their heated exchange only when Madeleine called, concerned about the way Janet is developing. "It's happening more and more with Sister Janet," Madeleine complains, "this insubordination."

"Wait a minute, Madeleine. You could interpret that differently. You could see Janet as assuming more responsibility for her values, becoming more mature."

"I'd be more open to her 'maturity' if she weren't so confoundedly dogmatic and critical about the way things have been done in the past."

"I know what you mean," I said. And I did. Janet has an excellent eye for what she calls 'system problems' in the order, but she can't understand any delay in addressing them. "On the other hand, don't you admire how she thinks for herself? You've got to admit, she's not easily swayed by others." Unlike sweet but insecure Angela, or fastidious Jeanne

Marie, I thought.

"I worry that Sister Janet is so independent that she may never fit in," Madeleine continued. "We need sisters with community spirit, Sister, team players, not lone rangers."

"But in the future we will also need creative young sisters who can work independently, with much less support from the order," I said, remembering predictions about how orders like ours will look in the years ahead: smaller, leaner, each sister more autonomous than now, in professions other than teaching (possibly in law, public health, social work). That calls for more young women like Janet, not fewer, I feel.

I hang up from that exchange with Madeleine fearing that my affection for Janet had led me to protest too much. The truth is, I envy Janet. She's made me wish I were twenty years younger, with her zest and clear-eyed view of what she wants in her own future. She knows our changes aren't simply to make the life more attractive for newcomers, or to hold on to disgruntled sisters. She grasps the reason behind all the reforms—of allowing us to work more effectively with those who most need us—what our foundress had in mind at the start, many think. Janet sees this more clearly than either Madeleine or me, caught as we are in the centuries-old style of convent life, the only one we've known. My worries for the future lie more with the emotionally fragile Angelas and the rigid Jeanne Maries than with the strong Janets.

After Mass I detour to the infirmary on my way to supper in the refectory. I linger a bit longer than usual, reminiscing with a few of the older nuns, most of whom find the Church's new approach to Holy Thursday disconcerting, to say the least. As far back into their childhood as any can remember, and certainly during all their years in the order, Holy Thursday has been a day of penance and fasting. It's the night Judas betrayed Christ, so, like Good Friday and Holy Saturday that follow, Holy Thursday has been a time to concentrate on the sins of the world and the price Christ paid to redeem everyone. Until now, it's been a grim day in a grim week.

The laughter they've been hearing from the refectory at this late hour is hard for the old ladies in the infirmary to accept. The rule they've observed their entire religious lives defined the refectory as a place of strict silence, dispensed only on important feasts and then only for actual mealtime. Nothing about Holy Week has ever called for this kind of dispensation. And never before have we called this meal our "Passover celebration." But the refectory is as different this Holy Thursday as the chapel. The austere cavern of a room has been transformed into a colorful, cluttered dining room. From the beginning of time, the narrow linoleum-topped table segments have stood end to end, making three long refectory tables, with every seat assigned to a sister in the order of her profession, with every sister silent most of the time.

But now one of the "experiments" decreed by our recent chapter has changed all this: The long tables came apart, with individual segments placed every which way. Assigned places disappeared and, with talk at lunch and dinner, there's now no official end to the meal. That's why this evening, at almost nine o'clock, sounds of merriment are still disturbing the infirmary's quiet. And why it's possible now, an hour or so after the close of the Mandatum service, that Janet and I, although separated by almost twenty years of professed life, are sitting across from each other at one of the small tables.

I am less than thrilled for Janet to be at the motherhouse tonight. Sister Madeleine could easily interpret her absence from St. Raymond's on such a feast as more evidence of her lack of "community spirit." Because I care for Janet, I count on her continuing presence in the order, and I worry that she isn't aware of how thin the ice beneath her is. She sits, cradling a coffee cup, staring intently into the small bouquet of garden flowers on the cloth between us while I work away at my plate full of braised lamb and other Passover trimmings. She'll keep me company, she says, for by now most sisters still in the refectory have almost finished dinner. Still feeling a glow from the Mandatum, I'm lighthearted. But not Janet. At first, I think her puritanical streak disapproves of the tablecloth and flowers, but it's something else.

"Big deal!" she utters with scorn. "We put our 'help' up there in the sanctuary, like rich ladies. Why not twelve sisters? Christ washed the feet of his friends. So why can't we?" My mouth is full, or I would protest that I don't want to sit up there in front of the whole community, struggling to remove my still unfamiliar pantyhose. "We fiddle with details, congratulating ourselves on our 'progress,' and then miss the main point," she continues, now working her coffee spoon back and forth across the linen.

"Which is?"

"To ask the hard questions: Why are we here in the first place? What's the point of being a nun?" She gestures around the dining room, at the white tablecloths, the flowers, the banners, and buffet table. "And all this niceness: What's the point?" I wait to hear her answer her own question. "Jesus sought out the smelly and sick, the lame and the halt. Yet we're satisfied with those nice suburban kids who come to our nice parochial schools." Again, I keep eating, swallowing my desire to remind her that well over a third of our sisters work with the poor.

"Instead of all this stuff about clothes and whether we do or don't switch to English in the liturgy, we should be asking, What can *we* do that others in our society cannot do? Or won't do? Why else do we give up family and kids to live in community?" She twists around in her chair, gesturing at the huge room behind her now filled with mostly empty chairs and tables. "With our nun power, we could afford to take the risks others can't. Like the risk of siding with the poor and powerless."

Janet sinks back in her chair, finally, it seems, ready to hear me. Yet the replies I've been squirreling away have by now been replaced by perplexity. Why, when I am so hopeful, is she so dispirited? Because I'm older? Or that I am more of a thinker than a doer? Or is it that I have never, even when most idealistic, identified myself, as she does, with the truly poor?

"We need to reinvent ourselves, get rid of our ritzy hospitals and our academy for rich girls." I should remind her that it was in our academy that she herself—on scholarship!—learned about Christ's mission to the poorest. "What do these high-class 'businesses' have to do with Christ?" She sighs deeply, lowering her voice to add, "We should be where no one else wants to go. That's where Jesus is: poor with the poorest. In Latin America, the inner city, with immigrants."

I can't contain myself. "You forget what's behind the changes you scorn. 'Fiddling with details' allows us to have a say in the work we do, to begin taking responsibility for our choices. Today, the choices may be only between kitchen or laundry duty. But one day they'll be more significant. Then sisters who want to can choose to be 'poor with the poorest.'"

She sets her coffee cup, sans saucer, on the table with a thud. Hunching closer to me on her elbows, she covers up the markings she's been making with the end of her spoon on the white table linen. Such transgressions of etiquette would definitely have alerted superiors during my years of training, while the poor were not even discussed.

"We've been talking about renewal ever since I joined the order, but what's it come to? For us at St. Raymond's," she continues, pulling a leg up under her, breaking more etiquette rules, "it means every spare moment this week, we've had to help Sister Ignatia make her special fudge, for Easter baskets, for our benefactors! I don't see why Sister Augusta

doesn't just tell the local superiors they've got to start sharing their authority."

"You want her to dictate democracy! *You*, the great de-
fender of free choice! Hasn't the fudge project been Sister
Ignatia's thing for years? The way yours now is Olympia
Village?"

"But I don't expect Ignatia to go down there with me. Yet
I've got to spend my free time making her damn fudge!"

"I imagine Sister Madeleine's trying to accommodate
all the sisters," I say, smarting from having to defend Madeleine so much when I basically agree with Janet.

Just then, Sister Stanislaus, in full traditional habit and
looking very cross, makes her way through the maze of tables toward the kitchen area. As she maneuvers her way
past five or six sisters still bunched around a table at the far
end of the refectory, she directs at them that frozen look of
scorn practiced on generations of misbehaving youngsters.
Clearly, she does not approve that long after their meal, they
are still locked in lively, noisy, conversation. As she passes
the two of us, she mutters in disgust, "You'd think they were
schoolgirls."

"Would that we were," Janet quips. "Schoolgirls don't
struggle with the frustration I feel."

My own fear, like a sudden quiver of pain, shoots through
me: Maybe the only way to keep the Sisterliness of old is not
to grow up but to remain schoolgirls, caught up in the romantic ideals of our novitiate.

"It's not *all* Sister Madeleine's fault," Janet admits. "Nor
Sister Ignatia's. It's the monsignor's. He's got this hold on us.
Everyone pulls back because of him. Even Sister Madeleine.
At times she reminds me of my mother, swallowing her own
plans—like a good wife, she's submissive." Janet looks up, as
if pleading. "I thought being in the convent meant not having
to put up with that 'father knows best' crap. Excuse me, but
you know what I mean."

I do, of course, know. However, I reply only that, "Sister Madeleine has great respect for Monsignor's priesthood." A true enough statement, and probably all too much to the point.

"Sister Madeleine's too old or too tired or too something for what's needed right now," Janet says.

"She's my age!" I protest.

"I can't imagine that she was ever young or ever got excited about anything."

"Oh, you're wrong, Janet, so wrong," I say sadly. Suddenly, I want everything to be the way it once was: refectory tables in a row, stripped bare, silent except for the quiet opening of drawers beneath the table as we took out our plain crockery and placed it carefully on the table (lest we interfere with the sister reading from the corner lectern), then ate food as uninteresting as most of the reading. Everything, always A.M.D.G., *ad majorem dei gloriam*, for the greater glory of God.

By comparison, Janet looks coarse and ordinary to me when I remember the loveliness of young Madeleine, that teenage Noreen Becker with her endless energy for helping anyone in need. How I wish Janet had known her then. Or later, to have seen the excitement of her mind when we were in the midst of our college studies, debating long into the night about the subtleties of Jacques Maritain's aesthetics, or whether Graham Greene can be called a Catholic novelist when his main characters were often adulterers.

Would Janet have found our enthusiasm laughable? I'm not sure. What is clear to me, however, is that little love is lost between Madeleine and Janet, two people I dearly love.

The chapel stays open all night Holy Thursday so we can "keep the Lord company," as his apostles failed to do the first Holy Thursday. Following their Passover meal, Jesus spent the night alone praying in the garden of Gethsemane before being led off to Golgotha. So, throughout the night, until noon on Good Friday, we take turns paying homage to Christ in the Blessed Sacrament. This much of the old way remains.

When I enter the chapel around midnight to take my turn, the air is still heavy with the scent of roses mingled with incense. Because the darkness is lit only by candles at the side altar, I cannot at first tell whether or not anyone else is sharing that watch with me. When finally a half dozen or so shadowy forms emerge, they are so indistinct, they could easily be in the traditional habits. With darkness and silence, it is once again the chapel of old.

Up front in the chapel, a hornlike nose-blowing startles me. I'd know it anywhere. It's Janet's; she's been weeping. I feel guilty for not being more sympathetic with her in the refectory. I wish now that I would have shared with her my own early frustrations at St. Pat's and others later, when certain aspects of convent life seemed at war with others. Is it because of what Sophie said about me, that I'm scared to share my feelings, especially my "not nice" feelings? Or what Suzy describes as our Byrne sense of superiority over more "emotional types"? As I kneel in the darkened chapel, it becomes obvious that the need to defend Madeleine, to urge patience on Janet for "her own good," is my defense against letting Janet see that vulnerable part of me—which just might give her hope.

Maybe it is, after all, unfortunate that her growing up in community is happening just as the order itself is growing up. I have often envied her this accident of history—especially when I recall my own tears at St. Pat's—which now seem such a waste. At least she struggles with problems emerging from the realities of our day, not from some misguided piety. When her sniffling again reminds me of her presence in the dark, I think at least she doesn't suffer from the sense of failure that still haunts me. I can't imagine her personal relation to Christ causing even a flicker in her soul. Janet is so sure Christ is among the poor.

I have to admit that my twenty-three years of community living haven't given me what Janet's five years have given her: a fierce preference for the poor, for those without a voice, for the abandoned. Her affection for whatever will make her more like them can be annoying at times, but edifying. Others can dismiss her penchant for cast-off clothing and her disregard for the nuances of grooming as the "style" of her generation of university students, whether at Columbia, Berkeley or Paris—or right here. Yet I know how she longs to identify with the least of the brethren because that's where she believes Christ dwells.

Easter Monday, 1968
"Why are you off to New Orleans, Sister, just as these meetings are getting important?" At the depot, Madeleine looks very much the sister superior in her modified habit. And I, in my simple skirt and flat shoes, very much the schoolgirl being interrogated.

"Because I promised to," I respond, "way before the community meetings were scheduled." My back stiffens, my tone turns testy. "I promised months ago to chair one of the small sections on Wednesday." True enough, but not nearly as strong a reason for going to New Orleans as the hope of recharging my professional batteries—and seeing my old CU friends. From the time it was announced last year, I got permission to travel to New Orleans for the American College Personnel Association convention after Easter. Much later, Augusta announced a special community-wide meeting for that same time. An interim evaluation of the various experiments underway within our order these last eight months. She wants to test our earlier, widespread enthusiasm for reform.

"Will your priest friend be there?"

"As a matter of fact, Dan will be job hunting during these holidays," I answer truthfully, if somewhat curtly. When I add he probably won't even get to New Orleans, though, I'm less than candid. Dan will get there if he can, I know. Why else would he have asked for my arrival time?

Will it still be easy to talk to him, I wonder now, as I stand squeezed into the aisle of our coach inching its way into the New Orleans train yard? I rest my bags on the arms of a seat, thinking over the two years since I've seen Dan.

From our phone calls and letters, I've learned he's flourishing as a secular (diocesan) priest without even a twinge of regret about leaving his monastery. He's definitely back on track, with dissertation and degree behind him, finished with his "days as a schoolboy."

Still, letters and phone aren't the same as face to face. Distance and time, different occupations and associates, these can open chasms in otherwise solid friendships. Maybe that's happening with Madeleine and me, or why else do I hesitate sharing all my travel plans with her? Can she ever truly understand about Dan? Probably not, I admit, reluctantly.

When the crowd in the aisle finally gathers momentum, I find myself surprisingly clumsy. I struggle with luggage, fore and aft, to avoid inflicting injury on myself or others. When my shoulder purse slides off its perch, I have no hand to retrieve it, so it just dangles at my side, banging out of sync against my ankle. What a paradox: Our switch to secular garb is supposed to bring greater simplicity, yet here I am, more encumbered than I ever was traveling in the habit. Gone, alas, are the days when a nightgown and toothbrush stuck in my briefcase sufficed. Now I needed outfits.

Once out of the train and into the muggy New Orleans evening air, I pull aside from the crowd bearing down toward the exit sign. I need to take off my sweater, which means reorganizing my cumbersome load. In the process, purse strap, arm, and cardigan get tangled up. I'm completely flustered—mortified to have become so ungainly. Suddenly, my embarrassment turns into cold fear when, from behind, a deep male voice startles me. "Need some help, miss?"

I press my purse close against my body as sweater and briefcase fall to the ground. I assured Madeleine that I had no apprehension about this first-ever train trip without a sister companion. Yet now I'm frightened—and ashamed of the fear—that keeps the "no, thank you" stuck somewhere in my throat. But then I recognize Dan scrambling to pick up my sweater and spilled briefcase—Dan in a blousy sports shirt with swaying palm trees rippling across his back. It's the same blue as my sweater.

"So it *is* you," he says, straightening up. "The real you. I thought I might have trouble spotting you." He's eyeing me up and down, looking neither startled nor surprised. But I'm startled at how different *he* looks, softer and more youthful, although there's more gray now in his hair. Is it the clean-shaven face or the clothes? It's the first time I've seen him in something other than jeans and dark turtleneck—or his black clericals. I'm tickled to see that we match in our khaki and soft blue, but all I say is, "You got rid of your beard."

"And you dumped the habit," he replies. As he leads me off toward the exit sign, I have the oddest sensation of feeling like the whole of me is smiling, inside and out. The fatigue, the awkward self-consciousness, the fear have all melted away.

My mind's a jumble of things I want to share with him, yet I'm incapable of anything like conversation. The crowd thins by the time we reach the parking lot, and Dan picks up where he left off in the last letter. For some months, I've heard about Bird, the 1959 Thunderbird he acquired for next to nothing. Because he'd gone into such detail about this project of his, I'm able now to ooh and aah intelligently about upholstery, white walls, and bucket seats. I even ask about the rebuilt carburetor—while allowing the contents of my own heart to settle somewhat.

"She looks better at night than in direct sunlight," he says proudly, and I hope the same is true of me. I marvel how he has exactly the right term for every little thing on his car, how he can explain so simply what to me is quite mysterious. This way of his, being unpretentiously smart about any number of odd things, has always intrigued me.

While he maneuvers out of the parking lot, talk of our current lives weaves its way into the car talk. Yet we have barely touched on the subject of his job search by the time we reach the hospital nursing school where I'm staying. So, after depositing my bags, I agree, despite the hour, to continue our catch-up with a quick walk over to the French Quarter. "No place gives you a feel for the magic of New Orleans like Bourbon Street," he says, "especially at night."

We pick our way carefully to the last two chairs in the darkened room. He discovered this place, he tells me, this small hole-in-the wall jazz club, on a previous visit to New Orleans. As he had Mrs. Lavery's guesthouse nearby, where he's staying. "Much more 'N'awlins' than that antiseptic hospital." Without his beard, his smile still surprises me.

Waiters in white aprons take orders and serve drinks with the silent reverence of altar boys. For the crowd packed into this small area, it seems indeed a sacred moment. They listen, as if mesmerized, to the plaintive strains of a brass horn that glistens in the spotlight. As soon as the piece is finished, Dan whispers, "Want a beer? Or one of those?" pointing to an exotic concoction nearby.

I'm hungry as well as thirsty, so I choose the one with skewered fruit sticking out of the glass. By the time our drinks arrive at intermission, Dan discovers I don't know a clarinet from a trumpet or a trombone from a saxophone, or how Dixieland differs from other jazz or the blues from calypso. So he launches into his concise lecture on jazz, New Orleans style, as I munch on the fruit.

Here it is again, I think, as the fascinating story pours out of him: Dan's detailed knowledge of worldly things. It shouldn't surprise me, for he had much more interest in "the world" than I did—whether it's cars and sports, or restaurants and wines, or, as I am just now finding out, the lore of New Orleans.

It isn't simply that his is an intelligent, retentive mind. He cares about these things the way no nun I know does. The way I never, until this moment, have ever wanted to. Because these are the things my family and others "in the world" care about. Part of what I left behind when I left that world. But sitting here in this stuffy jazz club, which looks quite shabby when the lights are up, sipping this luscious drink, I recognize, with a slight twinge, a new emotion. More than simple admiration for his ability to be passionate about things—not abstracted from them, as I often feel—it's envy that I feel. And resentment, that my own training as a nun encouraged me to keep myself so distant from the things of our world.

I recall Dan telling me one time that he didn't think men would put up with being "cut off from the world" the way nuns are expected to be, and that priests who lecture nuns about shutting out the world probably never even imagine themselves doing likewise. At the time, I only felt sorry for such priests, for the all-enveloping spiritual life I thought they were missing. But now, a little light-headed from having nothing in my stomach but alcohol and a little fruit, I recognize a smoldering anger at the inadequacy of my own training.

We were led to believe we could combine two incompatible styles of Christian dedication. To think of how Madeleine and I in our youth were enchanted by the austerity of those monasteries perched on mountaintops—at the same time we were chasing our tails in a too-full round of classroom, college, and community obligations. For too long, we tried to be more monk-like than the monks themselves. Madeleine is still trying. But there's something off-kilter, wrong-headed, in this ideal. Striving for the asceticism of the monk in the midst of our active lives is crazy-making!

The musicians return and start up again, this time to a livelier beat. I smile to think I was occupying myself with thoughts about asceticism while tapping and swaying and clapping to the beat of these wild drums. My whole body is telling me why Dan loves jazz so. However, a few moments later, just as he says things are starting to heat up, I suddenly begin to feel very strange. Whether it's the stifling room, or the "special Caribbean drink," I'm getting woozy.

"Better go slow on that," Dan warns, having noticed that I'm no longer responding to the music.

"I do feel a bit off," I say, as the room closes in on me.

"Come on, let's get some air," he says, helping me to my feet. With a firm grasp of my elbow, he guides me out through the haze into the mild New Orleans night.

The jambalaya does it, makes me normal again. Or maybe it's the strong coffee and gulps of water after each encounter with the hot, spicy stew Dan calls "typically Creole." I expected only coffee when we stopped at this all-night diner on our way back to the hospital. Once inside, though, the aroma from a large pot on the stove reminds me that I've had no real food all day. So we sit at the counter devouring a delicious, altogether new-to-me mix of rice, tomatoes, sausage, and seafood. Between mouthfuls, Dan explains the difference between Creole and Cajun cooking, which necessarily involves the tale of Louisiana's polyglot culture.

In the midst of explaining New Orleans's complicated role during the Civil War, he breaks off abruptly. "Forgive me, I'm jabbering," he says flatly. It's the voice of the serious, brooding Dan. For the first time since we met, he seems at a loss for words. "It's odd to be with you now—without your habit, I mean." Sitting at a counter under the glare of fluorescent lights, I'm glad not to be facing him directly, for I would be embarrassed to see him embarrassed. "Don't misunderstand, Elizabeth. I'm all for it, your change of habit. It's just that I feel, well, odd right now."

"Likewise," I say. Then an uneasy silence and I'm glad for once to see Dan reach for his cigarettes. "It's great just to be plain people, not being stared at while we eat."

"You can never be plain, Elizabeth!" I concentrate on finishing my bowl of jambalaya while he finishes his cigarette. "What difference is it going to make for you, to be dressed like that? Without the habit?"

"Someone just might offer me a cigarette," I quip, surprising myself. I wasn't a real smoker before I entered the order and don't particularly want to become one now.

"Excuse me," he says quickly, fumbling for his cigarettes. "Old habits die hard."

Once again, I am the seventeen-year-old imitating Bette Davis as I lean toward him on one elbow to light up. It's Joe's Joint, circa 1945. I twirl from side to side on the stool, letting my legs dangle, and concentrate on recapturing my old talent for perfect smoke rings, basking in the innocent wickedness of a high school ditch day.

"I know how self-conscious I felt when I first went out in civvies," he says. "But it wasn't the novelty it must be for you. We regularly switch into secular clothes. You never do." Wordlessly, he stubs out his cigarette, then reaches for another. "Eventually, of course, when I took off the monk's habit for good, it meant leaving the monastery and living on my own." His voice trails off. "I'm truly curious, Elizabeth, what will it mean for you?" He's twisted around to look at me.

"That we won't be so preoccupied with our set-apartness, our specialness, our differentness, that we can concentrate more on what we joined the order to do."

"We, we, we—what about *you*?" he asks, sounding irritated. His remark cuts deep.

"Me?" It's hard to focus. I'm distracted by the memory of how much I liked the ritual but not the taste of smoking. "Not much will change. I'll keep on teaching philosophy. They've paid too much for my education for me to ditch it for social work. And I'll probably stay on with the junior sisters. Speaking of teaching, why so few Catholic colleges on your list?"

"There'll be even fewer now that I've seen a couple of places—small, nunny places. What they want is some grandfatherly chaplain. It's not a world I want to be in anymore, Elizabeth."

"You're not grandfatherly enough? Even with your gray hairs?"

"Hardly." His head is down again, focusing on the coffee cup in front of him on the counter. "I want something much more secular, Elizabeth. This may shock you—I was going to wait until after the meetings to tell you this—but I don't want philosophy at all. Certainly not scholastic philosophy, or Thomism. It's too tied in with old theology for me, with old Church stuff." The waiter pours him another cup of the chicory-laced coffee. "I want to work more directly with people in need. Maybe on a secular campus, in counseling. Or social work. I want to get away from all the clerical, parochial baggage, to live and work with people who come to celebrate the Eucharist—not from guilt or routine or tradition, but because they want to."

I recognize his ideal of the anonymous priesthood, what

he's been referring to the last few months. Each time I wonder about his priestly status: What does he mean by "living on his own"? Is he free to accept any job he wants? Anywhere? Does he ever think about looking for a position in St. Louis? But now, almost twenty hours after the rising bell at the motherhouse, I am much too weary for these weighty questions, so I ask him to head me back to the nursing school.

⁂

Easter Tuesday, 1968
I'm still in Dan's company, in my secular clothes, this morning—at least mentally—addressing him emphatically: See, this is what it means to be a plain person. A few minutes ago at the hotel coffee shop, I stood anonymously amid a crush of habited priests and nuns from the convention, all clerically garbed. They had to be finished by nine, they informed the hostess, who deferred to them—the way one does to small children or the elderly—and then promptly seated them. But to me she was dismissive. "You'll have to wait, ma'am—twenty minutes minimum."

I felt released, and turning on my heel, pushed my way through the darkly garbed clutch of churchly convention people to rush down the street. As I barreled along through the morning foot traffic, I had no need for those censors that come with the habit, that have kept me oh-so-ladylike, averting my gaze, deferring to those rude enough to elbow their way ahead. But not now. In no time, I got myself waited on in the first coffee bar I came to. I stood there, munching on a beignet, watching the sea of ordinary people rush by.

I lick the sugar from my fingers without shame. You see, Dan, I can be plain.

⁂

"How about a real N'awlins lunch?" Dan says, as we both emerge from the annual association luncheon. Truth be told, I was so busy throughout the banquet catching up on Tom's family and Basil's new responsibilities—he's been made provincial of his order—that my rubbery chicken was hardly touched. I am easily persuaded to ditch the afternoon meetings for the sake of sampling some Creole cuisine.

We take off for the French Quarter, though not nearly as briskly as the night before because of my pumps and wool knit. We promise ourselves to be back for at least some of the afternoon sessions, surely for the business meeting at five-thirty. In the bright light of day, the magic of New Orleans seems rather tawdry and cheap—until we step inside Antoine's. There we relax in elegance with crusty bread and cool white wine. Eventually we move on to the *potage de jour,* with *truite meunière* and *salade vert*—enough mixed greens for a table of six in our refectory. Dan says we mustn't rush, that there's the rest of the afternoon and our bottle of Pouilly-Fuissé to finish, as well as crêpes Suzette and *café filtre.* He's right about the civilizing legacy of the French in New Orleans.

It isn't hard for Dan to convince me we needn't rush back to the convention, that we should explore a bit more of this wonderful city. Besides, I never knew I could so relish just talking about "unimportant things" with someone else. Our talk is effortless, a wonderful completion of our odd exchange over the last two years, when at times we've had to wait weeks to answer the other's letter. Much information has passed between us, in our letters and phone visits. But little of the give and take that creates the topic of conversation as it spontaneously lurches ahead. Which is what happens as we amble down streets named Bourbon, Toulouse, Orleans, and Chartres, with sounds of jazz and the smells of strange, exotic foods never far off. Again, Dan seems to know the names and have a story for everything. Especially when we arrive at Jackson Square.

For a while, we just stand at its edge gazing upon the

peaceful, park-like expanse that once was a working town square. Dead head of us is the Mississippi, and the buildings on either side of us reflect the successive regimes of Spaniards, French, and Americans. Immediately next to us stands the lovely old Cathedral of St. Louis, prompting Dan to wax prophetic about the demise of the hierarchical church. The whole square has a tangled history, he explains. In it, militia of various nations have drilled and settlers gathered for public executions, including burnings at the stake, beheadings, and hangings. An equestrian Andrew Jackson, meant to dominate the area, is at that moment upstaged by street musicians, artists with their easels and a juggler charming a group of tourists. "Do you still feel like you're ditching school?" he asks.

"I do! And I love it. I would have dozed through the afternoon talks anyway."

"You look plenty wide awake to me," he says, looking intently into my eyes. My own impulse to chatter is slowed by his stare, whose focus moves to my hair.

"You've got a forehead," he says, gingerly brushing aside hair that now replaces a starched headband. "And a widow's peak!"

"Maybe we should walk some more?"

"Whatever you like." Yet neither of us moves.

After a moment, he shifts his weight a bit, stretches an arm out along the bench behind me and lays his other hand over mine in my lap. It's such a simple gesture, yet it panics me. I cannot tell whether it's his hand or mine, but something at the end of my sleeve is throbbing furiously, turning my face and neck scarlet. So I disentangle to remove my jacket, which I've been wanting to do since leaving Antoine's but haven't because the thin shell underneath doesn't seem like a proper blouse. Removing the jacket doesn't help though. I'm still burning with a heat I'm embarrassed to have Dan notice.

In the silence between us, he begins, ever so lightly, to brush the nape of my neck. "You've got another one back here, another widow's peak," he says. "Such a hairy beast!"

"Look who's talking." I laugh. For one of the first things I noticed at the train station is how the Louisiana humidity curls the hair on his hands and arms into tight ringlets.

"I can see you haven't been uncovered long." He's switched his attention from the back of my neck to my forearm, where he's playing with the dark hair that resists his attempts to twist into curls. I'm chagrined at how deathly white my arm is next to his, but even more at how strong the impulse is to stroke his tanned arm with its furry hair now bleached a reddish brown.

Maybe this is why the coifs and veils and inner sleeves of our habit were invented. So that if some nun should happen to consume too much Pouilly-Fuissé, then sit on a park bench next to a fascinating man, while listening to a saxophone singing "Smoke Gets in Your Eyes," she'd never be able to experience his tickling around her neck or know the delicious feeling of his hairy arm resting next to hers, setting her whole body ablaze.

"C'mon," he says. "There's a flea market I want to show you before the rain starts."

He leads off across the square, then up one narrow street and down another. The area is quietly residential, a secluded world away from the carnival of Bourbon Street or the easy camaraderie of Jackson Square. We pass Old World mansions, some that look decrepit and abandoned, but many in the process of being transformed into quaint hotels with walled gardens. Their majestic iron gates invite peeking. We are stopped en route by a crack from the heavens, then an enormous explosion of thunder. "We're never going to make it," he says, taking my hand, turning us away from the flea market, and back toward the way we came.

With heads down, we push against the force of pelting

rain, darting around a corner, down a short block, until, breathless, we pull into a large, gated entryway. A balcony overhead shields us momentarily from the sheet of water washing down the street. The cloudburst, though, has already done its damage, more to me than to Dan. His windbreaker and sturdy hiking boots have saved him from turning into the bedraggled mess I've become. Yet neither my wet head nor soaking jacket nor collapsing pumps keep me from noticing the strange but pleasurable scent that winds around me as we huddle together under that balcony.

"C'mon," he says, holding open the heavy gate for me to step inside.

"We can't just walk in," I say. "This is someone's home."

"Elizabeth! It's Mrs. Lavery's." He sounds impatient, as if I haven't quite learned my lesson. "It's the guest place I told you about. She's bound to have some extra towels—or a hair dryer. Or something. It rains like this all the time here."

Still, I stand there, craning my neck, examining the facade. It bears no indication of a commercial establishment, with only a smallish oval plaque up high to the left of the gate, beneath the iron-worked balcony—white numerals on dark blue porcelain, just like the ones I've been admiring throughout the French Quarter. Old World, I guess. Dan will know.

His "C'mon" becomes more urgent. So I step through the gates, guardedly, into a musty-smelling, high-arched carriageway. I feel uncomfortable intruding on this private world. In the dark of the passageway, intensified by gray and rainy skies, I stumble a bit on the cobblestones. My pumps are no match for either the weather or the terrain. For the briefest moment, I long for the comfort and stability of my well-worn nun's shoes. But then Dan grasps my elbow firmly and guides me through the carriageway to the entrance to an enclosed courtyard.

"Wait here a moment," he says and disappears, while I

stand, sheltered, at the edge of the drafty passageway, gazing at rain pelting the courtyard beyond. Though seedy, it's charming. A good part of the main house boarded up; how on earth did Dan manage to find a spot like this?

I have the sense of being in a cloister, though one more sensuous than any cloister of my experience. The sheer exuberance of overgrown life packed within this decaying mansion is haunting in its beauty. I stand awestruck at the sound of the rain as it splashes over a fountain in the center of the courtyard, into a lily pond, washing leaves and blossoms before sweeping across the flagstone path and up against the buildings. The steady, insistent rhythm, rising from the rain striking metal gutters, is broken only irregularly by the squawk of a tropical bird I can't see. Nothing suggests human habitation. I am filled with the desire to praise and thank God for the wonder of His creation.

The familiar words of the poet Hopkins sound in my soul: "Glory be to God for dappled things." But out loud it's Dan I thank, when he returns carrying a small hair dryer and an armload of towels. I shiver from the cold, but pulling the wet jacket up around my neck doesn't help. It only releases a trickle of water down my back, and I shudder again.

"Look, you need to dry off," Dan says. "Let's make a run for it—you can't get any wetter than you already are." With the towels bundled inside his windbreaker, he leads the way out into the courtyard through the pounding rain. "Just across the courtyard to those stairs," he shouts. "Follow me."

When we talk about it later that night, returning to the hotel for the awards ceremony, neither of us can recall how it all started. We remember the scene vividly enough: standing there on the balcony in front of his door—in what he said had been the servants quarter—joking about how each of us so carefully packed an umbrella, giggling at Dan's bushy hair plastered against his skull, and my blouse clinging like a second skin. We recall, too, our argument about the best way to dry our sodden clothes and whether or not it's all that important to make it back to the hotel for the five-thirty business meeting. Yet neither remembers exactly when, in this tiny white room with its peeling paint, we knew we would not return to the business meeting. I was already in the robe from his bathroom—where I sequestered myself as soon as we came in, dripping from the rain—when Mrs. Lavery knocked. "An extra one—for the missus," she announced, thrusting another large terry robe into his arms.

The door's barely closed when Dan's gentlemanly demeanor cracks with a guffaw, and I'm tickled by how jarring the matronly "missus" sounds, for at this instant, I am right back inside the skin of that hooky-playing young woman at Antoine's, all warmed and wined, needing to reach out and touch the man she's with. We practically fall into each other, laughing and tumbling onto the old iron bed—I in my heavy robe, he still in his damp clothes. We roll about with abandon as a thought floats like a distant refrain: How on earth is this happening? But it floats out again just as easily. I'm astonished by how natural it is to play with him like this, how much a continuation of our friendship, and how amazing to have lived so long without it.

Horrified, my brain suddenly clears. Even as he makes me tingle with excitement, I know: This is exactly what I promised myself, promised God, I would not let happen! I pull away, protesting to Dan—to myself—that we must stop, though I feel about to explode.

"You are so right—we shouldn't go on like this without protection," he murmurs, and says he's going out to get some.

"We shouldn't go on at all," I reply. Protection hasn't even occurred to me.

"It won't take long. I'll be right back."

"No, Dan, we mustn't." Though sleepy, I am, by now, lucid.

"The rain's stopped," he says when I awake. "Come on out." He's leaning against the balcony post, smoking. He assures me not another soul is about, so in bare feet and bulky robe I join him to watch the dying sun—and to drink in the strange scent I now know as his. The mellow silence between us seems surreal, without perspective. It's as if we are, just the two of us, planted in the midst of this courtyard's extravagant tangle of colors and scents. I am enthralled by the wild profusion of plants now ripening in the late afternoon sun. For the first time, I feel truly a part of this physical world. A world "charged with the grandeur of God," that "bursts like shining from shook foil."

"So much for the business meeting," he says glancing at his watch. "It's already half over."

"You're sorry?" I ask.

He starts again to kiss and cup my breasts—what had triggered our earlier tumble onto the bed. He lets me know that he has the protection he went out to get. Now, though, I'm very clear: We cannot continue this way. I cannot. Though I ache to finish what we started earlier, this way of loving Dan doesn't belong with my life in the order, with being a member of the community I've pledged to help renew. This I'm sure of. "C'mon," I say, "let's get back to the Roosevelt."

With the awards ceremony starting at eight, we scramble about, finally leaving for the hotel in clothes not yet thoroughly dry. "Wait." I reach on tiptoe to smell the jasmine trailing from the balcony roof. He picks a tendril and holds it against my cheek. Once again, the rush of desire floods through me.

"Sure you want to go back to the meeting?" he asks gently.

"Yes, I'm sure." I manage to sound more confident than I

feel. "We—at least I—must go back."

"And I'm more sure than ever that I love you and want to make love to you. But, yes, we probably should go back."

Easter Wednesday, 1968
Stuck to the lectern when I arrive to chair the morning session is a note from Dan. "Can you join me and Bird for lunch out at the lake? We need to talk."

Suddenly, what I'd crammed into my brain since rising early this morning leaves me. *However do women manage,* I want to cry out, *after an afternoon like yesterday?* How do they contain themselves within these fitted skirts and jackets? How do they pull their lives back into practical shape? But there's nobody to answer me right then, for the room is slowly filling up with black-suited clericals and a lone nun, fully habited, in the rear. I hold tight to the lectern, the better to steady my fluttery hands, and draw a deep breath. Gradually, as I calm myself, the information on the speakers returns to me and my face retrieves its old Sister Mary Joy smile. Yes, indeed, we do need to talk, I say to myself, as I calmly fold his note and slip it into my pocket.

Yet neither of us is talking much when, a couple of hours later, we thread our way by car out of the business district, up along the Bayou St. John. It's a part of New Orleans Dan doesn't know, so he needs prompting from the maps and guidebooks in my keeping. When we reach the curving drive along Lake Pontchartrain, he pulls in at the first parking bay, switches off the motor, and slumps over the steering wheel, as if collapsing from exhaustion.

"Then you didn't get much sleep either?" I ask. But when he turns to look at me, I know it isn't simply fatigue that grips him. He begins again to whisper my name, as he did at Mrs. Lavery's, and soon we are twisted together over the gearbox in an altogether uncomfortable yet delightful embrace.

"Look," I say, finally extricating myself from him and falling back into the maps and guidebooks, "we do need to talk."

He nods. "Then let's walk." For a while, we walk silently along a path, actually the top of a concrete seawall hemming in the lake. We are striding in step—again in unison, I think—and gleefully squeeze his hand. "Elizabeth, I need to know where you are in all this."

"And I you," I say.

"I feel like there are two parts to my brain," he begins, gesticulating broadly, "two levels. One is business as usual, efficient, organized. I think about our drive today, and how we'll get hungry. So I dash over to the French market, getting the stuff for lunch. I even remember the year of that Pouilly-Fuissé you liked. I think of our drive up to St. Louis, what Bird will need, what we will need. I mark the maps, cash some traveler's checks. But then, clunk! Suddenly, like some heavy metal bolt falling through my neat and tidy mind, it rattles around, threatening everything: What in the hell will it mean to spend the next two or three days—and nights—with you? What—"

I interrupt, shocked at what he says. "We can't do that, Dan. Can't drive back together." My words give me a resolve I didn't have just seconds ago. "I've got to take that five o'clock train, this afternoon."

"I was afraid you'd say that."

We are sitting now on one of the concrete steps that form the lake side of the levee. I've taken off my shoes and am dangling my feet over the water that breaks gently below us, glad that I decided to change into the khaki outfit, and to go barelegged. He takes my hand, lifts it to his face, then begins kissing—wrist, knuckles, fingertips. "Your hands were the first thing I noticed about you from that lonely spot in the corner of Schneider's class. On Aristotle's *Metaphysics*. Remember?"

"I remember that you always sat in the back, separate

from the rest of us."

"They're so strong, yet womanly. For the longest time, I fantasized about holding and kissing them." With his index finger, he slowly explores my hand, tracing around its edges, then up and down each finger. "I love your hands, Elizabeth. I love you. How does this fit with who we are?" He gazes out to the lake's horizon. "I am a priest. I stand between God and man. Offering back to Him His creation, loving Him through His creation. And then you come along. You, you, Elizabeth. You are the best of His creation for me. He has given you to me, to love and take care of. Through you I love Him. For a long time I've known—you are my way to God. Then yesterday...."

He sinks over, elbows on his lap, with hands on either side of his head. I reach over, rest my hand on his back and feel silent sobs. His voice is husky when he sits up and says, "You're at the center of my life. In the place where I am a priest." He turns finally to look up at me with pleading eyes. "Can you understand? How being a priest, and being with you, how they go together for me?"

What he's said makes me both happy and pained. I have no doubt what I must answer, but only a whisper emerges. "It's different for me, Dan. None of this fits my life either. Celibacy may not be essential to your priesthood, being, as you say, only 'a disciplinary rule,' about to be overturned, but it is for me, essential I mean. For the community I love and want to remain part of." I force my voice into a firmness that barely covers threatening tears. "Not because celibacy is superior to marriage, God knows. Nor because of the other highfalutin things I believed when I took my vows. Certainly not because I think sex is sinful." I pause, almost hoping he'll interrupt my incomplete thought. "Even though it's only a discipline, as you say, it's a discipline we sisters still need. Even with our reforms. It's our glue, Dan. Without celibacy there isn't any community life."

Drawing a deep breath, I spit out the rest of my resolves from last night's turbulence. "My situation is quite different from yours. Yesterday does not go with my life—old or new." Even as I say this, though, I long for what I know is impossible. I want to be proved wrong in what I've just said, to be shown some miraculous way I can be with Dan and still be part of my community of sisters. To have it all. For now I know—as I did not before yesterday—how incomplete I feel, how strong is my longing to love and be loved by Dan.

"A lot of guys feel the way you do," Dan says, "that celibacy is so tied in with their priesthood they've got to give up their ministry to marry. But I don't believe that. Marriage and priesthood belong together. They're both sacraments of love. Soon they'll be together—officially. It's only a matter of time. You and I are just 'anticipating' a bit."

We're both sitting upright, staring straight ahead, yet I feel his smile returning and hear again a tease in his voice. "The Church has always gone easy on engaged couples, Elizabeth. That's what we are!"

Engaged? Hasn't he heard what I said? "Sometimes, I think I've never been engaged," he says. "Never. Not whole-soul, whole-body engaged. I've always been an onlooker. Part of some group commitment. Celibate life is a great place for that, you know: learning how to extend yourself to what's bigger than the self, being committed to causes beyond your own self-interest. Yet that's not the same as commitment to a person. You can identify deeply, personally, with the group and its work but never commit to any one person, including maybe even Christ. That's far worse than breaking promises about celibacy."

"So I'm your chance for personal commitment!" I blurt.

"Maybe. And maybe I am *your* chance."

Talk of commitment brings back old feelings of having failed in my personal relation to Christ, what is supposed to be the center of a nun's life. Am I, as Dan just said, using group commitment to substitute for personal commitment? The questioning from last night erupts once again: Would a deeper faith—or whatever people mean by "intimacy with Christ"—have kept me out of Dan's arms? Or is this experience of loving him a beginning of real commitment, for which all the rest has been a rehearsal? I ache for him to hold me and comfort me, yet I can only mumble, "They don't go together, Dan, not for me."

"Maybe not now." After a light but lingering kiss on my neck, he pulls himself up and me after him. Arm in arm, we walk along the levee until we find a spot where the receding tide has left enough beach for us to stroll along the water's edge. Ankle-deep, we splash water back and forth at each other, as I try in vain to summon a clear answer to him. Instead, memory intrudes.

"Just before I left home, I remember Dad choking up— the first and only time I ever saw him cry—when he told me I didn't know what I was giving up when I gave up marriage. Now I think he was trying to talk to me about how the love between a man and woman is so total, so much body and soul."

Dan turns me around to face him. Taking hold of my head in both his hands, he gently kisses my forehead, then my hair and neck. "It also has to do with hair, and necks. Your dad was right, Elizabeth, wasn't he?"

We walk on for quite a while, playfully kicking the water at each other's feet. The space between the water and the wall has widened and we find ourselves a clear spot in the dry sand where we sit, contemplating the enormous expanse of lake.

Finally, he breaks our silence. "The way I see it, the changes we've each made are our only course corrections toward our original goal. I feel freer now than ever to fulfill my priestly vocation. More grown-up, not needing the brotherhood of the monks as much. Isn't it the same for you?

Convent life preparing you for wider ministry?" He draws my hand to his cheek. "Listen, Elizabeth, whatever you decide, you know I love you and am committed to you. And after yesterday, I know you return my love. Someday soon we'll be together—for good." With that, he gets up and sprints off toward the car to fetch our lunch.

I sit, mindlessly scooping up sand, sifting it through my fingers, mulling over something he said in Antoine's yesterday. I'd asked him about our priest friend Brian, "Why doesn't he get a dispensation and marry his lady friend? Plenty of priests are doing just that."

It had ignited Dan. "Because he's *called* to be a priest! He can't just amputate himself from what gives his life meaning, Elizabeth. Besides, that's what she loves about him." Would that it were the same with me, that Dan's priesthood is what I love about him. But it's not. My love is in spite of, not because of, his being a priest.

My resistance to Dan's romance with the priesthood has old roots. Early in the convent, I deliberately distanced myself from those nuns who I felt fawned over priests, especially the newly ordained. With tears in their eyes, they'd beg for the traditional new priest's blessing, then kiss his newly consecrated hands. This reverence for the clergy gave rise to a Priests Dining Room at the motherhouse where regularly we served steaks, fresh salads, and ice cream on an array of hand-painted bone china, while in our refectory, creamed beef, canned peas, and Jello-O salad ran together on our thick brown plates. As early as St. Pat's, I became aware of this nun-mystique surrounding priests. It turns perfectly sensible women into smothering nuns, as charmed by the authority of some as by the little-boy ways of others. It's always repelled me.

I squirm in the sand, fretful. Am I being unfair, letting this old disgust color how I hear Dan's dream of a new church? Priests will be different from what I've known, he tells me. But is this really possible? Will churchmen ever give up their claims of privilege and return to Jesus's way?

My disturbing reveries are broken by Dan returning, breathless, with bags of food in each arm. Without unloading, he kneels beside me, kisses my hair, and says, "I keep forgetting to tell you: that detour to Mrs. Lavery's yesterday wasn't planned."

"At least, not consciously," I reply. I split open the paper bags and spread out their contents while Dan busies himself with the Pouilly-Fuissé. "Hardly Antoine's," he says, discovering he has forgotten cups.

"But still very French." I use his Swiss army knife to slice some overripe pears, and then arrange them alongside some smelly cheeses, a slab of pâté, and a still fresh-smelling baguette.

"It could be hard on you at first, Elizabeth, having to be secret about how we feel, waiting for Rome. But it won't be long, believe me." I trade the Swiss army knife for the wine bottle and take a swig as he continues. "There's hope again. Recent news from Rome, official and unofficial, looks good. At last that papal commission on contraception is being allowed to do its work. Any day now—most likely before the summer—the ban will be lifted, at least on the pill. It's a foot in the door.

"Once the pill is okayed, it will be a whole new ball game. Soon we'll have married clergy and women priests." He ponders a moment. "Women priests may take a bit longer. But when they see the positive influence wives have on priests." He leans over and playfully plants a light kiss on my cheek. "Once they're assured that having a wife doesn't ruin a priest's ministry, it's only a short step to the ordination of women. We may very well be the first two-priest couple, Elizabeth."

How can he say that—even in jest? Can he possibly think I want to be a priest? I'm dumbstruck. Doesn't he remember my distaste for the whole idea? My misgivings about being any kind of "official Church person"?

As we make our way back to the car—not on the levee this time, but through the park bordering it—Dan puts his arm around me and, touching my cheek, asks gently if I have any regrets. My heart so wants to have it all, to be in unison with him for good, to play with abandon, to smother once and for all whatever discordance there is between us, that I answer him only with a kiss. Which means that right here in the open, in full view of Lake Pontchartrain and Bird, we once again melt into each other. As he holds me close, prolonging the sweetness, I can feel him swelling with desire. I want him in me.

"Let's get back to Mrs. Lavery's," he mutters as we collapse on the ground.

"No," I groan. "It's time for me to get on that train."

Madeleine looks like her old self. As I step off the train, she emerges from the crowded platform to help with my bags. It's the exuberant, perky Maddy of the good old days. "You don't know what you missed!" she explodes, her cheeks flushed with news of the three-day, community-wide meeting just concluded. She takes my heavy bag and leads the way through the crowded station, leaving me with only my ungainly purse and briefcase. I want to say, you don't know what you've missed. "It got pretty nasty at times," she starts, "reformers clashing with conservatives." Her tone seems odd to me. What normally would disturb Maddy, doesn't seem to now. She seems at peace with this news.

"Johanna and her friends, I presume? They've never been much for change."

"Many more than Johanna, Sister. Or the usual conservatives. Lots of other naysayers, too. They're distressed by all the brouhaha around our reforms."

"You mean our 'experiments.'" My brain shifts into the intricacies of our renewal language. A critical distinction, I feel, between steps in a process and its final conclusions.

"It's all the same, Sister. It's change!" Peace-loving Maddy is more than a little peeved and faces me squarely. "Mother Augusta's being forced to defend—again!—the whole thing: Vatican council, our own chapter, its decrees, the whole nine yards. Because whatever you call them, they're very troubling. For a lot of sisters, we're changing stuff they've always considered sacred." Was Madeleine referring to herself?

When we finally reach "her" station wagon, she opens the door for me, placing my bags in the back. Its fierce Bulldog emblem on the dashboard dramatically reminds me that, of course, the car is part of St. Raymond's parish fleet. As soon as I settle into the soft leather seat, an annoying but unmistakable guilt awakens: Had I not gone to New Orleans, maybe my well-known support of Augusta's position could have helped this mess Maddy's been describing? Odd that I never felt this way during those lovely hours with Dan.

Maddy sits with the key in the ignition, staring calmly ahead. Clearly she needs to say more. "It was a major setback, Sister. At least for Mother Augusta. It's obvious to her, and maybe to everyone else, that we may be going too fast. Reverend Mother needs to find out how each sister really feels about all the changes."

"Oh, bull," I blurt out, surprising myself at how easily I've picked up Dan's expletive, and just as easily edited it. "What about all those meetings? Those questionnaires and position papers? For five years!! Everyone's had a chance to be heard; we don't need any more of that!"

At last Maddy starts the car, and says sadly, "Mother Augusta's really worried, Sister, more than ever now. About the rank and file."

I shut up for the sake of getting us back to the motherhouse, to the quiet of my cell. I need to flop on my bed before Vespers and digest it all—those three short days in New Orleans, the stimulation of all kinds. I can't deal with all this messy community business. Not now. Yet my soul mate is so obviously troubled. Could Maddy herself be doubting the wisdom of what we're doing, attempting to reform our centuries-old style of life? I've never doubted she shared my convictions about the order's need to change, yet now that it's under way, I wonder. "Am I missing something here, Maddy? Is this something you want, this referendum on our reforms?"

"I wouldn't call it a referendum, Sister," she says slowly, carefully, her voice tightening. "It's just that there's been no chance for the not-so-vocal to be heard, to get their reaction to the changes. The *experiments,* if you will. At least not since that IHM thing blew up in California."

Ah, so that's it, I think as I settle back once again into my comfortable seat. The reality of that dark news from out west, my friend Sister Christine's news, is something I know only too well. It silences us both as we head for home, Maddy deftly weaving her way through the late afternoon traffic. I begin to refocus this gloomy picture of our own community that she's been giving me against the even more sober story of "those California nuns."

Sister Christine has been sending me cassette tapes with her newsy updates fairly regularly since she finished at CU and returned to Southern California. Her news is indeed dramatic—and disturbing: about how her nuns are being fired from the Catholic schools of LA by their conservative cardinal. Despite all the directives from Rome, and their own order's elected chapter, this flinty cardinal who thought the council so "dangerously liberal" that he left early, is using his status as employer-in-chief of LA's parochial school nuns to fire *all* the IHMs in "his" schools. This means close to eighty percent of her group's active healthy nuns will be out of work by next summer. The news of his edict has spread like wildfire among nuns across the United States.

"I just can't believe it," I say, "all because they're experimenting with how they *look*?"

"Right. He wants 'real nuns' in his schools! Meaning ones who look like nuns—in habits!" The bite of Maddy's sarcasm warms my heart. Maybe we're not so far apart, after all.

The nasty details of this feud playing out with Christine's group of LA sisters and their cardinal has been detailed in both *Time* magazine and *The New York Times*. Yet for all of us cheering on this group of beleaguered sisters, I understand how others are frightened. Because of course we all know it has to do with much more than their habits. Other pastors and bishops will feel much as that cardinal does. But Madeleine? Seems hard to believe.

In the silence of our twisting and turning through the traffic, the old cardinal's words about looking like real nuns plays in my mind and once again I am distracted by how my good friend Maddy looks. When I first spotted her in the station, I was struck by how unbecoming her "modified habit" is. Like those matronly English nurses in old World War II films, I thought. Of course, it doesn't help that always-slender Maddy has put on some weight during the years I've been off at CU; but it didn't make much difference in the old habit. For all her progressive thinking, Maddy still holds on to the ideal of the habit—modified, if necessary—as signifying our otherworldly goals. Compromise is possible, she says. Yet that skirt at midcalf and that skimpy little veil just don't cut it—some compromises just don't work. For the first time since I've known her, my beautiful friend looks awkward and ungainly.

At the motherhouse, though, my ruminations on vanity instantly vanish as I retrieve my suitcase from the rear of the station wagon. For there, stuffed into the back, are some physical realities of Madeleine's life, more important by far for her than the clothes on her back. "What! You've got Sacristy duty, too? On top of everything else?" I say, spotting a huge golden candlestick protruding from a pile of Bulldog paraphernalia. It's from the high altar, and I instantly judge that her pastor Monsignor Sweeney is once again taking advantage of Maddy's reliable generosity by piling on yet another responsibility.

"Heavens, no," she says matter-of-factly. "It's just that Jeff—he's our star forward—broke one of those huge candlesticks when serving Monsignor's Mass last week. He couldn't bring himself to confess; it might have cost him his place on our team. So I took it. Sister Charlotte could make it whole again. But there hasn't been a good time to ask her."

That's quintessential Madeleine. The suburban-housewife–mother superior–counselor–principal of an eighth-grade, 300-plus-student parochial school, plus psychological guide for a house full of nuns, a guide who knows what is and is not a "good time" to approach fragile Sister Charlotte, or the all-powerful monsignor. That's the real Maddy, I think as we climb the old motherhouse stairs to my third-floor room. Generously spending these last hours of her "free day" to play taxi for me, while all I can think of is a nap! How different we are, and how different our nun-lives these past five years. In some ways how much more complicated the challenges of Madeleine's convent life compared to mine.

We've lived our nun-lives very differently, which can't be more clear than when we finally step into my room and behold the generally cluttered state of my domain. For besides the usual stack of volumes for my class preparations, with three or four opened journal articles laid one over the other, that usually free space on my convent bed is now cluttered with the cast-offs from packing for my first venture out in civilian clothes—since I left in a rush without straightening up my cell. I'm embarrassed for the ever neat and organized

Maddy to see what to her eyes must seem to be a mess. Yet she simply clears a space for herself on-the bed and settles in. She's in no rush.

"Before we part," she begins, deliberately, "I want to be sure you got the final, the main, message from Mother Augusta's meeting. Last night, at the final assembly, she asked us all to take these next weeks of summer to deliberate on a weighty issue. We are to evaluate our vocation, each of us—prayerfully, personally. And the order's as well. What are we as a group, as a community, are called to do. In each case we must ask ourselves, 'Are the changes okay? The experiments—helping or hindering our goals?'"

"Again?" This is how we started the ball rolling five years ago! Can she possibly be forgetting how all this started, with Good Pope John back in 1962, urging us to open the windows and let the fresh air in, to look out at this world and see what it's asking of us?

"Here's what's new, Sister: Now we are to reflect in private. No more distributing of 'position papers,' no more lectures from visiting 'authorities,' workshops, panel discussions, or 'targeted seminars.' Through our own personal reflection, our prayerful meditation, we are literally to 'examine our conscience' these next few weeks. She called it 'discernment.' Very grass roots, very Vatican II, don't you think?"

What I think is how ironic if our liberation ends up curtailing the very freedom of expression it's making possible. "Surely Augusta's not letting a few malcontents frustrate the will of the majority, is she?"

Maddy snaps back, "Just who are the few and who are the majority? That's the question."

We sit silently for a moment. Rarely has our back and forth been this uncomfortable. She recovers a calm more quickly than I. "What disturbs a lot of us, Sister, what disturbs Mother Augusta is that some sisters may be just too afraid or too shy to speak up. With all the bickering, who knows what the majority truly wants?"

More likely a minority is scaring the majority, I think to myself. Could Madeleine herself be scared? It doesn't seem possible. Yet I have never experienced what it's like to live under parish authority like that of her blarney-spewing Monsignor Sweeney. Nor have I confronted Sister Johanna in such a hostile atmosphere. But the votes won't go Johanna's or Sweeney's way. They can't. We've come too far already.

"There's more, Sister. After deliberating, we are to vote yes or no, every sister, in private, on each of three questions and put it, in writing, to Reverend Mother Augusta by July 15. 1. Do we go forward with the experiments? 2. Do we cancel all change and wait for orders from Rome? 3. Compromise—keep educational experiments and leave for later any structural change?"

"But structural change is the basis for all the rest!" I interrupt, furious that she can mention this keyword so casually? Why no outrage in her voice? I think of all our discussions when I was at CU, about the dangers of pyramidal, top-down structures like ours—like those in asylums! How can Maddy not be outraged that so fundamental an issue could be delayed? She's still not finished instructing me, though. Fiddling for a moment with the car keys, she seems to be searching for a way to tell me more bad news. "Some sisters feel intimidated around the more 'enthusiastic' reformers." She glances accusingly at me with the kind of knowing smile I recognize only too well.

"I wonder who?" I smile back.

"And local superiors are no longer to sponsor group discussions about any of this. There have been some pretty ugly scenes in a few convents. So she doesn't want anything that could be construed as authority influencing more impressionable sisters—either for or against a position."

"You mean I can't argue with you anymore?" I say teasingly.

"She isn't asking for miracles." Her quirky smile returns. I smile back, yet I feel a wide gulf opening between us. Could the days of seeing eye to eye with good old Maddy be over? I hope not.

May 1968

Time is closing in on me as the countdown to term's end begins in both university and convent life. There's a scramble of term papers to check, exams, and student conferences. Most immediately, though, I need to prepare for summer session, which is just weeks away. There's also physical dislocation. Next week, when the high school academy students vacate their rooms, I will move myself, body and books, over to their wing of the motherhouse for the six weeks of summer session. There I'll be "mistress" of our fifty-four junior sisters, which leaves little or no occasion to discuss with Maddy or anyone else the issue that so irked her at Easter. Not that I've forgotten her distress, or what caused it. Just that I'm buried in busyness, as I jotted in a note to her yesterday.

Truth is, I love this new phase of my teaching life, busyness and all, because teaching means way more than classroom performance. Preparation itself is rich: reading these great philosophers, watching as each constructs his unique universe of meaning, then sharing these worlds of meaning with students. For virtually every student, it's an exciting experience of discovering how seriously different thinkers have understood "reality."

I also see this academic work as fueling the extra effort I've been putting into our order's renewal this past academic year, primarily because I can never forget that first miserable teaching year at St. Pat's with those seventy-two innocent little kids. It still haunts me, and drives me now to make sure this doesn't keep happening to our beginning teachers. It is the most obvious of the structural changes we need to make: to see that our nuns are trained before entering the classroom. I know Maddy agrees with me on this.

Amid the busy days, Dan also is very much on my mind. One might think that "living the life" in our motherhouse would be impossible after what I experienced at Mrs. Lavery's. Or that I'd be disconsolate at being separated from the person I love, pining for him and for the pleasures of that balmy afternoon in New Orleans. Or crippled by guilt over my transgressions. Yet none of this is true. I tell myself we are like those wartime couples separated by something greater than their personal wants and needs. But I don't fool myself. I know I am growing closer to Dan. Especially in his phone calls, when I hear him growing in hope, letting go of some of his darkness.

He has been hearing—on the QT, of course—about the developing progressive views within the Church, especially on birth control, as well as a recognition of developments in the science of human sexuality. From his privileged clerical grapevine, Dan has been learning that both the Church's hierarchy plus an expanded papal commission of laypeople have taken on this thorny subject.

"He's put laypeople on that commission," he tells me. "Men and women. Imagine that. Women. On a papal commission! Only five or so out of more than seventy men, but still, they're having a say. For the pope's ears. And word has it he's actually listening to them."

Dan is as excited as I've ever seen him about renewed dreams for "a reinvigorated Church," and within this new Church, with its windows opened wide, "a new priesthood." Clearly he's counting on some pretty strong winds! Much as I rejoice with Dan on these hopeful bits of news, I do wonder how it addresses the problems the nuns are having. But he's convinced a new pope will straighten things out soon. "The guy's finally coming around, m'dear. Seems to be catching the spirit of Good Pope John. *Aggiornamento* may yet happen—even in California!"

It's not his words so much as the form of his body that drifts off with me to sleep each night.

⁂

June 5, 1968

I'm up later than usual this hot muggy St. Louis night—in my nightgown, plotting out reading assignments for my summer course, Introduction to Existentialism, starting next Monday. My tiny room over here with the juniors is even more cluttered that it normally is. Why unpack when it's only for six weeks, I tell myself. So most books are still in boxes, an extra nightgown and changes of underwear in the suitcase—with only my new outfits hanging in the tiny closet: two skirts, two cotton blouses, and an Irish cardigan, a gift from my dad.

I'm immersed in Camus's *The Rebel*, when a sharp cry jolts me back to the reality of my job with the juniors. I grab my bathrobe and fly down the darkened hallway, berating myself, why did I let them prop open that fire door? And where are those emergency numbers?

As I round the corner, fear gives way to a different and terrible shock. In the student rec room, everyone is staring at the TV. A couple of junior sisters clutch each other, one sobbing audibly. Others quietly slump in their chairs. I had forgotten some of the juniors decided to wait up for the results of the California Democratic primaries. Now I stand, frozen just inside the door, watching an Ambassador Hotel out in Los Angeles go wild. There on television, another Kennedy tragedy plays out.

Janet's leaning against the wall with her hands on either side of her head. At first I think she's covering her ears, then realize she's holding her thick glasses to keep them from sliding off her face in the wash of tears. Speaking to no one in particular, she's stomping her feet and crying, "That crazy city! That crazy, stupid city!" She is neither challenged nor supported by the others and continues lashing out. "It was stacked against him. From the start. Just like that cardinal out there. The powerful never want change."

I want to tell Janet to shut up. For as we hover, shocked, around the TV—listening to tidbits of news woven into the endless conjecture about Robert Kennedy's wounds—there's little doubt that we're losing another hero. Another Kennedy. Then Sister Jeanne Marie kneels down, quietly starting the rosary, and we all join in. One by one we gently say our Hail Marys over the TV words—about an ambulance, a receiving hospital, then another hospital, then surgery and bullet fragments. Janet eventually joins in. When at last they tell us Robert Kennedy has lapsed into a coma, there's nothing to do but go off to our rooms.

It seems wrong to sleep when out in LA so many are working through the night to keep this young man alive. I lie on top of the bed fully clothed, waiting for the 5:30 rising bell, thinking about the old saying that bad news comes in threes: JFK, Martin Luther King, and now Bobby. All still so young, not much older than me. I feel numb and tell myself this sort of confrontation with death is supposed to lead to deeper faith. But the formulas of religion don't help right now. They feel, instead, like a distraction, an escape.

When finally I drag myself to chapel for the six a.m. Angelus, Janet's anger at the evil in LA, including the Church's evil, is still with me. The chaplain comes on the altar for Mass asking us to pray for the dying Senator and for those who have taken hope from his life. As I have. As I had from JFK and Martin Luther King and Good Pope John. A hope that threatens now to slip away while this peculiar day wears on. Bobby clings to life, yet I seem unable to get on with my own. I return time and again to the chapel to join in the perpetual rosary being said for him. Is it faith, or drowsiness from too little sleep last night? Or simply the need to be surrounded by people who feel as bereft as I do?

The rhythmic "Hail Mary, Holy Mary" finally loosens my tears. Bobby used his years well. What have I done with my forty? Nearly twenty-three of those years handed over to others—my parents, the order, the Church. Is there anything in my life of adult choice like his? Anything? Maybe those hard choices in New Orleans?

I recall that December Child's message that's stayed on my wall all these years, "that each of us is responsible for our faith." It never stops haunting me. But have I really listened? Or heard it? All day, I battle the temptation to think of my "youth" as lost. I have to force myself back to a common-sense truth: "That the order has been a good place for me to grow up." Life in the Byrne tribe would have kept me a child much longer. Once the reforms take hold, I tell myself, my community of sisters will be an even better place to keep on growing. Still, my tears for Bobby continue.

I'm leafing through the education section of the *Post Dispatch* when a small headline catches me: INDIANA NUN SCHOLAR LEAVES ORDER. It's Sister Charles Borromeo. I'm stunned. This theologian-journalist is—was—a Holy Cross nun from Notre Dame/St. Mary's and the one of Suzy's college profs from years ago, one whom she could "really dig." Though closer to home for me and my community is her book *The Changing Sister.* With it, she's helped us all to imagine a new kind of nun-life following Vatican II. I've been using it for evening discussions with the juniors this summer. They think of her as a hero. As I do. Yet now she is giving up on it, the life we have in common.

My feelings fluctuate wildly as the news settles in. At times I'm sunny, congratulating this woman on her choice to step outside her expected role. I've never met her, yet through her words I feel I know her as a sister. But other times, I'm engulfed in shadow. One of our leaders is giving up, one who had the same hopes and expectations as I have, a sister the juniors think of as leading them to embrace this way of life still new to them. How will this affect them and their choice to renew or abandon their vows?

By the time I meet with the juniors after night prayers, there's yet another shock of news to digest with them. For just before dinner, Augusta shared a letter with me from my long ago teacher and inspiration, Sister Marie Gabrielle, a letter she thought needed some special handling with the junior sisters before they see it posted on the refectory bulletin board. For my inspiring high school English teacher, Gaby, that lover of poetry, after more than thirty years in the order, is leaving to join another order, a cloistered order of nuns up in Canada.

My job is to make clear the message Mother Augusta wants to stress: that Gaby's choice is *not* because of all the changes our experimenting has caused. Her move is unusual, yes. In our order no one has ever switched over to an "enclosed order." Still canon law does allow for it, because the life of contemplation is considered "higher" than our "mixed" way of combining spiritual and corporal works of mercy. It's not that Gaby, as I will always think of her, is rejecting our reforms, Augusta stresses; it is because of these reforms that she has the courage to make this move.

Indeed, as her letter reveals, she has desired this move for years, starting as a novice, probably when I met her in Kansas City. But she was told then it was prideful of her to want this higher way. Now, though, the freer spirit of Vatican II allows her to act on her desire. So with clear conscience, and the Church's blessing, she's quitting her life as the principal of our highly respected, award-winning high school in Kansas City to begin over again as a novice in an order whose only secular work is making altar breads and vestments for priests.

I recount for the juniors my childish fascination with the pink-cheeked young novice in Kansas City, even as I've always felt sad at not getting to know her better. Our paths crossed only occasionally and briefly these past twenty-plus years. If I had known her better, I could have watched this choice growing within her, maybe even challenged her. I feel sad to see her move away just now when the new life we have worked so hard to create is getting started. Yet, when it comes to bedtime and my personal night prayers, I can only thank God for letting me know so courageous a woman.

As sisters cluster at the bulletin board to read Gaby's farewell the next morning, there are both sniffles from a few and harrumphs from others. Sister Johanna takes the news as proof that these "so-called reforms" are destroying our religious life. "Others will follow, mark my word."

Yet Gaby tells us it is *because* of the new openness, and a climate that encourages choice, that she has been able to reach her decision. Her words of appreciation for Sisterly love during her thirty-six years among us bring tears and steal any appetite for a hearty breakfast. My remembrance of English teacher, lover of poetry, explainer of *religio* merges with those images of my beautiful fantasy dancing partner in that long-ago Kansas cloister.

By the following week, another bombshell greets me, in block letters, from the top of Brother Basil's handwritten page: I'M GETTING MARRIED. Quickly, I learn more. Her name is Marguerite, his secretary for the last two years while he's been the provincial superior of his order. She's thirty-five, divorced, mother of five-year-old Mark and soon, he hopes, mother of their kids. He signs off simply as "Jack." I stand dumbfounded in the middle of the community room during the busy hour of evening recreation. Around me, a couple of foursomes concentrate on bridge, while a knot of older nuns, knitters and embroiderers, hovers near the TV. Others like me are busy with mail. Many more chat aimlessly, glancing from time to time at Huntley, then Brinkley. I shut them all out, listening closely to Basil, now Jack. He's taking advice he once gave me about not despising the good for the sake of the best.

It might be best to stay in the order, he confesses, volunteer for Latin America or the inner-city slums, like many younger brothers. But he isn't up to that sort of thing. Too middle-aged? Too set in his ways? Too selfish? Maybe all of these. But also afraid of himself if he stays with the order, he says. Afraid he'll indulge in the overly comfortable bachelor's life their reforms now make possible. "We've made our brothers' life more human, more sane," he wrote, "but we've also made it easier to be mediocre. I saw an all-too-human side of our order in my provincial job. It really got me down. Men I once considered 'model brothers' became childish and self-indulgent, reveling in 'reforms' that were supposed to mature them. This place is now more like a country club than the marine barracks I joined."

It's his closing line that stays with me when the bell for Vespers rings, ending the recreation period. I join the silent group making its way to chapel but I can't silence those words, "It's not where I want to grow old, Sister."

People leaving orders doesn't exactly surprise me. The exodus has been making headlines in the Catholic press for the past several months. Until now, though, they've been at a distance from me—like journalist Father Charles Davis. Or they've been like those of our departing junior sisters who seem to me clearly "not suitable" for either the traditional religious life or the new kind we are designing. But not these three. Not Sister Charles Borromeo, Gaby, and Brother Basil, each a model of "living the life"—whether the old or new way. They are not walking away because they have to, because of ill health, "moral turpitude, mental, or emotional instability"—the reasons allowed by canon law for dispensing final vows. They're leaving because they *want* to.

Yet Basil is different from the others. How could anyone around me in this chapel understand the way I've loved him, not the way I've loved anyone else in this world, certainly not the way I love Dan. More like the way I love Maddy or Carla or Christine—but different. And I just can't call him Jack.

We move through Vespers into Compline, ending with the soulful "Nunc Dimittis": *Now thou dost dismiss Thy servant, O Lord.* Old Simeon accepting his death. At this point each night, I bid the day farewell, knowing each night is a rehearsal for the final farewell of my own death. Tonight, I also say goodbye to three very special people who are departing—each for such different reasons—from the life we all chose long ago. Each hurts in a special way.

I stay slouched over the pew long after prayers end, my knees bolted to the kneeler. I feel burdened with an unfamiliar weight, resisting the climb up two long flights of stairs to my room. I'm not ready to sleep or meet with junior sisters, or even talk with Dan. He's been calling most nights since New Orleans, shortly after the end of evening prayer.

My brain snags on the memory of Dan. Am I avoiding the obvious—that I must choose between the order and him? How are we any different from Basil and Marguerite? I've long since abandoned any conviction that celibacy is a higher or better way to practice Christian love, as we were taught. I've told myself that my love for Dan fits what I do believe about my vow of celibacy, that it is a way to direct *all* human love to God. My love for Dan is part, a very special part, I admit, of my basic Christian commitment to love. So there's no contradiction between my feelings for him and my commitment to the order. No need to reject one for the other. Or so I tell myself. Yet, am I simply deceiving myself? Rationalizing? Indulging, perhaps, in what I am hearing from Sartre about "bad faith"? Don't I have the guts to admit that I'm in the same boat as Sister Charles Borromeo and Charles Davis and Brother Basil? Have Dan's airy speculations—about "the Church of the future" including married priests—seduced me? Am I deluding myself, imagining that I can inhabit both worlds?

My musings are as uncomfortable as the stifling heat, now that the fans are off. The chapel is deserted except for me and the sacristan who's turned out the last lights and is rattling her beads somewhere behind me—a well-understood convent signal that it's time to lock up for the night. Trickles of perspiration roll down my back, but I resist returning to my room. So I detour down the back stairs to Carla's hideaway in the basement. Although she's acquainted with Basil only through me, she certainly knows Gaby much better than I do. And she has shared the speakers platform several times with Sister Charles Borromeo.

I find her at her silkscreens—as I have so often these past months—working late in the motherhouse basement, her studio. In a few days, she's off to Scotland for three months, meeting with English-speaking nun-artists and educators from all over the world. It's a great opportunity for her, but also a sacrifice, for these weeks of summer have always been her best chance to work at her art. It's a sacrifice for me as well. To whom will I turn when she's gone?

I watch her for a few moments as she rhythmically pulls the squeegee over the frame of silk, forcing a lump of orange paint through the fabric. After each pull, she hangs the wet print on the clothespin drying rack, the one I helped her build twenty years ago. It's a ritual as familiar to me as her appearance is not: A handsome chignon holds her graying hair, giving her a distinguished air oddly incongruous with her leg-revealing skirt. I wait for her to finish that color run before thrusting Basil's letter at her.

Carla pauses from her work, drawing up the old garden bench that has become a fixture in her underground studio. We sit side by side as slowly she digests the contents of his letter. "Poor baby," she says, stretching over to hug me when she finishes the letter.

Her soothing touch and the cool dampness of the basement help relieve the burden I've carried down from the chapel. "I feel as if I've been slapped in the face. It's crazy. Why do I feel so wronged? I believe in free choice, so why am I so angry at the three of them?"

"Because they're deserting you—deserting all of us—don't you see? We've all been in this together. They've believed what we believe—in reform, in change. Yet now they're giving up. You're not crazy." As she leans over to drag the fan closer to us, I notice her wrinkling neck, something the coif had hid, and hear her weary sigh. "I feel as you do, Sister."

But would you if you knew about my time with Dan in New Orleans, I say to myself. I watch silently as Carla returns to her printing, plopping bright blue paint onto another frame of silk. With her firm grip on the squeegee, she begins again to smooth the color over the tightly framed silk cloth, forcing the paint onto the paper below.

"We've made the group thing so personal," she says "Now, when key people quit, it feels like a personal affront. Like they've done something to us personally."

"They have," I murmur. I sit, empty-headed and exhausted, as I watch Carla gracefully complete another color run. Only after a long silence do I notice that she hasn't been printing on clean, white paper as she usually does. She's printing over other serigraphs from long before. "You didn't like the old ones?" I ask.

"They were okay. For then. But for now we need new art."

⁂

Late June 1968
Madeleine calls it "the invasion of the chattering masses."
She's right. Our motherhouse, generally very silent, is being
transformed this summer. Especially the refectory at noon,
with extra tables and an extended lunch hour. Each weekday, both before and after their summer-session classes at
the nearby university, sister students flood into the motherhouse from outlying convents. And, yes, despite the rule of
silence, our chatting is noisy. This seems to bug Maddy.

For me, it is not only understandable, it's encouraging.
For many sisters, especially the young ones, this is the first
opportunity to freely discuss, outside the confines of their
small parish or hospital convent, the experiments begun
after a vote by our elected delegates last summer. These
were our beginning attempts to open some windows as the
pope had requested, to let at least some whiffs of air ruf-
fle through our long-practiced ways. Now, though, July 15
looms, the date when each sister must vote whether or not
she thinks these experiments should continue for another
school year. Reason enough, it seems to me, for sisters to
use these weeks of summer school to talk things over with
good friends. Perhaps a friend assigned elsewhere—maybe
a novitiate classmate, or a sister chum from a previous assignment or college course, or a trusted superior or college
professor. Anticipation fills the air.

⁂

"Why does it bother you so?' I ask Maddy. She's been increasingly fretful since that talk we had Easter week when
she picked me up from the train. For me, the hubbub is kind
of exciting, gives me glimmers of hope after that dismal report of hers at Easter time.

"Because we were told not to, remember? 'Ordered not to proselytize' was how Mother Augusta put it, as I recall. Which is exactly what all this smells like to me."

"But how can you tell? When you see a couple locked in heavy talk, maybe they're simply sharing? Clarifying their own thinking? Or possibly, trying to discover how they do think? I don't know how you can call it 'proselytizing' unless you know motives?" When she doesn't reply, I push on, reminding her, "It's hard work, trying to wrap your mind around new ways of thinking." If I sound pleading, it's because I can never forget my own struggles at CU—and the resulting delight—when I was finally able to *digest* new, foreign ideas. Or this past year, as I witnessed the same kind of effort in students struggling to try on ideas very "foreign" to them, as strange and different, and rewarding, as Plato or Karl Marx or Descartes.

"You and your philosophizing." She cuts me off abruptly, though without losing her friendly tone. "I think you flatter our chattering masses. You know what I'm getting at."

Of course I do. She senses a worrisome political flavor as sisters nudge one another toward this position or that. Still, I wish she could share the challenge I feel in those evening discussion groups with the junior sisters, when we work to "try on" ideas from some of those Vatican II thinkers Maddy and I have been sharing for years—Rahner, Kung, Suenens, for example. The juniors' questions are not always the same as mine—or yours. Like the other night, when sharp-eyed young Sister Jeanne Marie asked how "shared decision-making" in the Suenens or Goffman books might play out in our community. "If we're going to share decision-making, can we still speak of our assignments as 'God's will?'"

"It's one thing to talk of choosing what clothes we wear," added young Sister Alma. "But what about choosing the vows we make? Can we pick and choose? And how can we even talk about 'final vows,' when everything is up to choice?"

Hardly what Maddy or I would have asked back in the day. Nor would we have questioned the use of "formation,'"convent lingo for the training period of a young nun. Yet Sister Janet critiques it right away: "Seems the opposite of that self-direction being urged on us these days? 'In formation' seems more like a military, lockstep style of training."

And it isn't simply the challenge of these erudite theologians that's revving me up this hot summer. It's also, perhaps mainly, the equally foreign world of my Existentialism class this summer. For each of the thinkers we're reading, personal choice is center stage in their philosophies. Happy accident for me, I say, just as the "open windows" enthusiasm throughout the Catholic world is taking hold in our community. Or so I'd like to think.

Maddy continues, however, to give me pause about the universality of this enthusiasm. She's on my mind again this morning as I take off on foot for the university. I've chosen this quiet time right after breakfast each day, before the heavy heat of St. Louis summer, for this solitary walk. I must be late today, though, since the cooler air and lighter traffic are gone—with only the fumes and muck blown my way by heavy traffic. A noisy bus, then a smelly garbage truck, and suddenly I'm engulfed in fetid air. Could this be why Maddy's so reticent to celebrate our "open windows" opportunity? Imagining, maybe, that only putrid odors would blow in if we opened the windows—as Good Pope John told us to do?

My university class is comfortably small: five laywomen, a couple of grade-school nuns from another order, a high school Latin teacher nun from our order, a hospital sister, a couple of teaching brothers, and a single Vietnam vet. An even dozen, they cluster around me as close as possible to the on-again, off-again air conditioner hanging from one of the tall windows in this ancient third-floor room. "Returning

Adults," the university calls these students. After some years in the "real world," they are here now, either resuming work on their BA or working toward an MA.

One student's returning is particularly special for me. JoEllen is not simply returning to college after years of marriage and child rearing (a story common to all five laywomen in the class), she's returning to *my* classroom, choosing to take a second course from me after being in my large Introduction to Philosophy lecture course last fall. In all my years of teaching, this has never happened. Grade school or high school kids don't get to choose their teachers, at least not in Catholic schools. I'm flattered. It feels good, in unexpected ways. When I first encountered JoEllen last September in that Intro course, it was my first semester teaching after finishing at CU and returning to St. Louis. She stood out then in appearance from the rest, not so much because of her face or figure—which were indeed strikingly beautiful—but because of her decorum. In both dress and manners, JoEllen exudes elegance amid coeds of casual, almost careless, if not sloppy, appearance. Yet she fits right in with this small group of adults—all youthful, yet neatly fixed in grown-up ways—except, perhaps, me: still awkwardly outfitted in khaki skirt, nondescript white blouse, and sensible shoes.

By the time I arrive, JoEllen has arranged a cluster of lecture chairs to accommodate us. As I take the chair next to her, the faint scent of her cologne at first startles, then delights me. She's the picture of calm composure—school paraphernalia neatly stacked under her chair, her yellow pad at the ready, and her bare, tanned legs crossed as she immerses herself in the tiny print of her paperback copy of *Being and Nothingness*. Can she really be forty-five? Five years my senior? We dive into our discussion, and I relish the intelligence and thoughtful questions of my students.

"I've got a hunch what he means," JoEllen says, tentatively, when she comes to my office toward the end of the first week. She wants to discuss Sartre's "burden of freedom." Her bright, intense face looks vexed as she sits facing me. "That waiter fellow sees himself only as a waiter, lets others see him that way. He's just a 'thing' who waits tables." Her glance is fixed in a frown as she stares at the pencil she's been twisting. Then a deep sigh, as she confesses, "I understand that, Sister. Because I've done it. For a long time. Become a 'thing.' Let myself become a thing, a thing who mothers and housewives."

She stops—at the strangeness of her made-up verbs? Or because she can't finish her thought? She seems uncomfortable, as I am, hearing this grown-up woman confessing. My mind wanders—how she reminds me so of Madeleine when we first met as postulants. The same confident stance, reddish-blond hair pulled back, face virtually free of makeup, and straight-ahead, clear-eyed look hinting at practicality mixed in with otherworldliness. Would Maddy look this elegant were she to experiment with civilian clothes?

"When our last kid left for college, I decided to get a job. But what had my years as super-mom prepared me for? Nothing. Except maybe to help others do the same." A cynical laugh, then her resigned words, "So, here I am, back at college to become a 'marriage, family, and child counselor.' Now Sartre tells me I'm just looking for another role. Like his waiter switching to ticket-taker. Replacing one 'thing' with another 'thing.' He's making me crazy with all this, because I'm not just a 'thing.' Okay? But now what? I'm to embrace my—" She stops, uncomfortable with where Sartre's leading her.

"Your 'no-*thing*-ness'?" I provide the word—and with it the thought—and immediately regret it. My long-practiced teacher-habit is out of place right now.

"Right," she replies, "my no-*thing*-ness...." Her voice

trails off. She seems uncomfortable. And it's more than the strange word. When she drops her head for a moment, I fear she could be weeping. Yet after an uncomfortable pause, she raises her head and in an exasperated tone delivers her conclusion, *"That's* the burden he wants me to accept?" Clearly a troubling message for her.

"Yes." I say, uncomfortable at her discomfort, and I launch into my teacher role again. "To say 'I am nothing' sounds trivial, doesn't it? Hardly a 'burden. In fact, we often brush off something by saying, 'Oh, that's nothing,' but Sartre is using these terms literally: We are no-*thing.*" I allow the word to linger in the air between us, promising myself not to interrupt again.

Finally, JoEllen looks up at me, her eyes pleading for a response, yet I remain silent. Then she lowers her gaze and slowly spells out her insight, staring all the while at the palms of her hands, as if Sartre's lesson were written on them. "Okay, then, Sister: If somebody—if I—refuse to identify myself with a role, with myself as a thing. If I let myself see myself as not-a-thing, or in his words, *nothing,* then I'll be able to see how I've been choosing, all along, who I am." She looks up, as if for my approval. "That's freedom? Owning up to my choices? All of them, those past and now?" I'm nodding in agreement.

"That's heavy, Sister. He's so right," she says, sighing slowly, as if relieved of a burden. "At least about this much: It is a burden. A heavy burden."

"And so easy to deny," I add. "We can just slither out from under the weight of our choices." The way she's looking at me lets me know I'm no longer interrupting her. "It's easy to blame others, including God, for how our life develops."

How did that just slip out of my mouth, bringing that awkward silence between us? Then JoEllen spots the brown sack all neatly folded inside my briefcase, the lunch I've been packing lately to avoid traveling back to the motherhouse at the hottest time of the day. "You've packed your lunch? Can we lunch together, Sister?" The usually self-assured JoEllen suddenly looks flustered by her own request. "I presume nuns do that now? With all the changes?" She gestures toward my skirt and nyloned legs.

"I'd love to," I say, relieved to be putting Sartre's burden aside. Eating with seculars is allowed now—providing it "extends our mission." One of our experiments. No doubt, she is my mission right now.

And so it becomes our routine when class is over, as we brown-bag together in a dingy little room in the basement, in the company of beverage and candy machines. JoEllen insists on bringing "surprises" from her kitchen, and in no time she is supplementing my brown bags with an array of foods more intriguing than could ever be found in either a convent or Byrne kitchen—cold saffron soup, wild rice, Greek cheese, tabbouleh, gazpacho—as well as the familiar tuna, potatoes, and beans, transformed now into marvelous summer salads. The convent lunch staple of canned fruit cocktail buried in Jell-O never shows up. Can't say I miss it.

One day, out of the blue, JoEllen interrupts our recipe discussion. "What you said the other day, Sister, did you mean that you have blamed God for how your life has turned out?" Her question, so piercingly direct, catches me off guard and I'm tempted to move back into my teacher-talk on Sartre's thought. I resist, though. She's asking about me.

"Not blamed, really. More like forgot. Or as Sartre might say, 'choosing to let myself forget.' For a long time, at least on the surface, I've let myself see my convent life—in all its particulars—as God's choice for me. 'Forgetting' that it was my choice in the first place to see it that way." I pause, hoping she will question further. But she sits silent. "Forgetting is easy," I add, flashing back to the heated discussion with juniors on this very point a couple of nights ago.

"Tell me more."

"It's habitual in the convent." We both smile at the play on *habit*. "Trying to see the hand of God in everything. Now, though, I'm coming to see how our convent reform will mean examining all our habits—not just those of cloth—even 're-forming' some habits of thinking when necessary. Or maybe most of all, our habits of thought." What I was hoping to share with Maddy the other night about trying on new ideas. "They're homemade, after all." I touch my denim skirt. "This morning I had to choose between khaki or denim. I love it! Though I imagine it could be a nuisance."

"Is it ever! It's a pain, Sister, having to choose what to wear every day. I've always envied the way you have it all decided for you. Or used to, anyway."

"Point taken. Still, I love being able to choose right now." I finger her small container of dried cranberries and various nuts. "Some choosing is fun."

It's been on the tip of my tongue during our lunchtimes, to say I wish she'd stop the "Sister this" and "Sister that." Just call me Elizabeth, I've wanted to say—another of our experiments that I'm sure will be voted in. Now, though, I wonder if JoEllen may be confiding in me because I am "Sister."

"Something you should know, Sister," she says. "I'm far from the good Catholic you may think I am. Some choices that I've blamed others for, blamed the Catholic Church for, would shock you. They shock me." She looks straight ahead, her face again taut, but then crumbles a bit as she mutters, "It's hard for me to let go of it, to think differently about all this. So much harm—not from you personally, of course, Sister—but definitely from Church people. And I don't mean way back in the Inquisition either. I mean now—with people I love."

I'm troubled by her obvious pain as I watch a muscle in her neck twitch and her face tighten with anger. "The Church has made me a liar, Sister. It's still making me a liar.

And I hate it for this! Sartre says I've been choosing to let the Church do all this to me, choosing to let this happen." Again I want to interrupt, but can't. "For so long I've lived with this—being a liar about that first sex. Up even till now with those little white pills. And everything in between!" Her head is bent and her words have become mumbled, yet after a few slow breaths she straightens up, her face tight and eyes dry. "How's that, Sister: a great record, no? For somebody from a good Catholic family!"

And a family of prominent Catholic donors, I think, recalling names I've noticed on a brass plate outside the university president's office.

"For years I've felt dirty, Sister. Years blaming everyone: my soldier-boyfriend, his going off to war, the war itself, my father. He had connections, he let me know, at a Catholic adoption place up in Michigan. 'No one need know,' he assured me. It made me mad then, and ashamed ever since. Mad at how the Church makes us such liars, such manipulators. Even now. I lie to my husband, another 'good Catholic jurist,' about those little white pills. I have to. I feel my lies are moral, the right thing to do. The only thing I can do!" Her voice verges on desperate.

"And Dave knows nothing about any of it, not about that soldier boy, let alone the abortion. He is so proud of his large brood. And of being a Knight of Malta. Just like my dad. Both staunch defenders of the Church on everything, including birth control and, certainly, abortion. Opposing them, I mean."

Her voice quivers, the hot tears finally come along with, "Now Sartre says I've chosen all this—that I'm still choosing. I'm letting the Church make me a liar."

"I think I see."

"How can you?" she lashes out. "You don't—" She stops, hanging her head, attempting, I imagine, to swallow the harsh words and forceful tone directed at me. Yet she is so right. I am only too aware of not having had anything close to her experience. I lack the courage to tell her this. She grows more composed and lifts her head, and says, with a far gentler tone, "Ever since that early stuff, I've been angry at the Church. But I just can't accept what Sartre says: that I'm to blame. I think it gets even worse as I'm coming to see more of how the world works: watching my kids grow up, listening to them. I grow more and more angry with the Church and all that business of 'increase and multiply.' I just had too many too fast—four kids in just six years. It's simply not right. Not that I could imagine being without any one of them now. I love my kids, would die for any one of them. But back when it was so important, I couldn't give each one the attention they needed. It's criminal."

Her quivering voice has hardened as she pronounces with judicial firmness, "And it's all the Church's fault. The Church is responsible for this crime. Sartre says I am. But he is wrong! He is so wrong."

I am uncomfortable with the silence between us and can only utter the obvious, "You're being hard on yourself, JoEllen. You've made some courageous choices." I speak softly, feeling ashamed at the contrast in our lives. The same Church she hates describes my life of vows as "the more perfect way," superior to marriage, etc. Yet if devotion is measured by what you are willing to pay for something, she's certainly paid more for her Catholicism than I have. "I admire your courage, JoEllen. I admire *you*." My voice weakens in the presence of this heroic woman.

"Thanks. I've blamed others for forcing me to make those choices, Dave especially. Almost as much as the Church. And it's become a habit with me, this anger."

"You know what I think about *habits*," I say, drawing my denim skirt more firmly over my knees, to still a bit my self-consciousness. "Maybe nuns won't be alone in discarding habits these days."

She resists my attempt to lighten our talk. "Maybe I've made it sound too black and white, Sister. I love Dave. I'm with him now—for twenty-three years, and not because the Church forbids me to leave but because I love my children and want to be with them. And with him. They need him. I need him. I do love him...." Her voice trails off and I wonder if this conviction she's repeating is another habit.

"But it's very hard, Sister, very twisted. What my family calls sinful were for me *moral* choices, including that abortion. Or my refusal now to play Vatican roulette: Every morning I reach for those little white pills that I've hidden so carefully. Pills that would shock Dave, and now my Jesuit-educated sons, were they to know. They believe those pills send women like me straight to Hell! They say it's "intrinsically evil," with no forgiveness for this sin—the way there is for his drinking, and whatever else he confesses every Saturday."

I ache to tell JoEllen how edifying I find the life she's made in the midst of such enormous struggles. "Courage" is the right word, I think. In her presence I feel the discomfort so often experienced at my family gatherings, that tension never spoken about around my two Byrne families: kid sister Suzy with her two well-spaced children and my sister-in-law with her brood of eight stair-step kids, all wonderful. Together we Byrnes present a set of contradictions right in front of us all—the "higher way" of my life, spoken of as a life of "perfection" because my vows involve sacrificing sex and family life; yet these young mothers, each living her Catholic life so differently, are more burdened in their sexual lives by the very Church that places my way of life "above" theirs.

I want to tell her how my problems seem so trivial compared to what she and other women face, that I'm almost in the league of those mean nuns of her childhood she's told me about—the ones who spanked kids for chewing gum. Yet I can't get the words out that would let JoEllen see just how little a Church person I really am. In these moments I feel more in sync with her than I do with Maddy, or even Augusta.

~

July 2, 1968

The slow tolling of the chapel bell announces the death of Sister Zita, Carla's tray sister. She's lasted well into her high nineties, as so many of our nuns do. For the next two days, our world fills with that mourning-mixed-with-joy that surrounds the death of a sister. She's left us, but she's home with God. The full-throated Gregorian chant "Te Deum Laudamus": "Let us praise the Lord" floats out chapel windows into the heavy summer air. We're letting the heavens and earth know with what gusto we send off little Zita.

Three days later, the sanctuary of the motherhouse chapel, usually void of male presence, is packed with priests. Zita prepared for Holy Communion, trained altar boys, ironed linens, and counted the Sunday collection for an amazing number of local clergy in her long years of teaching K through 3. She's eulogized as sweet, long suffering, humble, and, most important, childlike. She's a model, Monsignor Sweeney tells us, of those who are chosen by God to be nuns.

Coming as he does from the same county in Ireland, though a generation later, the monsignor has long been a confidant of Sister Zita, which is why he was invited to be the celebrant at her funeral. He stands now, with Mass finished, at the head of her open coffin for a final blessing. On Zita's head lies a simple lily of the valley wreath, reminding us all that she is a spouse of Christ. On either side, altar boys swing incense until Monsignor indicates he's ready to address us.

I'm accustomed to turning a deaf ear to priests who insist on instructing us about our way of life, authorities who have never themselves lived a communal life. Today, though, I'm caught by the sparkle of Monsignor's elegant cuff links as I hear Sister Zita described as the Biblical "child who can lead us" out of our present confusion. In the same Donegal lilt as Zita's, he speaks of her sadness at seeing the community she loved become "so secular."

"Let her death recall for you, my dear Sisters, the essentials of your religious life. Because, first and foremost—I must remind you—you are 'daughters of the Church.' " His proclamation hangs in midair. After a dramatic pause, he continues, "The logic of nun's life rests on a central truth for all Catholics: 'God and His Church are one.' This is basic—for every Catholic. But especially for a nun." The cuff links come together, the praying hands signal pious submission. He bows his head, as if to sniff those dratted cuff links, and continues in staccato phrases, "To be chosen by God, to be a nun, is to be a daughter of the Church. It is to live in a special way, under the loving authority of Holy Mother Church. It's that simple. A matter of faith, of obedience, of *truth*."

His tone turns chatty. "Of course, the intellectuals among us can always complicate this basic logic. But that's pride, plain and simple. The sin of pride. Not the humility of God's chosen ones. You must never forget that Christ and His Holy Church care for you. Like the 'birds of the air and the lilies of the field,' you need not worry for the morrow. You have your Holy Rule the Church gave you when you freely accepted Christ's call. What you were told then is still true: 'Keep your Rule and the Rule will keep you'!"

His voice rises with his emotion and now, flinging his arms upward, he pleads with a flourish, "You are brides of Christ! Daughters of the Church! God's most beloved children! So cherish your Holy Rule, my dear Sisters. Live it. Persevere on the path God's Holy Church has shown you. Then, like your dear Sister Zita, you will be welcomed into God's presence on the last day."

Another dramatic pause as the cuff links come together and his head bows in silent prayer. Then finally, his eyes lifting to the choir, a nod lets them proceed with their long pleading response, "*Libera me, Domine.* Deliver me, O Lord, from eternal death on that awful day." He readies us for the final blessing of Sister Zita's earthly remains. But his words that stick with me as he drones on are how we are all *children*, daughters of the Church.

Indeed, the Zita I knew did seem like a child, always so submissive and compliant, so sweet, willing to take another's words, any convenient voice of authority. How typical of the accounts we're given of the saints, especially female saints so innocent, so pure, so like children. I chuckle to myself remembering those few times I substituted for Carla bringing her tray, how she seemed to revere me as an authority because I was tall! Was she ever adult? Can nuns ever stop being "children" to our various "fathers"?

With all those bodies packed into the chapel now for almost two hours, the air has grown too heavy for the fans to make much difference, and I begin to feel a bit light-headed. Instinctively, my nostrils turn away from the incense, hoping by chance to catch some of the fan's meager stream. It doesn't help. But then I've never gotten on well with incense, especially in the humidity of our St. Louis summers.

And now this funeral incense is bringing back the feeling at Mimi's funeral, the summer before I left for the novitiate. Everything outlined in black, my face and arms turning cold and damp. I was shaky, embarrassed then at having to sit down and wondering, Is this how it is when you're dying? How Mimi must have felt? What pulled me out of my trembling that frightful morning was recalling Sister Marie Gabrielle's words about nuns starting here on earth what the angels do for all eternity. Death is not terrible for them, she claimed, because by their religious profession they start living their eternal vocation here on earth.

The memory jolts me. I stay kneeling but lean back to let the pew support me. Then, like the incense I am unable to avoid, a simple yet awful question forces itself into my mind: Has the convent been that for me? A great escape? An escape from the terrible uncertainty of that last day? That day of reckoning "when the heavens and earth shall be moved: when Thou shalt come to judge the world by fire." What I wanted to escape on that dreary morning at Mimi's funeral? Of course, I was overwhelmed by all the unknowns ahead of me in life, but isn't that how it is for every teenager?

Now, again, it's the monsignor's turn: *"Kyrie eleison. Christe eleison*; Lord have mercy, Christ have mercy...." His Irish tenor is truly magnificent, something he must have been told hundreds of times, including by Zita. The image of her adoring, upward, little-girl look drifts through my mind as slowly, solemnly he intones the Pater Noster, maneuvering himself in his bulky golden cope twice around the casket, incensing continuously. Another two times around and he concludes triumphantly, "Lead us not into temptation," lingering on the lovely, elongated Latin of *temptatione*, and once again I am focused.

The real temptation, as I can see now, the real hell, is to continue escaping responsibility for my own death. For my own life. No one—no order, no church, no authority—can ever relieve me of this burden of my existence. A simple truth, now confirmed, and I can sing with my sisters a hearty "amen."

I join the recession out of the chapel. With my sisters and assembled clergy, we process behind Monsignor out of the chapel, singing the lyrical "In Paradisum"—"May the angels lead you into Paradise." It's a lovely send-off for this little girl/old lady, the angels leading her into paradise, the martyrs receiving her into the holy city of Jerusalem, the choirs of angels surrounding her as she joins Lazarus, to rest in peace. Over and over, we sing the exquisite chant for as long as it takes the entire procession to wind its way out of the chapel, through the cloister garden, and back to our cemetery at its far end.

The fresh garden air with its medley of scents revives me and lets me indulge my fondest memories of this beloved garden. In reality, as in metaphor, our "garden enclosed" carries the meaning of the convent life I've known for the last twenty-three years. Stretching out from the rear of the chapel to the far end of our property, the garden duplicates in shape and size the chapel itself—its long rectangular grass garden matching the nave, its semicircular cemetery a copy of the sanctuary. A continuous hedge trimmed a head or so above the tallest nun walls us all in, and shades one side a bit. Low boxwood hedges mark the many interior paths, while a string of rose vines separates the graveyard from the rest of the garden, as the altar rail divides sanctuary from nave in our chapel.

Even in spring, when winter's gravelly beige of dead grass gives way to lush carpets of green, when bulbs spring up and vines blossom, it's a fairly spare garden—aesthetics at the service of contemplation. As it should be. The garden was designed as an extension of the chapel, an open expanse where we regularly come to pray the rosary or the Divine Office while pacing back and forth. Except for once-a-month Visiting Sundays or major celebrations, it is a place of profound silence.

Despite it being midday, with pockets of the requiem's incense lingering in, the heavy July air, I relive the wonderful sights and sounds and scents of this garden enclosed: On crisp Advent nights the haunting "Veni, Veni Emmanuel" pleads for our Savior to come; on Christmas Eve, our carols and candles fill the midnight chill; in the spring, after the reception ceremony with the heavy scent of Easter lilies, parents and nuns visit with the newly habited novices; on Vow Day in mid-August, the garden again fills with nuns from every convent in the order to welcome with hugs and kisses the newly vowed junior sisters. Sweet memories, all.

But with nostalgia come, at last, the tears of sadness that have been welling up since Mass in my shaky self. Without the veil to hide under, I feel exposed. Yet others would understand, wouldn't they? Don't they too weep for the romance of it, for the old ways of acting, the old comforts of believing—that we are brides for whom Christ has prepared a very special garden enclosed? I long to be able to believe, literally, the comfort of those promises from the Apostles' Creed we pray each day, about "the communion of saints, the forgiveness of sins, the resurrection of the body, life everlasting."

Silently, we cluster around the huge, stone crucifix at the far end of the garden. After a short flurry of prayers and blessings, the casket is lowered into the freshly dug-out ground, and then slowly sisters disperse, some lingering prayerfully at the graves of loved ones or quietly whispering with one another as they make their way back toward the refectory for lunch. There will be laughter and special feast-day treats at lunch to complete the joyous celebration of Zita's entrance into Heaven.

I'm lingering at the grave of Aunt Maggie when Sister Johanna comes up from behind to clasp my arm, engulfing me in the antiseptic aura of her fresh hospital whites. It seems ages since our long train ride together, and only a year after the revolutionary General Chapter last summer where she and I locked horns constantly. A painful chill separated us then. Apparently she's forgotten all that, however, and is well into the gaiety that runs high whenever we bury a sister.

"You must catch me up on the Byrnes," she bubbles, once again the chipper family friend, inquiring about my parents, especially about my eldest niece, Sheila. "I hear she graduated with honors. Like her aunt! Your dad tells me she looks like you. What's she doing with all that talent? I hope you're encouraging her, Sister." When finally she looks directly at me, noticing tears, she tightens her grip on my arm. "Don't cry for poor Zita, dear. She's the lucky one. She's left all this behind." She moves me more briskly than my body wants to go toward the refectory.

"I need to wash up a bit before lunch," I say, pulling away and heading toward the far wing of the motherhouse. I need to get away, get up to my room to the typewriter, and gather my thoughts for that letter with my vote. It's due in Augusta's office by the fifteenth. Sweeney's words have clarified what I need to say. I need to let her know I'm with her, that I support our efforts at reforming our community...at opening wide our windows and letting fresh air clear away what's no longer needed or helpful. All the debris of accumulated generations.

My tiny cell is stifling, so I leave the light off and push up the window as far as it will go. When I settle before the old Royal, the words come easily: "I vote YES on #1—Proceed with changes. And NO to all other options." I sign my name proudly, uttering a silent prayer of thanks for Augusta and her strength. After folding the slim message into its official envelope, I print "REVEREND MOTHER AUGUSTA—PERSONAL & PRIVATE" and stick it on my door at eye level. No way to miss it in the morning, even with my six a.m. sleepy eyes. I'll deliver it to her office on my way to Mass.

Now I can relax. My legs are still quivering from the steep climb up here, and I stretch out on my narrow bed, yanking the fan up from the floor, and setting it behind me on the bed. As the gusts blow my hair against my ears, tickling my neck, I think how useless our headgear was, like so many accepted restrictions of convent life. We don't need them for what we are about, any more than we need Sweeney's logic.

The knock is Madeleine's. She's missed me at the after-funeral celebration down in the refectory, worried the day's heat had gotten to me. More urgently, though, she needs to see me before I send in my vote to Augusta, so up she trudged with a bundle she unpacks now, picnic fare from the refectory. As she places it next to my Royal in easy reach from my perch on the bed, I see she herself is hardly in picnic mode. Her whole body is as tight as the grip she'd had on the food. It doesn't relax as she moves my chair away from the desk so she can sit facing me.

I rush to thank her, but she dismisses my words with a swoosh of her hand. "Look, you told me earlier today you hadn't yet written Reverend Mother. Though I guess by now you have." She gestures at the envelope on the door. "So just eat up and hear me out, okay? I need to talk with you." Her severe words don't sound like Maddy.

"It's more like apologizing, or at least explaining," she says. "I've been cranky all summer, Sister, I know that. I've been angry. Might as well say it. And I'm sorry about that—very sorry."

I start to break in with my own apologies, but again her hand raises to stop me. "Look, friends can have different takes on things, even important things. I know that. This is different, though." A slight smile almost manages to break through. "We could cancel out each other's vote, but I hope not."

Whatever is locked up in Maddy is obviously painful, so I resist further probing. We face each other with the uncomfortable information she delivers: That after so many years of sharing opinions on serious matters—differing only on more superficial aspects of controversial subjects—we now differ in some major way. Or so she is implying. "I'm not sure of my motives right now, Sister, but I heard some distressing news at the CAA last month. Very distressing," she starts, referring to the nationwide conference for Catholic-school administrators she faithfully attends each year. "News you need to hear, because I believe it's relevant for us—especially for the junior sisters you're working with. Seems there's more to that trouble out in California with those teaching sisters, the order your friend Christine is part of, right? Their problems aren't all because of that crusty old cardinal." Her words become measured and careful. "It's also about how their order, or many within the order, got more than a little 'off' in their renewal efforts by embracing that California-style, 'person-centered-psychology.' It was part of their college's teacher training, but then found its way into their parochial classrooms. And finally into their convent lives."

I think how very different her story is from what I've heard from Christine. Yet I stifle any desire to defend one friend's convictions by arguing with another, even older friend.

"When the Vatican II renewal business started out there," Maddy continues, "it seemed natural for the order itself to use sensitivity workshops and focus groups to 'renew itself.' 'Focus on the individual,' it urged the nuns. What do *you* feel, what do *you* need, how do *you* see *your* future in the community? The results have been disastrous. For their community life, for everything. 'Renewal' for this order has come to mean the expansion of self-development—*self indulgence*—the very enemy of community life!" She lets out a deep breath, relieved, it seems, to have spilled out her bad news.

"That's the report," she says. "From someone I trust! Finally, I had a name for what's been getting under my skin these past many months, what I've been seeing among the young sisters at St. Raymond's this past year, and now this summer, heard all over the place here at the motherhouse. It's that culture of self—do your own thing." Maddy's voice has again grown tight in a way that makes me think she might just weep. "Yet it doesn't seem to bother you, Sister. You seem content, maybe even happy, that our renewal has become all about personal decision-making and the structural changes needed to allow this to flourish. Our community, our order seems for many to exist as an aid for personal ambition. Yet isn't this just the opposite of how we saw our lives back when we were at their stage? We asked then, What does the community need from me? How can I contribute? How can I be part of the team, working as a group to be creative about bringing Christ into some small part of the modern world?"

We sit in silence, the pain hanging in the air between us. "It's been awkward this summer, Sister, knowing you and I think so differently. I've been cranky, I know. I am sorry about that. But seeing how enthusiastic you are about restructuring, about doing away with the pyramidal form of authority has made me desperate to share how—why—I think we're missing the whole point. Of renewal."

"You mean, how *I* am missing the point," I say.

"Okay, yes. Yes, I think you are," she says slowly, in great pain it seems. Yet she continues her personal credo in measured words, "From the start of my life in the order, I have been clear about the great good thing we have to give to this world: It's our witness of community. This is what we should be focusing on, figuring out how to do it today in our modern world. Not giving up on it! Yes, let's open those windows the pope told us to. Get fresh insight on how we can accomplish this. I'm all for this. But not at the expense of community!"

We both digest her words in silence for a moment. I can't doubt those words, though her urgency escapes me. "Of course change is needed," Maddy confirms, "but the vows must remain, because they make community possible. Which is what we are all about, isn't it? Our vows aren't so much about cutting off, or giving up, as they are about making possible a fuller, richer life through community, a community the three vows make possible. A community able to take on tasks beyond the capacity of an individual.

"But you know, Lizzie, something I've never really shared with you, or with anyone, is my own personal association with all this. It goes back a long way, long before I decided to join the order. But it's why I did. You know about our rural farm life, how I was the eldest of the kids. Mother had all eight of us at home. With a midwife, of course. I was there for it all, gradually becoming aware of what was going on as I grew, and especially with the last three. And definitely with the youngest. My brother Frankie—you've met him on Visiting Sunday. But I was seventeen when he was born. A turning point in my life.

"Mother had a really tough time with him, more than with any of the others. She ended up in the hospital afterward and almost died. That was June 1944, on D-Day, just before midnight. The radio was telling us that troops were landing at Normandy—at last! Everyone was rejoicing. Not Mother, though. She was terribly upset, apprehensive really. She was so sure her young brother Frank was one of those GIs landing, and being killed, on that French beach. She kept screaming his name all through her labor. It was her most difficult birth.

"Turns out she was right. He was there, and he was killed that first day. My Uncle Frank. Twenty-three years old. We didn't find out for some weeks, of course, and by that time Mother had recovered and was home safe with a new son. So of course she baptized him *Frankie.*

"I'm telling you all this because I saw what my mother went through to build our family, our community. My father, too, of course. But most of all Mother. I saw in the most intimate way how bringing new life into our world is the most wonderful thing a human being can do. Yet I chose to walk away from it—from family life. And so did you, Lizzie. Why?" Maddy inches closer, staring directly at my face like the meanest of prosecuting attorneys. "If parenting is the most Godlike, richest thing a human can do, why did we walk away from it?"

Maddy relaxes a bit. "During those endless hours, when I lost track of morning and night, snatching sleep catch-as-catch-can, I saw those hospital nuns going about their labors. They were a team. A team that allowed my mother to live. Let my new little brother Frankie live! Ordinary women, every one of them. They were new for me, those hospital nuns. Of course I wouldn't have spoken of their 'community life' then. More like the military, I thought. What I'd heard my uncles talk about from the start of the war. Especially Uncle Frank, who was a medic. How ordinary guys working as a unit could accomplish amazing things, things beyond what anyone alone could accomplish. He was proud of what he was doing, joking often about how he was winning the war by emptying bedpans!

"So when I feel that sense of 'community first' is being tempered with, I become angry, very angry. And that's what's been buzzing in my mind since I first heard you so worked up about structural change, something I believe will mean the death of community, the end of our own great army."

What can I say to Maddy's challenge? Or is it a complaint? I can't find the words. Our talk is over. Her beautiful tale has silenced me; the truth of it all, undeniable.

"You look tired, Sister. I've worn you out with my tale," she says, looking washed out, yet finished.

"I'm so glad you did. I could tell things weren't good," I say.

"Less so now that we've spoken. Thanks."

But I haven't spoken...not really. And I had so much I wanted to say to her. Instead, I give her a hug as she's leaving and move my heavy, hot body over to the window.

It takes some doing to wedge myself between the bed and wall so I can perch—my favorite spot for thinking, sitting on the edge of the bed, heels hooked on the iron springs—my chin resting on folded arms. But thinking is not possible right now, and I cave downward over my arms. The dark feelings are too dark, especially what Maddy stirred up about the "privilege" of my grad study and those years "away" at

CU. To me, those years are about a hard assignment success-fully completed. But now I wonder, have I been looking for Maddy to thank me, or what? Somehow she's stirred some strange and unfamiliar feeling. Is it guilt?

As the hot tears bubble up, I know it wouldn't be honest to deny entirely what she was getting at. Here and there, I've felt that privilege myself, especially around my family, and when Kevin's Rosemarie confided in me about their worries, weeping about how on earth were they going to afford Kev-in's years of expensive study, without a real job. And what about employment when he's finally got the PhD? Especially with the new baby. Yes, I knew even then I was "privileged."

And I've felt the privilege around Sophie as well, when she had to drop out of the doctoral program and switch to law school. That also was because of finances. She teased that I was lucky to have God paying my bills, and, more se-riously, she'd often said something to the effect, "You need your community more than it needs you." At the time So-phie's crack made me mad, but of course she was right, and of course Maddy's right. But what has this to do with the vote Mother Augusta's asked us for? The vote I've already made, sitting there in that envelope. Is Maddy trying to get me to change that vote through guilt?

July 29, 1968
I've lingered with students longer than usual after class, in-dulging in the pleasure of hearing students caught up in the thinking of the philosopher we've just been reading. With four of our six-week summer session complete, I am at last feeling that kind of pride I used to feel when tenth-graders could see, really understand, for instance, why it's impos-sible to "square a circle." But when I sit down for dinner, a note I discover in my refectory drawer shocks me out of that pleasant feeling. "*Please,* I need to see you. Can we meet

after dinner? I'll wait for you out at the pergola. Thanks!" So I grab an apple and ask my companions to set aside a plate for me. It's Janet, I know, though I am surprised a bit by her tone. She's impetuous, but hardly demanding. Not like her.

We've barely spoken this summer, which I've taken to indicate that she has no worries about her upcoming final vows. As the summer progressed, she seemed calmer, less intense. Even during the tennis tournament, where she's always been a fierce competitor, she was noticeably more peaceful. Of course, that neat tennis dress, instead of her awkwardly pinned-up habit, had something to do with it. Still I've felt convinced that the many changes afoot in the community are the cause of her peace.

The summer has definitely transformed her, I think, as I approach the old pergola looking now so neglected and forlorn. As Janet herself looked only a few months ago. Now though, she's a symbol of the order itself and its transformation. That bush of unmanageable hair, cropped now, reveals a lighter face; her heavy denim and woolly sweaters, chunky shoes, and knee socks have given way to a cotton shirt, hanging loose now, with sandals and bare legs. Most of all, rimless light glasses have replaced those dark heavy things. The simplicity is lovely.

"May Jesus Christ be praised," I say, our traditional greeting, though mumbled because we are in the midst of a day of silence.

"Now and forever," she replies, just as traditionally, though not so hushed.

We hug and I whisper, "What's up?" We sit side by side on the wide, splintery plank that runs the length of the forlorn arbor.

"Look, Sister. I want you to know first. I'm leaving. Not renewing my vows."

When I don't reply immediately, she hangs her head, muttering, "I'm sorry, I'm so sorry." She looks about to weep.

"Oh, please," I say. "Please." Why haven't I seen this coming? Have I been so tied up with my own concerns that I haven't noticed something obvious in a person I'm supposed to be "mothering"? Truth is, I've never doubted Janet's place among us.

"I wasn't going to do this." She sniffles and removes her glasses. Her easy tears have always embarrassed her. "I hate letting you down."

"Janet, Janet. You're not letting me down. Please. Don't think that way. Of course I trust you." My voice is low and calm, confident—a voice of motherly authority. "I am surprised, though."

Truth is, I feel ripped apart. For all my writing and lecturing about our renewal, how it's all about making adult choices, taking responsibility for our lives, growing past Sweeney's good daughter's "father knows best" mindset, for all this, her news stabs at my gut. I am about to be abandoned by one of the very people I have most counted on to be a leaven in our renewed community. "I've watched you lately, Janet. You are at peace, aren't you?"

She laughs, sniffling at the same time. "Yes! Oh, yes, yes. I've wanted to tell you, but I had to think this through by myself."

"Of course you did." I reach for her hand as she pours out details, her tears vanishing. With glasses off, her clear green eyes hold my attention and I hear her plans: She will join a group of ex-nuns from another order out in Colorado who live together in simplicity and poverty, doing the good works their former orders could not allow.

"They live in public housing and support themselves as social workers," she says, sounding triumphant. She pulls her freckled legs up under her, stretching her spine up tall the way she does when preparing to dive into the pool. "I've been so angry for so long, at everyone and everything that didn't change. Or at least *want* to change the way I thought necessary. Maybe especially Sister Superior. Sister Madeleine. I've been hard on her, and I'm sorry. Really sorry. She's a good person, a good friend of yours, I know. But I just can't understand her rigidity. When she goes on and on about that destructive 'culture of the self' and the crime of enriching ourselves—what else do we have to give others, but our self? Isn't it our duty to make ourselves as rich and talented as we can! In the service of others of course, but—" She stops herself, recoiling with effort into a more Zen-like position of composure. "But that's all over now. I'm not in that place anymore."

I am grateful not to have to defend Maddy's convictions, to explain to Janet why Maddy feels so threatened by this "culture of the self." It's long passed the time to think any of this could matter for Janet.

"But it's all so different now, Sister. During Zita's funeral, I felt this incredible freedom—and peace. No more struggling to fit in. It's over! Amen! But I also feel I need to tell you." Her voice grows shaky again. "I'm so grateful to this place, to all of you. To the community itself. And you, Sister, especially you. You've had faith in me, Sister, from the start."

Her eyes are on her hands resting peacefully in her lap, and her voice is solemn and slow. "I've learned about Jesus here, and the truly poor. I might never have known this had I not joined the order." She hunches up her shoulders in an enormous sigh, then blurts out, "Now, though, it's all different! I've got to move on." The tears return, yet after bowing her head for a few moments, she conquers them.

"Of course you do," I say, my own tears rising.

"But please don't tell anyone else right now—unless you need to alert Mother Augusta, of course. She spoke to me about the possibility of a high school assignment. So she should know not to count on me. You understand?"

I do understand, I assure her. I too am diffident about sharing her news with the juniors—or with Maddy, for that matter. She will be dejected. Even when she's questioned, and challenged, Madeleine knows Janet epitomizes the kind of young person we need if the order is to reinvent itself and flourish. We sit in the shade of the ancient vines, once green and flowery, and still woven thoroughly into the trelliswork overhead. Exactly how I'm feeling: dry and withered as I've listened to this young woman so eager to describe her epiphany.

"Remember how I fumed about that cardinal out in LA and how he was treating those nuns? All that punitive crap about 'stripping them of their canonical status' and 'rescinding their vows' and 'reducing them to lay state.' It made me so mad!

"The next morning," Janet reveals, "I woke up thinking, 'What's so bad about the lay state? Who needs to be a nun with the hierarchy telling us what we can or can't do, when the poor are everywhere and always need what we have to give?'" She stretches herself up again. "Then I read about this group in Colorado. They do exactly what I want to do. The decision was easy."

With the bell for Vespers, we stand. A snag in my stockings from the splintery plank develops into a run and tickles down the back of my leg. I gather Janet in my arms for a real hug. Suddenly she feels so slight and frail to me. I worry for her. Yet I am proud of her. Maybe this is what religious writers mean by becoming "spiritual mothers" to our charges?

It's quite late by the time I locate Mother Augusta out at the Lourdes grotto, almost time for the Grand Silence. I hesitate to approach, as I see her pacing up and down on the path, concentrating on her large clipboard. A final look, I imagine, at her "mission list" (convent lingo for our yearly assignments). By tradition, these are posted by the close of the junior sisters' retreat, which was yesterday. She's already late, probably finished with the assignments, including that difficult-to-fill high school slot for Janet. Why I must interrupt: Janet's news can't wait.

The grotto has been one of my favorite spots ever since I came here with Mimi to visit her beloved daughter, my young aunt and novice-nun, when I was very young. I thought of it as a secret hiding place, watched over by the life-size statue of Mary, as she appeared at Lourdes. I would stand on the kneeler and gaze upward at the Mother of God high up in the cave-like grotto amid reddish boulders. Ever since, it has remained for me that lovely cool place, even in the heavy heat of St. Louis, with its circle of stately pines surrounding the rocky tableau—a place to gather my thoughts, away from the feel of other people close by. As apparently Augusta is doing as well on this particularly lovely evening, still light with a cooling breeze moving through the tall pines.

"I seem to be the repository for unpleasant news tonight," Augusta replies after I deliver my news about Janet. She lets out a deep sigh and moves over to one of the old wooden benches. Odd that she seems so nonchalant about Janet, I think, as she brushes off the place next to her for me. "I've got news for you as well, Sister. Bad news, and then some more bad news." The early evening air is still sticky. I watch as Augusta straightens up, folds back her veil, away from her face for more air. Her eyes are more puffy than usual, her generally pale complexion an unhealthy gray. Of course she turns fifty-five this year, certainly no longer our "young" mother general, but not old either. "The Vatican's announced its decision on the birth-control issue—with a new encyclical. There's to be no change." She looks stricken as she repeats the news delivered hours ago by her editor friend at the *National Catholic Reporter* in Kansas City. "There was a press conference in Rome this morning. The Catholic world is shocked; the pope's ended all speculation; using the pill is a mortal sin. It's all spelled out in his new encyclical, *Humanae Vitae*."

Her professor-priest friends at the university, along

with that NCR editor, must have given her the same hope that Dan gave me: that this ancient teaching was about to be updated following the work of that special papal commission that's been meeting now for months. The news has been leaking out the last couple of weeks that a majority vote will come down on the side of modernization, that an affirmative decision from the pope would come any day...but now this. My thoughts go to Dan immediately.

"This is not good for reform-minded Catholics," Augusta says dejectedly, her shoulders drooping, her eyes on the ground, "in any arena." When she finally straightens up, she's regained her voice of authority, "Which brings me to my other bad news, right here at home. In their letters to me, the sisters—a majority at any rate—are rejecting our chapter reforms, or at least the significant ones." Her heavy news sinks in, and then she adds, "I've heard from a good majority by now. And it's clear: They are against any serious change. It's unmistakable."

"But couldn't this just be a 'go slow'? We can't just stop what we've started!"

"Oh yes, we can, Sister. What we've been doing thus far are trials, remember?" Her tone of rebuke is firm, unmistakable. It seems painful for her to go on, still she continues. "I'm glad you came by," she says, not looking the least bit glad. "There are some immediate implications for the juniors—and you." She reaches over, resting her hand on my skirt, and with an uptake of breath continues, deliberately, "I've just spent a couple of hours praying over this, Sister— what I should do, how to do it. Much as I wish it were different, the truth is, a sizable majority of sisters now oppose the basic thrust of our reforms. So I'll be posting an order: By August 15, all experiments will stop."

Madeleine's predictions flash through my brain. I still resist believing she could be right. "Those experiments were voted on last summer by a majority, by properly elected—"

"We are *not* a democracy, Sister. We're a *faith* community, daughters of the Church. No, we cannot go on. The Holy Spirit speaks through those letters."

"You really think it is the Holy Spirit? And not just politicking from the likes of Sister Johanna?" I continue, sounding more demanding and petulant than I would like. I've also snagged my other stocking when I twisted to look at Augusta directly. Clearly I'm not yet accustomed to the fragility of pantyhose any more than I am to questioning the highest authority in our order.

"We all breathe the same air, Sister," she responds. "No doubt about it. Conservative sisters have filled a lot of our air with their fears. But your friends have, too. And my friends, as well. So, yes, I believe it is the Holy Spirit. Working through the free choice of each sister." Her carefully measured words roll on, the result of her hours of prayer, I don't doubt. But they're floating over me now, because my attention has been seized by those last words of hers. The "free choice of each sister." Of course, why didn't I catch it—what our "reforms" are all about! Giving each sister a chance to *choose* how she wants her life, her community, to evolve. And now, the reality, Augusta tells me: The majority are choosing *not* to have more choice in their lives. They have made their choice, as Janet has. And as I am becoming more and more aware of my own choices. The burden of our freedom. Of our no-thing-ness.

"The sisters have definitely pulled back from where they were during last summer's chapter," she says sadly. "Remember all the talk about greater autonomy, more professional training, opportunities for new works, different forms of governing, different schedules? More *choice*." She lets out a deep sigh, and once again I see just how painful this realization is for her, too. It's hard to see energetic, ageless Augusta look so beaten. "But not now. Now they are choosing to put all that aside. Maybe sisters still feel this way in their heart of hearts, but just not now. There's enormous ambivalence now. There's fear."

"It's that fiasco out in Los Angeles, isn't it?"

"I'm afraid so." She sighs, sounding thoroughly weary. "Sisters have been chastened, not just here but everywhere. Better not to anger—or is it threaten—the hierarchy." She shakes her head, disbelieving. Her hands rest, listless, in her lap as she slumps in the enveloping dusk. "That cardinal has sent a terrible, terrible message to sisters across the country, that those sisters in Los Angeles are deviating from the essence of religious life. You may be sure that sisters everywhere have heard it, and heard as well that the higher-ups in Rome have backed him up. Our community is no different, Sister."

We remain in silence until she speaks the difficult truth: "There'll be more Janets, Sister. We'll lose more of the young."

"And more of the not-so-young," I add.

We sit sadly with this specter of defeat, Augusta continuing in a meditative, almost dreamy voice. "Some were fearful the proposed reforms would put our parochial schools in jeopardy. Irony is, that without our changes, we'll probably have to withdraw from parish schools anyway." Then just when she seems to have touched bottom, she lets out one of her wry chuckles and says, "The comments about the habit are outrageous! Even those who claim to be 'open to change' emphasize they do not want 'secular clothes.' They want a 'modified habit,' in effect, another uniform! All the same, again!

"Oh, great," I groan. "So much for shared decision-making." "Do what Mother wants. Be good girls! All neat and clean in a uniform Mother chooses!" Which are more likely than not to be ugly, I think, recalling Madeleine's get-up.

"Though I must say, I was struck by one young sister who wrote that she feels ashamed to work among the poor in her habit. Said she felt like a queen or a rich lady with her sweeping skirts and soft, flowing veil." At the moment, Augusta appears anything but an elegant lady in her heavy habit. It seems ages since I've carried around that weight of serge and starched linen, which seems now to be weighing her down. She brightens a bit as she recalls another response that includes the phrases, "witness to community" and fear about a growing "self-improvement" culture. I recognize Maddy's words. "She's right to be concerned, you know. I myself have probably been overly identified with these reforms, like the mother who's too strong-willed about what her children should do with their lives."

"But you've been scrupulous about respecting individual choice."

"Maybe that's why these letters threw me: Sisters opting for fewer choices!" Even Augusta's faith in the workings of the Holy Spirit cannot erase from her voice her utter incomprehension. "One thing's obvious now, we'll lose some because we've gone too far, others because we've not gone far enough."

I wonder about Augusta herself, and most likely she's wondering about me, yet neither of us broach the personal in this raw moment. How can she continue to lead a group when what she's worked for is being dismantled? As if sensing my question, she stands and announces, "I'm taking a cue from President Johnson, Sister: I will not seek and, if asked, will not serve another term."

It's late by the time I get up to my cell, where the sister next door tells me my phone has been ringing off and on throughout the evening. It has to be Dan; he will be livid about the pope's decision on birth control. Yet I can't bring myself to return the call. I simply don't want to talk or listen to anyone right now. Too much is clamoring for space in my brain to give Dan the kind of attention he will want.

As I toss about before sleep, jagged pieces of today's news

replay themselves: Janet weeping with joy at her choice; the pope putting aside the majority opinion of his birth control commission; Augusta fatigued and probably angered, or at least deeply disappointed, by her sisters' choices. Most of all, though, it's Maddy's choice that challenges. How I wish I could talk all of this over with Carla, now far off in the English countryside. Undoubtedly she knows of the pope's pronouncement but probably not yet about our own reversals. I wonder what she'll make of it all. I miss her so.

August 1968

My own decision to leave the order is not like Janet's. There's no morning, or any other time, when it becomes clear as a bell what I need to do. Rather it's a pit-of-the-stomach feeling that the whole world around me is changing. By day, I witness those "Returning Adults," as they struggle to grasp—each in his or her own way—how their "existential choices" have been, and still are, "creating their lives." And in the evening, it's much the same, with the junior sisters preparing for their solemn Vow Day on August 15. For on that day, each young sister, by choosing whether or not to renew her vows, will be deciding how she chooses to live the remainder of her life on this earth.

The choice has become particularly fraught because of Mother Augusta's recent decision to cancel our "experiments." With this edict, many of the junior sisters are motivated to try harder and recommit themselves to the order's struggle for reform. Some few are simply relieved, happy that the group they are committing themselves to stay with until death will soon return to "a more normal convent routine." Still others are deciding to delay final vows for an additional year "until things settle down." Only three out of twenty-eight in this third-year class, including Janet, are deciding to withdraw from the order completely.

One of these is a genuine surprise—providing a good laugh in this otherwise humorless week. When young Sister Angela, who never hesitates to boast of her Sicilian heritage, heard the pope's unmistakably Italian voice extolling the sanctity of marriage and the blessings of fecundity, she took it as a sign that God was directing her personally to procreate. "I must marry, bring more Italian Americans into this world. It's God's will!" But only she and Janet are so sure about their choices.

And Dan. His calm surprises me. I haven't heard from him since those huge protests a couple of weeks ago at CU after the pope's unexpected decision, or lack of a decision, on birth control. I presumed he was part of that loudly protesting crowd, even searching the TV screen for him in the endless coverage. He would be among those clerical voices shouting about what a terrible mistake the pope is making, I thought. No doubt about it.

When he does call, it is a completely matter-of-fact Dan. "It's no use. The Church as an institution is bankrupt, my friend. Keeping the Roman machine running is more important for the hierarchy than for the people of God." A long sigh, then his careful words, "I'm making some hard decisions, Elizabeth. Things I want very much to talk with you about. Just not yet." He'll be coming through St. Louis in a couple of weeks, he tells me. He's accepted a teaching position at a Catholic college in San Diego.

"Thought you were finished with Catholic colleges?"

"I am. Just not yet."

"Will that place tolerate your kind of Catholic?"

"They'll never know, m'dear. I'll be living in a parish rectory and can keep my mouth shut for the short time I'm there. Listen, I can be as clerical a parish priest as Bing Crosby. *Would you like to swing on a star, carry moonbeams home in a jar, and be better off than you are"*—it's the old Dan, and a fairly realistic Bing—*"or would you rather be a fish?"*

I imagine him acting out the verses and giggle shamelessly.

"I miss you, Elizabeth. I miss your laugh."

"Listen, I miss my laugh. Things aren't exactly laughable around here." It's the perfect moment to tell him about Augusta's decision to stop all experiments and about the upheavals it's causing in the lives around me. But the rustling of books and papers coming through the transom remind me that some junior sister might be waiting to see me. In less than a week, their retreat in preparation for Vow Day begins. Anxieties are high. So I say goodbye.

Finally, the pressure is off me. Summer classes at the university are over and the juniors have made their decisions. Even the weather brings relief. After days and nights of sweltering, record-breaking temperatures, a night of rain brings a fresh, cool morning. It's my favorite kind of summer morning. With the rising bell just after daybreak, my first prayer is on my knees facing a window where the sun is beginning to light up the sky. "This is the day that the Lord has made, let us rejoice and give thanks." Never has the psalmist spoken so clearly in my own voice.

I make my way circuitously to the chapel. Walking through the cloister garden, I see water still lingering on leaves, puddling delicately on rose petals. And by the time I enter the chapel for morning meditation, the garden's damp smell fills the air. Tall windows along both sides of the chapel are cranked wide open with overhead fans rippling the veils of sisters at prayer, and the hair of those still experimenting as I am with secular garb. The breeze is delicious. Yet by seven-fifteen, as the parents of the junior sisters start to join the community, heavy scents from the flower-decked altar are becoming oppressive. How great to be free of the heavy habit!

Many of us who can do so climb the steep circular

stairway to the chapel's choir loft to make room for more parents. Then at exactly eight o'clock, the junior sisters—all of them in the traditional habit for the ceremony—begin to process up the long aisle, in single file, toward the altar. There, facing the congregation in all his clerical finery, the archbishop awaits, while the entire chapel chants the many verses of *Veni Sponsa Christi* until all reach the sanctuary.

"Come, bride of Christ, receive the crown
which the Lord has prepared for you for all eternity;
for whose love you have shed your blood.
And you will enter into the Paradise among the angels.
Come, O you my chosen one, and I will set my throne
within you:
so shall the King have pleasure in your beauty."

They stand, side by side, each with bridal wreath and lighted candle, just outside the railing that circles the altar. Then, one by one, they come to the center, genuflect and kneel before the archbishop who, in the name of the Church, receives their vows. A packed chapel listens intently as each individual—in a voice now delicate, now strong, now euphoric, now somber—pronounces the simple formula of the vows. At this moment every August 15, I've always repeated within me these familiar words, as I have every morning at communion.

But not now, not this morning; the words just won't come. The scene unfolding below me says it all: This is what nun is—veiled, cinctured, head covered, bowing low before this prelate of the Church, separated from him by a railing. A daughter of the Church, just as Monsignor Sweeney says.

As if for the first time, the reality hits: I am a child of the Church, a daughter, a bride. Yet my place is outside the main action. That's what these vows in the presence of the bishop mean. *Veni Sponsa Christi* rises from all the assembled as I silently edge my way through the packed choir, and down the stairs. As they chant, I rush the other way, down the hall-way, not entirely sure of what I'm doing or where I'm going. Only that I must go. I pass the toilets, continuing down the long hall toward the academy side of the motherhouse. Once through the heavy swinging doors separating the cloistered section of the motherhouse from the academy, the singing voices grow fainter, and I am conscious of the steady click-click of my civilian/secular pumps on the tile floor.

My un-nunlike clicking echoes up three flights of this silent stairwell, validating, it seems, my march into a new world. During these "empty" days of August, when I've of-ten found myself alone in this deserted space, normally bub-bling with teenagers, I'm often aware that this, my home, is in fact an institution. Though one of my own choosing, I've always stressed, when protesting to Madeleine, and one that I prefer to her more homey parish convent.

I've insisted to her that I thrive on the bustle and busy-ness of this old place with its always too much to do, its blend of old and young, its mix of girls and nuns, and, yes, even its ascetic, inconvenient quarters that mean long treks for shower and toilet, thin mattresses, never quite adequate heat or hot water, and boringly plain food. Yet I have loved it. Perhaps most of all, I love that it's big enough to escape occasionally, unnoticed, into my own cocoon.

Which is exactly what I'm doing now, I realize, as I drag myself up the last flight and stand for a moment at the top to catch my breath, as I almost always must lately. The drama unfolding in the chapel seems a world away, while the drama of my own decision rests a bit more peacefully in my heart. This is no longer home for me.

It takes me a while to locate the form I'm looking for once I reach my cell, the form I keep on hand for those occasions when a junior sister is asked to withdraw from the order or decides on her own to leave, the form one needs to apply to Rome for a dispensation from her vows. Now it's for me.

As I start to fill it out, I'm stopped by the shock of its demeaning language—something I never noticed when handing it out to others: "Most Holy and August Pontiff.... Humbly prostrate at your feet...your devoted and humble servant, though unworthy to address Your Holiness...earnestly begs your forgiveness." Forgiveness for making a thoughtful decision! A decision of my conscience! I cannot believe it. Two entire pages, framed in language presuming that I've transgressed some law of God, or some law of nature, or possess some character flaw making me unfit for convent life.

From under the bed comes the old Royal—easier right now for my shaky hands and racing heart. Quickly I peck out a "Dear Pope" letter. "I no longer choose to live as a nun," I tell him, "because the life as currently regulated by the Church is an impediment, rather than an aid, to my life as a human being and therefore as a Christian." The relief is palpable. The stiffness in my neck and shoulders seems to slip away, and the frown etched into my forehead relaxes. I make it back to the chapel in time for communion with a decision firmly resting in my heart: I will deliver my decision to Augusta as soon as possible. Which can't be until after night prayers, so full has been the day for us both, with festivities celebrating the newly vowed sisters and their families.

She's alone at her desk when I finally find her later, after night prayers, poring over papers in front of her. "May Jesus Christ," I start, more formally and awkwardly than I have in years, placing my Dear Pope letter on top of the papers she's studying. She picks it up and stares at it in silence for an uncomfortable few moments before opening it. I am unable to read her reaction.

"So, it's come to this," she says, finally looking up at me. Again she scans my typed words, fingering the page as if to test its authenticity, and then puts it down. After smoothing it with the palms of her hands, she looks again at me. "I suppose I expected this, Sister. Still—"

I lean toward her, eager to explain what I couldn't put into the letter. But she raises her hands, fingers spread wide, as if to say stop. Silenced by her reaction, I pull back. She clears her throat, gets up and moves over to the window. Suddenly I feel covered in shame, realizing how my own turbulence has allowed me to forget about her and her feelings. In the midst of all this upheaval in the order, how does she feel when a comrade in arms like me pulls away? Does she feel deserted? Betrayed? Maybe even deceived? As I did—at least for a moment—with Janet's decision? How to explain that until this morning I myself wasn't clear about something she may have noticed in me long ago? There's so much I want to tell her! I need to tell her. Yet she's telling me not now.

Augusta turns abruptly and, like my high school teacher she once was, thrusts my Dear Pope page back at me. "This won't work, Sister. If you want a dispensation from your vows, swallow your pride and use the form they provide." Her face is rigid, her lips tight. "Bureaucrats work faster with boilerplate. And they're not particularly swift where this is going." I mumble my thanks, say I'll be back, and turn to go. "There's a packet going out to Rome tomorrow, Sister. Special selivery. Get your documents here tomorrow before Mass and they'll be included."

I know her well enough to recognize that her stern manner is a way to avoid any show of feelings. It's what was said of her repeatedly when the sensitivity craze swept through our convents. I've never minded Augusta's reserve, though. It's been a comfort knowing that she's counted on me, that she's been proud of me. Which is why, right now, I have such a sinking feeling. I'm disappointing her, letting her down—just when she needs me.

Making my way back to my cell, I realize that, until this moment, I've never before left her presence feeling worse than when I went in. The confusion and chagrin stay with me through my quick filling out of the Roman form and its delivery back to Augusta's office. Even at this late hour, I discover her occupied with another sister, and slip the filled-out form under her office door. Oddly enough, I feel relieved to be denied direct contact.

In the midst of all that busyness yesterday, Carla returned. She was seriously sleep deprived, wiped out, from all those flights in and out of airports for the last twenty-four hours. But today's a new day, and I head for her basement hideout, only to be brought up short when I get there. Stacks of huge boxes block the hallway and entrance to her boiler-room-turned-studio. Coming in closer, I spot her, behind her barricade, in the midst of all the clutter.

"Welcome home, stranger!" I call out, as I angle my way around what I now see are packing crates. But when we hug, I'm startled, as I was with Janet. How small each of them feels in civilian clothes! Not weak or frail, just bony and lean. Amazing the amount of padding we've been carrying around. Good in case of an accident, I guess.

"What does all this mean?" I ask her. I haven't been down here since she departed a couple of months ago, so I'm baffled by all this unpacking—or is it packing up? "Are you coming or going?"

Her crinkly, striped dress is short and full and unbelted—the same simple pattern as the habit we all learned to make in the first months of our novitiate, as well as the pattern for all those surplices worn by altar boys. Yet Carla's current outfit could never be mistaken for any sort of church outfit: The heavy wooden medallion, with its crudely carved PAX, hangs around her neck on a leather thong. It rests on a bosom of bright colors, thanks to the Indian bedspread she cut up to make her dress. Her rolled-up sleeves reveal arms muscled and, like her bare legs, quite tan. A most unusual image, but very much Carla. I like it.

"Both coming and going, I guess." Carla finishes the label she was working on—which I see is going to Boston—and comes over to sit on top of one of the lower crates. Pulling her sandaled feet up under her, yogi fashion, she bids me sit opposite her. "I'm taking a sabbatical, Sister. From the university and from the order." Her voice is heavy, the voice of dread—or maybe relief? And she looks beat, pale and round shouldered. I had expected to see her tired from the long journey home from Scotland. Yet this looks like more than fatigue. Could all those altitude changes have aggravated her blood pressure? I worry about her.

Our lovely, cool August morning has turned heavy and sticky. Though her basement spot is the coolest in the motherhouse, the day's heat still lingers. Yet I know right away that it's more than the heat. "Travel is tough—at least for this now fifty-plus lady!" Carla says wearily. I move the ancient fan on to her worktable to let the breeze hit her directly. "Struggling through those crowds in Glasgow, then Heathrow, then the absolute worst, New York, and, finally, good old Lambert. Made me think of that quote you gave me from one of your philosophers about life being a series of 'perchings and flights.' "

"Uh, yes, William James."

"Well, I've had too many flights these last forty-eight hours—not nearly enough perchings. Too much moving around, Sister. A metaphor for my life, maybe. For years now, I've let myself get too busy, too stretched out, preoccupied with what we should do. We nuns—how we should change; how we could make ourselves more relevant to the world. Now, though, I just need to perch."

"Remember when you told me that it was an art to know when to keep on challenging the accepted way of doing things? And when to give up?" It was her long-ago lesson for me, the one that got her stuck with Zita's Christmas chain for years after.

Carla exclaims: "I said that? Well, I still believe it. When I heard the sad news about those California nuns with that cardinal challenging them, and then Augusta's decision to retrench here at home."

"It wasn't really her choice, you know."

"I know. The naysayers got to her, didn't they?"

"Mostly they were scared."

Carla shakes her head, exasperated. "That whole mess told me I need to get away for a while. Breathe different air. Like those ancient monks who took themselves out to the desert."

"To fast and do penance—in Boston?" I tease, and then quickly see she's not really in a teasing mood.

"No...well, in a way." She sighs, and I see a faint smile with her slow answers. "That's when I thought of a sabbatical, Sister. I've never taken one." Carla is tenured at the university, so this benefit's available for her. Something most of our nuns can't even imagine, surely not our sisters working in parochial schools. Nor is it a choice for me, a lowly new hire. Tenure isn't even imaginable. But it all makes great sense for her. She's worn out. It makes me sad to see her so low, and she sounds every bit as weary as she looks.

"I just want to hide out and paint, Sister. Paint simply. The way I did as a child. Watercolors. Without all this...." Her hand sweeps the room to include it all. "Paint and read and think. Perch. I'm tired of worrying about mankind. About the Church and its changes. About nuns. About all of us, our community. I need to think about myself right now. About this particular nun." As she sits there silently, her strong stubby hands covering her face, I wonder if she's about to weep. But then she pulls back and straightens up to look at me. "Sounds selfish, doesn't it? Well, it is, Sister. I need to be selfish—for a while. I'm in no condition right now to make a decision about the rest of my life."

She'll take a year's leave of absence from the order and the university, she tells me. A "sabbatical" in academic language, *ex claustration*—or EC—in church lingo. It's a term all too familiar to me from Dan's frequent mention of some friend "on EC"—and at one point, a possibility for himself. It means a kind of limbo, living outside the cloister, apart from the community, but still a member, without having to decide one's long-term status in the order.

"I'll be perching for a year, in Boston, with one of my brothers and his wife. They've got an extra bedroom—perfect for my perch."

"It's just the opposite with me," I say, leaning over close, finally spilling out the news I can no longer keep inside. "I'm leaving, Sister. Last night I filed the form—requesting to be dispensed from my vows. It's on its way to Rome as we speak, special delivery."

After a moment of uncomfortable silence, she blurts out, "Not *ex claustration*? You're that sure?"

"Very sure." And then my deepest choice spills out, one I wasn't able to share with Augusta, let alone Maddy. "I just can't be a Church person anymore, Sister. A daughter of the Church, that's what a nun is, I've come to see. What's being enforced right now out in LA. Tangibly enforced. No, the Church is not changing, Carla, despite all the hopeful talk during and after the council. And it's just not a choice for me anymore, at least not here, not in this convent I love, with sisters I love."

"You're so sure?" she interrupts. "But, Sister, the council *has* mattered! I saw it. Both in Scotland and England, even Ireland. I was there. Mass in the evening, in English, a meal together—at times even with home-baked regular bread and tasty red wine, even sometimes regular dinner!" The color in her cheeks has returned, rising with the intensity of her voice. "The Lord's supper, we've always called it. Yet it's only been a *priest's* performance. We've been the silent audience following along, sometimes not even knowing what all the mumbled words mean. Until now, Sister. Now it is changing!"

She leans out toward me, exuding a delight that was missing just a few minutes ago. "Believe me, it's really different now! Now it's like it was with Jesus and those twelve fellas at their Seder meal—only now there are women and kids speaking up as well. We're all part of it now. I've experienced it, Sister. Folks visiting with one another, sharing the Gospel message, exploring what it can mean in our world. I know how wonderfully alive and real our Church can be."

"Wait, Sister, wait." I reach over rest my hand in her lap. Much as I'm happy for her, even feeling some of her joy and hope, I need to get at something deeper. "Look, Carla. Sorry to interrupt, but I must. Let's be honest. You're talking about the liturgy. Important as it is, it's a detail of the larger reality of the Church. And though wonderful, beautiful—everything you say it is—it's not the Church.

"The Church itself, its structure, is *not* changing—not as an organization, and for sure not in its relation to nuns, to us, to women. It's still what it was in the Middle Ages, Sister. It's clerical, paternal, a perfectly tiered hierarchy! An organization like General Motors, that business school professor—what's his name?—said, with *all* men and *only* men, at the top. We are its children, Carla, the minors! Or maybe the worker bees. Or the customers. But whatever, we don't count. Not really. Not where it matters!"

My middle-of-the-night thoughts pour out of me now, in a voice much louder than normal. Good thing we're isolated down here in the basement, as I press on to tell her about the funeral she missed, of her longtime friend Zita. Especially that message from Monsignor Sweeney, about how we are "daughters of the Church." "That ceremony says it all, Carla. All those lovely young veiled women, kissing the ring of that grandly attired bishop, chanting in beautiful Gregorian *Veni*

Sponsa Christi."

I'm frantic now as I try to share with her this sobering scene and my even more sobering thoughts the scene triggered. They've been roiling about in me these last twenty-four hours, and I long to share them with her. "We are the Church's obedient little women, Carla—*all* women are, or should be. Think about the birth control decision handed down just a couple of weeks ago. The pope said he wanted to hear from married folks, so he appoints a commission of married folks, all kinds of professionals, all good Catholics, including medical doctors, women and men, even that 'pill doctor' Dr. Rock—remember him? They work for months, then tell the pope, by a huge majority, that birth control is the correct, moral choice for married couples, that the Church's current teaching is not only not healthy, it's immoral.

"But then, out comes the pope's answer, and guess what? The 'voice of the faithful' means nothing! *Nada!* There will be no change! He's gone with the minority report from a handful of elderly cardinals. Forget those married men and women. The Church *is* the hierarchy!"

Carla moves over beside me, putting her arm around my shoulders, yet I push on. "So what's the message from on high? 'Shut up and obey. Follow Church teachings. There can be no change! Not for women! Listen to my exalted men—my celibate men in their fancy hats—obey them.' All this after a council that was promised to bring worldwide reform. Especially for the laity. Yet for us it's still about blind obedience, crazy talk from old cardinals that literally don't know what they're talking about."

Ever so gently she tightens her hold on me, and says, "I have missed you, Elizabeth, missed your thoughts. Yes, even your anger. But I don't feel as you do. I just can't dismiss what I've seen in the Church this summer. It was so much more than what you call a detail."

Resisting Carla's solicitations, I continue. "You know

what one of those Roman hierarchs said after news of the encyclical was given to the press? 'A husband could no longer respect his wife were she to use birth control.' What does that say about his view of women? That old cardinal! About his respect for wives and mothers. For all women! Men like him are framing the Church's rules for all of us—for wives and mothers *and nuns!*" Finally, exhausted, I reach up for her arm. "Oh Carla, am I just one of those angry feminists?"

"I hear you, Elizabeth, and I do understand, or think I do. Hope I do. And, no, I'd never confuse you with Betty Friedan or Gloria Steinem! However...."

She loosens her grip as we sit silent while I simmer down, letting myself remember that helpless nineteen-year-old in this very room, so grateful for this tiny older sister willing to share her clay and her ideas. Happier, smarter kids came from her art, plus someone finally feeling like she could be a teacher with a smile on her face. She's been with me all along, I think, even this summer with those bookmarks cut from her old Christmas cards: "No institution can do it for us: bring light out of darkness."

"You're still helping with my teaching! You and your art," I tell her and launch into tales from my class this summer with those RAs. How pondering together those existentialists and their words finally gave me words for what I've been trying to tell her today: that for me to remain here means living in bad faith. To continue as a "daughter of the Church," as a *child*, someone whose choices are made for her, is something I can no longer freely choose.

How I wish I could have shared this with Maddy, or Augusta. Along with Carla, they've been my chief listeners and understanders during my years in the order. But what's been inchoate is now clear as a bell: "We are not children, Carla. I don't think like a child, or believe like a child."

"So you must 'put aside the things of a child,'" she says, finishing St. Paul's words for me. She understands!

"Yes," I murmur.

"And take flight?" Her tears spill over now, and I reach over to hand her my handkerchief to dry her eyes. We hug firmly. I love her and want to let her know how much she's meant to me, in all the important twists and turns of this life. "Who else has these anymore?" She interrupts my nostalgic daydreaming with her chuckles, as she touches the hand-hemming on my huge Irish linen handkerchief, its name tape almost completely faded from its twenty-three years of convent bleaching.

"Large enough for two," I say, picking up another corner of the same huge hanky to wipe my own tears, "allowing for true Sisterly sharing! These came with me in 1945. They were required—men's linen handkerchiefs, two dozen of them—but, of course, no one could get them because of the war. Except me! My grandma Mimi's trunk had ample supplies of her beloved Irish linen."

"You've been privileged from the start!" The teasing, smiling Carla is back. "With hems already rolled for you?"

"More likely for all her possible sons and grandsons." Once again I let slip into the recesses of memory that awareness of privilege I've experienced, even within our community life. It's something Maddy has hinted at, something that still tickles my conscience. But for now I let it simmer as Carla and I sit, comfortable at last with our silence. She seems to be brooding and soon shows me again her brow-wrinkled face, her serious look.

"Curious," she speaks deliberately, "that you see yourself as a child, because that's the opposite of how I see myself—in this new flight I'm about to take, to perch for a while. I feel we all may be suffering from an excess of 'adultness.' I certainly am. Which reminds me...." She's up and heading for the small lavatory outside her basement studio and returning with—surprise!—some cold beers. "Since we are both so adult. Some art majors hid these down here and told me I was welcome to them."

The slight exertion has brought beads of sweat to her face, so she moves over by the fan, flapping her full dress till it billows out from her like that girl with her umbrella on the old Morton's salt container. It's all the encouragement I need to pull off these uncomfortable pantyhose and sit barefooted and cross-legged on the cool stone floor. That, plus the cold beer, and we're both refreshed.

After her first few sips, Carla sits back down on her crate and starts rolling the chilled bottle over first one cheek then the other. Her face is pensive once again. "I like to think of us all—all nuns working at reform, bucking up against the strictures of ages, as artists trying to refashion our lives. For the last four or five years now, we've tried to see things afresh, rework with clear eyes all the old stuff. Obstacles inspired us to take another tack—and another, and another. Then it got messy. Certain people felt threatened. Finally, here in our own little corner of the nun-world, our sisters, or at least many of them, said 'STOP, no more change, the old is more comfortable, we don't want any new art.'"

"Like that Christmas Madonna you wanted to put in the refectory years ago."

She nods, slowly sipping more of her beer. "They preferred those childish chains," she remembers, shaking her head ruefully. We sit in silence for a few moments, enjoying the cool drink. "You know, Sister, many artists have cupboards full of unfinished stuff stashed away for another try on another day. I've done that, am doing it now." Her hand gestures over the crate next to the one she's sitting on. "At times, though, you just have to give up and start something altogether new."

"Do you feel guilty?" I venture.

"Not really. It's part of creating new art. A painful part maybe, but a part." She turns to me. "Do you?"

"Yeah, among other feelings. In the middle of the night,

I sometimes feel cowardly, like I'm quitting now that the going's got tough, abandoning Augusta, especially—"

"What about 'quitting now that it's over'? While there's time to start again?"

"I do wonder about that. Because I always had a hard time with endings. Or was it beginnings? Maybe I put off this decision, or came to it so slowly, because I'm afraid of the new?"

"Everyone's frightened by the unknown, by *new art.*"

"Each term at school, as a kid, then as a teacher, I held onto the term that was ending, not wanting the year to be over. I remember once being the last one left in the building as the school was being locked up for the summer."

"When they still did that! I'd forgotten how we used to padlock the schoolhouse for the summer." Her hearty laugh returns. I'm glad. "Listen, Sister...." She slides down from her crate onto the floor opposite me, pulling the fan down with her. "It's normal to feel bad when a good thing's over. This place, the struggle for renewal, has been a good thing for both of us. We'd be nuts not to feel sad. But sad is not the same as guilty."

"Mother Augusta. That's where I feel guilty. She looks so tired and old, so discouraged."

"Well, she is tired. And old. Older than I am! And she is disheartened. Poor baby. But your staying or leaving can't change that. We need to start over again. Start our lives over again—you, me. Create new art, new lives!"

We remain there on the floor, letting the fan whip up our hair. The future as my creation, my art, just like that new twist on Sartre that JoEllen saw so clearly. We're not responsible for just our past; we're responsible for how we choose to shape our future.

Finally Carla breaks the silence. "When I was spending a lot of time working clay, I used to work and work on a pot, and then sometimes, I'd have to break it down and start over, reworking the same clay. Other times, though, I'd give up entirely and start with fresh clay."

"Finally giving up on potting altogether," I remind her, "switching to printmaking."

"There, too. Right. Sometimes I'd make a new serigraph over an old print. So, yeah, I know what it's like to let go, to start over."

"But this letting go—it's different, isn't it?"

She gives me a long hug. I sniffle a bit, but when we separate, it's Carla's teary eyes that are blinking rapidly. "Now, it's watercolors for me," she says, with even more conviction in her voice. "I need to paint simply. The way I did as a kid." Putting down her beer, she stares into the fan, her loose hairs lifting away from her head. "I did this as a kid, too. Worrying my mom, no end. Funny, isn't it? I'm trying to get back to my childhood, and you're trying to escape yours."

August 18, 1968

When Madeleine appears at my door, she looks like her old self again. She's flushed, out of breath from her climb to my third-floor aerie. Yet she's playful—the way she was as a novice. Gone is the pensive, peeved face of recent months.

"Thought maybe you could use a little break," she says, holding up a book bag clinking with something clearly not books. But the doorway's blocked with boxes—as are the bed, chair, dresser, and desk. The message is unmistakable. I'm packing up and moving on. Clearly Madeleine is not surprised. But neither is she angry. I'm grateful to be spared the anguish of figuring out how to tell her, my old novitiate pal, of my decision to leave the community. "Let's get out of his mess," she announces in her best take-charge voice. I promptly dump the files I'm holding, take hold of her outstretched hand and step over the litter to join her in the hallway. For once, I'm grateful that neither of us is particularly good at sharing our feelings. Hugs and kisses would only embarrass Maddy. My delight in her cold Cokes will have to suffice.

We head for the kitchen at the end of the hall, the boarding students' hangout during the school year. Except for the home ec lab, it's the only spot in the motherhouse where non-refectory fare, including ice cubes, can be indulged. So I knot up a dish towel full of ice and then hang it over the fan, while Madeleine extracts the Cokes from her bag. To my surprise, she also produces a bag of cookies.

"They're still warm! You just made these?" As it turns out, she'd baked all morning and then, in the midday heat, drove in from Ladue to be with me. Ever the generous and thoughtful Madeleine. Her largess touches me.

"As soon as I heard, I wanted to come. Help. This is all I could think of."

I look across at her pale eyes, tearing ever so slightly— and causing a heaviness in my own throat. In our postulant days, she was scolded for being "kind to a fault." Now I'm glad she's never reformed. "Looks like you need an extra pair of arms. There are *days* of work down in your room. And you don't have days, do you?" Practical person that she is, Maddy's figured out that one of my immediate problems is that I'll be without a room by the end of the week, since my name has already been removed from the various motherhouse assignment sheets that generate the Room List. She reaches across the table to take my hand. "Remember, St. Raymond's has a guest room—and you are *always* welcome with us."

"Thanks, Sister." She's cut right through our personal, political and theological views to provide exactly what I need right now. "Tomorrow I hope to finish straightening out my things."

"And then? What are your plans?"

"I'm not entirely clear about everything. Only some things."

"Like?"

"Like getting out of St. Louis. Away from everyone here—and from all the Byrnes, too."

"You're not telling your family?"

"Not right now. Eventually, of course. I'm just relieved that everyone's out of town until after Labor Day. My parents are on a cruise up in Alaska, and Suzy and Tom are with their families up at the lake."

"What about your priest friend in DC?"

"Dan. He's heading out to California, coming through here the middle of the week."

"Wanting you to go with him?"

"Most likely," I say, relieved not to have to hide what I haven't been able to share with her these past two years.

"He knows about your decision?"

"Not yet. I had to do this alone." Echoes of Janet. There's a comforting quiet between us, and, while I no longer feel the need to hide Dan's importance to me, I don't feel I need to elaborate either.

"Listen, thanks for your help with this stuff," I begin hesitantly. "Once my belongings are organized, maybe I can straighten out my thinking. I'm aware of big decisions ahead. But I can't concentrate on them while that room is such a mess." Her questioning face relaxes.

"This much I know: I need to get out of here, out of the Midwest, live alone, live near the ocean. Some ocean, go east or west. I've only seen one ocean on that quick trip with Mom and Dad out to California in 1945." My own words startle me. Maybe I'm not as undecided as I conveyed to Dan in our last talk. Maybe my feelings have been sorting themselves out while I thought I was only sorting books.

"What about a job? And money?"

"It's too late to get a decent academic position for the fall term—or even the spring term. I'll concentrate instead on strengthening the odds for a good position next fall." I don't mention that positions are still available in a number of small, Catholic women's colleges that I am deliberately avoiding, nor that I feel keenly the need to secularize my curriculum vitae during these coming months.

"Being near an ocean won't put food in your stomach or pay your rent," she says. Ever the practical Madeleine.

"Somewhere in a bank there's a bunch of war bonds that I bought with my earnings when I was in high school. Dad refused to cash them in when I entered the order. Surely, they've matured by now. I probably have a half dozen or more."

I can see Madeleine quickly calculating. "That won't get you far."

"Also, long ago, Mimi set up a trust for her grandchildren's education. I've heard my cousins and Suzy talk about 'cashing in on their inheritance.' I can probably do that, too." I don't mention that the trust fund is primarily for foreign study and travel, Mimi being a great believer in both. Among my fantasies these last forty-eight hours is the chance to go abroad in the spring. To Dublin or London, or maybe to Paris?

"Your family doesn't even know about your decision?"

"They will by the time I need to get a loan. For the immediate future, I've got that 'dowry,' remember?" As novices, we used to joke about our "dowries," the five hundred dollars our parents had to come up with when we entered the novitiate. Even in 1945, it wasn't much. "Sister Augusta returned it to me last night."

"With interest?" We both laugh at the absurdity.

"She even offered me a plane ticket—when I decide which ocean I'm going to."

"So many decisions," she says with a sigh, and stands up. "We need to get back to those easier decisions down the hall."

For the next couple of hours, we struggle together,

deciding which things go back to the university, which to the community room, which to the incinerator, and which to my trunk in the basement. There are voluminous files of academic notes, family letters, community memorabilia, and, hardest of all, twenty-three years of retreat notes, journals, and letters from dear friends, including, of course, Dan. My impulse is to cart all these treasures off to the incinerator, but Madeleine persuades me not to decide anything so drastic right now.

"Lock it all in your trunk. I'll ship it to you once I hear where you've settled." Her easy way of involving herself in my move out of the motherhouse—and, quite possibly, out of her life—soothes me. And touches me in a way I can't let myself attend to right now. For one who says she wants to live alone, I'm far from tranquil at the prospect of actually doing so. "You won't be needing this any more," she says gently, but firmly, as she holds my well-worn copy of *The Holy Rule*. Much of what bound us so closely in our early years, and then estranged us later, grew out of our personal interpretations of this slight volume.

"I guess not," I reply, feeling oddly detached from this little book that I've revered since receiving it on the day of my first vows. It's been on my dresser, next to my crucifix, where I've kissed it each morning after donning the habit. It was supposed to 'keep me' if I kept it. "That's over for me, Madeleine. What it was supposed to create, though, will stay with me always." Is she remembering right now our countless discussions about whether and how this or that rule stifled or fostered the main goals of our order? How we questioned whether Christian charity might not be compromised by this very set of rules? "You will stay with me always," I finally say. Her eyes begin to fill and we step toward each other to hug, each of us sniffling unashamedly now.

When we relax our hold, I stoop over to extract a small velvet pouch lodged safely in the box of things I plan to take with me "to the ocean." "I'd like you to have this," I say, open-ing the drawstrings of the pouch. It's a gold medal, the size of a fifty-cent piece, with the smoothly worn image of the Sacred Heart of Jesus on one side and "SPONSA CHRISTI 1890–1940" engraved on the reverse. "My Aunt Maggie—remember old Mother Mary Brendan?—she gave it to me before she died. It had been a gift from her sister, my grand-mother Mimi, on her Golden Jubilee as a nun. It's the only thing of value that I have. Will you take it?"

"So you're going to let *me* break the Holy Rule now? Monetary old Madeleine." And she laughs with this refer-ence to our rule's prohibition against owning "silver or gold of any kind," mocking her own reputation as a keen mon-ey person yet personally extremely non-materialistic. She takes the medal, running her finger over the worn image of Jesus, inspecting the print. "Thanks," she murmurs, "this means a lot."

With sleeves rolled up and melting ice hanging over the fan I bring from the kitchen, we work steadily until after nine o'clock. Down and back we trudge—to the trunk room, the community room, out to the parish car from St. Ray-mond's, parked in the back. Madeleine offers to return my library books "so you can have some peace and rest before your friend arrives."

August 21, 1968
Ten o'clock and it's already scorching. I wait for Dan by the Sea Lion Basin at the zoo. Impulsively, I move over to the ice cream vendor setting up business under some trees. The first frivolous expenditure from my dowry! Once again, I'm little Betty, using her milk money for a popsicle. I struggle to keep it from melting all over me, as some little kids push and shove me away from the cart in their efforts to get their own

treat. (As they never would when I was clothed in the habit.) Then I spy him, smirking at the kids' disrespect for "Sister."

"Help me, it's going fast." I hold the messy, dripping handful up to his mouth.

He gulps down what's left. "What a mess!" He wipes his face with the back of his hand, then leans over to kiss me.

"Kind of dumb in this weather," I say licking my fingers. "It was ninety-seven when I stepped off the bus."

"I like this kind of dumb," he says running his fingers down the side of my face. "Besides, m'dear, you look beautiful when you're hot."

"So do you." I smile and study a tanned face, framed by sweaty ringlets. Handsome all right—and definitely not clerical. Without waiting to hear the news he's promised to bring me, I spill out my own. "I've left the order."

"Oh, Elizabeth," he says tenderly, and puts his arm around me. Again. Together we push through the crowd toward some picnic tables far away from the crowd; he tightens his hold on me.

"Thanks for not saying, 'I told you so.'"

"Would I say that? Listen, what your group was doing was great. What you are doing is great." We're stopped now at the tables, and he brings his other arm around to envelop me, whispering, "I'm sorry for your sisters, for their loss, but happy for me!" Then with a squeeze and closer hug, "And I'm really happy for you, Elizabeth."

He slowly, gently kisses my head and neck and shoulders and then steps back, holding me at arm's length—to look me up and down. Another hug tells me I've passed inspection. We move over to sit side by side on an old park bench. He picks up my hand, studying it as if it were wounded. In the hours since packing with Maddy, I've alternated between terror and excitement at being on my own at forty, with no job experience, no knowledge of finances, and very little practice cooking or keeping house. Next to him, though, I feel confident.

"And your news?" I am curious about what he couldn't say over the phone that last call.

"I'm going underground, Elizabeth." The term startles me, my immediate association being with war resisters off to Canada. "I've lost hope, Elizabeth, for the Church— at least as it is now. It's going to be a long time before any real change takes hold. Those responsible for reversing that birth control decision won't stop. They're powerful. And our new pope is no match for them. They'll force him to squash any of the 'liberal initiatives' from the council. We'll both be old and gray before there's another pope like John."

I reach over, touching the cluster of gray in his hair made bushy by the humidity. "We're already going gray, silly. There's more salt up here now than pepper," I say, inspecting his mop. "And I'm not far behind you."

"Let me show you just how young we still are."

He leans over to kiss me but instead I ask, "So what does it mean to 'go underground'? Is that your California plan?"

"I'll be laicized, out of the official ministry. Resigned from active duty."

"But still in the Church?"

"Absolutely, the underground Church."

"And still a priest?"

"Absolutely. Once a priest...."

"Yes, I know. But how will you manage at that place?" I'd done some checking since his last call. The college in San Diego where he's going is a very conservative Catholic place.

"The underground part won't be right away, probably not for several months, maybe even a year or more. Not until I'm finished with my teaching stint. While that's going on, though, I plan to take classes in social work at San Diego State—nights, Saturdays, summer—until I get some credentials for the real world. Then I'll quit teaching. But that's down the road a way.s Right now, I'm moving into a parish rectory. I'll keep the collar on, teach scholastic philosophy to good Catholic kids...."

"The Bing Crosby part?"

"Right. Then, when I've accumulated enough social work units to get a certificate, I'll look for a job and enough cash to get my own place. That's when I'll go underground. Probably by next summer or fall. I'll resign from the ministry—the officially recognized ministry—and begin real ministry." Again, he leans toward me, taking my hands in his. "Listen, Elizabeth, this is what I couldn't say over the phone. I want you to join me in San Diego. We can marry the minute I'm laicized."

I draw his hands up to my face, kiss his long, tapered fingers, and then hold them tight against my cheeks. I can't speak. He leans way over to place a gentle kiss on my mouth. "There's lots to be done out in California, so many people overlooked by the official Church," he says. "There's that huge immigrant population. Just the sort of ministry I feel called to, Elizabeth—without all the bureaucratic claptrap of the official Church. It's tailor-made for us!"

His plans are so firm, so clear. It's staggering, that same sense of direction I heard from Janet. Dan is still so much a priest. As Janet is a nun. Despite their disenchantment with the official Church, each is unambiguously a Church person. And Dan presumes I feel the same way. "Things have happened faster than I planned," he says. "I can't provide for you just yet. After this trip, I'm broke. In a few months, though, with a regular salary, I'll be able to get us a decent apartment near the university. Maybe you'll want to look into social work, too? Or continue teaching? I'll be able to arrange something, at least part time, for you before I bail."

He brings my hands back up to his face and covers them with kisses. "This must seem sudden. I know you need time to think things over. But wouldn't it be great to wait out this crazy time together? In the sun. By the ocean. In California!

It'll be a long time before there's a new pope. Our kids will be in college, or having kids of their own!"

Ministry, social work, marriage, *kids*. He's going too fast for me. His images clash abruptly with those that were so vivid when I was with Madeleine, those of a windswept, sun-drenched solitary self by the ocean. Too many choices. One choice presses me at the moment, though: the need to get out of this ferocious St. Louis sun. Dan reminds me that his car is air-conditioned, so we amble back to Bird, and sit for a while sipping a lukewarm soda, listening to some soothing Mozart. Sure enough, the radio interrupts, St. Louis temperatures are still hovering around 100 degrees, with the humidity holding at ninety-eight percent.

He's the first to speak, apologizing for the shocked condition he's put me into. "My timing is terrible, Elizabeth. Sorry. With what you've just gone through, with all your own decisions, I shouldn't be asking you all this right now."

"I'm okay. It's just this awful heat. You'd think after all these years I'd be able to handle St. Louis in August."

"Look, Elizabeth, you don't have to anymore. In fact—" He brightens and turns the key in the ignition. "I'll help you get out of this heat for good." He heads out for the airport and chortles, "A ticket to California is what you need!" I don't object, as he steers through the afternoon traffic until we reach the highway leading out to Lambert Field. "Don't worry, m'dear, there's no rush. We'll get you an open ticket. Then you'll have it when you're ready to move."

The air conditioner has begun to revive me. I'm dismayed by what he's proposing, though the urgency to respond recedes as I allow the comfort of Mozart to blanket me. I accept the simple joy of being enclosed with him in his beloved car, maneuvering through traffic, feeling his occasional brush on my cheek or squeeze of my hand, then reaching over to respond, all the while reading quiet pleasure on his face. This must be what it's like to be an old married couple, I think. This is what California promises. My RA women students spoke often about "a good man being hard to find"—especially at a "certain age." Still, I wonder—California? Marriage? Kids?

We drive without speaking for a few minutes, speeding past neighborhoods I've never much noticed during a lifetime in this city. For the umpteenth time, I think about the privileged life I've had, comparing the bunker-like apartments I see with the memory of Mimi's house, our Byrne home, and the various spartan but adequate convents I've been assigned to. But then I am brought up short by the simple scene of a man in shorts out washing his VW van with three little kids playing around him, delighting in the spray he occasionally sends their way. What kind of domestic scene would we create, I wonder, Dan and me?

We're within sight of the airport when a newsbreak informs us of a drama unfolding in the streets of Prague. Last night, minutes after midnight, Soviet tanks entered the city's outskirts and within an hour filled the streets of the capital. A lightning maneuver, it's being called, Moscow cracking down on a small country's attempt to create "socialism with a human face."

"Goddamn it!" Dan explodes. This past year Dan has been keenly interested in that particular portion of the sealed-off communist world, probably because an ex-monk buddy of his is Czech, with family still living there. Often during the last eight months, he has told me stories of the excitement among European intellectuals about this bold experiment going on behind the Iron Curtain. He likened it to the changes in the Church, changes we both see disappearing now.

We pull into the airport parking area and stay put until the report on Prague is over. Each of us knows the background story only too well: of Alexander Dubcek leading his fellow Czech Marxists in a "quiet revolution," wanting a healthier, stronger socialism. We'd been reading, over the last several months, reports that civil liberties had been restored, censorship lifted, artistic freedom revived. There was celebration everywhere. By spring, Dubcek had reported to the world press that Czechoslovakia had regained control of its destiny and that a bright future beckoned. "I'm still an optimist," he'd announced to the world.

His optimism had resonated personally with both of us. In this "peaceful uprising," we saw parallels with the revolution Pope John had started in our Church. The political goals were the same: decentralized government, greater autonomy at the local level, more diversity, more choice, greater freedom all around.

"I really thought it would work," Dan finally says.

"Didn't we all."

"But I said that about the Church, too." He lowers his head to the steering wheel. He's been clutching it with tight fists since the first news.

"And I said as much about the reforms within our community," I add.

We leave the car, moving through the airport's air-conditioned vastness to its bar and TV. We sit mesmerized as film footage smuggled out of Prague is played and replayed. Students with handheld cameras have recorded Soviet troops taking over the state radio and television stations. Excited voices from "hide and seek" radio operators tell of a pitched battle at Radio Prague. Staff are barricaded inside and local buses jammed outside to thwart the tanks. At first the resistance is carnival-like, with students hurling flowers at the oncoming tanks and playfully switching street signs to mislead the invaders. Then the scene turns grim: A huge tank swivels its gun and fells a peaceful protester. The filming gets more erratic until, finally, a bloodied Czech flag is all the camera captures.

We sit for more than an hour while the smuggled tapes play again and again. Dan's hands tighten around his beer, as

I fold and unfold the cocktail napkin. Finally the screen goes back to American baseball, and Dan suddenly bangs the table. "SHIT! This is exactly like the Church! Things got better right after the council, remember? Messier, but better. People were actually becoming adult in their faith. Questioning, exploring, growing up, for God's sake! But Rome can't stand that any more than Moscow can. They're threatened, so bam! Bring on the tanks." He slams the table again, and I look around me, but no one seems to have noticed.

"It's back to those old, crude methods of control." His face reddens, and he spits out, "You'd think freedom's some kind of virus that's about to infect everyone. So they protect us like this!" He gestures angrily at the TV, even though Prague and its mayhem are gone. "And that bulletin at the end. The Reds are calling this invasion a 'security measure' to 'restore order.' Because a 'few radicals' created this 'civic disorder'! So they send in tanks and guns. What a perfect metaphor for how the Vatican is acting."

My attention, though, is still on that anguished face of the young Czech student running away from the group by the statue of King Wenceslas. He was breaking rank with his group, but why? Is he a hero, maybe one of the runners, like the one who smuggled the film tapes we've been watching? Or is he a coward, an informer? Or simply a person who's had enough? Enough battling for what is obviously a lost cause. Maybe in the midst of the mayhem he saw the inevitable: that for him to survive, he had to pull away, struggle on his own terms. Create new meaning? Make new art...like me?

Dan pays the tab, and we walk over to the coffee shop for hamburgers. He looks thoroughly dejected, even as my heart lifts. Because I know now how I must respond to him. I'm more like the Czech boy than I am like the protesters with whom he identifies. I need to remove myself from old struggles, from St. Louis, from my family, from the order—from him. Whether I'm a hero or a coward, I don't know, nor do

I care right now. I've had enough of the struggle. Dan is still enlivened by his tangles with the Church, maybe he always will be. But I'm not. Not any longer. I need to be on my own. To create the new art Carla talks about.

We eat and chat and occasionally stop to touch each other. I know I'll be flying off tomorrow, but it won't be to California, not with Dan's ticket. I'll take Augusta up on her gift and go in the opposite direction. I'll fly to Washington. To see Sophie. A comfortable waystation until I figure out what I want to do.

It begins to rain, and the approaching thunderstorm dramatically colors the afternoon sky. We walk over to the glass and stare at the arriving and departing planes. As lightning cuts through the purplish heaven, Dan puts his arm around my shoulder and tells me he'll always love me no matter what I choose. Has he somehow become privy to my silent decision?

August 22, 1968
TWA Flight 30, departing St. Louis at 3:50 p.m. I am on my way to a new life. My carefully gathered bag of brochures remains unopened on the floor. In it are recent issues of *Jobs in Philosophy,* notices about post-doc grant applications, and bulletins on "Careers Suitable for Academics Transferring into the Corporate World." Threatening, and challenging, yet I don't look at any of them. They're too much in the future, too specific. I need to absorb the immediate, what's happening at this juncture between two lives. I sit gazing at the void around me, letting images of my life below the clouds float through my mind. One by one, I gently say goodbye, and close these chapters of my life. Whatever providence has brought so much beauty, adventure, and love into my first forty years will, I pray, bring new life and love into the years ahead.

Last night was mostly sleepless, with only a brief nap after packing and writing a few letters. The letter to Dan was made easier by our slight exchange when finally, close to midnight, he dropped me back at St. Raymond's convent, with its guest room that Maddy had offered. "You need more time," he'd said, almost apologetically. "I can see that." He played with my hair, then pleaded, "Please write soon. I love you, Elizabeth. I need to know your plans."

So I began with his letter. What I wrote him, though, turned out to be not that different from what I wrote Augusta and Carla and Madeleine and Janet: about how I need to leave much more than just the convent. How I feel very much like the way I felt twenty-three years ago, leaving home, coming into the order, full of excitement and anticipation about a new life, and not a little fearful about the path ahead. How their friendship is the greatest gift I am taking with me on this new journey to create new art.

I slept so little last night that tears come easily when recollections surface. Memories and tears, the poetry of Hopkins—in Gaby's voice—also bubble up, words that spoke for me in that long ago time of deciding to join the sisters. I hear them now, embedded in my brain: "The world is charged with the grandeur of God. It will flame out, like shining from shook foil." Beauty, grandeur, love—above and below these clouds. May I keep Hopkins's sense, now my own, that "nature is never spent," and that "there lives the dearest freshness deep down things."

The summer sky grows dark as we approach Washington, the purplish pinks of this long day replaced by a lavish array of blues. Blue is Mary's color—I learned that as a toddler from Mimi. Up here, as the night sky deepens, the ancient evening hymn at the close of Vespers sings itself in me: *Salve, Regina, mater misericordiae: vita, dulcedo, et spes nostra, salve.* "Mother, queen, mercy, hope"—sweet words all, borne on lilting chant. I hope it will always be my evening plea, "mourning and weeping" in this "vale of tears."

The Latin continues to roll around my head as easily as the Aves of the rosary, or the grace before meals. Or the thousand other relics fixed within me from that spot on earth we called the motherhouse. As much as my sister friends, or the words of my poets and philosophers, they are forever part of me.

About the Author

Dorothy Dunn has been a philosophy professor, a corporate executive, a geometry teacher, and a nun. While a nun, she taught both elementary school and high school, later earning a doctorate in philosophy from St. Louis University. After leaving the convent in the late 1960s, Dunn taught philosophy at the university level, then worked in business. She lives in Los Angeles.

CPSIA information can be obtained
at www.ICGtesting.com
Printed in the USA
BVHW031337081221
623415BV00029B/246